AIDAN SONG

ZACK MASON

AIDAN
SONG

ZACK MASON

Dogwood Publishing
Lawrenceville, Georgia

Published by Dogwood Publishing
Copyright © 2012 by Zack Mason

Library of Congress Cataloging-in-Publication Data is available upon request from the publisher.

ISBN-13: 978-0-9886524-5-3

Manufactured in the United States of America.

9 8 7 6 5 4 3 2 1

First Edition: March, 2021

Cover Design by Matt Smartt

This book is dedicated to
God,
the Author of History and Founder of Freedom

-and-

to Joshua, Rebekah, & Ashley,
the greatest gifts He's ever given me.

In 1135, after the death of King Henry the First, England descended into anarchy as his daughter, the Empress Maude, and his nephew, Stephen de Blois, battled for control of the throne. The civil war that erupted tore the nation apart and lawlessness reigned for almost twenty years.

As one prominent chronicler of the era reported, it was a time when "Christ and the saints slept."

Prologue

September 1118 AD - Becca's Well, England

Lord William Falconer peered closely at the new parchment, tipping his candle a bit to better examine the words he'd just written.

As he did, a solitary drop of crimson wax splattered onto the desk beside it and splintered into tiny droplets, a few of which landed on the document. He blotted at them hastily with a cloth, hoping to minimize the soiling.

He sighed as he replaced the candle in its holder. He really should just throw that one in the rubbish. It never gave enough light.

Though he knew why he didn't. *Willful waste makes woeful want,* his departed mother had always said. She'd been a Scottish *dame,* and a dutifully frugal one at that. Many of her pithy wisdoms remained with him even today.

He rose to fetch a few more candlesticks so he could work without straining his eyes.

Just three months prior, his wife had blessed him with their first child, a son.

Aidan.

The boy was an immeasurable treasure, confirmed always in the giggles and coos of the ever content baby. Of course, he'd dutifully supplied his wife with a wet nurse, but Marie constantly insisted on taking care of their child herself. Like his own mother, she was descended from Scottish nobility and had inherited all the hard-headedness that came with that blood. Not to mention the fiery temper.

Yet, she was half-Norman as well, so she was equally capable of subtly bending him to her will through the coy use of her eyes.

Not that she had to try very hard. He spent as much time with her and his new son as possible.

Which is why he was up here in the tower studying the books so late tonight. With his new family obligations, he'd been neglecting the business of the barony recently and needed to catch up.

So far, the numbers were pleasing. The harvest would soon be fully stored, and all indicators said it would be a good season. For years, he'd longed to release the villagers into a little more freedom so they could spend more time laboring on their own holdings. Next year, that might finally be possible, it seemed.

He dared hope the king might even grant him that large acreage to the north he'd had his eye on for so long as a new fief. It was very well-watered, and the king had yet to assign it to any barony. With an addition like that, he'd have enough resources to retain an additional knight. Such a thing could be the beginning of a true legacy for his family.

Life felt good right now. He was starting to dream . . .

Outside, there was a bright flash followed by a sharp clap of thunder rumbling sonorously.

A bolt of lightning had struck closer than was comfortable.

It rattled the inkwell on his desk and shook him from his reverie. Dark, ominous clouds had been rolling in all afternoon and now they were finally letting loose.

The crisp patter of cold rain slapped against the glass of the study's tiny window. He paused and watched the flow expectantly.

Sure enough, a thin rivulet began to seep out from under the sill, pooling on top of older water stains. The carpenter had supposedly fixed that leak three times now.

William withdrew his dagger from his pocket and sliced a wedge of wax from one of the thicker candles. He moved to the window and worked the wax in the palm of his hand until it was warm enough he could ball it up. With meaty fingers, he stuffed the wax into the narrow crack beneath the sill, pressing and stretching it along the void until the water stopped. It would hold for a while, at least until summer when the sun grew hot again.

He returned to his desk as another flash streaked through the glass. The thunder was so loud this time, it battered his chest and the very stones of the keep.

He shuddered.

Once its echoing remnants died off, he settled back into his chair, determined to finish his work and join his wife in bed.

"Evening, brother…"

William stiffened. The gravelly voice was behind him.

"Richard, what are you doing up?" he replied without turning, "I thought you'd retired."

His younger brother circled to the front of William's desk and stood silently, as if expecting something.

William flicked his eyes up. Even at twenty-nine years of age, thin slashes of grey already lined Richard's dark hair and the otherwise black goatee besieging his mouth.

"Have a seat," William offered smoothly, motioning to a plush chair across the room. "I'm just finishing up my review of the accounts." He turned back to his books.

"I think I prefer to stand, if that's all right."

Now, William fixed his attention upon Richard as another flash of lightning bathed the room in a flickering bluish-white glow. Tonight, something different lurked behind his brother's eyes — something unfamiliar.

"What troubles you, Richard? You seem intent."

"Indeed, I am. I'd like us to speak of young Aidan."

Instantly, William tensed.

"My son?"

"I shall arrive straight at the point." Richard tossed a small scroll onto William's writing desk and took a few steps back.

Still, he did not sit.

William cracked the seal and began to read, immediately shocked by the heading which read "Last Will and Testament."

"Why . . . this is *my* will . . ." he stammered, reading further. "It disinherits my son and bequeaths my entire estate to you!"

"Yes, that is a fair summary." Now, Richard finally took a seat and crossed his legs with a smooth flourish of apathy. He scrutinized his fingernails one by one as another rumble of distant thunder rolled in.

"*Are you out of your mind?* Why would I *ever* sign such a thing?"

"Because I have certain documents in my possession that would cause you great harm should they be released."

"Stop preening yourself and face me like a man, Richard!" William's eyes narrowed. "What is your game? What are you talking about?"

"Of course, dear brother, you are confused. You'll remember how our father disinherited you for cause before he died and willed the Falconer estate to me. I know you've never acknowledged that but . . ."

"I remember no such thing!"

"Well, I've certainly pressed you about it repeatedly over the years . . ."

"You have not! Are you daft? You've never mentioned this before! Our father died ten years past, and you've said nothing since. There were no problems, no issues. He loved me and made no changes to his will!"

"I *do* have his will, William. The real one — the *last* one. The one that replaced you as heir in favor of me. Three of your knights, Sir Hugo, Sir Roger, and Sir Walter were all witnesses at the time who signed to bear testimony as to its validity . . ."

"None of those men were even knights under my father! Walter was just a squire and Hugo and Roger were still in Normandy . . . *this is ridiculous.*"

William shook his head vigorously and pinched the bridge of his nose between his fingers as if to prevent the onset of a migraine.

"Oh yes, they were knights under our father, brother. And they stood at his bedside when he passed."

"No, they weren't! Have you turned lunatic? *Anybody* will attest . . ."

"*Who* will attest to that, brother? Who?"

"Why . . . why . . ."

"Yes, *now* you see it, don't you? There's no one left from that time is there?"

William cursed and stood abruptly. This was no silly prank on his brother's part. It was a real attempt to usurp power. He'd always known Richard lusted after the Falconer estate. He'd also known his brother had a dark side, but apparently, he'd underestimated its depth.

"There are plenty of servants and villagers who were here then . . ." William said.

Richard waved him off dismissively. "A handful of servants and yeomen. The serfs aren't worth the paper they'd try to make their mark on before the council. Regardless, if any of that chattel stood up for you, well, they might just disappear." He flicked a piece of lint off his sleeve.

"You wouldn't dare!"

"Not I . . . *we*. And yes, we would . . . *dare*, that is."

"I knew you were low, Richard, but I never dreamed you'd stoop so far."

"Yes, well, that's all in the past now, isn't it?"

"This is treason!"

"Treason? I'd say not. Betrayal maybe. Treason would be against the king."

"I'll take this to the king!"

"To Henry? Ha! You know he's not exactly thrilled with your light-handed practices around here, William. He would welcome my taking over the estate. You are simply entrusted with the land at his pleasure, need I remind you?

"And, as you know, the king has been otherwise occupied on the Continent for the past year. In his stead, the chancellor will defer you to the full Exchequer, and when they meet at the end of the month, they'll believe whatever the sheriff tells them."

William grimaced. The Sheriff of Derbyshire and Nottingham, William

Peverel the Younger, was as corrupt as they come. Naturally, Richard had always seemed to get along with him better than he.

"Plus," Richard continued, "You should also know that we have documents revealing your plots to conspire against the king."

"*What!* Of what lunacy do you now speak? There are no plots!"

"Now, now, brother, stay calm."

"*Of course! You've invented more lies!*"

"Not lies. Documented evidence, well attested to."

"Let me guess. Attested to by Hugo, Roger, and Walter."

Richard lifted his palms and dipped his head slowly, acknowledging the accuracy of the guess with feigned humility.

William gripped the sides of his desk until his knuckles turned white. "I will fight you to my dying breath," he seethed.

"No need for that, brother. I do not intend to take the estate from you now."

"What is it you want then?" The baron growled.

"I'm a patient man. I knew you'd fight. Just sign this new will assigning to me all inheritance rights when you die, and I'll leave you alone."

"And how much would my life be worth to you, dear brother, after I sign such a thing."

"Don't look at it that way. See it as surety for your son. After all, who would feel the need to harm young Aidan with no inheritance in his future? Surely you can see the benefits."

William dropped himself heavily back into his chair. He stared vacantly at the document.

Too much of what Richard inferred was true. It was a fact that he was not a favorite of the king. Their regent preferred sterner men. Those three knights were close friends with his brother and favored Richard over himself. He should have kept a closer eye on their relationship. Hugo was certainly capable of murdering innocents, and Walter was an oaf, though Roger's betrayal did surprise him. That meant that out of Falconer's four knights, only Bart was left to him.

However, parting the fog now swirling through his mind was the veiled threat to his son's life. He'd not missed the sick flicker of relish in Richard's eyes, verifying the threat was real. That risk scared him more than anything. His brother was more dangerous than he could have ever conceived, and he'd realized it too late.

With his knights willing to testify to falsehood, even treason, and the king assured to side with his brother, he needed to buy some time.

He could not tell Marie. Not now, at least. He would have to find a way to beat Richard at his own game.

In the meantime, he needed to diffuse the threat.

William's hand shook with frustrated fury as he picked up the quill and dipped it several times in the inkwell.

"Where do I sign?"

Chapter 1

8 years later – April 1127 AD – Becca's Well, England

The flowers were in full bloom, inspired by early warm winds from the south that had chased away the frigid winter. The expanse in front of the Falconer keep was flooded with carpets of white wood anemone blossoms, but eight-year-old Aidan paid them but a passing glance.

He was determined to reach the brook as fast as possible and try out the new fishing pole Sir Bartholomew had made him.

He passed through several meadows and fields, but then stopped short when he spied a strange wagon and driver headed into town in the opposite direction.

As it neared, he studied the vehicle's craftsmanship. It was a finely made wagon, not one of the simple, rough-hewn carts used by peasants. Most unusual of all, a thin frame of narrow sticks stretched up tall from one sideboard, curved over above the cart, and then dropped to the other side, terminating at the opposite sideboard. The frame was covered in tanned leather, so the effect was to enclose the wagon's interior like a giant rounded tent.

A team of large coursers pulled the coach. The driver, dressed in a black fur cloak, was obviously a man of means, probably a baron of some sort, but Aidan did not recognize him.

Aidan strained to see inside the coach as it passed. He was rewarded with the briefest glimpse of chestnut hair and a light-skinned, slender face as a young girl peeked from within only to retreat again and disappear a moment later.

The wagon rolled on, popping rocks under its wheels.

He dropped his pole and bait box next to the path, taking mental note of where he left them, and then ran as fast as he could back to the keep. A man like that could only be going to meet his father, and he knew a shortcut that would get him home before the visitors were even halfway through town.

He raced along the outskirts of his village, took a sharp right and then ducked under a small footbridge. He splashed without caring through the cold stream flowing underneath and then scrambled up the slippery bank on the other side. A few minutes later, he'd reached the stone keep that served as his family's home.

Sure enough, he'd beat it. The carriage was just exiting from the village on its way to the castle.

It swayed up the path while Aidan waited dutifully. Eventually, it passed through the main gate and then halted when it reached the keep's entrance.

The driver jumped to the ground. His tight lips revealed a certain sternness, but gentler eyes hinted at a general decency behind it.

The man turned and held out his hand. Small, feminine fingers emerged from the covered wagon and gripped it. A young girl, about his age, stepped out and dropped down as delicately as possible from that height.

To her belonged the fair chestnut hair he'd glimpsed —and she was clearly this man's daughter.

Aidan's feet felt rooted in place. He stood still, fascinated.

"Tis rude to stare, boy," the man barked as they passed, moving to the front door.

He'd taken Aidan for a servant, which wasn't surprising given the ragged attire Aidan wore whenever he went fishing, or, for that matter, did just about anything.

Aidan spun away and rushed around the side of the keep, searching the grasses there hurriedly. Near the rear corner he found was he was looking for — a bright yellow sprig of Cowslip blossoms. He knew he'd seen it here yesterday. Unusual in that it had flowered a full two weeks early for this time of the year.

Aidan plucked it and gripped the stem in his fist while he ran back around to the front of the manor. The guests had already been admitted inside.

He found them sitting in the parlor before his father and mother. The stern man did not see Aidan approach, nor did his parents acknowledge his arrival, aside from the critical eye his mother flashed his way, having noticed his rough choice of dress.

"I notice you have no undercroft . . ." The man was saying.

"We do," William replied, "Our stores are in the level below us, but since the hill slopes down behind the keep, the entrance to it is back there. Makes for easy access to our living quarters up front."

"Do you not fear for security?"

"The king's peace has been held for many years now, and we have the curtain wall . . ."

The young girl sat beside her father. Aidan crossed the room and extended the blossoms to her.

She looked mildly surprised but took the sprig and smiled. Aidan didn't understand what he was feeling, but he marveled at the smoothness of her cheeks and the sparkle in her eye.

"Lord Nicholas Fontaigne, this is my son, Aidan."

His father had seen the gift and shot Aidan a disapproving glance. "Aidan, this is Baron Nicholas Fontaigne. He holds land in Miller's Dale to the northeast of here. And this is his daughter, Priscilla."

Of course, his mother had seen his offering too and blushed, but smiled pleasantly. Aidan strode to the front of the chairs and offered his hand to the unfamiliar baron.

"It is a pleasure to make your acquaintance, sir."

Baron Fontaigne stood and accepted Aidan's hand. "The pleasure is mine, young man. My apologies for outside. I mistook you for a servant."

"Not to worry." Aidan bowed as a gesture of respect.

"Aidan, would you like to show young Priscilla around?" His mother asked.

"Yes, mother."

Chapter 2

There's a devil at your door, and he grows, he grows...

"I Followed Fires"

~Matthew and the Atlas

October 1127 AD - Becca's Well, England

L ady Marie Falconer tilted her gaze toward the stars, relishing their cool, sparkling beauty amidst the blackened, late-autumn sky. She loved to ascend the castle walk in the evenings before bed to gaze at them. She fancied them as tiny jewels scattered across the heavens and never tired of their artistry. They never failed to inspire her thoughts to grander things beyond the mundane of the day past.

Tonight, the air was brisk. She tugged her woolen shawl tighter around her shoulders, thinking the chill might force her back inside too soon.

Marie inhaled deeply, enjoying the faint smell of wood smoke drifting up from the villagers' chimneys, always a clear sign winter was near.

She ran her fingers across the rough stone wall at her waist that separated the walkway from a twenty-five foot drop on the other side. From her vantage point, she could see most of the sleepy village.

It was her husband's liberal policies toward his serfs that had allowed the village to prosper so. Before him, the barony had been nothing more than a humble thatched-roof manor attached to a smallish, square stone keep and a few scattered dwellings lower down on the hill.

Of course, the town's prosperity had prospered her family as well, and William had since torn down the older, more rustic manor house and built the current two-story stone castle.

Though such prosperity also brought risk.

She feared for her husband. The wolves always seemed to be nipping at his heels. Three of his four knights were anything but loyal.

William never said anything to her about it, likely so she would not worry, but she saw the contemptuous glances, the conspiring chats. She heard the hearty jokes laced with veiled disdain. Only Bartholomew was faithful. He was the most capable of the three, yet he was aging and less politically connected.

Her brother-in-law was clearly the alpha wolf of the pack. Richard's greedy eyes did not understand her husband's wisdom was the source of their growing wealth. He only saw resources to be plundered, and she knew he coveted the barony.

She feared even more for her son. Aidan was the only progeny she'd been able to give William. He was training Aidan intensively, but for many years yet, their son would still lack the experience he'd need to stand up against a . . .

"Evening, Milady."

The raspy greeting sent an involuntary chill down her spine.

Lady Falconer turned to face her loathsome brother-in-law.

"*Richard* . . . to what do I owe the pleasure?"

He slunk toward her, oblivious to the distaste in her eyes as he advanced. "Such a beautiful night, is it not?" He stopped by her side and turned to face the night, as if enjoying the view as much as she.

"It is."

"Do you come up here often?"

"What brings *you* up here, Richard?"

"I happened to be walking along the yard below when I saw your pretty face above the parapet. Thought to join you."

She grimaced. The man slithered everywhere he went and generally disgusted her. The sound of a personal compliment escaping his lips was repulsive.

She was dismayed to know he'd discovered her private evening walks. Not that she'd thought to hide it from him, or anybody else for that matter, but maybe she should have. Tomorrow, she would no longer hesitate to speak to William about asking Richard to find a new place to live. It was long overdue.

A frigid finger brushed her cheek as he reached to tuck a tress of her hair behind her ear.

She startled at the unexpected touch and jerked her head back.

"Richard! What are you doing?"

"Forgive me, Milady, but you look so beautiful in this light. The harvest moon becomes you."

He stepped closer and clamped a hand on the back of her neck. He pursed his lips and began pulling her face towards his.

"Richard! *Stop!*" She squirmed and struggled and somehow managed to get an elbow into his stomach before he could succeed.

Wincing with pain, Richard withdrew. His face twisted into a sneer.

"What . . . are . . . you . . . *doing?*" She spat the words. Vigorously, she rubbed her hand across the back of her neck and then flung it toward the ground as if trying to wipe away the remains of his cold touch.

"You want me, Marie. I know you do. I know the signs."

"You're out of your mind! William will hear of this!"

Richard's eyes narrowed to daggers. "*William?* What will your husband do? He's a weak man. His knights are all with *me.* You know this is true. I have the king's ear too. Your husband does my bidding for the sake of your son."

"*Aidan?* What are you talking about?"

"Yes, your husband has already designated me as heir in place of Aidan. Didn't he tell you?"

He read the shock on her face.

"Ah, I see he did not. Doesn't surprise me. As I said, he's a weak man. Yes, your husband does my bidding, and I, in turn, make sure that nothing untoward happens to your son. And you will too, Marie. You too will do my bidding . . ."

He advanced toward her again, lecherous glee flooding his face.

"I will not!" She backed up, stumbling on a loose rock. "I will never submit to you. You are *nothing.* A nobody! William *will* hear of this and I guarantee you and your traitorous knights will be removed from this castle by morning!"

At the moment she spat that word — *nothing* — fury slashed him like a vicious scythe.

There was no choice now. He would not, could not, allow her to go back down those stairs.

He rushed her and shot his body low, embracing her legs in a vice-like hug. Then, he heaved upward, clearly attempting to flip her over the wall.

She saw what he planned and desperately grappled for a grip on the stones, bracing herself against his strains. It was all she could do to resist, but he was too strong, and she was slipping.

"He...will...defeat you," she breathed through gritted teeth.

"I don't think so," he hissed.

One final, mighty heave and she was up and over, falling freely.

He was already moving to the staircase before he heard the expected, sickening thud. Her screams had never registered.

A single shadowy hall lay between the bottom of the stairs and his bedchamber. Within moments, he'd be in his bed and would pretend to be groggy when they came and fetched him.

***

The sky did not match Aidan's heart.

It should have been overcast, coated in dark, dreary grey swaths of cloud, shedding rain like teardrops. Instead, the actual bright blue hues ripped at him. Today, the grass was too green, and the dark mound of loose earth they would use to fill in her grave smelled entirely too rich and fertile.

Aidan did not recognize the wrenching in his chest, but he understood it. They hadn't let him look upon her face but had sealed her up in the box away from all prying eyes.

He knew why.

The fall had hurt her beautiful face, and now he could not see her. He would never see her again.

Already, the nuances of her smile were fading from memory. The only permanent image that remained was the large portrait of her his father had commissioned a year ago, but the painter had not really done her justice.

Staring at the open, gaping hole in the soil, he trembled.

He longed to rip the lid from the coffin, but his child-sized fingers would be useless. The men had already looped the ropes under the box. Any minute, they would lower her down, cover her in dirt, and then she'd be gone forever.

The priest chanted something unintelligible in Latin.

Aidan looked to his father. He'd never seen the great man so broken. Dark bruises encircled his grief-stricken eyes.

It had been so sudden.

All morning, Aidan had heard whispers floating around the castle, dirty, unrepeatable whispers about suicide, scary whispers of something worse. His father said she'd fallen, but that parapet was almost chest high on Aidan. Granted, it would have only been up to her waist, but how could she have just fallen?

He studied the backs of his hands. They were shaking. A lump caught in his throat, forcing him to gulp involuntarily.

Still, the tears did not come. He couldn't seem to let them out. Instead, they burrowed deeper into his heart while his throat constricted to the point of choking.

A cool, gentle touch interrupted his sunken thoughts.

He looked up to see little Priscilla. Her young eyes shone kindness yet were full of sympathetic pain. Her chestnut hair sported a blond streak in the front, a lock lightened by last summer's sun.

She smiled faintly and held out a blue-petaled flower. He took it in his fingers and stared at it blankly.

He didn't know its name.

***

9 years later – May 1136 AD – Becca's Well, England

A glint of sunlight flashed off the twirling sword as it swung toward Aidan's head.

A sharp clang of metal welcomed its approach as he parried. The opposing blade then dipped and sliced at his knee, but Aidan fended that off as well. Three more times the sword threatened him in vulnerable places, but his wrists were loose and flowed to counter each attack with his own.

Finally, Sir Bartholomew lowered his blade and stepped back. A bead of perspiration trickled down through the grey stubble lining his jaw. Aidan thought he could detect a definite heaving of the chest as the older knight caught his breath.

"Ha! I made you sweat this time, Bart!"

"That's *Sir* Bart to you, you impertinent little cuss," he grunted, launching into a surprise swing at Aidan's neck.

Aidan flipped his blade up and successfully blocked it, but the blow knocked him off balance. He stumbled back and landed on his rump.

Sir Bart was already arcing another blow down, so Aidan let himself fall all the way onto his back, held his blade at an angle to block again, and then swiftly rolled to the side. He stood up outside of the knight's range.

"Now, now, *Sir* Bart. Let's not get testy about it."

"Young man, it is a hot day today. *That* is the source of my sweat, not your weak attempts at battle."

Sir Bartholomew was the only one of his father's knights that he liked. In fact, he was the only knight his father had entrusted with Aidan's training. The others always flocked around Richard like some conspiratorial cabal.

Sir Bart was not only his father's favorite, but one of the top knights in the land. In hand-to-hand combat and archery, he never failed to take first place in every tournament within a hundred miles. In jousting, he usually managed second or third, but who cared about jousting? *Real* battle ability was what mattered, and Sir Bart was the best of the best.

He'd been training Aidan in the art of combat since Aidan was twelve, and he'd grown to love the older man like a true uncle, a second father even.

Before this month, he had never bested Bart, not even once. Their sparring over the years had simply meant a long series of black bruises and sore muscles for the young Falconer. The knight consistently refused to be easy on Aidan, pushing him much harder than would be expected of any normal squire.

Truth be told, in the beginning, Aidan had cried himself to sleep most nights from exhaustion and pain. Now, at seventeen, he was strong and competent — and *confident*. Though Bart might say cocky.

Today made the fourth time he'd beaten Bart in swordplay, and *that* meant something. The knight never gave him any milk. If Aidan won, it was a real victory.

"Yeah, yeah," Aidan smiled. "You ready to go again?"

Bart walked over to him and laid a hand upon his shoulder. "Honestly, Aidan, you're ready. Today, you are a man."

Aidan flushed at the unexpected praise.

"What do you mean I'm ready?" he asked.

"I mean that you are well-trained, ready for any adversary. Why don't you take the rest of the day off?"

He was shocked. Bart had *never* given him the day off before.

"You're not going to stop training me, are you?" Aidan asked, alarmed.

"No," Bart laughed heartily, "I've still got a few tricks to show you, but you've got an admirer. Why don't you go spend some time with her?"

Priscilla de Fontaigne had watched from afar, mesmerized by the flickering sweeps of the sword in his hand, and the evident power behind it. As she studied his taut back muscles bulging and dancing in tune with his movements beneath a glistening, sun-kissed skin, something stirred within her that she had not felt before.

She was impressed by how well Aidan fought. Sir Bart's reputation for prowess was renowned. She almost laughed out loud when the older knight caught Aidan by surprise and knocked him on his rear. She flushed visibly when they both glanced her way, and then Aidan began walking toward her.

She quickly straightened and brushed her tunic flat with her palms, trying to pretend she hadn't been staring quite as intently as she had.

"Hello, Priscilla," he grinned — a little too smugly.

His perspiration shone on his chest in the sunlight like pressed olive oil.

"Don't you think you should put a shirt on when speaking to a lady," she quipped, embarrassed by what he had made her feel.

It was his turn to blush. "Oh, sorry." He crossed his arms across his chest, unsure what to do with himself now.

"Hold on," he said and raced the hundred feet or so to fetch his shirt, slipping it over his head as he ran back to her. Deep inside, she really didn't want him to put it on, but she'd never tell him that.

Bart threw his head back in laughter at the sight and walked away.

"So, what brings you out to the manor?" Aidan asked, still grinning, but not quite with the same level of assuredness he'd had a minute ago.

"Greetings to you as well." She curtseyed. "My father is visiting yours today, so I accompanied him."

"Well, I'm very glad you did. Do you have time for a walk?"

"I do," she smiled.

He loved the way her face lit up when she smiled.

Chapter 3

Sailing down behind the sun, waiting for my prince to come.
How will I know him? When I look in my father's eyes.

"My Father's Eyes"

~ *Eric Clapton*

4 Months Later – September 1136 AD – The Road to Becca's Well

"You're right!" Aidan roared "We might as well put his name on one of the stables!"

Thomas Weaver was Aidan's best friend, and he had just noted quite publicly and loudly for all the world to hear that Sir Walter's girth had become indistinguishable from that of the fat old horse named Barley they kept in the barn.

To be fair, Walter had only put on twenty pounds or so in the past year, but the joke's punch line was exaggerated by the number of steins of mead he and Tom had just downed at the Wayfarer's Inn.

Tom always made Aidan roll with laughter. It was one of the reasons he liked him so much.

Tonight's ride home was no different. Aidan's stomach already ached from laughing uncontrollably as their horses clopped along the moonlit path, oblivious to any random cottages they might be disturbing.

Tom was the son of the only weaver in Becca's Well. When Aidan was still young, his father had brought Tom to the castle as a live-in, dedicated to Aidan's service.

Yet, Aidan instinctively hated being served, so he'd always shared in Tom's chores. It usually meant they would both be done early, so they would spend the rest of the day playing together at some game or other.

Later, when Tom was old enough to apprentice with his father, the weaver, and Sir Bart took Aidan under his wing for training, Tom had returned to the village. Still, their friendship had always remained strong.

Suddenly, Tom's face turned uncharacteristically serious.

"Speaking of Walter, Aidan . . . did you hear what he did a few days ago?"

"No..." Aidan replied, puzzled.

"He tried to force himself on one of the maidservants. In the kitchen, after hours."

"*What?* Which one?"

"Juliana."

"That . . . *that* . . ." Aidan's cheeks burned with heat. "I will speak to father about this immediately."

"Do you honestly think it will do any good?"

"What do you mean? Of course, it will. Father will not tolerate such things."

"Well... and with all due respect to your father, Aidan...Walter is a known brute and your father just doesn't seem to . . ."

"What? He doesn't seem to what?"

"It's just . . . he doesn't seem to . . ."

They were interrupted by the faint rumble of hooves racing toward them on the road. Someone was pushing their mount at breakneck speed.

The moment the rider saw them, he hauled back on his reins hard and stopped his horse short right in front of Aidan.

It was one of the hostlers from the castle.

"Aidan, come quick! Your father's ill!"

***

They thundered up the road as fast as their mounts would carry them. Dozens of torches atop the castle wall flamed brightly, which only made Aidan's heart race faster. At a little past midnight, all should have been extinguished a while ago.

They passed through the front gate. Aidan leapt from his horse before it fully stopped.

The moment his feet hit ground, he was off and rushing into the keep. Servants huddled everywhere, in small clusters, along the halls, whispering among themselves.

Upstairs, he found his dad.

His father's body was laid out upon his bed, seemingly asleep. His skin . . . so pale, so . . . *not like him.* Like a waxen figure carved to give the appearance of his father, but badly made in such a way as to not truly represent his likeness.

John the Steward and his uncle Richard stood by the bedside, faces drawn with grief.

Aidan rushed in and moved toward the bed, but John blocked him with an arm across the chest.

"Don't, Aidan. He has already passed."

"What? How can that be?" Aidan choked back an involuntary sob. He pushed the steward aside and knelt by the bed, grasping his father's hand in his own.

It was cool to the touch. Too cool.

Lifeless.

The dam broke and grief burst through. Aidan laid his forehead on the mattress and wept with abandon.

So sudden. Why?

"What happened?" he managed to croak.

John laid a hand on his shoulder. "We don't know. He complained of stomach pains shortly after dinner and retired to his chambers to rest. Two hours ago, he screamed for me to come, and I found him in tremendous pain. We sent for Brother Henri to bring his medicines, and then for you. Henri has still not arrived."

"How long . . . ?"

"About thirty minutes ago."

Deeper sobs assaulted him and won in spite of his efforts to control himself.

He stood and lifted his father's eyelid with a gentle finger. It was his father's eye, but there was no longer a soul behind it. It just stared into nothingness. Aidan let go, but the eyelid remained open, so he brushed it closed again. He leaned forward and hugged his father's head to his breast.

First his mother, now his father.

He was alone.

"Leave us!" he barked.

John and Richard turned and exited the room. John closed the chamber door behind them. Aidan needed to grieve.

"Aidan's of no mind to speak at the moment," Richard said to John, "We'll discuss arrangements in the morning."

The steward nodded and left. Richard marched down the hall and found Sir Hugo at the other end.

"Did you dispose of the cup and the vial?" Richard asked him under his breath.

"The vial, yes," Hugo replied, glancing to the side. "The cup is his favorite though. If it disappeared there would be suspicion, but I scoured it several times. You can't smell a thing."

Richard nodded.

"Good. Order Roger to man the front gate and intercept Brother Henri. Send the monk back the way he came. His services are no longer required. Tell Walter to lock the steward up in his room after breakfast tomorrow morning. No one is to leave this castle unless I say so."

Chapter 4

Give me to the road upon the heart that I had sold
Warm my heavy hands, my heavy hands, for you to hold...
Now the low lakes have frozen, away from home I'll go

"I Followed Fires"

~ Matthew and the Atlas

A sharp knocking interrupted Aidan's nightmares.

He sat up and groaned, aching from stiffness in his back and neck. He rubbed his temples vigorously, trying to massage the cobwebs from his mind.

The rude knocking repeated.

Whoever's hand was responsible for that, he found himself wanting to rip it from their body.

He'd stayed by his father's side until nearly five in the morning, unwilling believe it was real, unwilling to be consoled. John eventually persuaded him to get some sleep.

Every dream had been filled with scenes of his father pulled from his arms over and over.

The strong morning light streaming through his window let him know he'd long since slept through breakfast.

Not that he cared. Food was the last thing he wanted.

Aidan got up and yanked open the door.

Sir Roger stood outside.

"Get dressed," the burly knight barked. "Your uncle wants to see you in your father's study."

Aidan tensed.

He could not stand Roger. The man always spoke to him like he was still a child.

"Father's study? What is he doing there?"

"Just get dressed."

The knight spun and left.

Aidan closed the door and grumbled as he threw on some clothes. He hated thinking about it right now, but he was lord of the castle now, and these knights would have to learn to respect him. Didn't they understand he just wanted to be let alone? He needed time to himself.

He supposed there were probably things that needed to be decided. Arrangements to be made.

He found Richard seated at his father's writing desk, framed by his father's books on shelves behind his head. Sir Hugo had stationed himself stiffly on one side, like a sentinel.

"What are you doing in my father's chair?" Aidan demanded.

"Your *father's* chair?" Richard laughed. "Well, young Aidan, that is precisely what I wish to discuss with you. Though you do not yet know it, and I am here to inform you of it, this is now *my* chair."

His words registered swiftly. Aidan's cheeks burned hot. Fire flowed into his limbs.

Slowly, he clenched and unclenched his fists.

His father's brother or not, he despised this man and that was never clearer than today. Richard's presence had always been an odious feature of the castle, but to see him sitting in his father's chair, acting like he owned it, was beyond the pale.

"What are you talking about?" Aidan growled, instantly regretting the way the very question weakened him.

Richard rocked back in the seat and used his father's letter opener to pick at something in his teeth.

"There is much you do not understand, Aidan. I begged your father to explain it all to you many times, but he was always such a procrastinator. Alas, now it is up to me and under such unfavorable circumstances." He sighed dramatically.

"Speak clearly, *uncle*." If the man said one more disrespectful word about his father, he might lose control.

"You are not heir to Falconer Manor. I am. My father, your grandfather, left it to me in his will, not your father. William hid that from me for years, pretending to be the rightful heir just because he was firstborn. When I discovered the truth, I graciously offered to allow him and your mother to retain possession of the manor as long as your father was alive. It was on the condition, however, that William would change his will to reflect me as heir instead of you. Which he did."

"You lie!"

"Now, now, Aidan. I feared you would react this way. This is why I pleaded with your father to tell you . . . Oh well. What is done, is done. Serves me right for trying to be gracious. I have the will right here that bears his signature . . . if you wish to see it."

"I'll see you *buried* is what I'll see." Aidan turned to leave but bumped against the thick chest of Sir Roger.

He could feel the hard bulk of mail under Roger's leather tunic. He was dressed for a fight.

Without hesitation, Aidan swept a foot behind Roger's ankle and shoved him hard in the chest. The move caught the knight off guard. Roger had underestimated Aidan. The combination sent the man flying onto his back.

The way now clear, Aidan stormed from the room.

"There!" Aidan heard Richard call out behind him as he walked away. "You are a witness, Hugo! He threatened me and attacked Roger!"

Aidan reached his bedchambers and raced to the cupboard where he kept his weapons. He flung the doors open wide.

Bare. Cleared out.

His heart raced.

They were a step ahead of him.

Stop and think.

He needed to get to the armory.

He ran back into the hall and saw Richard, Hugo, and Roger coming up the hall. Thankfully, they were still forty feet away.

"It's no use, Aidan!" Richard called. "We've taken precautions!"

Aidan rushed down the stairs and into the Great Hall.

Several of the servant women were there, setting bowls and cups on the table for the midday meal. Wilfred, one of the menservants, was stoking the fire in the great hearth at the north end.

Aidan had entered through the south entrance, but to get to the armory, he needed to cross the entire hall diagonally and exit through the door to the right of the fireplace. However, before he made it halfway, his pursuers entered through the north entrance to the left of the hearth and cut him off. They'd come down a different set of stairs.

Hugo and Roger separated to cover both northern exits while Richard stood in front of the fireplace. Aidan continued to advance until he was just ten feet from Richard.

Wilfred backed away from the hearth, drawing a distasteful sneer from Richard, and then fled the great room. Several maids gasped at the unexpected confrontation.

Aidan had to get to the armory. If he couldn't, he was as good as done.

"This doesn't have to be so difficult, Aidan," Richard cooed.

"Tell your lackeys to get out of my way, Richard."

"You will leave this manor immediately, young Aidan. I am now the lawful lord, I have the king's backing and that of all the knights as well."

"Sir Bart is not your man."

"Bart is old and inconsequential. I tried to deal with you reasonably, but you have threatened me and attacked my knight. You will leave this castle with nothing but the clothes on your back and never return."

Marion, one of the servant women, dropped to her knees at Richard's side, pleading. "No! Please, milord! You might as well send him out naked!"

She'd been like a surrogate mother to Aidan since his mother had died. Aidan's heart broke seeing her so distraught.

Richard gave her a sidelong glance, disgusted and annoyed by the outburst.

"Please, milord, I beg you! He is the son of your brother. Do not condemn him to the life of an outlaw. At the very least, give him a horse."

Richard's face turned purple at the woman's impudence.

He glanced around the dining hall. Rather than flee, more servants had entered to watch. How Richard behaved here would be reported around the shire.

"Very well, Aidan. Because I am generous, I will grant you a horse," he hissed, forcing himself to try and sound reasonable. "It will be waiting for you outside. Hugo, Roger, please escort the gentleman to the courtyard."

Richard jerked his head at a servant as if telling him to go fetch the horse.

"And some silver," Marion interjected, "Please don't leave him penniless!"

"You will learn your place, woman!"

His eyes bore into her and then turned back to Aidan.

"Very well. Here!"

He pulled a small pouch from under his tunic and tossed it to Aidan.

"That's about ten pence. It should tide you over for a time. Now, I have clearly been *overly* gracious . . ."

"Ten pence? Why that's barely enough to . . ."

A slap rang out as Richard struck Marion across the face with the back of his hand. She collapsed to the floor.

"You've got all I'm giving, Aidan. Now get out of here!"

Aidan still hesitated, so both the large knights drew their weapons and advanced. The shock of what was transpiring finally broke, and Aidan knew he had to retreat. These men were strong, more experienced, and he was unarmed. He pocketed the pouch of silver and backed toward the southern entrance, away from the armory. After a few steps, he turned and began to walk faster.

The knights accelerated their pace as well to keep up and make sure he wasn't headed anywhere but the front gate.

Though sunlight blared into his face the moment Aidan emerged from the manor, it did not warm him.

He shielded his eyes and saw the hostler was bringing around his favorite white stallion. Richard grimaced, irritated by the choice of mount, but he could say nothing.

"What is the meaning of this?" A familiar voice bellowed.

Sir Bartholomew plowed his way through the main gate in the castle's front wall. His eyes were afire with fury.

"I said, *what is the meaning of this?*" He demanded again.

"None of your concern, Bart," Richard stated flatly.

"If anything is my concern, I'd say this is it! Your brother's barely a day deceased and you seek to usurp his manor!"

"This castle and everything in it belongs to me, Bart, and I have William's sealed testament to prove it."

The old knight turned to Aidan, "Where are you going?"

"He's threatened me and attacked my knights," Richard answered for Aidan, spitting the words, "He is no longer welcome in Falconer Manor. Yet, I have generously provided him with a steed nonetheless, now stand aside or face judgment yourself!"

"Traitors!"

Bart slid his sword from its scabbard in a smooth movement. Its metallic ring echoed off the stones encircling the courtyard. "Get to the armory, Aidan," He commanded, "I'll hold them off."

Hugo and Roger didn't wait for an invitation. Both knights raised their blades and leapt at Bart. The older man handled their parries with finesse and expertise. As strong and vicious as they were, Bart was abler. He slapped a devastating blow into Roger's side, and though it deflected harmlessly off the knight's chain-mail shirt, it still took the breath from him. He doubled over in pain, gasping for air.

"Ha!" Bart shouted victoriously. Yet, his triumph was cut off by a terrible grunt.

He stumbled to one knee.

Fifty feet away, Sir Walter held an empty crossbow in extended arms. The shaft of his loosed bolt jutted rudely from the side of Bart's chest.

The warrior sat down hard in the dirt, awkwardly, and then rolled to his back.

"You've killed him!" Aidan shouted, rushing to Bart's side. He fell to his knees to cradle his friend's head, but Bart wrenched his torso and stretched his arm out to Aidan, as if to ward him off. His face was twisted with agony. Blood flowed from his mouth.

"Run, Aidan!" He choked, "Run!" He jerked his body back and forth, trying to wave his stiff arm in the direction of the gate.

Aidan hesitated, but in one last demonstration of strength, Bart heaved his entire body Aidan's way to get his attention.

"Get out of here! *Now!*" The knight gurgled.

He stared for a split second, burning a last impression of his dying mentor's kind face into his brain. He would never forget its strong lines, or the ferocity in his eyes.

Aidan snatched the reins from the servant, swung up onto the stallion, and dug his heels into its side.

The horse leapt forward and Aidan did not look back.

In less than twenty-four hours, he'd lost everything.

And he didn't mean the castle.

Chapter 5

Praying for the healing rain to restore my soul again.
Just a toe rag on the run. How did I get here?
What have I done?

"My Father's Eyes"

~ Eric Clapton

Before Aidan had even rounded the first bend in the road that led into the forest, cold rain erupted from the clouds overhead.

In town, villagers had stared in shock at the slumped, defeated Aidan passing through their midst atop a stallion with its head hung.

Word of Williams's death had reached the village earlier, but they didn't yet know of Richard's take-over. One young lad raised his hand in a silent wave, but Aidan was oblivious.

In no time, his clothes were drenched, pasted thickly against his skin. Steady drops dripped from his boots and the tip of his nose. Chilled rivulets of wet flowed down his neck and back, evoking regular, involuntary shivers.

He patted his horse on its flank. A heavy slop of water splashed up between his fingers from its soaked coat.

When he reached the forest, the leafy canopy protected him from a lot of the downpour, but occasional heavy droplets still pierced through to pelt his head and shoulders like grief-borne needles.

He rode for hours, wandering aimlessly.

Eventually, the rain tapered off, but dark boiling clouds continued to threaten another outbreak any minute.

The weight of his loss was too much. Bart, his trusted mentor — dead. They hadn't even allowed him time to bury his father. His *father* . . .

A lump caught in his throat at the thought. He had to block memories. The pain was overwhelming. All the anger he'd felt earlier had been drowned by it.

Where could he go?

The only refuge that came to mind was Fontaigne Manor, but he was embarrassed to let Priscilla see him like this. Soaked, unarmed, helpless. Not an image he wanted her to remember.

Still, he had nowhere else to turn. He desperately needed a fire to warm himself. Unless he wanted to camp in the forest unsheltered tonight, he had no choice but to head to the Fontaigne house. Catching the wasting sickness from exposure wouldn't help his cause any.

He entered a clearing, and it suddenly occurred to him how much he'd been wandering.

He reined his horse to a stop.

Alert again, for the first time all afternoon, he twisted back and forth in his saddle to gather his bearings.

He decided he thought he had a good guess as to where he was. He guided his mount toward a path leading off to the left that he thought would lead to her house.

Suddenly, a swift breath of air passed in front of his face, followed by the solid thunk of an arrowhead burying itself in a tree trunk to his right.

Aidan reacted instantly. He flung himself from his horse and into some shrubbery. He scrambled around a tree trunk until he felt it was between him and the most likely location of the shooter.

He peeked around the trunk. He saw eight men, all armed with bows and swords. They were advancing with clear intent toward him.

Then, the sharp tip of a blade pricked his back.

Aidan craned his head around. A very determined looking man held the other end. The man jerked his head toward the clearing, meaning Aidan should move back toward his horse.

Aidan obeyed, hands in the air.

"Ho!" Their leader called out with far too much joy in his voice, "No need to be so dramatic! Twas just a warning shot, after all."

"A warning of what?" Aidan grumbled.

"A warning to stay put while we take everything you've got," The man smiled. "Name's Red. Martin the Red."

"You're outlaws!" Aidan accused.

"Yea, and you're our next generous donor, rich boy. Although . . ." The man circled and scrutinized Aidan's appearance. "Something's off here. You are unarmed and half-naked. Not at all the way I'd expect a spoiled whelp to travel."

Aidan glared, but remained silent.

"Perhaps you stole this stallion, then? It seems entirely too good for the likes of you. No matter, he belongs to us now either way. How about silver? A rich boy would never travel without silver."

Aidan lunged into the outlaw at his side, throwing him off balance, and then leapt back onto his horse.

Another arrow whizzed by his head and nicked his ear before slicing into a tree.

"The next one will be true, friend," Martin assured him firmly.

A different blade slipped itself under Aidan's chin and followed him all the way down as he dismounted for the second time. Its bearer was especially grim-faced.

He saw his attempt at escape had caused the outlaws' jovial spirit to sour.

"Search him, Ranulf."

A large, oversized outlaw with meaty fingers rummaged through Aidan's pockets and beltline and discovered the money pouch.

"Aha!" cried Martin, "You were holding out on us!"

"Feels kind of light, Red." Ranulf tossed the pouch to the leader.

Red caught it, opened it up, and spilled the contents onto his palm. He looked surprised.

"What is this? Ten pieces? What kind of rich boy travels with so little? You risked your life to protect a few pennies?"

"It was my horse I wanted," Aidan said.

Red studied the horse. "Yes, he is a fine animal, I'll give you that."

"He's all I've got left."

"Oh, that just makes me want to cry," The outlaw whined, mocking him. The others laughed heartily at Aidan's expense.

"I do believe you stole this horse after all. Nevertheless, one thief deserves another. Your transportation and your funds are now ours. Hand over your attire too."

"What do you mean?"

"Down to your underwear. Now!"

The tip of the sword pressed harder into Aidan's throat, so he began to undress.

"This is truly despicable," Aidan muttered.

That just made the outlaws laugh even harder, so Aidan silently vowed to keep his mouth shut from there on out.

"Boots too," Red commanded.

Aidan grimaced, but took them off and handed them over.

Bare-footed and bare-chested, they left him with nothing more than his long, woolen underpants. Those reached down to his ankles at least and would protect him from some of the briars.

Ranulf mounted Aidan's stallion and soon the merry outlaw troop had melted back into the forest and disappeared.

He was alone again.

The chill that set in thereafter was much worse than before. The rain had let up momentarily, but it could begin pouring once more any second.

He folded his arms across his chest, rubbed his shoulders for warmth, and began to walk.

His objections to seeking refuge with Priscilla's family were now greater than ever, but he had even less choice after being robbed. He didn't even have a flint to make a fire.

Gingerly, he picked his way down the path. For the time being, the chill was his only problem, but if he wanted to make it to her manor on foot before dark, he would have to take a short-cut that was choked with brambles that would tear at his flesh.

It began to rain again.

***

The grey drizzle did not let up the entire route to the Fontaigne fief.

Thick, muddy slop surrounded the thatched home. Aidan was so numbed by the time he reached the front door, he barely noticed the sludge slapping and clinging to his ankles. Heavy streams running down the roof's grassy eaves dripped onto his forehead and ran down his cheek.

He raised a hand to knock . . .

. . . and pulled back.

Finally, he lifted his hand once more and, before he could change his mind again, rapped swiftly.

Muffled voices and then the door swung in.

Baron Nicholas, Priscilla's father, filled its frame, blocking the warm firelight from the hearth inside. His brow creased in puzzlement upon seeing a half-naked man standing at his door in the pouring rain.

Then, recognition dawned. His confusion changed to shock.

"Aidan Falconer? *Is that you?* Please, come in."

Aidan stepped inside, suddenly aware of the filth adorning his feet. He tread lightly, not wanting to dirty the floor, as Nicholas closed the door behind him.

"Uh . . ." was all he managed.

Priscilla leaned around her father's body to see the visitor from her seat by the fire.

"Aidan? What happened to you?" She stood and moved toward him.

"Fetch him some of my clothes, daughter," Nicholas commanded.

She disappeared into a bedroom.

"The question is appropriate, young man. Where are your clothes? Where is your horse?"

Lord Nicholas Fontaigne had never been a fan of Aidan's, which Aidan did not understand. The lesser baron had always had an amicable relationship with his father, but for some reason he'd never given Aidan a chance for a second impression.

"My father has passed."

The older man's face pinched into an expression of heart-felt pain. "Yes, we heard as much this morning."

"Yet, you remain here?" Aidan chastised.

Nicholas' pain converted to irritation. "*Weather* permitting, we had hoped to make a visit in the morn. Explain, Aidan. What is going on?"

Priscilla returned with a set of dry clothes. Aidan thanked her and began to put them on.

"Why don't you change your pants in the bedroom?" Nicholas gruffed. "Then, tell us."

Aidan obeyed and then returned dry and somewhat warmed.

"It's my uncle Richard," he explained. "As soon as my father died, he took control of the castle. Hugo, Roger, and Walter are with him. He said that father disinherited me and that our lands are now his to rule. He ran me out of the castle with nothing but the clothes on my back and my favorite stallion."

"And what happened to those?"

"Outlaws," Aidan muttered under his breath, hoping Priscilla would not hear.

"I see." Nicholas sighed and sat down at the eating table that adjoined the main room.

"So, it has begun then. I'd heard whispers of such, but I doubted he had the guts."

"What are you talking about?" Aidan asked.

"Your uncle. There have been rumors circulating for a while that your uncle planned to take the barony from you father by force. He's been flattering the king up for years. I warned your father several times, but he always brushed it off. Said he could handle Richard. Now I see he couldn't."

Aidan was in shock. He'd never liked Richard, but he never suspected he could have been capable of something like this.

"What of Bart?" Nicholas asked.

"He died at my feet defending me." Aidan's eyes turned glassy from the memory.

"I see," Nicholas sighed again. "Very well." He drew himself up straight and stood. "You may warm yourself by the fire and have dinner with us, young Aidan, but then you must be on your way. I am sorry for your loss . . ."

"Father!" Priscilla interjected.

"I'm sorry, darling, but he may not stay."

"Father! May I please see you in the other room?"

They left Aidan standing awkwardly by himself, listening to the hurried whispers between them in the master bedroom.

A minute later, they returned. Priscilla's eyes drooped in sadness. The tears welled and fell intermittently.

"Aidan, as I explained to my daughter, you are now a man without land."

"I have land! Richard is a usurper!"

"That may be, but Richard holds the castle while you stand here with nothing but mud between your toes. Your only ally was Sir Bart, and he is dead. I have a better idea than you just how entrenched your uncle is, and I tell you, your predicament is dire."

"Then, why don't you help me, sir? You may not care for me, but surely you cared for my father."

"Indeed, I did, but it's not about caring. Your uncle is now a tenant-in-chief to the king. I have much lesser holdings and owe fealty to Earl Ranulf, who also happens to be a friend of your uncle Richard. If I were to be caught harboring you . . ."

"But Father . . ."

"Enough, daughter! You will mind your tongue as long as you are under my care! Is that clear?"

"Yes, Father," She mumbled, looking as devastated as Aidan felt.

His words numbed Aidan's mind beyond what his body had endured in the elements. He would receive no help from the outside world, he realized.

"Then . . . what is to become of me, sir?" Aidan asked meekly.

"I do not know, nor is that of my concern . . ."

"Father, please," Priscilla pled with her eyes.

He glared at her, then finally relented. "Very well. Seeing that you have nothing, I will bestow upon you my long bow so you will not be defenseless. Though, should you get caught, you had better not reveal the source of it! Beyond that, I can only recommend you direct your path to St. Alban's monastery. Perhaps they will take you in."

Chapter 6

There is hope that it will change
With the turning of another day
No I won't go back, back to them
With the weight of Winter's hint

"Evening's Wake"

~ The Native Sibling

E n route to the monastery, the rain finally ceased. Slowly, the loud roar of the leaves being pelted from above diminished to a soft trickling. By the time Aidan reached the front gate, only a smattering of glistening beads still dripped from the foliage.

The scent of freshly fallen rain revived his senses but did nothing to alleviate the residual chill that seemed to have embedded itself in his bones.

Before rapping his knuckles on the thick oaken door, Aidan checked his feet and saw they were once again covered with mud. He swiped some water from the leaves of a bush next to the entrance and vigorously scrubbed them until they were presentable. Monks could be a fastidious lot, and there was no need to antagonize them right off.

With no results after the first attempt, Aidan knocked harder. He heard the echo of his call ricocheting off the monastery's interior halls and then thought he detected a series of faint, answering footsteps.

After a minute, the heavy door cracked ajar to reveal a man in a black tunic through the slit.

His face was youthful, yet strong. He was clean-shaven, including the hair on his head, except for a narrow strip encircling its circumference, as was the custom of most Benedictine monks.

"Yes?" The monk's brow creased with concern as he noted that Aidan was soaked and barefoot.

"I come seeking shelter."

"Your name?"

"Aidan, son of William Falconer."

"Wait here."

"Can I come insi . . ." But the monk had already shut the door firmly in his face.

Aidan rocked his weight back and forth on tender feet, exhausted from the day's events and the tortuous terrain borne by his bare soles for hours on end.

After a period of time that felt like an eternity, but was probably just a few minutes, the door swung back open.

"Come in," The monk waved Aidan past him into the entrance hall. "I am Brother Aelfric," he said, "This is Prior Andrew and Brothers Thomas and Geoffrey."

A trio stood in the center of the foyer. The center man was the oldest and obviously the prior. At first impression, he seemed stern, though he certainly possessed a lighter shade of the stuff than Nicholas Fontaigne. His eyes spoke of quick wisdom birthed from hard experience that allowed him to swiftly dissect truth from the profane.

"You are Falconer's son?" The prior asked.

"Yes."

"I heard of your father's passing. You have our condolences. He was a good man."

Aidan had only visited St. Alban's once before on a trip with his father. He'd been very young at the time and barely remembered it.

"What brings you to us in this state?" The older monk inquired.

Aidan began to explain with fractured sentences, stuttering from a combination of nerves, cold, and exhaustion.

The prior held up a hand for him to stop. "Come with us," he said.

He and the other monks led Aidan down a short hallway to the chapter room. There, a roaring fire blazed in a hearth that almost filled an entire wall. One long table was in front of it and many smaller desks and chairs were scattered around the room so monks could conduct their studies and keep warm at the same time. Two of the desks were currently occupied by monks doing that very thing.

While many monasteries were groupings of buildings called a cloister and centered around a courtyard, St. Alban's was primarily one large building with many of the normal cells and rooms incorporated into it. Beyond the chapter room were hallways leading to the dormitory cells, the scriptorium, refectory, lavatorium, and other rooms. The building was still organized around a courtyard, but it was a very small one and simply served as a prayer garden.

Prior Andrew motioned for Aidan to move toward the fire.

He didn't have to be told twice.

"Warm yourself and start again. Though we are only in September, the past few days have been unusually cold."

He could already feel the warmth seeping back into his pores. It felt delicious.

Aidan began again and told them the story from start to finish. The prior did not speak for several minutes after he ended, digesting what he had been told. The other monks remained silent until their leader had issued his verdict. In spite of the heat reviving his core, Aidan found the silence increasingly unbearable.

Finally, the man spoke. "And do you intend to seek vengeance?" He asked.

The question threw Aidan off guard. Thoughts of his uncle made him seethe, yet shock still dominated and benumbed him. He hadn't had time to think about anything past finding shelter for the night.

Vengeance? In the morning, it might sound sweet. Today, he was too tired.

"I don't know. I am without resources," he replied.

The prior considered this.

"That is a truthful answer, I imagine. Very well, you may stay for a time, but we will not harbor you for the purpose of exacting secular revenge. If you ever decide that is your aim, you must leave us."

Aidan nodded in assent, grateful to hear a bed might greet his weary back soon.

"You will turn your weapons over to . . ."

"I only have a bow . . ."

"Which is a weapon. You will turn your bow over to Brother Geoffrey for as long as you are here. You will also be required to work seven hours of manual labor in the gardens each day except for the Sabbath."

Aidan nodded again.

"Very well. Welcome to St. Alban's."

His smile was grim and wary.

***

The young man looked more distressed than most that showed up at the priory door. Beyond the obvious cold, hungry, and tired, there was a clear shade of fear brimming in his eyes. The kind of fear that only occupies the destitute and insecure, those who've lost their belief in safety.

Prior Andrew knew that feeling. His parents had been poor and unable to feed all their children. They'd dedicated Andrew to God and left him at another monastery when he was only eight years old.

That had been almost fifty years ago now, but that insecurity took a while to go away. A person doesn't forget that moment when the world is first turned on its ear, when you realize the firmness of the ground beneath your feet is only an illusion.

A monastery was a place of refuge though, an oasis of surety in a world of paper-thin promises. Andrew had learned that in God there is peace. Only in His service had he found a solid foundation on which to walk. As Solomon had once said, all else is a vapor, vanity.

He knew the Falconer family. They were a good family — or had been one at least. He remembered when Marie had died so unexpectedly. There had been whispers of suicide at the time, or even murder. The priest in Becca's Well had declared it an accident, which had satisfied the sheriff, even if it hadn't fully satisfied Baron Falconer.

Prior Andrew had only seen William Falconer on a couple of occasions. He'd met the man before his wife's passing and then encountered him again twice after. In those later instances, his eyes had seemed haunted, the lines of his face deeper.

Over the decades, many young men had passed through St. Alban's front door since Prior Andrew had first joined its brotherhood. All of them looking for a place in life, a purpose. Scared they wouldn't find it.

Though there was something different about Aidan. While the fear in his eyes was normal for someone of his age who had just gone through such a traumatic upheaval, there was a clear steeliness of spirit still shimmering behind it.

He's going to need every ounce of that strength.

Long before the events of this week, murmurs about Richard Falconer and his dealings had reached Andrew's ears, and if half of what he'd heard was true, Aidan was up against some powerful forces.

In the months to come, if he chose to not join their brotherhood — and Andrew suspected he was not the type — then Aidan would truly need a miracle to overcome them.

A miracle, Prior Andrew could not provide, but hospitality, he could.

It was their duty as followers of the Rule of St. Benedict to provide shelter to those in need. They could help with the cold, hungry, and tired parts, but as for his larger struggle . . . Aidan would have to find his own way.

***

The Benedictines maintained a cautious eye, especially during the first days as he settled into his daily routine. They kept him busy in the fields surrounding the monastery, pulling fiercely-rooted weeds from the furrows and caring for the crops.

The harvest would begin soon. He was sure they would work him like a dog then.

After a few weeks, they grew used to his presence, but he could feel he remained an outsider. He was a trained warrior, and they were men of the cloth. Oil and water.

He itched to pick up a sword and practice, but they didn't have one — and even if they did, picking one up would likely get him thrown out on his ear.

Aidan stewed repeatedly over what had happened. As sorrow faded, he began to feel cheated. Anger seated itself firmly within his heart. His uncle had not only left him landless, but also status-less.

Under Sir Bart's tutelage, Aidan had only been months away from being knighted. Yet, without that ceremony officially offering entrance into the brotherhood of knights, and without his uncle's sponsorship, he was in limbo, without position in society. No better than the outlaws who'd stripped him in the forest.

Aidan sank his fingers deep into the soil in search of the roots of an especially stubborn weed. He winced as a fingernail caught and bent on a hidden stone. He pulled it out and examined it. The nail had split, and it hurt.

One of the brothers had left a pail of water next to the well, so he went and poured some over his fingers to try and clean it. He bit at the nail until the split section was gone. The soil tasted rich on his tongue.

Soil.

Land.

It was the essence of power in England. Without it, one was powerless, moneyless.

And he could see no way of getting his back. If those closest to his father, men like Nicholas Fontaigne, would not take up his cause, then how could he expect anything different from those in distant authority.

Aidan spat out a tiny granule of rock and got back to work.

Chapter 7

I'm giving everything I've got
God knows I know it's not a lot
I'm headed somewhere but I don't know where just yet

"Back to You"

~ Wild

February 1137 AD – St. Alban's Monastery, Derbyshire

Months passed. Aidan grew leaner, his muscles turning sinewy from the stingy portions the monks allowed themselves and the lack of available meat. They did not hunt and so relied on passing traders to bring the occasional cut of deer or sheep. The strenuous labor of the harvest followed by building maintenance throughout winter kept him in shape and strong, but his type of strength was changing. His muscles held more endurance, but he rued the lack of power he now felt in his arms.

In the evenings, Brother Aelfric spent countless hours in the chapter room teaching Aidan how to read by candlelight.

Honestly, he'd already known how to read. His father had deemed it important and instructed the priest to begin tutoring him in his letters a few years ago.

But he'd been rusty and not very good at it. Those lessons had always taken a back seat to Sir Bart's, and frankly, he hadn't cared that much for learning back then. Aelfric helped him with his speed and also taught him something of history and philosophy.

Most of Aelfric's books were in Latin, but he had some in Norman French and even a couple in English. Aidan dug into the works of both languages and actually found himself preferring the English tomes, though he was Norman through and through.

His favorite by far was an English translation of the Gospels done by some abbot whose name was also coincidentally Aelfric. His Aelfric only let Aidan read small portions of the Bible, however, and those were on the sly. He said the prior would have his hide if he knew he was letting laymen read the Holy Scriptures in English. Only those learned in theology were thought to have enough understanding to profit from it.

Aidan didn't know why that was. The writing seemed fairly straightforward. Illuminating too.

Prior Andrew entered the chapter room and turned his palms to the fire in an effort to warm out the chill of the night. Aelfric and Aidan paused in their studies to see if he wished to speak, and then resumed when he didn't immediately.

A few minutes later, the prior did break the silence.

"Aidan, Spring will soon be upon us."

"Yes, Father."

"I have watched you closely and am very pleased with your progress. Both in labor and in your studies here with Aelfric. I know he's allowed you to take a peek at the Gospels from time to time. What are your thoughts?"

Aelfric turned a bright shade of red.

"Uh . . . they seem . . . they are powerful writings indeed. Full of truth," Aidan answered.

Andrew studied him, then smiled and nodded.

"You must soon decide what you wish to do with yourself. Will you stay with us and join our order, or will you venture out on your own?"

Aidan had known this day was coming. He could not stay here indefinitely and knew they would want him to become a brother or move on.

"I remain ever grateful for your hospitality, prior, but I do not believe my path lies here among the brethren."

"Very well, then. I thought as much. You have behaved admirably during your stay, a true gentleman. Not once did you grow impatient, nor impertinent in spite of your former entitlement. Not once did you ask me to allow you to practice with a weapon, though I know your hands must ache for the familiarity."

Aidan bowed his head, embarrassed by the unexpected compliments.

"Yes, you have shown true humility. Humility I never would have expected from a Norman of your position."

"Thank you, father."

"In the Spring, once the land has thawed, it will be time for you to leave."

Aidan nodded.

"Follow me then."

The prior left the chapter room into the hall through the rear entrance.

Taken off guard, Aidan rose and followed along with Aelfric, who could only shrug his shoulders and looked just as puzzled when Aidan prodded him for answers in whispered tones.

Andrew led them to the scriptorium. Here, built-in shelves and nooks holding scrolls and books lined most of the wall space. A few study tables and desks were distributed around the room as well. A recently stoked fire in the hearth flickered strong light through the small study, bathing it in dancing shades of orange.

The prior moved to one of the bookshelves and began to remove its books until he'd cleared off at least forty from one row and stacked them on one of the tables.

"Aelfric, stand guard and make sure no one comes in."

Now, they were even more puzzled. Aidan peered around the prior and saw a rectangular crack in the wood panel behind the shelves, hinting at a possible secret compartment hidden there. Sure enough, Andrew pushed on one of the corners and a section of the panel popped off to reveal a long, narrow niche behind it.

Immediately, the glint of metal shone out from the dark cubbyhole.

It was a sword.

The prior reached in, lifted it from a pair of wooden hooks, turned, and showed it to Aidan.

The blade looked ancient.

It was a long broadsword. Very long. In fact, he'd never before seen a blade of that length.

The shape was odd too. The blade was flatter and wider than a normal arming sword. It had a raised ridge running down its center, and the shape was slightly rounded. Its edge lines curved inward a short way from the hilt, then flared out again, remaining wide for the rest of its length until tapering off at the point.

The metal did not shine like a recently-forged blade, but someone had clearly made an effort to keep it polished. The hilt was tarnished silver with a straight, unadorned crossguard. A single ruby gleamed from the hilt's center.

Prior Andrew hefted it up, one hand under the blade, the other under the hilt and nodded for Aidan to take it.

Aidan lifted it from his hands and was immediately surprised by the weight. Most swords weighed between three to five pounds. Sir Bart had always made Aidan train with a seven-pounder to build muscle and increase his agility when holding a more standard, lighter weapon. This blade weighed more than that.

"Where did you get this?" Aidan asked, eyes pouring over its surfaces.

"Its origins are old and mysterious, but now it belongs to you."

He was shocked. "You're . . . you're *giving* it to me?"

The prior nodded and folded his arms across his chest with hands resting in opposing sleeves.

"I thought you said I couldn't have a weapon. That was a rule."

"As I said, I have been watching you, Aidan. You are a good man. You have not allowed revenge to grasp your heart, yet neither are you a soft man. You are not meant for a life here in the monastery. Your purpose is other. That sword came into my hands many years past. Until now, I had not found a worthy owner.

"Your father has been taken from you, so perhaps it is for me to be a father to you now in whatever limited way I can."

Aidan's eyes watered and threatened to spill over. He had never guessed the prior felt any affection for him at all. He choked the sentiment back.

"I am in your debt, Prior. Thank you," Aidan bowed his head in respect. He hesitated, but then ventured another question. "May I practice?"

The prior nodded again. "Please keep the existence of this sword a secret from the other brothers. Only Aelfric knows of it. Hide it under your bedding and you may practice at night, after Compline. You will be excused from Matins, but," he wagged a finger, "You must still be up early for your morning chores."

"Yes, Prior," Aidan laughed.

"And you must still leave at Spring thaw."

"Yes, Prior."

***

The sword was heavier than any he'd ever held before. He credited that to its abnormal length and width. At first, his weakened, sinewy muscles were no match for its mass, but he kept working at it.

He convinced the prior to also give him back his bow and let him hunt for meat. After he promised not to shoot any of the king's deer while living at the monastery, the prior assented, and Aidan soon found enough rabbit and other wildlife to contribute extra meat to the meals of the entire cloister. Of course, this increased his popularity among the brothers.

The prior even authorized extra portions of bread and gruel for Aidan's meals and he soon found his strength returning in full force.

March entered with blasts of violent southern winds clashing with walls of cold resistance from the north. Spring was on its way and Aidan knew his time was short.

He worked himself four to five hours every night, slicing and swooping, dodging imagined foes and thrusting at the conceived gaps in their armor. After each session, mere seconds lay between his head crashing to the pillow and being overcome by a hard sleep. The next day, he would again put in a full day of work for the brothers.

Then, one morning, he awoke without the chill of pre-dawn winter air paining his lungs. His heavy wool blankets, which were normally barely adequate, today felt stifling enough that he pushed them off his legs.

He rose, washed his face with water from the laver, which was also warmer than normal, and got dressed. Better weather was finally here.

He donned his shirt and noticed that it was harder to button up. The material stretched tightly around his muscled shoulders and biceps. Either it had shrunk, or he was growing thicker. He pinched the skin under his chin and at his lower side but detected no flab.

He would speak with Andrew this morning, but he feared he already knew what the prior would say to him.

And he was right.

After breakfast, Andrew and Aelfric approached him.

"Aidan, my son, I am afraid it's time." The cleric seemed sincerely pained by the parting.

"Yes, I thought today would be the day," Aidan replied.

"Please know that you are welcome to visit here any time," the prior said.

He and Aelfric each wrapped Aidan in an embrace, and then Aidan retrieved his few belongings from his bedchamber.

He'd rigged a scabbard and sling for the sword to hang diagonally across his back. Its extra length caused the hilt to stick out higher than normal above his shoulder and the tip ran down to the back of his knee. He'd practiced drawing it hundreds of times and, in a pinch, could now do so swiftly.

The other brothers gathered to see him off. Aelfric gifted him with a small book of poetry and told him to look at it later. Aidan thanked him and slipped it inside his small knapsack. Brother Geoffrey, the priory's cellarer, gave him a loaf of black bread and a small flagon of wine, which he also put in his sack. They said their goodbyes and then Aidan left for the trail.

Moments such as these mark divisions in a life, yet they rarely feel momentous in the moment they're made. One minute, he was embracing friends, the next he was off to begin a new life. No trumpets from heaven heralded the dividing second. It passed anonymously like any other moment of time, yet infamous in the starkness of its reality.

He had no idea what lay ahead on this path. His body felt ready, but his mind was unsettled.

He hadn't yet decided on the best course forward. Richard had acted very adeptly. There was honestly little hope for recovering what was his by birth. At least, not for now.

He couldn't even appeal to the Court of the Hundred. He sensed both the sheriff and the constable would favor his uncle's arguments.

Aidan's largest problem was that he had yet to be knighted. He had to become a knight to secure his financial future. Now that his hereditary manor was off limits, his options to gain a knighthood were limited.

He had to distinguish himself before another lord and be taken into their service. There were only two ways to do that: Hire himself out as a mercenary and achieve a notable honor in battle, or through victory in tournament games. For either, he would need full armor, weapons, and a horse. Without those, he couldn't enter a tourney, nor could he be considered more than a commoner in battle.

He'd decided he would make his way south toward London and see what life brought his way. He could hunt and keep himself fed. He just needed a path. An opportunity.

Aidan was well into the forest now. When the road had split, he'd chosen the right fork, which led away from Becca's Well and his heritage. It would take him at least seven days to reach London, if not more, depending on delays and time lost hunting.

A twig snapped somewhere behind him.

"Stand fast, man!"

Aidan froze.

A band of outlaws, at least twelve strong, slipped from the brush on all sides and took up positions in an arc in front of Aidan. Their merry leader had a small scar above his right eye and his face was all too familiar.

"You again," Aidan growled.

Martin the Red threw his head back with laughter. "Well, I'll be! If it ain't the little rich boy come to pay us another visit. Once wasn't enough for you lad, eh? Well, we are happy to receive repeat customers. What have you for us today? You managed to acquire a sword, I see. She'll soon be ours at any rate."

Aidan shifted his feet into a better position, eyes scanning the men behind Martin and their weapons.

"I will fight you for it," Aidan replied grimly.

"Very well." Martin moved forward, drew his blade from its scabbard and readied himself in a fighting stance. There was about a foot of space between the tip of his sword and Aidan's chest.

Aidan waited. "May I draw mine?"

"Stand down, men," Martin called out, "It'll be a fair fight. I like your spirit, boy."

Aidan drew his blade swiftly, its movement a blur. The point came to rest against Martin's throat right above his Adam's apple. It broke the skin and drew a thin trickle of blood.

The outlaw chief gulped visibly.

He had vastly underestimated the length of Aidan's blade. With nothing more than a flick, Aidan could end his life, and the outlaw could not lunge forward with his own weapon without impaling himself.

The rest of the outlaws tensed.

"I wouldn't," Aidan called.

Red waived them off with his free hand.

"Well, this isn't exactly fair now, is it?" he managed a weak smile.

"Nor is twelve against one."

"Touché. What do you want?"

"For starters, how about you lose your weapon."

Martin's sword clanged against a rock as it struck the ground. "Come on, man," he said, "How about we have a true fair fight. I sense you are a man of honor."

"And you are a thief."

"I have more honor than you might think," Martin answered indignantly.

"If you have even a smidgen, it's more than I would think," Aidan replied. "Very well, we shall fight. Have your men drop all their weapons and pile them up by that tree over there."

"You heard him, men! Drop your weapons!"

Aidan did not remove the point while they piled their swords and a few crude maces by a maple tree to his right.

"Bows too!"

The outlaws reluctantly tossed their longbows and quivers full of arrows onto the pile as well. Aidan watched them closely until he was satisfied they were truly stripped of missiles.

"And daggers?" Aidan asked.

"Oh, for the love of Pete!" Martin yelled at his troop, "Did you not give up your daggers?"

A wide assortment of long and short daggers emerged from pockets and joined the growing pile.

"Now?" Martin asked.

"Now," Aidan nodded and stepped back, giving the outlaw chief plenty of room to pick up his weapon.

Martin was quick. His movements revealed significant experience with swordplay, but he was no Sir Bart. Aidan easily deflected his efforts with superior skill, and the outlaw suffered a double disadvantage with the extra length of Aidan's sword. He had to put himself within Aidan's range long before he could strike himself.

They danced awhile. Martin was not going to give up without a fight. He was searching for a chink in Aidan's defenses, a flaw he could take advantage of creatively, but to no avail.

Aidan grew bored with their choreography and moved in more aggressively. The extra weight of his special blade was a powerful force in of itself. Even when Martin successfully blocked a stroke with his weapon, the sheer power behind Aidan's swings pushed the outlaw's sword down and away like a leaf before the wind.

Aidan landed blow after blow on Red, but each time, just before his blade struck home, Aidan twisted it so as to slap Red with the flat of it instead of cutting deep. Each slap sounded sharply and echoed through the otherwise silent glen. The power of the blows repeatedly threatened to knock the outlaw off balance. After a particularly nasty slap on the side of his thigh, Martin's eyes filled with water from stinging pain.

"Do you yield?" Aidan asked.

"I do not" Red was defiant.

"I can flip this blade around any time and start cutting instead."

The outlaw had no armor for defense. He knew he'd been defeated.

Finally, he sighed and tossed his sword into the dust.

"So be it. I yield."

Aidan relaxed and stood his sword on its end, tip to the ground, hands on its hilt.

"I would have the name of the man who defeated me," Martin said.

"Aidan of Falconer Manor."

"Aha! So, I was right. You are a rich boy."

"*Was* a rich boy is more like it."

Martin creased his brow. "Yes, word reached us regarding what happened to young Falconer. We had no idea we'd already met him. So, what do you want, young Aidan?"

"A hot meal and a place to sleep would be nice."

Martin looked puzzled.

"I thought you said I had no sense of honor?" he asked.

"I changed my mind," Aidan replied.

Then, he flipped his sword up and rushed forward, laying the point right under Martin's chin again.

". . . and I'll have your boots. Those are nice boots."

The outlaw grimaced, but when Aidan pressed harder on the blade, he awkwardly took them off, taking pains not to slice his own throat as he moved. He threw them Aidan's way.

"I'll let you keep your clothes," Aidan offered, "which is better than you did for me."

"I thank you for that."

"But you have to carry them."

***

Martin the Red marched to his camp in his underwear, clothes piled up in bundles on top of his outstretched arms. Aidan marched right behind him the entire way.

He'd allowed the other outlaws to rearm themselves, but Aidan insisted they travel ahead of him and Red to prevent them from posing any threat to Aidan from behind.

Red's mood alternated between great mirth at his unexpected turn of fortune and red-faced humiliation when he caught one of his men snickering.

Aidan decided he'd need to keep an eye on Big Ranulf. The over-sized man had a strong fondness for Red and, unlike the others, he saw no amusement in his leader's predicament.

After a mile, they turned off the path and onto an indiscernible route that wound deep into the woods. One of the outlaws suddenly dropped back.

Aidan tensed, immediately wary. Red calmed him, explaining his job was to spread leaves over where they had walked to conceal the way from the foresters or the king's soldiers.

The camp lay in an inconspicuous little dale in between a series of small ridges. Their homes were essentially small, timberless, wattle-and-daub thatched huts, a construction that was easier and less permanent than full houses, but more comfortable than a shoddy tent or lean-to.

Aidan was surprised to see a number of women milling around, making preparations for the noonday meal. He had assumed these men were living roughly in a cave somewhere, yet he saw that even children darted between the humble structures in play.

It was an entire hidden village.

Of course, the villagers quickly noticed the stranger in their midst. Universally stone-faced, they paused in the middle of their chores to watch Aidan pass, but ripples of laughter bubbled up from their ranks when the mostly naked Martin came into view.

Aidan passed all the way through and seated himself against a tree trunk on the far side of the village.

No one approached, nor did they salute or smile. They all returned to their business as if nothing unusual had happened, though the children made sure their game of Tag never flowed too close.

Later, a now fully clothed Red came over to him bearing a bowl of steaming gruel. Aidan dug into the meal, using his fingers to scoop it out and making no effort to disguise his hunger. Each bite lay thick and clumpy and tasteless in his mouth, but the whole was warm and filling in his belly, and that was where it counted.

Red crouched by his side as he ate.

"You are a skilled warrior, Aidan. Not at all the spoiled brat I thought you to be."

"I was to be a knight," he answered, "And being skilled in combat does not mean a man is not spoiled as well."

"It takes a certain discipline and dedication to become as good as you are. And what of these?" He turned Aidan's hand up and pointed at the lines of calluses running across his palm. "These over here are the calluses of a fighter, but these others and the dirt under your nails say you've been working a field."

"I worked for the monks of St. Alban's over the winter."

"As I said, you are not spoiled."

Aidan paused, staring him in the eye, then returned his focus to his food.

"Where will you go from here?" Red asked. He produced a piece of crusty bread, and Aidan used it to sop the remnants from his bowl.

He shrugged his shoulders. "I need to be knighted. I'll head south in search of a tourney or a lord who will retain me."

"Without hauberk or steed?"

With his knife, Aidan pointed at the very familiar, white stallion grazing on the opposite side of the camp. "You've got my courser over there. I'll be taking him with me."

"Still, you'll need armor, and that is no cheap proposition."

"Your point?" Aidan set his bowl down on some fallen leaves.

"We need skilled men here. If you're as good with that bow as you are a sword, we could use you."

"To rob wayfarers?"

"To survive. These are rough times. We try not to molest the poor."

"Seems to me you could do a better job distinguishing between those who have and have not."

Red swept his arms apart in dramatic flair and dipped his head. "You have my apologies, Aidan, but a man riding a stallion as fine as yours does not appear poor at first glance."

"It is no sin to be rich, Martin, nor is it a virtue to be poor. God distributes unevenly," Aidan said.

"There are some here who might disagree with you, but I am not one of them. Regardless, we are faced with the issue of our survival. We are men without land, without lord, trying to provide for our families in what humble way we can. In England, many of those who have much are sinners indeed, not because of their possessions, but because of how they came to possess them."

Aidan nodded in agreement. "Have you ever robbed from my family or its estate?"

"Most who pass through here are not headed toward Becca's Well. The only one I can recall was a knight by the name of Walter."

"Ha!" Aidan laughed, "Him I'll not begrudge you!"

"You are like us now, Aidan. An outlaw in status, if not by deed. Why not stay?"

Aidan considered the proposal in silence. To say yes could be to give up on ever becoming a knight.

"Perhaps you could steal a hauberk from one of your uncle's knights and then be on your way," Red offered.

"I'll think about it," was all Aidan was willing to say for now.

Chapter 8

I'm an ordinary man, a wheel on the cage
I've never been this lost, but I don't wanna have to stay
In the morning I'm leaving and I don't know where I'm going

"State I'm In"

~ Needtobreathe

March 1137 AD

Aidan remained with the outlaws for a few days while he waited for Spring to fully break through. They seemed to warm to his presence in tune with the weather.

His hunting proficiency helped with that too. He felled a couple deer and a half-dozen foxes. This allowed their families to feast on much needed meat. It was enough they were even able to share with extended family who lived in nearby villages outside the forest.

Hunting game in a Royal Forest, especially deer, was a capital offense. The thought of a noose or mutilation did not seem to bother Red and his followers though. Flaunting the king's laws regarding his forests was essential to their survival in their view — their lives were at risk either way — so why not? As long as they could keep the foresters from finding their tracks or their camp, they'd be all right.

Aidan had technically become an outlaw himself the moment he felled his first deer without license, but as long as this remained unknown to the greater world he could still move on when he was ready.

Not that he really wanted to. Red and his people were a warm bunch, friendly and welcoming once they realized he was no threat. They hadn't forced him to participate in their highway crimes.

Yet, every day that passed, Aidan became more convinced of the truth of Red's words. He had to get his hands on some armor. He'd be no better than a commoner in the eyes of a lord without it.

One day, he returned from a hunt dragging behind him another deer and a wolf. The people cheered the deer but insisted on burning the wolf. They refused to partake of canine meat. They had some kind of superstition about getting contaminated by it and becoming a werewolf.

After the evening meal, as the camp was settling in for a peaceful night's rest, he went to find Red.

"Red, I think I'd like to stay," he said.

The outlaw leader leapt to his feet and clapped him on the shoulder. "That's great!" he smiled, "We're lucky to have you."

"I have some concerns though."

"Name them."

"I will not be a part of robbing the general public."

"There are those who deserve it."

"There are indeed. But if we are to take from the corrupt, we should give our gleanings to those from whom it was taken."

Red considered this.

"What you propose is unusual, but I've heard of others who are doing this. Robin of Locksley leads men in Sherwood Forest who frustrate the sheriff to no end. They distribute much of what they steal to the people of Nottingham."

"Then they are our brothers in arms. Sheriff Peverel is as corrupt as they come and he is Stephen's man."

"You support Maud then?"

"I don't believe Stephen can claim the throne."

Several years prior, King Henry, a decent king by the opinion of most, had suddenly died. His only son had perished in a shipwreck fifteen years earlier, so before his death, Henry had made his nobles swear allegiance to his daughter Maud and her two-year-old son, also named Henry after his grandfather.

However, once the king finally died, his nephew Stephen had ignored the oaths of fealty and rushed to London to secure the throne for himself, with the support of his brother, the Bishop of Winchester.

Recognizing the mortal threat the usurpation implied to her young son, Maud had pulled back, but her supporters declared their determination to see her inherit her rightful claim.

One of them, King David of Scotland, had invaded northern England several times already, wreaking havoc and distracting Stephen.

Since then, England had slowly descended into anarchy.

In fact, his uncle Richard's support of Stephen was a major reason Richard had been successful in wresting Falconer Manor from Aidan. His father's tentative support for Maud as the rightful claimant had been well known.

"And you?" Aidan asked.

"Politics do not interest us. We here are too small to consider such things.

Starvation and injustice are the menacing threats that matter to us, not who rules England. In the end, when men have bled and died, whoever sits on the throne will make no difference to our lot."

"Henry was a good king, was he not?"

"Aye, that he was. But Henry is dead, Stephen is known, and Maude is not. It's all the same."

"Well, as long as you're harassing William Peverel, count me in," Aidan agreed.

The Sheriff of Nottingham, William Peverel, was grandson of William the Conqueror and lord of most of Derbyshire as well as Nottinghamshire.

"We don't see him too often in these parts — Nottingham is much more profitable to him than Derby — but we see his agents aplenty."

"As I said, count me in on men like those."

***

That night, the villagers threw a party in honor of Aidan's decision to join them. Roasted venison, rich vegetable stew, and steaming bread dripping with butter abounded. Someone broke out the mead, and hearty song soon followed.

Young maidens danced to the rhythms of recorder and lute, twirling in tune to fiery, swirling sparks ascending into the night sky.

Aidan laughed at the merriment, his heart lightened for the first time in far too long. Three of the girls, a brunette, a redhead, and a blonde seemed especially intent on catching his attention with their talents. He smiled whenever he caught one in a sly glance his way, but they were too young.

Another maiden with honey-colored locks, a striking lass of seventeen by the name of Alveua, was much more direct with her intent. Her smiles and attentions were hard to ignore, but Aidan found no room in his heart for anyone but Priscilla.

The men took turns slapping him on the back and welcoming him into their humble tribe. Yet, his camaraderie with them would always remain marked by a subtle distance they themselves inserted due to his nobility. Nevertheless, they made him feel at home.

After several hours, the mood slowly extinguished as the outlaws trickled back into their dwellings. One of them had generously offered to move in with his brother's family so Aidan could use his hut while they built another.

As the festivities wound down and the fire grew dim, Aidan made his way to his new quarters. He laid himself out on its rough bed of straw. His back muscles ached dully as they stretched out following a full day on his feet. He hadn't drunk enough mead to be heady from its influence, but he felt at peace.

Content for the first time in a long while.

He would sleep well.

Chapter 9

Aidan woke the next morning feeling good. He sucked in deeply the crisp, morning air. Its briskness invigorated him for the day's tasks. He stretched, stood, and began to dress. He'd wash his face in the creek after breakfast. He slung his sword across his back and picked up his bow.

A couple of the married women, Edith and Margery, already had the fire going strong and were reheating yesterday's gruel. Edith playfully began to badger him to find a wild boar for some bacon, but he'd only seen one set of boar tracks since arriving, and he wasn't that big a fan of pork.

He'd just begun to dig in to a healthy-sized bowlful of the stuff when one of the men ran into camp.

"Aidan! A band of knights is about to pass. Red wants you."

Aidan put the bowl down and got up. He paused only to fill his quiver before setting off on a jog to the outlaws' favorite ambush site.

He found Red partially concealed behind a tree on a small ridge, shoulders turned to form a line pointing to the road, bow drawn and arrow nocked. Red's attention was riveted on the scene below, though he broke his gaze for a second to acknowledge Aidan's arrival. Aidan spied a couple of the other outlaws in their hiding places and knew there would be a good group of them on both sides of the road.

"What's happening?" Aidan asked.

Red was grim-faced. "A scout came in late last night with news of a traveling band camped a few miles up the way. He reported two knights and a couple of apprentices, which wouldn't have been too bad. But we just realized that was wrong. It's actually one knight and five men-at-arms. And they aren't ordinary travelers, but a band of soldiers. I've only got eight men. I let the others go off on a hunt because we thought they'd be less formidable than they are."

"Why not let them pass?"

"We know for sure the knight is Sir Grunnald. Have you heard of him?"

Aidan shook his head.

"Last year, he burned an entire village when it failed to meet the Sheriff's quota after the harvest."

"He is the one who burned Wellsey-of-the-Dale?" Aidan's face darkened. "I heard about that."

"My men want to slaughter them before they even know to pull arms, but these will be experienced soldiers. We're outmatched without armor."

"Every death will increase the kind of attention on this forest you don't want," Aidan commented. He'd recommended to Red before that they keep the killing to a minimum.

"Better that than our own deaths," Red replied, lips tightly pursed.

Aidan moved himself behind the tree next to Red. "Go tell your men to steel themselves and wait for my signal. They should stay their hand unless these men resist."

Red hesitated. Then, he nodded and moved off into the trees.

Ten minutes later, the soldiers rounded a bend in the road and came into view. They were indeed six-men strong, all fully outfitted and armed. Five walked while the sixth drove an ox-led cart stuffed to overflowing with wool fleeces.

Right off, Aidan identified Sir Grunnald. Without a doubt, the knight had to be the pompous one with red plumes stuck in his helm.

Aidan waited until he felt the troop was probably surrounded by the positions of Red's men.

He slid an arrow from his quiver, nocked it, and pulled his bow taught. He released his fingers. A faint twang of the string and then the swift missile sliced through the air silently. It pierced the back of Sir Grunnald's hand effortlessly. Its point suddenly protruded from the knight's palm by a good six inches.

Grunnald screamed and clenched his hand tightly between his thighs, doubling over from the unexpected pain. Aidan stepped onto the road in front of them before the other men could comprehend the reason for Grunnald's cry.

"Hold fast, men!" Aidan commanded.

The men-at-arms froze momentarily, but Grunnald didn't hesitate.

"Thieves! Attack!" He garbled, scrambling for his sword with his good hand.

One man-at-arms was in front of the others and already rushing Aidan. Aidan slung his long blade from its scabbard on his back and clunked the man right on the helmet.

The rich clang resounded as the attacker stumbled to the ground, stunned. Arrows suddenly protruded from the chests of two others who'd drawn their swords.

The wagon driver pulled a crossbow from underneath the wool behind him but didn't have time to aim it before another missile hit him. His corpse slumped and then slipped from its seat.

The remaining man's slowness saved his life. He'd barely had a hand on his hilt when his comrades went down. Wisely, he changed his mind and lifted his arms to the sky in surrender.

Grunnald also gave up trying to free his sword with his left hand (Aidan had shot his right on purpose, recognizing from the lay of the man's sheath it was his dominant one) and reluctantly surrendered as well, though the ugly fire in his eyes betrayed an unquenched hatred.

"You will pay for this, brigand," he snarled.

"And you will watch your tongue or we'll have it out," Aidan replied coolly. The soldier he'd stunned was regaining his senses, so Aidan stepped on his chest and relieved him of his weapons.

"We heard what you did in Wellsey," he continued.

Grunnald grunted, his lips disappearing in a thin line. "We are Nottingham's men and now you have assaulted the sheriff himself!"

"Are you tempting me to kill the rest of you? Now, for the last time, still that tongue of yours or it will be mine, I swear it."

Aidan allowed the man-at-arms under his foot to stand and then shoved him back towards his surviving pal.

"As for Nottingham," he continued, smiling, "You boys behave and we'll send you home to give good old William Peverel a message for us."

"And what would that be?"

"Tell the sheriff he's got enough problems over there in Sherwood. Until he's solved those, he might want to stay out of Newhaven."

Grunnald spat.

"Now," Aidan cooed, "What exactly are six armed men doing guarding a cart full of wool?"

"Guarding it from the likes of outlaws like you."

Aidan laughed. "You mean Nottingham has nothing better to do with his men than to guard a batch of penny fleeces? I bet if I were to check under there, I might find something of value. What do you think?"

The knight glared.

"Anyway, it's time for you boys to strip."

"What?"

"You heard me. We want your armor, your weapons, and anything else of quality you may have. You can keep your undergarments and tunics. They're probably filthy anyway."

All three started to remove their helms and hauberks. They tossed them and their mail leggings in a pile.

Two of Red's men emerged from the trees and took charge of the weapons and other belongings and hauled them off into the woods. A third began a rude search under the fleeces. In short order, he hollered with success.

As Aidan reached the wagon, the man lifted a section of the wool to reveal the side of a locked chest.

"Pull it out of there," Aidan told him. "We'll get the wool for the ladies later."

One of the previous outlaws returned. Together, the two carried the chest into the woods, disappearing in the shadows among the trees.

Nottingham's men looked pitifully skinny without their armor, and a little cold as they stood there shivering, trying not to look as humiliated as they felt.

"That's it. You boys can go home now. Stay out of Newhaven. If we see you again, we might not be so kind."

The two living men-at-arms turned to go, thankful for the respite. Grunnald hesitated and looked like he was going to say something, but Aidan cocked an eyebrow, and the knight then thought better of it.

Once they were gone, Aidan went to join Red.

"How'd I do?" He asked.

Red pounded him on the back, a huge grin plastered across his face. "That was magnificent. Simply magnificent."

"We should send a scout to trail them and make sure they keep going."

"Already done."

"Good. Let's go see what was in that chest."

***

That night, the celebration was unparalleled. Couples danced with a joy Aidan had not seen in...well...*ever*.

The chest had been full of silver pennies. Enough coins to hire a small army.

There had also been a letter stuffed in one of Grunnald's pockets from William Peverel addressed to the Baron of Manchester requesting soldiers to help put down the outlaws in Sherwood and other brigands around Nottingham-shire that were hindering his ability to support King Stephen. The coins were to compensate the baron for the men he would provide.

The mini army the sheriff requested would not come now that Red's outlaws had intercepted the funds. Of course, the sheriff could simply forget about Manchester now and just seek help elsewhere, or he could send men with another letter by another route, but either way, he would likely leave Red's bunch alone. He already had his hands full, and their band was too far away from Nottingham to be a priority. In the meantime, these people would eat like kings for probably the first time in their lives.

Aidan sat perched on a tree stump enjoying the revelry. He watched the husbands spinning round and round with their wives and found himself longing for Priscilla.

As usual, a number of the girls were vying for his attention. A buxom brunette by the name of Ysabella invited him to dance, so Aidan gave her a whirl.

The round curve of her hip under his hand stirred longings a single man tried to forget, and the bounce of her wavy locks gleaming in the firelight intoxicated him. Her eyes were a rich, chestnut brown, as big as a doe's. She pulled him close, and the light aroma of lilac reached him.

Still, his heart would not relent. He could only see Priscilla's face. The romantic tension of the moment demanded a kiss, yet Aidan pulled back. He turned his face away as if looking for someone.

She sensed his reluctance and let him go with saddened eyes. Yet, he caught a flash of something else in them he'd often seen in his mother's. She hadn't given up.

She was an English lass, through and through. He was half-Norman, half-Scottish, but knew the stubborn fire that English blood could yield. More so if she too had a touch of Scottish in her.

His mind turned to other things.

If they could get a few more takes like today's, Aidan could begin to reestablish himself, and Priscilla's father might even let him court her. That was his dream now, his life's hope. To be with Priscilla.

Red and Ranulf emerged from Red's hut and headed his way. Aidan had tried to get Big Ranulf to warm up to him but hadn't been successful so far. Though tonight, there seemed to be a different twist to the big man's mouth. Several other apparent leaders of the outlaw band spilled out of Red's hut behind them and moved to join their families around the bonfire.

"So, what was the take, Red?" Aidan asked.

"There were over twenty pounds in there! Enough to hire a couple hundred men for several months."

Aidan whistled. It was quite the boon.

"We're going to do what you said," Red said. "We'll keep eight shillings per family and send runners with the rest as a gift to the people of Wellsey."

Eight shillings, or ninety-six pennies, was approximately two months of income for a normal worker, so the outlaws would all live comfortably, and the villagers Grunnald had burned out would be blessed too.

"That's good," Aidan said with a content smile.

"There's something more." A mischievous glint gleamed in Red's eye.

"What?" Aidan's suspicions went on alert.

"We met with the elders of our band to discuss you . . ."

"*Me?*"

"Yea. It was unanimous. We think you should lead us."

"Me? Lead your men? What about *you?*"

"You are young, but clearly a lord, Aidan, a man of noble birth . . ."

Aidan snorted. So was his uncle.

". . . And you're a man men want to follow. Just look how you've provided with the hunt. The way you led today and put Sir Grunnald in his place. We'd do well to follow you."

"You've got to be kidding me."

"Not in the least."

"And Ranulf?" Aidan looked to the big man, "Even you, Ranulf, want me to lead?"

Ranulf laughed and wrapped his arm around Aidan's shoulder in a bear hug. He gave him a hard squeeze and let go.

Aidan closed his eyes. A sinking feeling formed in his gut. He needed to think.

He had a mail hauberk now, and a quality one at that. Full armor, weapons, and his stallion. He was ready to enter a tourney and win the favor of a lord and be knighted.

To accept Red's proposal meant responsibility — responsibility that had nothing to do with Falconer manor or winning Priscilla's hand. Responsibility that might publicly brand him as an outlaw one day and forever prevent him from attaining either. Till now, all that he'd done outside the law had been done anonymously. He could still walk away with his reputation intact.

He watched the couples dancing in large circles around the fire, laughing in tune to spontaneous lyrics voiced by a couple of boisterous lads. When he'd first come here, these people had been starving, barely hanging on. If he left now, they would do well for a time, but later, they would struggle again.

Not to mention the constant risk they faced for thievery, for violating the king's forest, and now, for murder of the sheriff's men.

His dream's call pulled on him strongly, even more so now that it seemed within his grasp. He was ready now. He could go. Yet, that call wrestled against his sense of moral obligation and duty. Duty and honor had mattered more to his father than anything.

Duty and honor.

Duty and honor.

Duty meant responsibility for others. Honor meant choosing others over oneself.

He opened his eyes and fixed them on Red. His stomach twisted.

"I'll do it," he said.

Chapter 10

So, I've started out, for God knows where
I guess I'll know when I get there
I'm learning to fly, around the clouds...

"Learning to Fly"

~ Hills x Hills

As leader, Aidan's first order was for everyone to keep his true name a secret for as long as possible. He did this in part because he still hoped to protect his reputation so he could pursue knighthood later, but he also didn't want news of his deeds to reach Priscilla's ears.

Even more importantly, he didn't want Richard to realize he was still so near. This band of outlaws was not ready to face the onslaught his uncle might unleash in order to put Aidan down.

He started training the men, both in the art of war and the hunt. As a noble, Aidan had plenty of experience hunting with his father and others, but the royal forests had been off limits to peasants for so long now that most hunting knowledge had been forgotten among their ranks, having died off with their great-grandfathers who'd lived before William the Conqueror and the advent of Norman Law.

Aidan trained them in the methods of tracking, and several of the spry, younger ones took to it like ducks to water, especially a sharp-faced fellow of twenty by the name of Eric.

It wasn't long before Eric was spotting sign and tracks that were not even obvious to Aidan. He formalized these young men into a group of scouts and put Eric in charge.

Aidan had a total of twenty-four men, and a few more women than that, who were fit to serve. Outside of them, there were many teenage boys and girls, even more younger children, and some elderly and infirmed. Yet, none were free from work, for their survival depended on it. Thankfully, the children were mostly well-behaved, and when they did play, they did so close to camp.

Defense and security were paramount. Red showed him a cave a few hundred yards behind their makeshift village. It had a small entrance, inconspicuous in the forested hillside. A man had to bend over to get through the opening, but once inside, it widened beautifully.

The main chamber was large and high. It was as if the entire hill was a hollowed-out dome. Large fissures in the top of the dome were the perfect size and shape to allow smoke to escape from a fire burning inside, and tree branches hanging over the cracks filtered the smoke in a way that it would not be detectable from a distance.

He sent Eric and friends exploring with torches farther into the caverns and they located two additional exits that could be used as emergency escape routes if they were ever bottled up inside by an enemy. They blocked these small entrances with medium-sized rocks that would hide the opening from outsiders wandering by yet could be pushed away from the inside by a woman or large child on the run.

Along the darkened paths from the main chamber to these escape hatches, they left a series of new torches ready to be lit as people ran. Aidan ordered the main chamber stocked with loads of kindling and storable foodstuffs. They also kept the bulk of their money hidden in a cut-out among the rocks inside.

The ladies wove a curtain of vine, moss and leaves to drape down over the main entrance to prevent its discovery by others. At first, Aidan didn't see how their work could possibly achieve their goal, but by the time they were done, their curtain so resembled a natural hillside that even he could not believe there was a cave behind it.

They now had a solid refuge — a place to run and hide if the village were ever assaulted.

Clear commands were given to all to avoid running to the cave if they were within eyesight of enemies. It was not fair to put everyone else in jeopardy to save the life of one. If a person were fleeing and the attackers were too close behind, they were to continue to the river and swim across. Men in mail would be too heavy to follow.

Next, it was time to beef up the defenses of the village itself. They worked hard to eliminate any traces of a path to the camp. They constantly scattered loose leaves across the routes they actually used and tamped down leaves elsewhere, creating a number of fake paths that ran to nowhere, each leading far from the outlaws' home.

The ladies made more of their leaf "curtains" and Aidan had them installed at various intervals among the thickets and brambles that surrounded the paths they used to reach the village.

He identified the mostly likely approaches attackers would take if making a move on them. Then, outside the camp's perimeter, they dug lines of pits about three feet deep. In the bottoms of the pits, they imbedded stakes sharp enough to pierce a boot. Next, they covered these pits with thin branches and leaves or patches of moss until they were indistinguishable from the forest floor.

Every villager, including the children, knew the location of these boobytraps. Three pathways were left clear of traps so they could enter or exit the village from any direction without risk, but you had to be one of them to know where those safe approaches were.

These lines of pits would serve as an alarm system of sorts. Intruders would likely to scream in pain after stumbling upon one. It would give them enough warning to either arm and escape or dig in and fight.

They also dug out and camouflaged a myriad of hidey-holes around the forest so a man could conceal himself in a flash if he were being pursued. They cut special markings in the trees next to these locations so they'd be easy to spot on the run, but you had to know what to look for. They were set up so an outlaw could dive under a small overhang and cover his body with a carpet of leaves in a flash.

Aidan established a two-man policy. No outlaw was to move about the forest alone, and no robbery was to be undertaken against anyone except those wealthy noblemen who were known to be corrupt and deserving, and then only with superior numbers and the element of surprise in place.

He trained his men to handle a sword. He also worked with them on improving their skill with the bow, which, being peasants, was much better than their hand-to-hand skills. Some knights viewed the bow as beneath their sense of honor, but it was a more familiar instrument in the hands of many commoners — and *all* outlaws.

Seven of the men proved to be especially proficient bowmen, so Aidan designated them as the archer squad and teamed them up with his younger trackers for hunting. He put Martin the Red in charge of the combined group and tasked them with felling as many of the king's deer and other game as they possibly could. What their camp could not eat, they would distribute secretly among the neighboring villages.

For the most part, it was the stronger, more burly men who proved they could fight with a sword when tested. He put Big Ranulf in charge of this group and was able to outfit half of them with the armor and weapons they'd taken from Sir Grunnald's bunch. The other half would have to wait until they confiscated more. When they weren't practicing fighting skills, they dedicated themselves to making improvements on the village's infrastructure.

By May, Aidan breathed a little easier. He had a tiny army now, outfitted for both offense and defense. He was proud of the effort these people had put into every initiative. He found himself caring deeply for each of them. There didn't seem to be a bad apple among the bunch.

They confiscated moderate amounts of silver off a few knights and local barons passing through but hadn't yet had another significant take like Sir Grunnald's.

So far, Aidan's only real struggle was resisting the pleas of those who wanted to bring brothers, and sisters, and parents, and cousins into their circle. Just a few months prior, being an outlaw had been a miserable affair, but now the provisions and wealth were flowing.

Aidan remained firm though. All that they garnered could be shared with relatives, but security was paramount. *Anyone* revealing their location, even to family, would be viewed as a traitor and dealt with accordingly. Aidan allowed a blacksmith and a tanner to join their ranks because, frankly, they needed them, but it was better if their core number remained small.

Chapter 11

After an especially delicious meal of spiced venison stew and steaming rye bread, Aidan laid himself out on the forest floor, full stomach to the sky, and enjoyed the warm sunshine on his face.

He felt like a stuffed holiday bird. He shouldn't have eaten as much as he had, but they'd caught a nasty merchant yesterday laden down with spices from the orient. Such luxury was a rare treat. They were really going to eat like kings now.

"Aidan! Aidan!"

It was one of the scouts interrupting his reverie, calling out as he hurried into camp. He'd come in from the east.

"What is it, Tom?"

"A rich man has entered the forest . . . he looks wealthy anyway. Red said to fetch you."

"Why? If he's just one man, what's the problem?"

"He looks to be clergy. We've never stolen from the church before."

"Taking from a clergyman does not mean you are stealing from the church. If he's a rotten thief, he's no clergyman, though he may wear the vestments of one. Depends on his name."

Aidan followed Tom at a quick pace. As they neared the spot where Red and the others were set up for an ambush, Aidan slowed to a tiptoe so as to not accidentally alert their intended victim. Tom moved up the line to get more intel.

The man was fat, overly so, and had planted his plumpness upon a beautiful chestnut mare. His long coat was plush, lined with rabbit fur, and dyed in a varied pattern of gold, orange and red. He plodded along the road, seemingly oblivious to any danger. At least, he showed no sign of being aware of their presence.

"*Who is he?*" Aidan whispered.

"Don't know," Red replied, hand on his bow. "Looks too rich to be a prior. Bishop maybe? I don't know his face."

"Hmmm," Aidan considered the possibilities. "If he's a bishop, then why does he travel alone?"

Tom returned. "Bert says more men are coming, 'bout five hundred yards back around the bend. Some are armed."

"That must be his escort," Aidan said.

"Why are they so far back?" Red asked. "They can't do much protecting from there."

"Who knows? Maybe he got impatient and rode ahead. Come on."

As the bishop was about to pass, Aidan and Red slipped from the forest right in front of him. Aidan grabbed his reins.

"Hold!" Red cried.

The horse whinnied and retreated several steps. Aidan drew the reins taut, and it calmed.

Fear sunk into the bishop's face, though he tried to hide it. He'd rue his impatience now.

The man glanced back for sign that his companions might come to his rescue, but the path behind him was bare.

"Release my horse, ruffian!" His fat jowls reddened as anger replaced his fear.

"Bishop, we're not above manhandling you, so settle yourself."

The clergyman gasped. "Impertinence! How dare you speak to a man of the cloth that way," he hissed.

Aidan handed the reins to Red and positioned himself on the other side of the horse. Then, he bowed at the waist in an exaggerated courtly fashion. "We, sir, are outlaws, and the only thing that awaits us is a noose. So, you see, speaking disrespectfully to a bishop is the least of our worries."

The bishop clamped his mouth shut. He twisted around in the saddle again, desperately searching for a sign of coming aid.

"We know of your friends, bishop. They're still a long way off, but, if need be, we have others who will delay them. Still, time is of the essence. So, let's get to it."

"What do you want?" he glowered.

"What's your name and who do you support, Stephen or Maud?"

The bishop flicked his eyes back and forth between them, seeking a hint as to their sympathies. Perhaps he'd underestimated their importance. They could be soldiers belonging to either of the battling regents' camps.

"Don't waste time trying to figure out what we want to hear, man," Aidan said, "Answer for yourself and quick or we'll decide you're against us."

"I am Bishop Seffrid of Chichester."

"Chichester! You *are* far from home," Aidan exclaimed.

The bishop gritted his teeth. "As for my loyalty . . ." he hesitated, still trying to gauge them, ". . . *Stephen* is the rightful king."

"Wrong choice. Get off your horse."

The bishop did not obey. "You would rob the church?"

"If you are part of Christ's church, then I am William the Conqueror. This is your last chance, get off the horse or my friend here will knock you off."

Red moved in menacingly.

Seffrid was not happy, but he obeyed, realizing the threat was real. Red searched his saddle packs and shouted elatedly. He lifted a fistful of gold from the pouch and let the coins tinkle through his fingers back into it.

"Gold coins!" Aidan exclaimed. "Whoever heard of such a thing?"

The only coins available in England were silver pennies.

Red flipped one into the air, and Aidan caught it one-handed. He examined both sides closely. It bore no images, nor any lettering he could recognize, just a flowing, flowery, unintelligible script of some kind.

"Looks to me like the writing of the moors," Aidan said.

"How would you know *that?*" Seffrid spat contemptuously.

"Chichester's close to the sea," Aidan continued, "You probably got them from crusaders coming home. And I have studied more than you realize, *your arrogance.*"

"They're called *bezants*, you ignorant lout," Seffrid said. They certainly weren't going to squeeze the insolence out of him in just a few minutes time.

"What are you carrying all this gold for?"

The bishop's lips tightened into a firm, but silent line.

"Please don't make us take you with us," Aidan threatened. "We don't want to spend any more time with you than you do us. It will be unpleasant."

"I won't tell you even if you cut my tongue out!"

"Very well. I doubt your purpose is to feed the poor then."

Seffrid glared hard, but realized he'd said more with silence than he would have with a lie.

"Grab the packs, Red." Aidan yanked the bishop from the horse. He landed hard on the ground with a heavy, flat thud and a thick expulsion of air from his lungs. When the bishop caught his breath again, he used it to let loose a flurry of flustered curses.

Aidan took a leather cord and tied the bishop's hands behind a tree.

"Your friends will be here soon," he said, "We'll put your horse and the gold to good use. Thank you for your contribution. You can keep your fancy coat."

Aidan turned to the woods, leading the horse behind him. Red was already gone.

"Oh," he called back over his shoulder, "Be sure to let your men know we spared them and their armor. If they try to follow us, we'll turn back and take it all."

***

There were a little over 300 of the golden *bezants* in the saddle packs. Aidan estimated they were easily worth at least 25 silver pennies apiece, so it was an unbelievable fortune for the band. It was almost double what they'd gotten from Grunnald.

They sold the horse but melted the gold down into small earrings. They would keep some for themselves but planned to distribute most of it to peasants in the villages.

There was no doubt the bishop would report the theft, so constables would be on the lookout for rare gold coins showing up in somebody's shop. Nobody would be looking for earrings though, so they wouldn't be traced back to them.

Aidan remained conflicted about robbing an elevated priest, but he knew Seffrid's type. Many bishops were truly humble, honorable, dedicated men of God who served their communities. A few, however, were corrupt and worldly and only held their position because they'd been appointed to it by someone in power.

That sort had no heart for God or the church. Often, they were the second son of a nobleman and so would have no inheritance. Thus, their best chance for political advancement was as a bishop.

Seffrid was of this kind. Centuries from now, the church and Christians would be blamed for acts committed by men like him, men who'd never experienced a conversion, men who claimed the name of Christ only because they thought it would lead them to power and wealth.

Well, they'd just relieved Seffrid of a little of his burden, and the more Aidan thought about it, the happier he was with their taking. Who knew how many peasants had sacrificed to pay rents and donate tithes to give that man his money? He'd implicitly admitted he'd been up to no good with it.

Probably some attempt to support King Stephen.

It seemed the entire land had broken down into war.

Later that evening, after another amazing dinner (the hunting party had brought in another deer), Aidan called Red and Ranulf over to confer about next plans.

"I think we need to keep a lower profile for a while," he said.

"Why?" Ranulf asked.

"Because we've robbed from the Sheriff of Nottingham, and now we've robbed a bishop," Red explained.

"Yes," agreed Aidan, "As long as we were targeting lesser barons or the occasional knight, it wasn't so big a deal. But with these higher-class victims, it's liable to bring us too much attention. Those two takes may have netted us a pleasing amount, tis true, but if we become too strong a stench in someone's nostrils, we could find ourselves facing an army ready to invade the forest. We're wiser to lay low right now."

"But these monies were to support Stephen," Ranulf protested, "We can't just let such men pass through, can we?" Ranulf had not cared a lick about politics before Aidan joined the camp, but now he'd absorbed Aidan's outlook on the world like a sponge in water.

Aidan shook his head. "No, but we must be careful. We need to vary much more where we stage our ambushes, or we might walk into one of our own — and if we see any more parties that seem likely to be the bearers of much wealth, we'd do well to let them pass completely through the forest and ambush them elsewhere to deflect attention from here."

The others nodded.

"I'm sure the word is out about our exploits," Aidan continued, "So, we should choose wisely who we give these golden earrings to. We should spread them out among peasants in many different villages around the shire with the condition they keep their ear to the ground and alert us if they catch word of an action forming against us.

Chapter 12

Give me your heart give me your song, sing it with all your might
Come to the fountain and you can be satisfied
There is a peace, there is a love you can get lost inside

"Testify"

~ Needtobreathe

His heart soared the moment he saw her.

She was standing alone, in a field of wheat, smiling at him with such warmth. A wisp of her hair waved before the breeze in tune with the stalks at her waist.

His mother's face was angelic, just as he remembered.

He ran toward her.

But the field seemed to stretch on interminably.

She lifted her arms in welcome, beckoning him to a hug.

Oh . . . how he longed to feel her arms surround him once more. It had been too long. Her smile breathed love.

He pushed his legs faster, but he could not seem to draw nearer. At least, he could now feel the breeze that graced her also blowing upon his face. Yet, the distance lingered frustratingly. He ran harder.

A sliver of understanding broke through the fog of his confusion, and he realized he must be in a dream.

Mentally, he strained to alter the environment.

At last, the field began to shrink in tune with his pace, though still too slowly for the strength he was exerting.

He pushed hard and doubled his effort. Finally, the field gave up its fight against his will, and he suddenly found himself at her side.

She was so healthy, so happy, so at peace. He loved her smile. He remembered *that* smile. With desperation, he yearned to hug her, yet instead, found himself kneeling at her feet.

She touched her fingertips lightly to his cheek.

"Grow," she whispered.

He awoke with a start.

Grow.

The thought echoed through his mind over and over.

What did it mean?

He hadn't dreamed of his mother since he was a child.

She'd looked so beautiful . . . so real. More so than he could have consciously remembered. Her face had long since faded from his memory, yet the details of its lines were now fully refreshed.

He lay back down on his bed and sighed in puzzled contentment.

After a minute, he wiped the sleep from his eyes, stood, and left the hut.

It was still very early, so the camp was silent.

The soft, cool morning wind invigorated his skin. Leaves rustled loudly overhead as branches and thinner trunks swayed before it. The grove was fully verdant with the bright, lively greens of early summer. He saw a couple of squirrels darting back and forth, chasing each other around a nearby tree.

Normally, the camp was so full of activity, this peaceful morning was a rare opportunity for solitude among the outlaws.

Aidan grabbed his weapons and left the village, taking the path toward the river.

Instead of heading to the normal spot where the women drew water and washed their families' clothes, Aidan turned off onto an unmarked way that led farther upstream. After a few minutes, he topped a small ridge and then descended the secluded slope on the other side.

At the bottom, the air hung misty and thick amid the roar of falling water. The river dropped ten feet in a single, strong current from the top of a bluff until it crashed into a rounded pool below. The water was clear and fresh, and at its middle, the pool was deep enough for swimming.

Though directly underneath the falls, the depth was sufficiently shallow for him to stand under the torrent. He'd bathed here a couple of times. It was a heavy and powerful shower, but oh so cleansing.

He knew others bathed here too every now and then, which is why he'd come so early in the morning. He'd wanted to be alone.

Aidan stripped, folded his clothes, and laid them on a dry log. He left his sword and bow by the waterline for swift access. A knight never knew when a threat would arise.

He knew the water had not yet had time to be warmed by the sun. He gritted his teeth against the shock and dove in, plunging all the way under. The cold was chilling, but a minute later, his skin had adjusted to the new temperature and began tingling as if it were being lightly stimulated by hot water instead of cold.

He stood under the falls and let the current pour down over his head. The strength of it battered his shoulders and threatened to throw him off balance. He braced himself and steadied his feet, enjoying the sensation of streamlets running deep through his hair. It ran down his back and chest in drenching rivulets of cold fire.

This place brought him a magnificent feeling of cleanliness, as if the entire world were being washed off his skin and even from his very soul.

He rubbed his scalp to rinse out days of accumulated oil. Next, he scrubbed his arms and legs, erasing streaks of dirt with little effort.

Aidan stepped out of the falling water and swept the remaining wet from his eyes and face with his fingers.

An unexpected sweetness met his ears, and he paused…

…a beautiful lilting melody that sounded like the voice of an angel.

Whoever the singer was, she was not in sight, but somewhere over the ridge.

At first, he could not distinguish the syllables, for she was too far away and the water's roar still too loud.

Aidan moved toward the middle of the pool away from the falls. Now, he could make out the words.

As Hawthorns bloom in fresh Spring light
Beneath the skies of Derby
My feet rise a' dance, stirring clouds a' white
In glades of Spindle tree

He moved closer to the shore where the rush of the waterfall was softer. Hastily, Aidan ran his hands over his skin, scrubbing the dirt from his stomach and thighs as fast as he could.

O' golden morn' yer sun streams bright
For to banish eve's dark night
Young air crisp an' laden in the miry mist
Toes wet o' dew ere it lifts.

He stepped from the water, sloshed what wet he could from his hair, and slipped his tunic over his head.

I leave thee behind O' shady grove
And run to seek my love
And run to seek my love

The tune caught his heart, producing a lump in his throat. He tugged his boots on, one at a time. Not an easy task with damp feet, but somehow, he managed.

Whisper o' wind pass through the boughs
Hushed promises and lover's vows

He glanced up. Was it his imagination or was the wind swaying the oak branches above his head? He could almost hear their whisper.

Cheery lilts of thrush, wren and whimbrel
Beneath the skies of Derby
Birdsong trills flood the wood tranquil
Beneath the skies of Derby

Within his mind, he could suddenly hear the clear notes of songbirds. Aidan strapped his sword to his back and ascended the ridge.

He had to know who she was.

O' fragrant earth, Light laurel scent
Wake my sense, tell me how he went
As I run an' seek my love
As I run an' seek my love

The rich aromas of wet soil and wistful flowers unexpectedly teased his nostrils, as if they had always been there, as if the song had merely awakened him to their presence.

O' gentle river, melodious flow
Lead the forest e'er you go

He reached the ridgetop and looked down. Below, numerous trees were scattered across a smallish glen with little undergrowth beneath them. Instead, wide patches of grass carpeted the clearings between their trunks.

A beautiful young woman in a mint-green frock danced among them. Her long, auburn hair flowed, twirling and falling, trailing behind her as she moved.

She held the ends of a pale yellow shawl in each hand and was weaving it through the air in rippling patterns. Her eyes shone with joy of being and her face was lit by a radiant, smile.

Ysabella.

Clear waters lending life
Trees dancing midst their strife

She was unaware of his presence.

Her dance captivated him. The way the folds of her dress and the tresses of her hair curled in sync with her floating feet…it was as if she was borne up by the morning breeze itself. Her voice trebled clear and melodic, like the solitary member of an angelic chorus among the forest's pillars.

As dawn's rays at last break the line
Across the flowery meadow stands mine
My lost love, be there by the willow
Alone had I the sun's beams to follow

I found him 'neath the skies of Derby
O' neath the skies of Derby
I had only to run, my love
I had only to run, my love

She finished her song and bent to examine a lavender-tinted flower at her feet. Gently, she plucked it and began the song again.

Aidan retreated several steps behind the ridge to make himself less conspicuous, but not so far he couldn't see her. Her song . . .

If she saw him, the magic would be broken. He felt drawn to her, his heart a prisoner of her art, rooting his feet in place as if he were just another tree in the woods blessed by the grace of her swirling beauty.

He watched her for a long time. Ysabella sang several more melodies, none of which he'd heard before. She finally grew tired and left the glade to return to camp.

Aidan ran his hand through his thick, wavy hair in contemplation. It was still damp, but the sun had dried most of it out.

He wondered if she came here often.

Chapter 13

I like the way you hung the moon uh huh.
I like the way you know that dance...

~ *Drew Holcomb & The Neighbors*

Ysabella did not know her last name.

At least, not in the sense that most had a second name. A first name gives a person their character, the second defines them. In England, a second name often spoke of origin or occupation. A Jackson, of course, was the son of Jack. FitzJohn meant someone was the illegitimate son of John, born of a mistress. The second name could also refer to the place one was from, though more often it was their craft, like cartwright, smith, or tailor.

Ysabella's parents had been serfs on a manor up in Copeland. Tending the fields alongside her father, she knew what hard work was. Being serfs, it meant she also knew poverty, what it was to look upon the scraps a farmer fed to his pigs with longing in those times when the hunger was strong.

When she'd turned fifteen, her body had begun filling out in ways that caught the attention of the lord of her manor. She had not understood the fear in her mother's eyes then, though now that she'd experienced the world for herself, she did.

Their lord was a powerful earl who was not accustomed to being refused, and he had desired her, though in her innocence, she was ignorant of the meaning of his attention. She overheard her parents whispering about him. They'd hoped that he would soon return to his other lands before there was trouble, for he only visited Carlisle for a few weeks each year.

Yet, on the last day of his northern tour, he accosted her in a barn.

She would never forget the roughness of his hands on her wrists. He'd tried to force her into the hay, but she had resisted and fought her way free. She'd fled to the safety of her parents' house, and the earl had been so embarrassed at having been outwitted by a serf girl that he'd left without a confrontation.

Yet, her parents had feared it was only a temporary respite, that when he returned to check on his lands again, he would either exact his revenge or succeed in forcing her to submit to his will.

So, they'd sent her to her aunt in York to apprentice as a seamstress.

A few months later, David of Scotland had invaded Cumbria. His soldiers had acted without restraint, full of bloodlust, like wild fiends, massacring and pillaging wherever they pleased with no respect for the distinction between soldier and farmer, nor between man and woman. Even women heavy with child had not been spared and were ripped open.

Her parents had been killed in one of those attacks.

In York, now an orphan, she'd worked as hard as she could to make her own way under the tutelage of her mother's sister. But a year ago, her aunt had died in childbirth.

Thus, Ysabella's place in this world quickly became nebulous. Daughters rarely took their father's name for their second anyway, but any position she might have held in Copeland had been wiped away by the wild men of David. With the loss of her aunt, she had no other family, and there was no place in York for her, nor even among the seamstresses.

Having no occupation or husband meant sure destitution. Of course, there were certain people in York who had some crass ideas about how she could earn a living. She refused to lower herself into such depravity though. She would never choose that fate voluntarily.

The only path left to her then was that of an outlaw — and as she soon found out the hard way, a young woman traveling the king's highways alone is subjected to all kinds of abuses, disgusting, greedy men who would force her into the very depravity she'd refused in York, yet without being paid for their violations.

She'd stabbed a fat man once who dragged her behind an oak tree. She'd not waited around to see if he would die but left him to wallow in regret at having molested the wrong girl. Few others had gotten that far, and none had succeeded, due to her early decision to never let a long knife be outside of her easy reach.

She'd faced off a number of simple thieves as well, but they were a more timid lot than the more aggressive violators. Plus, she had nothing worth stealing, so that by itself lent her some protection from their ilk.

Then, came the day she met the man she could not handle.

She'd been following the road south, slowly making her way to London and hoping to get there before the hunger grew so bad she could not go on. She was sure there would be work to be had in London. Her thoughts were so concentrated on this hope that she failed to notice the man standing against an elm tree by the side of the road.

He was dressed in forest green, and she recognized the lust in his eyes. It mirrored the look she'd seen in the eyes of the earl so many years before, but now with many roads and hardships behind her, a more experienced Ysabella knew it for what it was.

He'd been swift, and she never knew his name.

Before she could slip her knife from a slit in her tunic, he had her arm pinned against her stomach and was pressing her backwards. She stumbled awkwardly as she tried to regain her balance, but he kept pushing her back until she slammed up against a tree and had nowhere else to go.

He dug his fingers painfully into her forearm, forcing the muscles there to loosen, and she'd lost her grip on the knife. She remembered the hollow sound of it clattering upon a stone at her feet.

She raised her other arm to strike him, but he grabbed that wrist and twisted her whole body to the left violently. She fell forward and hit her forehead on a rock.

The man in forest green had snatched her knife up and tucked it in his waistband. Then, he was on her, digging a knee into her back and pressing her face into the dirt with one hand while the other began tearing at her clothes . . .

Then, just as suddenly, the weight was lifted off her back as if the man had evaporated. A terrible crashing among the brush to her right followed.

Ysabella rolled over and scrambled to put distance between her and her attacker, yet she froze at the sight of a giant of a man peering down at her. Panicked, she shot her eyes around the glade for the man in green to see where he'd gone, but she couldn't find him.

Then, she caught sight of a patch of green cloth among the branches. Squinting, she could make out the rest of his prone, motionless form through the leaves.

The big man stared at her.

He'd swept the man in green off her with a single mighty blow and sent him sailing into a tree.

Just as the eyes of her attacker had shot threats, the eyes of this man only communicated concern.

"Ranulf," was all he'd gruffed, pointing at his own chest as he did.

That was the day she'd first met Big Ranulf. He'd led her here to the outlaw camp in Newhaven Forest where she'd met Martin the Red and all the others. They were a different bunch from most, a group that could recognize a soul who was on the down and out and make them feel welcome.

The younger girls had instantly taken to her, though the married women were a bit more standoffish. She was a buxom lass, and they didn't want their husbands to get any ideas or a wandering eye. Still, eventually, all had warmed to her.

For her, this small outlaw family gave her everything she'd been missing. Food and a place to be. A place where she could feel at home. A place where she had a sense of purpose.

She didn't know how long their little enclave could survive. Sooner or later, the king's foresters would evict them . . . or worse. For now, Ysabella was content to live a simple life, enjoying a sense of security she hadn't felt for a *long* time.

Deep down, she still longed for something more, for a companion to ease her loneliness. She had passions stirring in her soul, heart-felt movements of spirit that called for someone to share herself with.

Nevertheless, she tamped such feelings down. There was no sense inflaming a longing that could not be filled. She could be content with her lot and the peace she now had.

Several of the younger outlaws had sought to court her, but she'd gently rebuffed all of them. None lit the spark within she needed to open her heart. And there was no sense complicating camp life over someone she didn't really care for.

Then, came the day Aidan Falconer had walked in.

In the first instant she saw him, from the moment she caught a glimpse of his pulse-quickening eyes, the firm strength of his jaw standing guard over his broad shoulders, she'd never been the same.

She'd watched as lass after lass threw herself at him only to bounce off when he refused to return their advances (just as she'd done to many of her would-be suitors).

. . . And then she'd gone and done the same.

She'd put her own heart on the line, offering it to him, exposing it to him, and then he'd rebuffed her just as he had the other girls.

It hurt.

Of course, she saw the reason shining clearly in his eyes. It was impossible to miss. He loved another.

One night, while listening to him tell stories by the fire of how life had been on Falconer manor, she'd learned the girl's name: *Priscilla.*

She did not feel jealous. Not at all.

Instead, she felt a tremendous admiration for such a woman who could attract the affections of a man like Aidan and then pin them to her so fiercely that he couldn't let go even after a year of separation in the forest, surrounded by pretty girls who made their willingness known.

If anything, she wished she could learn what was different about Priscilla so she could imitate it, so Aidan might long for her in the same way he did for Baron Fontaigne's daughter.

In the meantime, Ysabella had no intention of giving up.

Chapter 14

Ysabella had never noticed Aidan watching her that day in the glen.

He was ever thankful for that.

Before that day, he'd only had eyes for Priscilla, and it didn't have to be said, he was still overwhelmed with love for her…

…but Ysabella's song had gripped his passion and touched his soul in a new way. It had almost been against his will, though truthfully in that moment his will seemed to have completely crumbled. The vision of her dancing among the trees had thrown open the doors of his heart to her.

Now, whenever she passed near, he found himself tracing her moves with his eyes, or following the changing lines of her smooth jaw as she spoke. It was a fascination that would not let up, though he tried to dissimilate.

He was glad she was unaware of his turmoil because he knew that she remained determined to win him, and, in spite of the confusing swirl of emotions within, his heart still belonged to Priscilla.

The other maidens in camp, some of whom were quite pretty, angled for Aidan to pay them mind as well, but they hesitated in the face of Ysabella's dominant personality and waited quietly in the background, hoping he might notice their soft-spoken spirits.

Which was a good thing. He didn't need new pressures complicating things. Instigating a series of love triangles would be a great way to start some disunity among the outlaws. As long as he didn't catch one of those girls singing like a bird in the woods, trapping his heart a third time, he would be safe.

Daily life progressed uneventfully. They guessed that word must have gotten out regarding their exploits because there was a distinct drop in the number of wealthy travelers on the roads through New Haven.

The exception was knights, many of whom were too full of pride to believe an amateurish band of ruffians could get the better of them. The numbers of those actually increased as they insisted on entering the forest alone or in pairs to prove their courage. Aidan's men were usually capable of disarming them without a fight.

Unfortunately, as they were not necessarily a rich lot, knights rarely had much money beyond a pocketful of pennies.

One band of three, however, had yielded a nice take. Those knights had been fresh from a battle up north with Scottish raiders and were burdened with far too much golden jewelry and other loot.

Aidan was happy to relieve them of the extra weight so they could travel faster and avoid other outlaws who might wish to waylay them farther down the road, and he told them as much, though they did not seem to appreciate the favor.

As it was, while most knights didn't typically have a lot of coin wealth, their armor and weapons were always worth a small fortune.

Aidan had now accumulated enough armor to outfit himself as a knight forty times over. One hauberk in particular was an especially expensive piece of finely made chain mail. When he was ready, that would be the one he chose for himself.

Red and Ranulf wanted to sell the armor, but Aidan refused. Instead, they stored it in the cave. Selling such items locally would draw a lot of attention and possibly expose their members to being tracked back to camp. Beyond that concern, Aidan could imagine a number of scenarios where having access to all that armor would be useful.

Word of the outlaws' generosity had also gotten out. Local peasants were so grateful for what had been provided, they not only offered their protection, but also a regular supply of wheat, barley, and fruits and vegetables.

It comforted Aidan to see the outlaws building a life for themselves, but he knew it could not last. Eventually, their numbers would grow too large, or they would harass the wrong nobleman. Eventually, they would be discovered. They might continue with impunity for a year or two, but they needed a long-term plan. Some way to re-establish themselves in society.

It was an odd turn. He'd set out to reclaim his own status, but instead, he'd now taken upon his shoulders the burden of reclaiming status for over thirty families.

His father had always said Aidan was prone to take on lost causes. At seven, Aidan had once found a bird — a robin — by the manor's wall that had been mauled by a dog. Both wings were broken. Aidan had put it in a basket and tried to care for it, but it was beyond any help he could give and died during the night. He'd cried for two days after burying it.

His mother had understood. His father had marveled, but then told him to man up and get over it. Which he did. His father had been right, of course.

There was nothing he could have done to save that bird.

Secretly, Aidan worried these people might be like that robin: *Unsavable.* And they might drag him down with them.

"Aidan, you've got to see this!" Eric the Hunter jogged over to him, visibly excited. "Tom and I made a marvel."

Aidan followed the young man to the camp's south side. Tom, another slender young hunter, was waiting for them. Of the three trails leading into their little village from the forest, this one was the most obvious to outsiders.

Aidan squinted, examining the path with a hard look.

"You've increased its visibility," he stated flatly.

"Yes, but don't pass judgment yet, wait till I explain . . ."

Aidan waved for him to continue.

"We made it visible on purpose, but only near the village. We kept a gap of hundreds of feet obscured with leaves and debris between it and the main trails. So, if someone searches for us while walking the main trails, they will never find us. But, if they happen to broaden their search off the trails, they would find this path and follow it."

"Exactly," Aidan said, "Why in the world would we want *that*? They would *find* us." He was more than skeptical. Their best hope at defense was camouflage.

"Because if a party of soldiers decides to search the forest off the trails on a wider scale, they're eventually going to find us no matter what. So, why not lead them in on the path we want them to take?"

"All right. I'm listening."

"Show him, Tom," Eric said.

Tom smiled and motioned for Aidan follow him closer to the path's mouth. The young man paused before it, but Aidan tried to keep going. Tom shot his hand out and gripped Aidan's shoulder, stopping him cold.

The young hunter pointed down. A narrow cord of animal tendon was stretched across the path about six inches above the ground. It was a trip wire, the kind normally employed in bear traps.

"You do *not* want to set that off," Eric warned.

Aidan followed its line with his eyes, straining to see what it would trigger.

"You know all those crossbows we have stored in the cave?"

Aidan nodded.

While crossbows were considered to be dishonorable weapons by many, a number of the knights they'd robbed had some, and they'd discovered three more on a supply wagon destined for Stephen's army.

The crossbow, otherwise known as an arbalest, was universally feared and respected for the power of its bolts was enough to pierce even the best-made chain mail. Aidan estimated they'd probably stockpiled at least eight of the weapons so far.

"Well, they're not in the cave anymore," Eric continued, "We've concealed them along either side of this path. They're anchored to boards buried in the soil and angled up to hit a man's chest. Each is aimed to fire down the path lengthways to maximize the likelihood of hitting a target."

Suddenly, he understood the full nature of their invention.

"And this tripwire sets them off?

"Yes. We wrapped a long cord of sinew down the line around each trigger, then connected the cord to an iron mechanism that Warin the Smith made us. When the wire is tripped, the mechanism will yank on the cord and all the triggers should fire at once."

"So, if a group of men were coming up the path to attack us, their leader would hit this cord and all the arbalests would let loose down the path at the same time . . ."

"Exactly! We've already tested it. Works like a charm. Quite a deadly crossfire."

". . . and the attackers would be in a disarray after such an unexpected assault . . ."

". . . and their cries would warn us in the village so we'd have time to escape or to arm ourselves," Eric finished, a triumphant grin pasted on his face.

Aidan smiled. The invention was quite innovative. Brilliant, actually.

"You approve?" Eric asked hopefully.

"It's a great idea! Good work. We just need to make sure everyone knows never to use this path, especially the kids. And we'll have to test it regularly. It will need daily inspections to ensure nothing's been thrown off . . ."

A commotion arose from the village behind them.

The three of them turned to see what was happening.

Two scouts emerged from the woodline, prodding another man along in front of them with the tip of a sword in his lower back. Their prisoner gave the impression he was a man of wealth, perhaps a merchantman. He wore an expensive white tunic with thin golden thread woven into its seams. They'd tied his hands behind his back and blindfolded him.

The scouts forced him forward until he stumbled into the village's central square. The villagers were already gathering around, curious about the new arrival.

Aidan made his way forward and stood in front of the trio.

"What's going on here?" he demanded.

"We caught this nobleman in the forest, and he refused to tell us his allegiance. Said he would only talk to you."

Aidan smiled. "Hello, Reginald."

"Aidan," Reginald dipped his head in salutation.

"Cut his bonds, men. This man is no crook, nor is he a nobleman. He has no allegiance other than to the wool market, as any wool merchant would. He's bought fleeces in Derbyshire and sold them in London for nigh on a decade."

One of the scouts untied the ropes.

"I'm sorry my men accosted you, Reginald. What are you doing in these parts?"

The wooler rubbed his wrists, restoring circulation. "I came looking for you, Aidan."

"What do you mean?"

"Becca's Well has not been the same since Richard took over Falconer Manor."

"I would expect not, but what has he done?"

"He's eliminated free tenancy and forced all into taking fealty oaths as serfs."

"That's outrageous! And against the law, I might add."

"The king is distracted, my friend, and looking to his nobles for support. Which means he tends to overlook such injustices as long as your uncle can provide soldiers. Every day we draw nearer to a full war between Stephen and Maud."

"But to take men's freedom by force . . ."

Free tenants were peasants who paid rent to a lord for the right to grow crops on his land, but they were always free to leave and give up their tenancy if they so desired. On the other hand, serfs were bound to a lord and his land. They were not free to leave, and they were required to work several days out of every seven on their lord's acreage for his benefit instead of their own.

Essentially, serfs were obligated to work instead of paying rent and had no freedom, while free tenants had freedom, but they had to pay money rent. Richard had stripped all freedom and forced everyone into serfdom.

"He still requires rent payments from all though."

"*What?* Is he then only binding them to the land without requiring their labor in his fields?"

"No, he demands both labor and rents. And the same from those who were already serfs. They have to pay rent now in addition to giving their work."

Gasps erupted from the crowd. What Richard was doing was unheard of and outright illegal.

"That is preposterous. Why do the people not appeal?"

"Why did you not appeal when he robbed you of your rightful manor?"

Aidan saw his point. A man like Richard would be oppressive anywhere, but in times like these, selfish, despotic men thrived even more.

"Tis even worse than that," Reginald continued, "People are now forbidden from gathering dead wood from the forest."

"How can they make a fire? How can they cook?"

"They gather dried cow patties from the fields, or whatever else they can find to burn. Richard has also appropriated the blacksmith, the tanner, and the fuller for his own use. The villagers can no longer repair their tools or full their wool without paying an exorbitant fee. Old Osbert tried to take his fleeces to Derby for fulling, but Richard's men caught wind of it and they whipped him half to death."

Aidan cursed.

"Just days ago, he confiscated all the sheep in the valley. When I arrived in Becca's Well to do my annual trade, he tried to charge me two pennies a fleece. Needless to say, I refused. There are other towns. I'll likely not be returning any time soon."

The going rate for a fleece was one penny. Merchants were not obligated to do business in any one village, so Richard's actions in that case seemed foolish.

The villagers murmured. The injustices were frankly unbelievable. Life for peasants was hard enough as it was. Richard's tactics would reduce them to utter despair.

"What would you have me do about it, Reginald?"

"I don't know that you *can* do much. Your uncle has strengthened himself considerably since you left. He now has eight household knights and over forty men-at-arms. There are rumors that he is allying himself with the Earl of Chester to acquire more lands, which means more knights."

"Eight knights? Forty men-at-arms? Where in the world is he getting the money to support such a retinue?"

"Much is from the taxes and fees he imposes on the populace. But you are right; there is no way he can afford so much from those alone. Becca's Well is already impoverished and he's only making it worse, so he has to be getting funds from somewhere else. He's remained a staunch supporter of Stephen, so perhaps the Earl of Chester, or even the king himself, is rewarding him for that service in some other way."

Aidan studied the crowd that had gathered to surround them. He felt a natural, paternal instinct for these entrusted to him, but he felt no less a burden for the citizens of Becca's Well. Though Richard had exiled him, his sense of duty to them had not been severed.

"I am powerless to stop him," Aidan sighed.

"Perhaps," Reginald allowed, "Regardless, I have fulfilled my duty."

"What do you mean?"

"While I was at the castle, your steward, John, approached me in a moment of solitude and begged me send word to you of what was happening. He told me I could find you in the forest . . ."

"*Wait* . . . how did he know I was here?"

"Aidan, word of your exploits has traveled far. Did you think it would remain a secret?"

Aidan winced.

Any hope he'd had to ever be knighted had just evaporated like mist before a strong wind.

"Anyway, he begged me get word to you. To what end, I do not know. He told me all that I have told you, and that Marion, your mother's handmaiden, is dead. Richard killed her right after you left the castle for embarrassing him into giving you your horse when you left."

"He didn't!"

"I'm afraid it's true."

Marion had cared for him after his mother died. He'd loved the woman like a second mother.

Heat flooded Aidan's cheeks. Fury entered in force.

The low murmuring that had filtered through the villagers with each piece of bad news tapered off into silence with this latest recounting. None of them had seen Aidan this angry before. They'd also heard him speak of Marion with affection by many a campfire.

Reginald bowed his head. "I am truly sorry to be the bearer of such bad news, Aidan. I only wish that were all of it."

"How could it possibly get any worse?"

"Richard's men are becoming unbridled. They've seen there will be no consequences for their oppression, not from Richard — and not from the king. Do you remember a servant girl by the name of Juliana?"

"Yes. She's a pretty lass. Helps in the kitchen."

"John told me that Sir Walter had been pressuring her to lie with him. When she kept refusing, he finally violated her by force. The beating he laid upon her after that was terrible. By all accounts, he forces her every night now. And those are only the stories to which *I* am privy. If Sir Walter is being given free rein in this manner, who knows what the other knights are doing. They're all the same quality of men. None are honorable as Sir Bart was."

Aidan lifted a hand to the merchant's shoulder. Reginald winced in slight pain under the grip, though he realized Aidan did not mean for it to be so strong. His muscles were tense under the stress of what he'd just been told.

"Thank you for coming," he said to the businessman, "I need to think upon these things."

Chapter 15

Well, I know it's not been easy
But easy ain't worth singin' about

"Simple Song"

~ Passenger

September 1137 AD

Themselves — he silver moon bathed the men's backs in pale, shifting hues and the barley stalks whispered against their thighs as they slipped through the field single file.

Aidan would have preferred a new moon for an attack, but they couldn't wait for that. They'd just have to risk being seen in the weak light.

The castle's dark walls loomed before them as they drew near. It was strange seeing his childhood home as an outsider. This was the first time he'd been back since Richard evicted him.

The villagers had gone to bed hours ago. They needed as much rest as they could snatch before the next oppressive day began.

Before beginning this raid, more news had reached the outlaws that Richard was also prohibiting his people, to the chagrin of the priest, from observing the Sabbath on Sunday.

He let them attend services, but after that, they were to work his fields. Many were required to labor their lord's lands as many as three out of seven days now, an unprecedented portion of their time.

Instead of passing directly through the village of Becca's Well, Aidan and his men had circled around it. They were approaching the keep through the fields to the north.

A barn owl's hoot echoed from the woods behind them. A man next to him shuddered involuntarily. The call had sounded hollow, like that of a phantom in search of the dead.

Aidan raised a hand to halt the forward motion of their line.

Torches blazed atop of the castle's front curtain wall. Two men-at-arms stood guard there, one on either side of the gate. The portcullis had been lowered for the night. Other soldiers milled about, patrolling the top walk.

Richard was wary of attack, not because of any fear of Aidan, who he considered to be nothing more than a bug to be squashed, but because of the political tension and strife rampant everywhere.

One guard was moving around the walk toward their side of the castle now.

Aidan silently pushed downward with a flattened hand, a sign for them to hit the ground. Slowly, they all lowered themselves into the barley. The moon was too bright, and they might be seen.

Once the guard had passed on, the troop picked themselves back up and continued their circle to the castle's rear.

More torches blazed on the wall here as well, along with additional soldiers standing at attention. These were not guards on patrol, but stationary sentries. They would have to be very careful.

Aidan quietly got his men's attention and pointed to a cluster of large rocks at the base of a hill about a hundred feet away from the wall. The cluster lay right outside the edge of the illumination created by the torches. They moved as close as they dared on foot and then dropped to their stomachs, crawling the rest of the way.

Right before they reached the rock cluster, the soft swishing of barley beneath their bellies was replaced by the rough grating of gravel. Aidan froze as the noise threatened to give them away.

Slowly, they lifted their bodies a few inches off the ground and inched forward on all fours until they were safely obscured from the view of the sentries by the height of the boulders surrounding them.

Finally, each man pulled up and sat with his back to the rocks, panting. Sweat dripped from their brows. That last thirty-foot crawl had been strenuous. More so for Ranulf and Eric, whom Aidan had insisted wear full sets of mail.

Now, they had to wait.

***

Juliana sat upon her rude cot, wringing her hands impotently, dreading the night that awaited.

Her bedchamber was small but better than most castle servants got. The rest had to cram themselves two or three to a room, and most were tinier than this.

She was not thankful though. She'd wondered at first why the steward had singled her out to have her own room, but now that she understood the reason, she wished it had never happened.

Walter would return tonight. He would return this evening as he did every evening. And sometimes twice an evening. She *knew* he would — because he always did, and each time was always worse than she remembered from the last.

It wasn't just his roughness, or the pain when he ripped at her or knocked her head against the wall. It was the feeling of helplessness, of total violation and loss of innocence. A sense of filthiness you couldn't wash away, and why bother because the unrelenting beast would just be back.

She jumped at each creak and rustle, sure it would be followed by the door cracking open to reveal his puffy, greedy face. When it wasn't, she still couldn't relax because she knew the next noise very likely would be. It had to be just a matter of minutes now before he showed.

She wished she could go back to a time before he'd ever noticed her.

But that, of course, was impossible.

So, she'd started doing whatever she could to make herself undesirable. She stopped brushing her hair; she let her tunic stay soiled rather than wash it. She even threw away her perfume water, but nothing seemed to diminish his leering.

There was no way out.

She was a prisoner of the keep, though her chains were invisible. She often had to go into the village to buy produce or meat for the castle's kitchen. So many times, she'd been tempted to simply disappear. Slip away between the rows of houses and melt into the forest.

It would be so easy.

She'd be living outside the law, but at least she'd be living — and even freezing to death might be better than her current torture.

Yet, she knew she could not.

The second night Walter had assaulted her, he'd sworn to her, whispering in her ear harshly with the most unwelcome intimacy, that if she ever escaped, he would kill her mother.

She couldn't bear the thought of that.

Of course, he was manipulating her neatly. But she knew he was truly an evil man, easily capable of such a thing. She had been there when Richard had ordered Marion killed. And if they were willing to kill someone like Marion, the lives of a lowly scullery maid and her mother would be of little consequence.

Her mother had also been given a bedchamber to herself. It was next to hers. Walter had promised that he would bless her mother with such favors as long as Juliana succumbed to his will without fighting.

That room was more of a curse than a favor though. Every night, Juliana could hear her mother crying herself to sleep over her daughter's predicament.

Though some nights, Juliana's own tears were all she could hear.

***

"Long live Queen Maud!"

The voice pierced the night.

The cry sounded like it came from the vicinity of the Becca's Well in front of the castle — and it was only a few minutes later than expected.

"Come on, you louts! Come get me!" The distant voice continued.

Aidan peeked over the rocks. The castle's rear guards were rushing toward the front to see what the disturbance was, just as Aidan wanted.

"All right," Aidan turned, "Now!"

He'd planned this distraction specifically because he'd expected there to be rear guards, and they needed cover while they worked.

He plunged an iron rod behind a medium-sized rock and heaved.

It rolled away easily…as it was designed to do.

Behind it stood a small iron grate. Ranulf and Eric tugged at the grate, and it pulled away from its casing with a soft clang.

Not enough sound to be heard from the front of the keep.

They laid the grate down, and the five of them poured into the tunnel that it had covered, crawling to get through the opening and then standing again once they were inside.

Aidan had known about this secret passage since he was a boy. His father had built it and shown it to him when he was eight. It was supposed to serve as an escape hatch for anyone inside the castle who wanted to get out during a siege.

Aidan didn't know if Richard was aware of the tunnel's existence or not — his father had been highly secretive about it — but even if Richard knew, he wouldn't be expecting anyone else who knew about it to be trying to get in tonight.

The passageway was pitch black, but there were darkened torches stored at both ends of it, so they grabbed a couple and lit them.

They proceeded about a hundred feet before coming to some steps. This stairwell rose up inside the castle's exterior wall, unknown to all but those who had traveled the tunnel. After climbing to the top, another twenty feet of flat walkway took them to a seeming dead end.

Aidan stopped and explained, "On the other side of this wall is the library. My uncle is the only one who would use it, and he's probably in bed or somewhere else right now, but we have to be ready just in case he's in there."

"And if he is?" Ranulf asked.

"When I open the wall, we all rush in. If my uncle is there, secure him and silence him as fast as you can. Speed is the name of the game."

They nodded.

Aidan ran his fingers over the rough stones, searching from memory for the right one. When he found its familiar surface, Aidan used both hands to silently slide it out of the fake wall. He laid it on the ground softly.

Next, he reached into the void and clasped the iron bar he knew would be there.

He looked back. His men were primed and ready, swords in hand. With a sharp twist and a great heave, the latch clicked open, and the heavy wall swung out. They rushed forward into the study.

It was empty.

The opposite side of the secret panel they had just opened was a bookcase full of books, a couple of which had tumbled from their shelves. Considering the thickness of the stone floor and the massive oak door that led to the hall, Aidan was confident no one had heard the noise.

Curiously though, a candle still burned on the writing desk.

That could mean someone was coming back soon, or it could mean Richard had just been careless.

Without extinguishing them, they inserted their torches in the grilled holders just inside the entrance to the secret tunnel so they could use them later. Then, they swung the bookcase around until it latched back in place with a soft click.

Aidan showed them the hidden catch that would open it again.

Ranulf was his biggest man, and Eric was one of his top fighters. Their chain mail could allow them to pose as men-at-arms stationed in the castle for a short time, delaying detection, but it would also make noise as they moved, and stealth was their main weapon for the time being. So, he had a different plan.

"Ranulf, you and Eric stay here and guard our exit. If anyone comes in, conk them, gag them . . . do what you have to do."

"Got it," Ranulf said.

"Red, you and Tom come with me."

They cracked open the door to the hall, and Aidan poked his head through. The passage was clear and well-lit. Aidan, Red, and Tom slipped out.

Aidan led the way. At the far end of the hall, they came to a set of curling stairs that led down to the servants' quarters behind the kitchen.

The rooms in this lower region of the keep were dark. The fading smell of wood smoke lingered in the air from the preparation of the day's meals.

They reached a short hall that had four doors, two on each side.

"Which one is it?" Red hissed.

"Not sure," Aidan answered, "Her friend in town said she was in that room there, but Richard may have moved them around since she was last in the castle."

A sliver of light shone from beneath the door Aidan had indicated. When Aidan pressed his ear to it, he heard the sound of soft sobbing.

Aidan pushed it open.

"Please! No! *Please*, no more!" She cried.

Juliana lay in a disarray on the shabby hay mattress that passed for her bed. As soon as the door had moved, she'd instantly tensed and sat up. Her hair was a tousled mess, and her nightgown was ripped at the shoulder. A nasty bruise bloomed under one eye, and some dried blood was smeared under her nose.

Wide-eyed with terror, she scrambled backward on the bed to get away, though the small room afforded her no escape.

"Juliana," Aidan whispered, "Don't fear."

She hesitated, puzzled by the unexpected voice. After a few seconds, her fear started to melt.

"*Aidan* . . .? Is that you?"

"Yes, we're here to rescue you." Aidan had grown up with Juliana. He couldn't remember a time when her mother had not worked at the manor.

He motioned for Red and Tom to follow him in all the way. They pulled the door shut behind them.

"I . . . I thought you were . . ."

"I know who you thought I was. That's why we've come to get you out."

She burst into tears, but these were tears of startled relief.

"I'd lost all hope," she gargled between sobs.

"You must be quiet now," Aidan soothed. "We have to get out of here without them knowing."

She nodded, visibly trying to calm herself. "I cannot leave without Ma."

"Where is she?"

"In the next room over."

"Same side of the hall?"

She nodded again.

"Red, fetch her mother."

Red slipped out the door and closed it behind him.

"Get your things together, Juliana. We have to be quick."

She rose and gathered her few meager belongings into a small sack. In less than a minute, all that she cared about in this world was packed.

"All right, let's go," Aidan said.

When he opened the door again, the fat, leering face of Sir Walter filled the void beyond. The ruthless knight had been reaching for the handle when Aidan opened it. Apparently, the man hadn't been satisfied with the abuse he'd dished out so far tonight and had come back for more.

Swiftly, Aidan slung his dagger from his belt and slashed for Walter's neck, but only managed to slice his cheek.

Aidan leapt back a step just in case Walter had a weapon in range, but the knight was stunned by the sudden appearance of Aidan and his attack.

He retreated and laid a hand to the side of his face. His eyes widened when it came away wet with bright blood.

"Aidan!" He cried, his senses finally catching up to reality.

The door down the hall opened, and Walter swiveled his attention to it. Red emerged with Juliana's mother in tow.

The older matron's cheeks were streaked with wet trails of broken-hearted tears. She'd known of her daughter's sufferings and could probably hear everything that happened in Juliana's room from her own yet couldn't intervene without putting both their lives at risk. It was the worst kind of suffering for a parent. Knowing your child was being harmed but powerless to do anything about it.

Walter's shock wore off fast. He realized he was unarmed and couldn't make a stand, so he turned to run.

Red made a wild dive with his sword fully extended, but Walter was too far away, so Red only managed to clip his calf. Walter cried out in pain and staggered off in a limping run.

"To arms! To arms!" he shouted as he went.

"That's it, boys," Aidan said. "Time to go!"

They raced back to the spiral staircase and ascended its steps two by two. Doors slammed open and footsteps thundered as Walter alerted the keep's denizens to the presence of intruders.

At the far end of the upstairs hall, four men-at-arms appeared, weapons ready. Aidan sheathed his dagger, planted his feet and drew his sword. Red was already prepared.

The soldiers rushed them.

Tom pulled his bow, but only managed to loose a single arrow before they were upon them. Still, that shot was enough to drop one of Richard's men out of the fight.

Tom grabbed the women and put them behind him so they'd be protected by his body.

The extra length of Aidan's blade was a nasty surprise for the second man-at-arms. He failed to brake in time and impaled himself on it before he'd even had a chance to swing his weapon down.

Hearing Walter's cries, Ranulf and Eric had cracked opened the library door. They'd seen the battle shaping up but waited until the soldiers passed by them before acting. Then, they stepped into the hall behind the attackers.

Fully engrossed with Aidan and his party, Richard's men never knew what hit them. From behind, Ranulf and Eric dispatched the last two men-at-arms before Red could even get a lick in.

"Would you leave one for me next time, boys?" he smirked.

With the hall now clear, they went into the library and locked the door after them.

Aidan removed the book that concealed the secret passage's release lever and yanked it. He replaced the book, swung the bookcase open, and they all rushed into the tunnel. Once they were safely inside, Aidan shut the fake wall behind them again.

That produced a collective sigh of relief, but the danger was not yet over. They still had to get clear of the castle.

Their torches were still burning in the tunnel, so they grabbed them and followed the secret passage back down through the castle wall and to its exit at the rock cluster.

A few minutes later, they stood free in the cool night air.

Unfortunately, while most of the guards on the upper walk had hurried inside when Walter raised the alarm, one had wisely remained outside to make sure what was going on inside was not a diversion for a greater assault from the exterior.

He hadn't seen Aidan's party yet, but only because they'd maintained complete silence, and for the moment, he was looking the other way.

Slowly, they slid the grate back in place. It was almost there when it scraped a rock. Sharp noises carry far at night, and the guard heard it.

"Halt!" He shouted. "Halt, halt! Men! To the gates!" He ran to mobilize more guards.

Aidan's troop raced for the barley rows at full speed. Their goal was the forest line beyond the field.

In just a matter of minutes, a fully armed cavalry unit streamed from the castle's front gate. Thankfully, by that time, Aidan and crew were safely under the cover of the trees.

Men on horses were no good in a forest. Even less so in the dark against those familiar with its intricacies, and he knew these woods and its paths better than any of Richard's peons.

Only once they were well within its bounds and the beat of hooves and shouting had faded away did they stop to take a breather.

Aidan peered into the darkness for a beat before turning to address the women.

"My ladies, you are now free," he said, "You can go where you want, but if you wish to come with us to our camp, we will make sure you are cared for."

Juliana burst into tears and threw herself around Aidan's neck in gratitude. He felt the hot drops rolling down his chest as she wept uncontrollably for several minutes.

Her mother smiled weakly through her own silent tears while the men looked on uncomfortably.

When Juliana finally let go, her mother wrapped her arms around Aidan too.

"Hey!" Red complained, "Why does *he* get all the hugs?"

Chapter 16

Cause troubles will come
But it's the best decision you're ever gonna make

"Tuesdays"

~ Jake Scott

The next morning, Juliana and her mother, Agnes, mingled with the other outlaws, looking rested and little healthier. Aidan called a meeting of the entire camp to discuss the turn of events.

Agnes' smile peeked through from time to time, but he thought it might be a while before Juliana had healed enough to recover hers.

Ysabella had taken the mother and daughter into her hut until a separate shelter could be constructed.

Aidan couldn't help but glance her way as he hopped up onto a stump. The voluptuous girl brazenly flicked him a wink when she saw she'd caught his eye. He was thoroughly unnerved by her forwardness, as well as the stimulating shiver that ran up his spine because of it.

He cleared his throat and began.

"Good morning! I'm sure all of you have heard of last night's events by now. Today, we can be thankful for the safety of Agnes and Juliana."

Everyone erupted into applause and cheers. They were not only glad for that, but also elated to see one put over on a baron. Especially one as nasty as Richard who had stolen so much from Aidan.

"I trust you all will make them feel welcome, understanding what they've been through. Eric, will you and Tom build them a place to live?"

"The very best, sir."

Aidan smiled. Eric had been stealing glances at Juliana all morning. He had that lost puppy expression every young man gets when he's smitten.

"Good. Now, the bad news. We can't expect Richard to take this sitting down. Walter will have told him about my involvement. Since everyone and their brother apparently knows I've been leading a group of outlaws, there's no doubt he'll send men after us.

"They're unlikely to find us here in the forest — we've done well at concealing ourselves — but as Sir Bart always told me: *the best defense is offense.* That means if we want to avoid an attack at home, we must go on the offensive. Till now, we've focused on those traveling through Newhaven Forest."

He paused and took a minute to meet the eyes of each of the men in turn, and then magnified his voice with conviction.

"But from now on, we're taking the fight to Richard! We'll surround Becca's Well and Falconer's Manor like foxes waiting to rob the hen house. When his men come out to search for us, we'll ambush them instead.

"We will frustrate every plan he makes and keep the battle centered around Becca's Well, so his men do not have to come looking for us in these woods where your families reside. And given the nature of the suffering of the men and women of Becca's Well, whom Richard oppresses like they are animals, we will distribute the wealth we glean from his knights to its citizens."

Another round of applause went up at that.

"Any questions?"

"How will we attack them?" The questioner was a thirty-year old man named Alan. A scar from a whip ran down the length of his neck.

"We'll study his habits and those of his men. If we can determine his plans, that will tell us how to hurt him the most. Mostly, we'll make small forays, not enough to scandalize other earls into coming to his aid, but enough to be a significant thorn in his side and keep his attention on the forest around Becca's Well, not here.

"Our primary objective is the protection of our families. Second is to mess up Richard's life. Third is to help the people of Becca's Well."

"Here, here!" Someone shouted from the back. A chorus of agreement went up. Aidan's smile widened.

He loved these people.

Chapter 17

Here's a simple song
Won't stop the rain from coming down
Or your heart from breaking

"Simple Song"

~ Passenger

October 1137 AD – Becca's Well, England

P *ssst!"*

The unexpected whisper made Thomas Weaver whirl in surprise.

"Aidan!" he cried, immediately recognizing his friend.

"Shhh. Keep it down." Aidan stepped in, closing the back door of the weaver's shop behind him. Thomas wrapped his best friend in a bear hug.

"How have you been?" he asked more quietly.

"Well. And you?"

His friend's face fell. "We've been better. Your uncle is a terror."

"I know. I've heard. Do you have a customer up front?"

"Customers? Ha! That's a rich one. Have a seat. Are you hungry?"

Aidan shook his head about the food but took a bench by the wall.

"We haven't had customers for a while."

"Why not? You used to do a brisk business."

"For starters, because Sir Richard has confiscated all the sheep and wool."

"Please don't call him sir."

"Sorry. Forced upon us to the point of habit. Then, he commandeered the fuller for himself. Nobody wants to pay the prices for his fleeces, and even if they did, why would they have me weave them? He has required that everyone who uses us for weaving must go to his fuller after but charges an arm and a leg for use of the fuller's mill.

"We've been without a single customer the entire month so far. Pa says we're going to have to appeal to Richard to take us on as serfs if we want to continue to eat. We had a little money saved, but it won't last much longer.

And the food tax is high."

"Food tax? What in the world is that?"

"Your uncle has declared that all food sold by outside peddlers must incur a tax if purchased by freemen like us."

Aidan had thought he couldn't be more outraged than he already was, but here was another reason. "The man is *mad*. He's bent on making everyone his slave."

"I fear you're right, but what can we do?"

"How will the people make their clothes if they don't come to you?"

"They're using what they've got for as long as it will last. Eventually they'll have to buy at Richard's prices, but in the meantime, we'll starve. Some have tried to secretly full their own wool within their homes, but after they put old man Simon in the stocks for it, no one else has dared."

"Then, why do you stay? You should come with me to the forest."

"Ah . . . Aidan, I've heard of your feats, and my heart swells with pride at each tale, but I cannot leave my father."

Lines of defeat were etched deeply into Thomas' face, a face that just one year prior had been so full of youth and vigor.

"Your father could come with us."

"He's too old and sickly. I cannot leave him to tend a field by himself, and Richard's knights catch most of those who flee to other towns and force them to return. The whippings are terrible. Why do you not return to Becca's Well and relieve us of this tyrant? The manor is rightfully yours, not his!"

Aidan shook his head woefully.

"He outsmarted me before I even knew there was a game afoot. He has documents signed by witnesses saying my grandfather willed the lands to him instead of my father."

"That would make your father a usurper, and everyone knows that is not true."

"Richard says he tolerated the 'abuse' out of a gracious spirit, but now that my father is dead, it is time for him to reclaim what is rightfully his."

Thomas grunted in distaste.

"He has the documents to back it up," Aidan repeated.

"But they must be forged! There are a hundred men here in Becca's Well that would attest to the truth of your claim."

"The word of commoners against the sworn testimony of knights . . . who do you think the king would believe?"

Thomas sank his face into his hands.

"Then it *is* hopeless. I am to be a serf after all."

The despair in his voice broke Aidan's heart.

"Don't give up, my friend. Talk to your father. Try to convince him to come live with us. We're not living in tents, but dwellings that are comfortable and warm at night."

They spoke for a while longer, but Thomas was trapped and had no hope.

Aidan left his friend's home with his heart heavy.

He pulled his hood tight over his head to obscure his face as he made his way down the main thoroughfare of Becca's Well. Richard's sycophants and soldiers were mostly holed up in the castle, but he was wise to take no chances.

So much had changed . . . and all for the worse. Becca's Well's normal hustle and bustle had diminished to a near trickle. Shops were boarded up. The tavern stood empty — a truer testimony to the hardness of the times one would be hard pressed to find.

A serving wench sat on a chair outside its entrance, waiting for passerbys who weren't to be had. She called out to him to come in for an ale, but he waved her off.

Then, he changed his mind.

He changed course and made for the tavern. The woman leapt from her chair and hustled to attend to her unexpected customer, slipping through the doorframe right before he reached it. She went behind the counter and waited expectantly.

Her hair was a very dirty blond and slightly unkempt. A lock of it dangled loosely down by her nose. He could tell she'd once been very pretty, but time and the rough nature of her job had dimmed her former beauty. Her pale skin was marred by a smattering of rosy acne blotches, and the tattered fringes of her thick skirt said her clothing had also seen better days.

"May I he'p you?" she asked, her voice twisting upwards in hope at the end.

"Have any ale?"

"Yes, sir," She replied, a certain nervousness dancing in her eyes.

"How about some food?"

"Uh . . . um . . . well, ah do have some gruel and rye bread."

"No meat?"

She shook her head demurely.

"I'll take the bread and the gruel."

"The gruel . . . it's not very thick, you know, but it's the best I've got."

"Bring it just the same. Do you run this place by yourself?"

She hesitated, probably gauging whether he was the kind of stranger that could be trusted with the truth.

"I do now. Pa passed winter last."

"How are you faring?"

"We are in hard times, to be sure. Few have a penny to their name." Her eyes shimmered with teary water. "Pa used to say a good ale would never lack the men to buy it, but . . . that's not the case anymore."

"Not when things are this bad," Aidan agreed.

She nodded and ducked behind a curtain at the back to fetch his meal.

The ale was watery and strangely bitter. Aidan choked it down, managing somehow to hide his distaste. It was no wonder she was dry on business. With silver hard to come by, who would spend it on a draught like this?

It was not her fault. Supplies were so meager. The gruel was also thin, like a stew — and a weak one at that. The taste was not as heinous as the ale, but still not the most pleasant of meals he'd had.

She watched him warily. She'd probably had a number of travelers eat and run of late, stiffing her on the bill.

"Would you like to go upstairs?" she asked.

She managed a smile and tried to wink seductively, but the effort was unsuccessful. She was not offering a free romp but trying to earn whatever extra income she could to make ends meet. She was clearly not a natural at the practice and had probably been forced into it by her predicament. Her father's passing had left her to fend for herself all alone in a town that was self-destructing.

His heart broke at her plight.

"What is your name?" he asked.

"Margie."

"Margie, I won't go upstairs, but I will take another piece of rye."

She turned and went into the back of the house again. Aidan pulled a bag of silver pennies from his traveling sack and laid it heavily on the bar. There were a couple of pounds worth in there, and they would tide her over for quite a while if she was smart about it and kept her wealth quiet.

He left before she returned, strolling among the crumbling stalls that had once been a bustling Market Street.

Chapter 18

Richard growled beneath his breath, seeking a target for his wrath.

Sir Hugo would not do. Hugo was his right-hand man — and Hugo was not afraid of Richard. The cold-hearted knight was loyal to Richard only because he enjoyed Richard's oppressive ways. At the moment, he stood stonily behind Richard's chair like a petrified vulture that could crack back into life at any second.

Roger had not been in the castle the night young Aidan had broken in and captured Juliana and her mother. He'd been on a mission to deliver a communiqué to Derby.

"Why would Aidan risk his neck for a servant girl, *Walter?*"

Richard knew Walter had been using the girl against her will, but that was neither here nor there. It did not explain Aidan's actions.

The plump knight blushed, and the inflamed pink lines ringing the long brown scab on his cheek turned a bright red. He was still limping from the wound to his leg. He'd been lucky not to have had his Achilles' tendon severed.

"I don't know. That Aidan is a weasel. A conniving . . ."

"Yes, yes," Richard seethed, "But *why* did he want the servant girl? Is he in love with her or something? Because that would have been a useful thing to know."

If he could discover where Aidan's sentiments lay, he could use them against the boy.

Walter stammered. "I . . . I have no idea. It could be . . . but I'd not heard of such."

"John! Step forth!"

John the Steward emerged from the corner where he'd tried to remain unnoticed.

"Yes, milord." He knelt and bowed his head.

"How did Aidan get in here?"

"I do not know."

"Do you *dare* lie to me?" Richard's face burned crimson. "There has to be some secret entrance. How did he do it?"

John remained silent. He knew this man's temperament by now and there was no way to calm him once agitated.

"Roger, take John downstairs and give him ten lashes, then put him in the stocks! Steward, we are going to search this castle from top to bottom. If my knights find Aidan's secret entrance before you sing, you'll have twenty more lashes from me. Only if your memory returns to you before then will you escape it."

John steeled himself as Roger hauled him up by his arm. He knew where the secret passage was, even which book in the library to pull to open its latch, but Richard would have to give him the full thirty because he wasn't about to betray Aidan.

"I see the fire in your eyes, Steward," Richard sneered, "but we'll see how you're feeling after the whip's had its say. Maybe you'll remember your place and who your true master is."

John resolved that there would be no time for that. As soon as he was given the chance, he would escape and not return.

There was no life for him here. He had a target on his back now and would become Richard's object of scorn until he killed him unless John got out while he could. He just wished he could have done so before they permanently scarred his back with the long, thin trails a scourging would leave.

***

News of ongoing developments in Becca's Well filtered into the outlaw camp sporadically over the next months. Aidan heard that John Steward had fled the castle and taken shelter among some relatives up by York. It pained him to know the scourging the man had endured at Richard's hand.

John had suffered thirty lashes and nearly died from blood loss. As soon as he'd recovered from the resulting weakness and fever, the steward had slipped away.

John was a good man and had served his father well. Aidan wished him the best.

These days, the outlaws distributed most of the wealth they accumulated exclusively to the citizens of Becca's Well. They still continued to gift family members in other villages with small amounts too, but the plight in Becca's Well was especially heinous.

While the revocation of free tenancy took away the people's *legal* freedom, the doubling up of rents on top of a serf's feudal obligation to perform labor on the lord's land made their slavery an *economic* reality.

The food tax sealed the deal. It was high and onerous, and now it applied to everyone.

Richard had recently declared that no serf could sell their harvested crops to any man but the castle. His stated reason was safety and quality. Only the castle, he claimed, could and would protect the public at large from contaminated or rotting foodstuffs. Richard promised, in an act of benevolence, to purchase all crops that were deemed acceptable. Crops that weren't were destroyed. Once the castle had inspected the products, everyone was free to buy whatever they wanted from the castle.

In an interesting twist, Richard paid a very low amount for the crops he purchased, as was expected, but he also sold the crops back to the town at the same low rate. The trick was the food tax he charged to cover his "expenses" in performing the inspection, which was equal to the value of the food being bought.

Outside produce peddlers were banned completely. Dealing with your neighbors for what they'd grown without going through the castle would cost you a hand. Growing your own small vegetable garden was prohibited.

All were serfs now and serfs could only grow large amounts of a single crop approved by the castle. They had to sell everything they grew to Richard and then pay double to eat what they had just grown.

It was an unsustainable system, one that would without a doubt drive the people into abject starvation. It made no sense to Aidan for Richard to injure his own manor in such a way. Common sense said that if your people could not eat, they could not work, and the lord's land would lie fallow. It was counterproductive.

Then, Richard announced a new program that illuminated his scheme behind the old one. Every man who pledged absolute fealty to Richard and the castle and turned their lands over to him for his use would be given rations of free food every day. They could keep their houses, though the land now reverted to Richard as tenant-in-chief.

Thus, instead of only two or three days, the people worked all seven days on Richard's land. In return, he fed them. Working for food was the lowest wage possible, and his rations were not generous.

The people of Becca's Well had been neatly reduced to complete slavery.

Aidan and the outlaws helped as they could. To Richard's great frustration, the contributions of bounty made by Aidan's band to the citizenry allowed many to pay the food tax and refrain from pledging themselves into Richard's service.

Aidan raided the soldiers collecting the food tax and returned the coins to the townspeople, but this only worked a couple of times before Richard ordered the people to start paying the tax inside the castle walls.

Richard had built a hut for his soldiers at the village's entrance to block unauthorized food vendors from entering Becca's Well, so the men-at-arms stationed there became favorite targets for the outlaws.

After losing several of their friends to random arrows birthed from the forest, the soldiers began to stay inside the small outbuilding at all times unless a peddler was trying to enter the community. Though whenever they did emerge to confront these merchants, the arrows would fly again.

When the soldiers began sending cavalry into the woods to rout out the bowmen to prevent this, Aidan and his men switched tactics and disguised themselves as the peddlers themselves. While knights on horseback struggled a hundred yards away in the dense brush searching for hidden outlaws, the wool covering of a wagon full of "goods" would be thrown back to reveal archers in its bed ready to dispatch the soldiers blocking their entrance to the town.

The castle was too far away from the front of the village to protect this small outpost. Short of constructing a stone wall all the way around the town, Richard had no way to permanently stop Aidan's aggression, and he'd hurt the town's economy too much to embark on such a project.

Eventually, the poor men-at-arms unlucky enough to be assigned guard duty at the gatehouse simply refused to come out anymore. Instead, they would call to wagoners from inside the hut and demand the drivers toss tax money in a sack towards the hut's door before proceeding, or they would order them to turn around.

If the vendor did not obey, they would be assaulted with bow and bolt from within the hut. The men-at-arms were doing their best to fight fire with fire, even to the point of using weapons they generally deemed beneath them.

Aidan's response to this tactic was to wait for a rainy day when the village and its homes were thoroughly soaked. Then, he and his men snuck to within range of the hut and fired arrows tipped with burning tar into it.

The bolts embedded themselves in the thick wooden door. The heavy rain and wet wood retarded the burn, but the tar still simmered and hissed in spite of the moisture. The deep thuds accompanying the impacts produced the desired result though, which was the door cracking open by a few curious soldiers who sought to know the source of the noise.

More flaming bolts followed the first round, but these sailed right through the ajar door and buried themselves in the much drier interior wood, with the exception of one that found a home in the chest of the man opening the door.

Within minutes, the hut was ablaze. The soldiers poured out into the rain and scrambled for the safety of the castle walls. The hut finished its burn thirty minutes later without damaging other homes. The rain had ensured no sparks would fly.

The burned-out shell served as a visible symbol of Richard's failed policy to ban outside vendors from the town, and that emboldened the people.

Instead of trying to rebuild the post, Richard began regularly dispatching his soldiers into the village on patrol. They marched up and down the streets incessantly, but Aidan harassed these too.

The end result was that, having heard of Richard's policies and realizing the people there would be likely to pay slightly higher prices if they could avoid the exorbitant food tax, many produce sellers did make it into Becca's Well to sell their foodstuffs.

Richard proved unable to stop the visitations, so the serfs sold all their crops to Richard, but refused to buy from him. They sold low and bought high, and became more impoverished in the process, but at least they ate and still maintained some semblance of freedom to choose their way.

Seeing his plan subverted on many levels, Richard began paying less and less for the crops he bought and sold them outside of the shire in order to gain income and pressure the serfs more.

Aidan raided several of these caravans laden with grain from the late summer harvest, and redistributed it to the people, who then sold it back to Richard again. Richard knew he was being had, but all he could do was lower the prices he was willing to pay once more.

Aidan knew he was becoming such a stench in his uncle's nose that Richard would soon be forced to make him the sole focus of his violent attention. With Aidan loose in the forest, the road to serfdom for the citizens of Becca's Well was frustrated. Without him, it would succeed. He was the only real obstacle to their full enslavement.

He knew the time for confrontation would be upon them soon, but the leaves had already turned, and winter was on its way. Aidan hoped the coming fight might wait until Spring. The longer they had to prepare, the better off they were.

Chapter 19

As winter's grip tightened, the outlaws settled down to hibernate, as did Becca's Well, Falconer Manor, and the rest of England. Aidan's people lived off the foodstuffs they'd stored from harvest offerings given by outlying villagers and the occasional game the hunters brought in.

Richard's activities seemed to relax with regards to the town, but Aidan knew this was misleading. Richard was merely building up his forces.

He'd sent messengers to London in search of new recruits for his modest but growing army. In response, sporadic groups of two or three soldiers arrived at the castle regularly.

By All Saint's Day, rumors abounded concerning Sir Walter's continued exploits among the castle's servant women. They'd heard that Walter was pressing Richard to dismiss some of the plumper, older servants and require the pretty young lasses of Becca's Well to enter into service within the keep. From Juliana, they'd learned that Walter had been abusing at least one other girl while she'd been there.

Aidan hesitated to repeat the feat they'd undertaken to rescue Juliana. He didn't know if the secret tunnel had been discovered, or what other precautions might have been taken since then.

Sympathetic informants within the village and castle kept them apprised of any significant movements by Richard, and through intermediaries, Aidan had asked several of the castle servants to let them know when Walter left the security of the keep, but they'd had no luck so far.

In December, a week shy of Christmas, the slate-colored sky hinted at dismal chills to come.

A thin blanket of snow had fallen the previous night, layering much of the forest floor in scattered white. A dusting still remained on the branches overhead.

Aidan was by the camp's main fire meeting with the elders of his outlaw band when he noticed a couple of obscure figures bobbing among the trees and moving toward them.

One was a female covered by a dark red cloak, the other a narrow-framed man. Aidan did not immediately recognize them. Cries of alarm spread among the camp, but Aidan quelled it as soon as he realized the girl was Priscilla.

His heart raced. She was always a vision to behold.

She'd pushed her hood back onto her shoulders. Thick, fluffy snowflakes that had blown off boughs dotted her warm, chestnut hair. Her cheeks were rosy from the cold, and her breath came out in steamy puffs.

The joy he felt upon seeing her, though, was dampened by the unease created by her father's trailing figure. Nicholas Fontaigne looked as stern as ever, and the strength of his severity swelled his physical presence beyond its natural size.

The rest of the outlaws emerged from their huts and gathered to see the visitors.

"Priscilla!" Aidan couldn't help the broadening smile that engulfed his face. "What brings you here? How did you find us?"

She curtseyed and smiled back. It warmed him to see her happiness upon seeing him equaled his own.

If it weren't for her father, he would have asked for her hand long ago — and he suspected she might say yes. Though, perhaps he thought more of himself in her eyes than he should.

"Your young Tom told us how to get here."

"Tom the Hunter?"

"Yes, now don't be harsh with him," she said, "He knew my name and who I am."

Aidan blushed and looked away. Tom only knew those things because of how much Aidan talked about her.

Ysabella caught Aidan's eye in that moment. She stood off at a distance by a large oak tree, her raven hair spilling down her back. Her gaze was fixed upon Priscilla, but she noticed Aidan looking her way and flashed a smile. He saw no jealousy in her eyes, but something else . . . something unusual.

Priscilla noted his glance and turned to look. Now, it was her turn to redden.

"I hope I have not come unwelcome," she said.

"Not at all!" Aidan assured, taking her hands in his. "You are most welcome! Most of anyone."

"Huh-hmmm," Nicholas cleared his throat and flicked his eyes to their clasp.

Aidan dropped her hands but continued to smile. "So, what brings you out in this cold?" he repeated.

She turned to Nicholas, "Father, I am going to speak to Aidan privately, if you approve." It was not a real question, more of a declaration.

Her father nodded. In many things the baron ruled, but clearly his daughter willed her way in others.

She took Aidan's arm and steered him away from the crowd, some of whom encircled Lord Fontaigne, peppering him with questions.

"I forced my father to bring me here. I had to see you. It has been too long."

"I am honored," he said.

"Don't be silly. You've known me since I was a girl. We're closer than that. . . I've heard about what you've been doing out here in the forest."

"I was afraid word might reach your father that I'd turned outlaw."

"You're no outlaw. What you're doing is noble! I think it's wonderful!"

Her words warmed him, but he didn't feel noble or wonderful. He felt like a man stuck in the woods with nowhere to go who just did what came naturally.

"What does your father say? Does he not think I'm an outlaw?"

"What he says does not matter . . ."

"He doesn't like me."

"I don't think he would like any man who stole my heart. So, don't you worry about what he thinks."

The weight of what she had just revealed made his heart jump and lit his face with the brightest grin yet. "Your *heart* . . ." His face dropped again, "But he won't allow us to marry."

"Not yet," She said, "You're right. He won't allow me to marry a man without a title, and he's quite firm on that point."

"I don't know how I'll ever become a knight now. Leading this band, raiding barons and bishops, who would ever convey the honor upon me?"

"But all that you've done has been in the name of Maud. Surely we have hope."

"Only if she prevails . . ."

"Then, may she prevail. I've never heard you sound so defeated, Aidan. Your confidence is normally overflowing."

"Only because I'm faced with the loss of that which I wanted most in life."

"Your knighthood . . ."

"No, what a lack of title prevents me from ever having."

"You mean land."

"I mean *you*."

She felt the passion of his words and choked up. A tear spilled down her cheek.

"God will provide, Aidan. My father has taught me that."

"*Nicholas?* What does he know about God?"

"Much, I tell you. He *is* my father, you'll remember, and I'll not have him spoken of that way." A flash of fire passed behind her eyes. "His heart is rough, but it is not hard. You would do well to learn much wisdom from him."

"Would it win me his approval?"

"He approves of you more than you know. He just wants the best for his daughter, good provision."

They strolled in silence.

"Did you know we took in a young refugee from Becca's Well?" Priscilla asked, "A young girl by the name of Lilith. She was a servant at Falconer Manor. It seems Sir Walter was abusing her."

"I know her . . . she arrived at your house?"

"Yes. After she fled the castle, a relative of hers in the village pointed her to us. I convinced father to let her stay. She's been through a lot, but I am happy for her company. We've become like sisters over the past month."

"I'm glad to hear it. I'd heard Walter had other victims."

She stopped. "And I've heard you rescued another girl from a similar predicament."

"Yes, that's true."

"Aidan, I don't think you know how special you are. What lord in this realm, much less an outlaw, would risk life and limb for the sake of a servant girl? It's why these men follow you. It's why I love you."

"You love me?" His voice broke.

"Yes," she said, her look intensifying.

"And I love you, Priscilla. I always have, ever since you were a young girl when I first saw you so many years ago. I always will."

A compelling attraction energized the air between them. She leaned in to buss his cheek, hesitated, then changed her mind and met his lips with her own.

The touch of their soft fullness surprised him. Electric tingles ran up and down his spine, and his vision swam as she pulled away. He was overwhelmed by a strong desire to grab her and kiss her again and again.

Instead, he turned his face up to the trees overhead. A light snow was beginning to fall, and the flakes looked like a shower of stars. He inhaled deeply the cold, crisp air and exhaled it again with a cloud of steam.

"Someday, I will come for you, Priscilla," he said firmly, "And I *will* marry you."

"I know. Now walk me back to the camp."

***

Upon their return, a strange thing occurred. Lord Nicholas Fontaigne asked for Aidan's permission to speak to his people. Puzzled, Aidan assented. Priscilla seemed to know what was going on but wasn't talking.

The baron leapt up onto a stump closest to the fire and called the outlaws to gather around.

"Men and women of Newhaven Forest," he began, "I would speak to you for a moment if you'll lend me your ears. That which I am about to say shall make me just as much of an outlaw as you."

He had their attention now.

"Many years ago, a priest, grateful to me for a matter I will not go into here today, gave me a book for my own personal use. This book was no ordinary book, but was quite special as you'll soon see, for it was an English translation of some of the Holy Scriptures!"

Gasps passed through the crowd. The church prohibited the Bible from being read in any language but Latin and translating it into English was considered heresy.

"Today, I stand before you having studied these Scriptures at length, and I wish to declare what they say so you may emerge from ignorance into the light. First and foremost, you should know that God created all men equal. According to the laws of England, I hold land and my title, but there are no noble ranks in God's eyes. From Adam and Eve until now, God has not declared a certain race of men superior to others.

"However, God's Holy Word also says that every man is a sinner, though I'm confident each of you is already painfully aware of your state before Him. Yet, you might be shocked to know that nobles, earls and barons, priests and kings, are all sinners too, no worse, yet no less than you yourselves."

Murmuring rolled through the people. These were truths they held in their heart, but to declare it publicly was scandalous.

"Yet, there is hope. Scripture says that every man and woman may approach God directly in prayer without any need for a priest or for a mediator."

A few exclaimed their shock. Others cried for calm to let him be heard. The idea of not needing a priest was . . . well, it was outside the scope of their reality.

"God's Holy Word says that all men and women need to do to avoid condemnation from hell is to trust in Jesus Christ as their Lord and Savior. Lord in obedience and Savior from your sins. To do this requires humility, repentance, faith, and trust in His love for you. If you do that, you will be saved and enter Heaven when you die."

The commotion among the people roared. They had never heard such things before.

"Those are my words, though they be based in the truth of God's. Take them or leave them." He stepped off the stump.

The people rushed forward and surrounded him, showering him with questions, some angry, some curious, some incredulous. Nicholas patiently answered each one in turn.

"Your father sure knows how to get a crowd going," Aidan commented to Priscilla.

"You have no idea how long he's waited for an audience."

Aidan's own heart burned with a turmoil sparked by the man's words. If what Fontaigne said was true, so much of the world Aidan knew was wrong.

He didn't know what to make of Baron Fontaigne. During his stump speech, the man was full of life and passion, but as soon as he descended off it, he'd regressed into his old, stern self, like a grand lion slouching until it could slip into the skin of a mole.

Chapter 20

March 1138 AD

Several months later, Aidan, Red, and a small band of others were headed back to camp from an uneventful patrol of the main road through the forest.

It was a bright and sunny day. The noonday air was warm, but not hot. Many of the trees had just loosed their first bright bursts of green, but the youthful leaves were still small and curling.

A heavy clopping echoed distantly behind them.

By now, Aidan's companions were used to reacting on instinct. The band stealthily melted into the forest line without a word.

Aidan turned and stood alone in the middle of the road to face whoever rode the approaching horses. The oncoming travelers might have caught a glimpse of Red and the others, but no matter. If so, it only meant the travelers knew there were at least five archers concealed in the woods with their bows at the ready.

The group consisted of five men riding destriers, the fiercest and most expensive of warhorses.

A nobleman, who in his manner carried the authority of an earl, rode the lead. Right behind him followed a monk in a rough brown tunic. Three knights in full chain mail rode the flanks in a protective formation.

The sight of the warhorses made Aidan nervous. Few had enough money to afford a destrier, and even fewer lords could afford them for their underlings like these knights.

The nobleman's tunic was scarlet red, finely woven, and edged with braided, golden hems. The clothes, the chain mail, the horses — without a doubt, this man was a very wealthy earl, and that meant he was also very powerful.

The most powerful they had encountered yet.

Aidan's outlaws had the advantage of concealment and the distance of an archer's bow but taking on a powerful earl was no trifling matter, especially if something went wrong and he were injured or killed. His heirs would move heaven and earth to avenge him, and Aidan certainly did not covet those kinds of enemies.

With the wealth this man displayed, he had to be a close ally of either King Stephen or Queen Maud. It was one or the other, and the first order of business was to determine which it was.

"Ho!" Aidan called.

The earl rode to within fifteen feet of Aidan before bringing his horse to a halt.

He held his countenance firmly level, even as Aidan blocked his way. His knights cantered up until they were even with their lord, while the monk remained a horse length behind.

"Who dares to block my path?" The nobleman asked, though not with the standard contempt Aidan's band had come to expect.

"I would ask the same," Aidan replied. "Tis our forest, and we require knowledge of those who would pass through it."

"It is the king's forest, young man."

"Whether he be king or not is in some doubt."

"Ha! So, you are for Maud, then?"

"I am, and devotedly so."

"You said *our*." The earl's horse sidestepped a few feet. "Who is we?"

"My men are well-trained archers hidden among the trees. We have you surrounded and will have answers to our satisfaction before you are permitted to proceed."

A knight with a thick, brown beard prodded his destrier forward aggressively. "How dare you threaten the earl?"

The nobleman stretched out his arm against the knight's chest, wordlessly ordering him to stand down.

"Do you have a silver penny?" Aidan asked.

"We'll not be robbed . . ." the rash knight continued, spitting the words.

The earl cut him off, nodding. "We do."

"If we rob you, I assure you it will be much more than a penny you lose," Aidan commented. "Toss one into the air then."

The earl removed a penny from a small purse and threw it up into a wide arc. Without warning, an arrow sliced from the forest, crossed the road, and clinked audibly as its point connected with the penny before driving itself into a tree on the opposite side.

"You see that we are accurate. Now, we'll have your names," Aidan said.

"I am Robert de Caen, Earl of Gloucester," he announced.

The blood drained from Aidan's face, but he did not budge.

The Earl of Gloucester was the son of the previous King Henry and one of the most powerful lords in all of England.

Aidan steeled himself. He would not fade, not even if facing King Stephen himself.

"And are you for Stephen or Maud, sir?"

"Have you not heard? I am for Maud, of course. That the throne should be hers was the clear will of her father, the king, as he abundantly expressed before he died."

Aidan stepped aside and swept his arm in a low circle. "Then we beg your forgiveness, Earl Robert. You are free to pass."

"And if I had been Stephen's man?"

"Then you and your men would have walked out of Newhaven Forest without horse, nor hauberk, nor arms, and your pockets much lighter to boot."

The earl threw back his head, roaring with laughter, and his men joined him. Even the harsh knight cracked a smile.

"You, my dear ruffian, are my kind of man," Robert said.

Aidan reddened. "I am no ruffian. My father was Baron of Falconer Manor, and my lands were usurped by my uncle, much in the same way as the king he supports."

"Ah . . . then I believe I have found the one I seek. You are Aidan Falconer?"

Aidan stood stunned.

He retreated several steps, his senses on full alert. His hand stretched instinctively for the hilt of his sword behind his shoulder.

"Relax, young Falconer." The earl lifted both hands into the air, and pressed his palms toward the ground, emphasizing to *remain calm*. "We seek you as a friend. Your exploits in Newhaven have reached my ears — even in Gloucester. I've also heard of the deeds of your uncle."

"Then, can you help restore my lands? Would you appeal to the king on my behalf?"

"My, you are a bold one," Earl Robert smiled and shifted in his saddle, "I fear that remains outside of my power. Richard is in support of Stephen, and I have become a thorn in the king's side. As have you, though the king's notice of you is minor. Nevertheless, Stephen would never rule in your favor. You may not realize what you have done here, but you have stolen many pounds that were intended to raise soldiers to Stephen's side. As long as Stephen is king, he will never restore your lands to you."

Aidan cursed.

"But that is neither here nor there. I come on a specific mission, young man. I've come to knight you."

A buzzing flooded Aidan's mind.

He was suddenly aware of the blood rushing through his ears. The shock of what the earl had just said was making it difficult to register the words.

"I . . . eh . . . beg pardon? *What* did you say, sire? You have come to *knight* me?"

"Yes, and I've brought this monk as my witness. May I dismount?"

Aidan nodded, and the earl stepped down from his destrier.

Red and the other outlaws emerged from the woods, bows relaxed and arrows returned to their quivers. The monk and the knights dismounted too, and the earl withdrew his sword from its scabbard.

He approached Aidan.

"Kneel," he commanded.

Aidan dropped to one knee in front of the earl, head bowed.

"I only regret that we have neither chapel, nor altar, nor time for you to pray. Do you, Aidan Falconer, swear to defend to your uttermost the weak, the orphan, the widow and the oppressed? Do you swear to always be courteous, to give women your especial care, to never give evil counsel to a lady, whether married or not, and defend her against all? Do you swear to never deal favorably with traitors and to observe the fasts?"

"I do."

"Then, I, Robert de Caen, Earl of Gloucester, do dub you, Sir Aidan." The earl slapped the flat side of the tip of his sword on each of Aidan's shoulders as he said this.

Aidan could barely believe what had just happened. He had title, even if his lands had not been restored, and by the Earl of Gloucester no less, whose word no one would doubt. He'd given up all hope of ever regaining legal status once word had gotten out about his living as an outlaw.

"What did I do to deserve your attention, sir?" Aidan asked. "Surely my importance in the scheme of things is low."

The earl replaced his sword in its scabbard on the horse and turned back to him.

"Your father was a good man, Aidan." Robert's eyes shimmered with water. "His son did not deserve the treatment he has received."

Aidan rose and thanked him. They spoke for a few minutes more before the earl and his entourage remounted to leave. Aidan felt a lightness of spirit that had been foreign to him for too long. Perhaps tomorrow the weight of his plight would re-roost upon his shoulders, but today it felt good. His future seemed as bright as the sun above.

***

And we spend our lives looking for things we can't find
Oh, but not a single day goes by where you don't cross my mind...

"Cross My Mind"

~*ARIZONA*

Aidan's horse leapt ditches and dodged trees as he raced to intercept the road that led to Fontaigne Manor. Faster and faster, he drove the courser, periodically ducking to avoid a low hanging branch that threatened to sweep him from the saddle.

The steed was beginning to lather. He'd driven him too hard. Once they reached the road, he let the stallion take a water break by a brook. He'd walk him the rest of the way.

Aidan knew he should have managed it oppositely — have the horse amble through the woods and then race ahead once it reached the straight road — but he was too anxious to get there and not thinking well.

He dismounted and knelt to drink from the cool water.

Straightening again, he pulled a small sack from his saddlebag filled with biscuits that Ysabella had prepared for the journey.

They were still warm. Faint wisps of steam swirled up when he cracked one open. Delicious and light, only some honey would have made them better.

He could only abide to let the horse walk for ten minutes or so before he ran him again. Still, it took him another hour to reach Priscilla's house, and he had to let the horse rest several more times on the way.

Her home was two stories, constructed of thick crisscrossing beams, stones, and plaster. On the lower floor, mortared stones lay behind the plaster, and a timber frame supported the upper. A steep thatched roof topped the house.

As far as houses went, it was much simpler than most barons had, but still much nicer than the average peasant.

Nicholas Fontaigne was what was considered a lesser baron. He held the title of baron because he held his tenancy directly from the king, but his lands were not enough to produce great wealth or even to support a knight. Three serfs and their families worked his lands for him, but Aidan knew there had been times when Baron Fontaigne himself had been forced to get muddy in the fields.

From Priscilla, he knew Nicholas could make the fief more profitable, but was too kind to his serfs. When times got tough, he let them focus on their own lands, knowing they would need every resource to get through winter. Aidan had trouble reconciling this softer side *she* claimed with the Nicholas Fontaigne *he* knew. He couldn't imagine the man being kind, but she swore he was. Just not to Aidan.

Regardless, her father was not by any means a poor man, and they lived comfortably. He spent the large majority of his time in the study of books he purchased from local monasteries.

"Priscilla!" Aidan called. "Priscilla!"

He didn't slow down as he entered the yard. The horse's hooves still thundered as he leapt from the mount.

He landed gracefully at the front door, and his knuckles launched into its oaken boards persistently, hoping against desperation he hadn't come while she was away. He'd been alone for far too long in the forest, and it was time to change that.

He flinched as it finally swung open, dreading the possibility it would be the stern baron who answered.

But it wasn't.

Priscilla stood in its frame.

She looked stunning.

Her dress was a pale yellow that reminded him of the wild Celandine flowers that bloom in March.

His cheeks ached as if they would burst from the large grin that barely contained his excitement.

"Aidan!" she gasped, "What are you doing here?"

Nicholas appeared behind her in the room. She stepped off the threshold to join Aidan outside and greeted him with a firm kiss on the cheek. Nicholas filled the opening in her place.

"I have been knighted!" Aidan exclaimed.

"Knighted?" Her eyes widened.

"*Knighted?*" Nicholas asked, "By whom?"

"By none other than Robert de Caen, Earl of Gloucester!"

Priscilla clapped her hands and squealed with happiness. She swiveled to glance at her father and then returned to Aidan.

"That is wonderful news!" She said.

"Slow down," her father hesitated, "How did this happen?"

Aidan explained about the encounter in Newhaven and how the earl had been searching for him since he'd heard about their efforts to support Maud.

"Tis true, Robert is a supporter of Maud," Nicholas conceded.

"Oh, Aidan! This is simply wonderful." Her smile lit his soul with more warmth than the sun overhead. She threw her arms around his neck and kissed him on the lips.

"Daughter! You will comport yourself!"

Blushing, she withdrew. "Sorry, father."

Aidan was elated. "So, I have a title now, and there's no reason we cannot be married . . ."

"Hold on," Nicholas interrupted. For the briefest of moments, he seemed uncomfortable with his own objection, but quickly shook it off. "I will never consent to such a marriage for Priscilla."

Her face fell. She turned to face him, shocked. "But father, you said I could not marry Aidan because he had no title. Now he does . . ."

"He still has no land."

"No land?" Aidan was incredulous. "My lands were stolen from me. You know that."

"Nevertheless, the facts of your state remain the same."

Aidan was stunned. "But . . . that could be years. It will be near impossible for me to receive a fief before this civil war is over."

"Young man, I will not have my daughter living in a primitive hut in the middle of the forest with a band of outlaws!"

Aidan reddened. This man got his dander up like few others, yet he had to do his best to get on his good side regardless of how difficult that might be.

"You speak a pretty word when you're up on a stump, Lord Nicholas. But it seems to me when you're on the ground with the rest of us, your talk of equality evaporates like mist in the morning."

His point hit home, but the baron wasn't budging.

"Yes, you heard my message well, Aidan, but when I die, who will carry it on for me if not Priscilla, and how will she do that if she's married to a peasant or a landless knight? No, she must marry a lord or the message dies with me. Not to mention the constant risk in which she would find herself among your people from those you've angered. I am sorry, but I must withhold my consent."

Priscilla flinched, devastated. A defeated expression clouded her visage.

"May I have a minute then, sir?" Aidan asked.

Nicholas nodded and withdrew back into the house.

Aidan took Priscilla's hands in his own.

"What are we to do?" he asked.

She was on the verge of tears. She knew as well as he how difficult the prospect of his coming into land was, and her father sounded like he might not even be satisfied with the holdings of a normal knight.

"We can pray," she managed finally.

"Prayer? What good will that do?"

"Prayer solves more than we can do with our hands."

Her father allowed them a long visit, so they sat on a fallen log by the wood line and talked. Nicholas even brought them a light lunch of bread, cheese and berries. He clearly felt bad about forcing their separation, but that didn't mean he was about to change his mind.

Her faith piqued Aidan's curiosity. It was a living thing, starkly different in contrast with the dry, unintelligible rituals performed by the priests each mass.

She spoke of all she'd learned from her father and other things gleaned from her own reading. Nicholas had taught her to read at an early age, and she'd read from the same Scriptures as he. Which surprised him — few in England were literate, and fewer of those were women, even among the higher classes.

And of those rare noblewomen who could read, how many had read the Bible written in *English?* Priscilla was truly a rarity.

Aidan's mother had also been a godly woman, but she'd been gone for so long he couldn't remember her words now. His father had been a man of deep, but quiet faith. He'd always endeavored to instill in Aidan a sense of honor and duty, which Aidan had understood was rooted in his father's beliefs, but he could not recall them ever having had a conversation about God or theology.

Aidan checked his gut. He instinctively wanted to reject the things Priscilla was saying, if only because he knew the ideas originated with her father, but he couldn't. The sheer logic and reason behind what she said rang true. Plus, she obviously held these beliefs near and dear to her heart, and they would likely become dear to him as well as he grew in his understanding of them.

The sun would soon threaten to dip below the horizon, so once the trees' shadows had stretched long enough for their tips to reach the house, Aidan bid them both farewell and began his journey back to camp.

He had a lot to think about.

Chapter 21

Rumors flew that the sporadic fighting between King Stephen and David of Scotland, who nominally fought in the name of Maud, was about to escalate dramatically.

Rumor also had it that Sir Walter was to leave this very day for London to recruit more soldiers into Richard's service for the purpose of augmenting Stephen's regiments.

Aidan couldn't resist the opportunity.

Walter was not worthy of the title he bore. He was an abuser, a violator of women. Aidan's jaws clenched at the memory of Walter murdering Sir Bart the day after his father died. Bart had been Aidan's mentor, as close to a second father as a man could have.

So, today, Aidan and Red were waiting for the lecherous knight in the middle of the road to London.

The sky above looked like dirty wool. All morning, it had threatened to rain, but so far, a storm had yet to break.

They'd positioned themselves around a bend in the road, out of sight from Falconer keep. Walter and his companions would turn the corner and ride into Aidan's ambush before they knew what hit them.

Seven of his archers were concealed in the forest behind where they believed Walter would approach to prevent the knight from retreating. Another five were stationed in the trees behind Aidan. Walter would be caught in the crossfire. Some might call it dishonorable to stack the deck so unfairly, but as far as Aidan was concerned, fairness had no place in battle.

He did not intend to rob Walter. He intended to make sure he never bothered anyone again.

However, Walter was running late.

According to their informant, Walter's group was to have left for London around nine this morning. Judging by the height of the sun in the sky, it had to be closer to ten by now.

No reason for alarm yet. The man was known for overindulgence and was probably recovering from an onerous hangover.

There wasn't much chance he could have chosen a different route. If London was their goal, all other roads would add at least a day to their journey.

At last, a clattering of hooves sounded faintly.

Aidan raised a hand, signaling for all to hold their position. It was just one horse, and whoever the rider was, they were racing at top speed.

Suddenly, Peter rounded the bend. In an instant, Aidan realized Peter had almost run his horse into the ground. The poor beast was bowing and dipping its head, straining for breath with each heaving pace. Peter towed back on the reins and leapt off, landing on his feet right in front of them.

"Aidan! You've got to hurry! Walter's not coming!"

"Slow down. What do you mean?"

Peter's eyes were wide with alarm. "The rumor about Walter going to London must have been a trick. They just wanted to get you away from the forest. At nine o'clock, a full company of soldiers armed to the teeth rode out from the castle toward Newhaven."

"How many?"

"At least forty, and they're off the trails, among the trees, searching for our camp."

Aidan's heart skipped a beat.

"They'll never find it," he said, "The forest is too big."

"That's the problem," Peter breathed. "They might. The hostler from Haddon told them where to look."

"*What?* Why would he do that?"

Aidan whistled, waving his hand in the air in a circular motion, a signal for the archers to come in.

"Richard found out he'd been supplying us with hay for our horses. They offered him a pound of silver if he told what he knew and threatened to kill him if he didn't."

Aidan cursed. "But he couldn't have told them much..."

"He'll get them close enough. They're searching the woods in stretched-out lines, and they're already in the right area. It's only a matter of time before they stumble onto our village."

Aidan's heart pounded in his chest.

The threat was serious, and many of his best fighters were here with him.

Most of the archers had joined him now and heard the tail end of the news. Aidan sent one of them up the road to fetch the rest of their horses where they'd stashed them.

Aidan mounted his courser and circled to rally.

"Men, we've been deceived! Mount up! Richard has sent men to attack our homes. We've got to move fast. Peter, jump on with me. Leave that horse to rest or he'll die."

Their expressions were grim, but they wasted no time. In less than a minute, all were thundering down the road through the middle of Becca's Well. Villagers peeked out from their shops and homes to see why fifteen horses were storming down their street with caution thrown to the wind.

Aidan would normally direct his men to filter into the woods and surround the soldiers stealthily, but Richard's men had too great a head start. They had to either catch these men from behind or somehow get ahead of them, and the only way to do that was to stick to the road. They could not keep up this pace among the trees.

As soon as they'd reached the line that marked the end of the fields tilled by the serfs, the weather broke. Sharp pellets of cold rain trickled through Aidan's hair to his scalp and rolled down his back and forearms with increasing frequency.

Soon, they found themselves in a full downpour. The chilled wet turned the leather of their saddles slippery. Peter tightened his grip around Aidan's waist to keep from falling off.

The road devolved into a muddy morass, forcing them to dampen their pace, but they pushed their coursers as hard as they could without losing footing.

Aidan was in the lead, and thus remained unsullied, but he knew the men behind were getting slopped with clumps of mud flying off the horses' hooves ahead of them.

The rain descended in sheets now, currents running like rivers across his exposed skin. It seeped under his leather tunic and soaked his undergarments in a cold and very unpleasant way.

They could only hope the cloudburst would dampen his uncle's men's will to continue their search. It depended on how hard Richard had pressed them. Unfortunately, given the effort put into the ruse to distract Aidan, they were probably quite determined.

Aidan's band raced on for several miles, only slowing for curves so their coursers wouldn't slip before the force of the turns.

Through the hazy mist ahead, Aidan spied the faint outline of a horse's brown haunches and the distinct, muted silver of a warrior's armor. As he neared, several fainter outlines coalesced beyond the first.

They'd reached the back of the attacker's line, but the soldiers were not yet aware of *their* presence.

Now was the moment of decision. They could pull back, melt into the forest, and try to surround them, or make a full-on assault.

Aidan did not slow.

He slid his sword from its scabbard and thrust it high. He waved his blade in small circles and then laid it forward, pointing the tip toward the soldiers.

He kicked his stallion in the ribs. It pulled a last burst of speed from its reserves and accelerated toward the soldiers' rear.

His men understood the silent order. Direct attack.

They too elicited a final forceful push from their horses and caught up with him.

Thankfully, the rain dampened more than just their clothes — it masked their noise for much farther along than they could have hoped.

Aidan's men went without armor whenever stealth mattered, and it had on this morning's mission, so Richard's men had the advantage of both armor and numbers, but Aidan's band had the element of surprise and longer-range weapons.

In fact, Richard's men remained unaware of their presence until arrows began plunging into their ranks. Three bolts soared past Aidan and arced overhead. One buried itself in an exposed gap in a soldier's mail; the other two bounced harmlessly off the armor of others.

The wounded man's cry stirred the soldiers' line. Their horses sidestepped and churned in disarray as Richard's would-be ambushers realized they themselves were under attack.

But it was too late.

Aidan sailed through them with his blade slashing in wide sweeping arcs on both sides. More arrows landed, some with reward, most fruitlessly. Red and several other outlaws followed Aidan into the middle of the enemy, their swords swinging as well.

One knight managed a counter-slash at the last outlaw in the piercing charge and felled him from his horse with a mortal blow.

Seven of Aidan's outlaws had no sword, so they leapt from their mounts before reaching the soldiers and disappeared into the cover of the trees to fight with their bows.

Aidan continued a short distance past the end of the soldiers' group and then whipped his horse around.

Both hope *and* alarm rose up within him simultaneously.

Only fifteen or sixteen of Richard's men were here. That meant they had a decent chance at overcoming them.

But Peter said around forty had ridden out from the castle. That meant there was a second group somewhere. So, the village was still in danger for however long they were tied up here.

The good news was that most of the knights, the most hardened and well-armored of the warriors, were here.

He twisted in his saddle to address Peter, who was still behind him.

"Grab another archer and warn the camp! They need to get to the cave!"

Peter leapt down from his horse and raced into the trees where he disappeared from view.

Aidan belted out a rally cry and dug into his mount's side, spurring it on again. Those outlaws who were armed with swords followed him into the fray once more.

He bore down at full speed. The enemy bounced in Aidan's vision in tune with the gait of his steed.

At the front of them, sitting stiff and tall, was Sir Hugo. The man's expression was one of pure contempt.

All the enemy held their weapons at the ready now.

Hugo barked an order and his men dismounted, steeling themselves for the coming charge.

Hugo's eyes shone like cold metal. He was a cruel man, yet one who knew how to control his emotions so as to be dispassionate before his enemies. A man who could focus completely on the defeat of his foes.

Aidan leapt from his horse while it was still in motion, knowing the move would be unexpected.

However, this time, his feet flew out from under him as soon as they struck the slippery mud. He slid and slammed into the ankles of a man-at-arms. The impact bowled the guy off his feet.

Aidan's slide came to a stop directly in front of Sir Roger. Unlike the suppressed Hugo, Roger's visage was twisted with hate.

He slashed down at Aidan's torso with a devastating blow.

Before it struck home, Aidan rolled to the side, and Roger's blade plunged into the sodden road. It clanged on a rock buried under the sludge and came back up heavily.

Aidan continued his roll, pulled his dagger from his boot, and rammed it into the calf of a soldier facing away from him. The man screamed in pain and dropped to one knee.

Aidan jumped back to his feet.

Another knight swung for Aidan's head, but he ducked and slammed a foot into the man's chest which drove him backward onto his rump in the mud.

For the moment, Aidan was clear of attackers, which gave him time to plant his feet in a strong defensive stance and appraise the status of the fight.

All of Aidan's men were afoot now. Red had been parrying with the man Aidan had stabbed in the calf, and when he'd gone down on one knee, Red had finished him off with a blow to the neck.

Including Aidan, six outlaws had swords and were going hand-to-hand against the more experienced knights. One outlaw lay face down in the mud where he'd fallen from his horse.

Presumably, Peter had taken one of the archers with him to warn the village, which left six archers in the forest. Their arrows were raining in, but the archers were limited in what they could accomplish. They had to be careful in their aim so as to not hit Aidan and their other companions, and their opponents were well armored, limiting where their shafts could find success.

To make matters worse, the rain had soaked their quivers, and the wet feathers of the arrows' fletchings made their aim less true.

Five of Richard's soldiers were down, one knight and four men-at-arms. That still left the outlaws severely outnumbered, and the element of surprise was now spent. They had to make up for it with fierceness of battle.

Aidan tore into them. Had he been leading the enemy troop, he would have called them to into a circular formation with their backs to each other. Thankfully, they weren't used to working together, and the outlaws could take advantage of their disorganization.

He swept low and knocked the legs out from under one, then whipped the pommel of his sword back into the face of a man at his rear. He parried numerous blows and circled around to a place where his back wouldn't be vulnerable. He felt a warm wash of pride at seeing his men using well the skills he'd trained into them over the past year.

Aidan took out a man-at-arms and then found himself facing Roger again, who wasted no time in swinging for Aidan's skull with all his strength.

It was an artless arc and Aidan fended it off with a little duck and parry. He stepped up the offensive against Roger, slashing and striking at every angle where the knight was not expecting.

Roger blocked many of the blows, but the ferocity of Aidan's attack cracked the angry disdain on his face and revealed stripes of panicked fear. Sweat broke out and trickled down the knight's temples as he fought to keep up. Aidan was easily ten years younger than the man, so he had the advantage of youth as well.

On the defensive, the knight was clearly struggling not to succumb. Several of Aidan's strikes landed, and though the glancing blows were prevented from biting into flesh by Roger's chain mail, their power still hurt. One smashed into his side with a flat clap. The knight winced and began to wheeze.

Roger was clearly not used to fighting against a weapon of such length or weight. Aidan could step out of range of his enemy's sword and still be able to land blows himself. He found himself falling in love with his unusual sword all over again.

Roger failed to step far enough back at the right moments, so the tip of Aidan's sword struck home several more times and sliced narrow slits through his mail. Roger's expression was full of fear now.

Then, fat Sir Walter tumbled into the picture. He rushed Aidan from the right with his sword raised high over his head, eyes burning bright with indignant, arrogant fury. Aidan's blade diverted its attention from Roger to intercept Walter and swept into that knight's side before his own weapon was in range.

Walter cried out and dropped to one knee, holding his ribs with one hand and his now drooping sword with the other. The look of arrogance had fled his face.

Still, Walter's arrival inspired fresh courage in Roger. Seeing Aidan distracted, he renewed his vigor. Aidan slung his sword back around and parried Roger's with a solid, electrifying ring of metal.

Aidan stepped to the right and slammed his hilt on Walter's helmet with another metallic clang. Walter groaned and slumped forward onto his face in the mud.

Aidan noticed Hugo trying to cautiously slip in from the left. Aidan glued his eyes on that vicious knight and maintained a dead-pan stare even as he swung for Roger again.

Roger responded too late, due to a combination of exhaustion and surprise at Aidan's unexpected ability to regroup so quickly after taking out Walter.

He had just enough time to get his blade up in front of Aidan's and defuse some of its power, but it nevertheless drove the flat of his own sword back into his neck limply, not harming him, but giving a visual reality to his impotence.

Sir Hugo was a careful and calculating fighter. Every move he made was measured, pregnant with intent.

If pressed in battle, Hugo never limited his response to defense, but would, with a flick like quicksilver, convert a parry into an offensive strike directed at some unexpected area on his opponent devoid of armor. Of all of Richard's men, he was easily the most skilled, and was perhaps one of the best warriors in all England.

The experienced and passionless knight needed no personal encounter with

Aidan's special blade to appraise its power. He'd immediately recognized its impressive length and instinctively knew how to adjust his movements to neutralize the unusual threat.

Aidan made an exploratory strike. He feinted for Hugo's head, but dropped the swing toward his legs at the last second. Hugo deflected both with lightning speed . . . and seemingly no effort.

To his right, Roger was still heaving for breath, but he'd raised his sword high to bring it down on Aidan's skull. Aidan swung up from Hugo's legs and drove Roger's blade up and back. With one continuous flow, he then curved low and cut into the man's knee. Roger lost his poise as that leg crumpled beneath his weight. Somehow, he managed to not topple over, but stayed up on one knee.

Losing no time, Aidan returned his attention to Sir Hugo, knowing the man would not lose an opportunity to catch him unaware. He was just in time to block Hugo's sword from slicing into his neck.

A flicker of surprise lit Hugo's eyes.

Aidan pushed Hugo's blade away and followed up with a slash at his side, but Hugo was also able to counter in time.

Without taking his eyes from Hugo, Aidan slung his blade back toward Sir Roger's neck and finished him off. The knight's body slid to the ground.

Chapter 22

Eric huddled in his hut, shivering against the chill that normally would have dissipated by this hour. Instead, the gunpowder sky had thickened until birthing this downpour. He and Tom sat gloomily, staring out their doorframe at the vacated camp.

Heavy rivulets of water flowed from lines in the thatch on every roof and dove into small craters in the ground underneath their ragged eaves. Small pools grew, merged with others, and then streamed out of the camp in small torrents like a miniature tributary system.

The camp's main fire had been extinguished by the rain, so everyone else was doing the same as they, sitting inside their homes waiting for it to let up, which didn't look like it would happen any time soon.

Eric chucked a stone out into a puddle. There would be no hunting today.

They had a small hearth inside where they might have started a cooking fire, but he hadn't had a chance to grab a flaming stick from the bonfire before the storm put it out. If they really wanted to cook something, he or Tom would have to run to another hut to fetch fire and get soaked in the process.

Maybe they'd draw straws to see who would go. His stomach was beginning to rumble.

He squinted, peering closer at the woodline.

A dark shape was forming in the grey, but it was hard to make out behind the sheets of water falling from the heavens.

It soon became clear the obscure shape was a man.

Then, a second figure appeared.

Two men were running toward the camp, probably trying to get to shelter . . . but they seemed to be headed straight for Eric's hut . . .

It was Peter and Fulke, two of their hunters, and they pushed inside the small structure without waiting for an invitation.

Water ran from their bodies like they'd just emerged from a lake. Both men broke forward at the waist, hands on their knees, gasping for breath.

"What's going on, Peter?" Eric asked.

He and Tom glanced back and forth between the two. Something was clearly wrong. Fulke had been with Aidan's group since dawn, but they'd sent

Peter out this morning to alert Aidan about Richard's soldiers leaving the castle.

Had something happened to Aidan?

"They're . . . coming," Peter finally managed to breathe, struggling with each word.

Eric leapt to his feet, brow furrowed. "*Who* is coming?"

"Richard's men . . . right behind us!"

Peter straightened, heaving his chest in and out as fast as he could, determined to recover quickly.

"How many?" Eric demanded.

". . . 25 . . . 30 . . . at least . . . all armed . . . they're on the path."

"Where's Aidan?"

". . . stuck at the road . . . fighting more of them . . ."

They'd never expected Richard's men to be able to find them so fast.

The whole village was at risk.

"How long do we have?"

"Minutes."

"Split up and sound the alarm!" Eric ordered the messengers, "Tell everyone to flee to the cave before the soldiers reach the camp. Once they're in sight, any who haven't reached it are to run into the forest. Get to Ranulf first! Tom, you're with me!"

Peter and Fulke fled back into the rain, each rushing to opposite ends of the village, pounding on the thin doors and shouting the instructions.

Eric grimaced. They weren't going to have time to inform the whole village at the rate they were going.

He and Tom had to slow the attackers down.

They snatched their bows and quivers and raced away from the village's heart toward the path Richard's men would likely use for an approach. He almost passed by the hut that belonged to another one of the hunters, Gervase, but thought twice and instead stopped and stuck his head in. Gervase was sitting at a table, eating some bread with his family.

"We're under attack!" Eric shouted. "Gather the archers! To the trees!"

From the corner of his eye, as he turned back to catch up with Tom, he saw Gervase moving into action, grabbing for his bow. Message received.

Unfortunately, they were too late.

He could see about thirty men already moving single file up the trail. A couple of them had spotted the village and were now breaking into a run. Thirty armored soldiers were a devastating force — *and no one was ready to fend them off.*

If they didn't do something quick to reduce the enemy's numbers or delay them, it would be the death of them all.

Mercifully, it seemed the main group of soldiers was right in the middle of the crossbow trap he and Tom had set up months before, though those men wouldn't remain in the sweet spot for long.

Eric elbowed Tom and pointed at the opposite side of the path where the head of the long iron rod that controlled the crossbow triggers lay nestled in the crook of a low branch. Tom immediately understood his thinking and veered off to the left.

Their captain, or at least the man who happened to be at the front of the soldier's line, was a tall knight with a dented helmet and a long stride. He'd just spied Eric and sped up to intercept him.

Eric raced forward, eyes fixed on that knight's legs as the man had just reached the trip wire that would set off the trap.

He watched in horrified fascination as the knight's feet came down neatly on either side of the cord without even brushing it. Then, just as quickly, he was past it and in the village.

Eric pumped his legs harder and curved toward the right side of the crossbow line. The knight pulled his sword and changed his course to match Eric's.

The second man in the attacker's line had now reached the trip wire.

Eric's heart leapt into his throat with anticipation as that man's shin struck the cord firmly and continued through it.

It pulled taut, and the soldier stumbled at the unexpected encumbrance, but he recovered and carried on.

No crossbows fired.

Panic overwhelmed him then. The cord had been pulled and it had not set off the trap. They'd tested it at least twenty times and it had worked every single one of them without fail . . . except . . . *they'd never tested it in the rain.*

The lead knight swept his blade through the air in an arc toward Eric's midriff. Eric twisted and dove forward, barely avoiding its tip.

His body slammed into the ground with a bone-jarring crash. Mud spurted into his face and eyes. Arms extended in front of him, the crash sent him skidding across the wet leaves at a high speed.

As he slid to a stop, his fingers were only inches from the mechanism that would engage the iron rod and set off all the crossbows on the right-hand side.

Five soldiers had spilled into the village now. In a matter of seconds, they would begin unleashing havoc on his people.

Eric struggled to get traction in the slop, scrambling forward on his belly, straining to reach the trigger . . . finally the tips of his fingers brushed it . . . he grunted . . . pushed forward an inch with his toes . . . his fingers were around it now . . . the lead knight was almost upon him . . . at last...

. . . A solid thunk told him he'd finally triggered it.

He couldn't see it coming, but he sensed the blow and rolled wildly to the right just as his pursuer drove his sword deep into the mud where Eric had lain a second before.

As he rolled, a chorus of faint, simultaneous twangs echoed in his ears. They represented the swift release of more than a half dozen crossbow bolts. The rain muffled the thuds of their impacts, but not the screams and groans.

Success.

He smiled.

He leapt up. Now, he had to put distance between himself and this attacker's blade.

Thankfully, the knight had paused, distracted by the unexpected shouts of pain from his comrades.

Eric was elated to see that at least four of his arbalests had hit home, and there wasn't any armor on earth that could resist the force of a crossbow bolt.

Tom had almost reached the left-hand mechanism, but he had to skip over a small bush to get to it, and when he landed, his feet flew out from under him on the slippery leaves. He slid sideways and rolled several times, body fully extended. The momentum took him further away from the mechanism.

The lead knight set after Eric again.

He attempted to ready his bow in defense, but there was no time to plant his feet and draw. He just had to run.

Tom made it back to his feet. Within a few seconds, he'd triggered the left-hand mechanism. The welcome whoosh of more bolts slicing through the air cut through the rain. Their eyes met briefly, and they both grinned.

Tom's secondary assault had been even more successful than his. After Eric's arbalests had fired, the confused soldiers had bunched up in the middle of the path to regroup and assess the unseen threat. Their decision to huddle had made them an even better target for the crossbows on Tom's side. All seven of his bolts found a home in some critical body part belonging to a knight or man-at-arms.

Their booby trap had just taken out a third of the attackers — even if they had had to set it off manually.

They weren't out of the woods yet though. The one knight was still chasing Eric. In spite of the fact the man was weighed down with heavy armor, he just couldn't seem to shake the guy. A few more soldiers who'd survived the death trap joined the pursuit.

A virtual wall of them were between him and Tom now. They'd seen Tom belatedly, so several set off after him to remedy that.

Because the remaining soldiers didn't know what other dangers might await them on the path, the rear of their line dispersed into the trees alongside it, but this caused them to approach the village in a much more disorganized manner.

A couple of those stumbled into the hidden pits the villagers had dug around the perimeter and pierced their feet on the sharpened stakes embedded in their bottoms.

Ahead of Eric, women and children were screaming and running for the cover of the cave, or the forest, whichever they could reach before being overtaken. Fathers and husbands brandished the hasty weapons they'd been able grab and rushed into the fray to give their loved ones more time to escape.

An archer that Gervase had alerted scrambled up a tree and reached one of the overlook platforms they'd built in the branches.

Several of those platforms were situated in different locations around the camp, the idea being to spot threats from a long way off — which was now clearly of no use — and to safely rain down arrows on said attackers if they ever breached the village — which they obviously had. Whether Gervase would be able to get enough archers onto the platforms in time to matter remained to be seen.

Suddenly, several arrows pierced the dirt around the knight's feet in rapid succession. A fourth passed through his foot, and a fifth buried itself in his upper arm. He cried out and hesitated.

Eric shouted for joy.

The slight delay gave him the break he needed. He turned, notched an arrow of his own, and finished the knight off with it.

Suddenly, a cluster of soldiers flew backward in all directions. Ranulf stood in their midst swinging a thick battle ax in wide arcs.

Where he'd come from, Eric didn't now, but the big man had apparently surprised the soldiers as well. Already, two of them were down with mortal wounds. A third gripped his arm tightly to stem the flow of blood from a lengthy gash and seemed out of the fight. The rest circled warily, hesitating before the ferocity they saw in Ranulf's eyes.

The mayhem lasted a few more minutes before a cry of retreat rang out among Richard's men.

They hadn't anticipated the village's prepared defenses. Between the crossbow trap, the hidden spike pits, the archers hidden in the trees, and

Ranulf's axe, they'd lost more than half their number in mere minutes, and they didn't know what other nasty surprises the outlaws might still have in store.

That sudden wariness, combined with the natural disorganization forced on them by the rain, pushed Richard's remaining men to tuck their tails and retreat back down the path as fast as their weighty armor would allow.

Some would be brave enough to return all the way to Falconer Manor and admit failure to their employer's face. Others would decide their mercenary skills were better employed by some other baron who didn't insist they attack crazy outlaws entrenched in a sodden forest.

Ranulf laid the head of his axe in the mud and leaned on its handle, catching his breath. It was a heart-warming sight.to see the backs of the remaining soldiers fading into the grey.

He'd only gotten two or three of them, which bothered him. If they hadn't fled so quickly, he would have gotten more.

Back home, people had known him as Ranulf the Ox, or just Ox as his friends called him. He'd earned the nickname when he was nineteen during some tough times.

One night before plowing season, his father's ox had unexpectedly died. Their lord had demanded they find a way to plow anyway and said if they couldn't get another ox, he'd put someone on their fields who could get the job done.

After a good harvest, they could have afforded to buy another animal, but not then, not at the end of winter when it was time to plow.

To make matters worse, theirs had been one of the only two oxen in the village, and they usually lent theirs to other families during plowing for a few pennies. Of course, the baron had insisted the second ox be dedicated to his fields, and it would not be released before the deadline he'd given Ranulf's family.

The other families made do. Most borrowed oxen from relatives in other villages, a few had given up and left for other parts.

Ranulf had done the only thing he could think to do. He put the yoke on his own neck and pulled the plow up and down those fields until every last row was furrowed. Not every row was as straight as an ox would have done it, but the job was done, and his father's fields were saved. The feat quickly became a local legend.

A few years later, his father had passed away, and his mother went to live with her sister. The baron had refused to let Ranulf take over his father's fields and instead forced him to become a man-at-arms and serve as a guard in the small keep he called a castle.

Ranulf couldn't stand the pompous jerk, but without land he was left with few choices — so he'd joined the guard.

He'd gotten some combat training out of it, which was good, but the more he saw of how the baron treated his people, the less he wanted to do with him.

Then, one day, a few loaves of bread had gone missing from the kitchen, and it caused a big problem. He knew the cook regularly snuck food out to her family, so he never understood why that day there had been such an uproar over those particular loaves of bread.

Didn't matter. For some reason it had, and the cook needed a target to deflect blame. So, she had accused Ranulf of the theft.

The moment he'd heard he'd been accused, he decided he wouldn't wait around to see whether or not the baron would suddenly develop a streak of justice or temperance.

Experience told him what was most likely about to happen, so he stole a horse and fled the castle. He grabbed his young wife from their hovel outside the walls and never looked back.

Soon, he met Red and a few of the other outlaws. That first winter, there had been only five of them, and they'd had to eat Ranulf's horse to survive. That was before he'd had any kids. Now, his quiver was full of young bucks.

The forest was the only place for him now. He'd carved out a nice life for his little family here.

He'd be damned if another selfish baron was going to take it away from him. He was done being pushed around. They might take his life, but that's what would have to happen before he'd give another inch.

Once he was sure they were in the clear of Richard's men, Ranulf straightened and began organizing the people to gather the dead. They'd strip their armor and burn the bodies.

The villagers rejoiced when everyone was accounted for. A true miracle. Their traps had been so effective in turning the tables against the ambush, only one outlaw had even been wounded, and not very seriously.

But what had happened to Aidan?

Chapter 23

Hugo retreated a few steps. He flicked his eyes back and forth and took a swift, but detailed assessment of the situation.

Roger was out of it, so Aidan was now unencumbered, able to focus his full attention on Hugo. Which Hugo did not appreciate.

Having no innate sense of honor, Hugo much preferred to have a clear advantage.

Walter had regained consciousness and crawled back to his horse. He'd gotten a foot in a stirrup and was now struggling to throw himself up and over onto his saddle.

The battle was still raging, but it wouldn't be for too much longer. Somehow, these upstart outlaws had overcome all of his men.

He watched as one of Aidan's younger ones, a scrawny lad with no mail or other defense, finished off another of his men-at-arms. Besides Walter, only four of his still stood.

One outlaw with a thick mane of flaming red hair caught Hugo's eye. He was leaning on the hilt of his sword, the tip of which was planted in the ground, calmly observing the fight between himself and Aidan.

Hugo did not particularly like what he saw in that man's unconcerned eyes: Pure contempt — and a certainty that Aidan was going *to win.*

His expression unnerved Hugo more than anything else. He'd already thrown some of his best moves at Aidan, and the boy had effectively blocked all of them.

So, Hugo made a decision.

He sheathed his sword and ran for his horse.

Aidan raced for his own, but it was further away than Hugo's.

He reached his courser and took off in pursuit.

It soon became apparent Aidan was slowly gaining. After a minute, the distinct thunderings of their hooves began to merge into one.

Hugo glanced back, a sneer cramping his mouth.

"Don't make me stop to kill you, Aidan!" he yelled, "Off with you!"

"I'm going to finish Walter, once and for all!" Aidan called back.

Hugo turned forward again, and they continued the chase. Walter rode pale and panicked, slightly behind and to Hugo's right.

Hugo glanced back again and saw Aidan had closed the distance even more.

He slid his sword from its sheath, twisted in his saddle, and flung the blade out in a wide, hard arc into Walter's chest.

Walter screamed and tumbled from his horse. He rolled for about twenty feet.

It was a bad fall. The knight lay motionless where he stopped.

Hugo dug his heels harder into his horse's side. It burst forward with renewed, violent energy, and momentarily increased the distance between him and Aidan.

Aidan hesitated.

Hugo was forcing him to choose which knight he wanted more badly. He couldn't go after both.

He chose Walter.

Walter was the one who'd shot the fatal bolt into Sir Bart's side. Walter was the one abusing the female servants in the castle. Hugo could wait for another day.

Aidan yanked back on his reins and rued the sight of Richard's right-hand man growing smaller and smaller in the distance.

He trotted back to Walter's prone form and dismounted.

Walter flopped over onto his back and groaned.

Aidan glanced down the road toward his friends. Red and the others had finished their fights and were now walking his way. The archers were also emerging from the forest. They'd only lost three of their fighters and none of the archers.

Walter was trying to lift himself onto his elbows but was having trouble.

"Mercy," he croaked.

Mud ran down his face in rivers as the rain melted it away.

"I cannot," Aidan replied dryly. "You've murdered and raped, and if you were to ever heal from these wounds, you'd just do it again."

Justice was a nasty business, never sitting right with the soul no matter how necessary its execution was. Yet, he sincerely doubted Red or any of the others would disagree with his decision.

***

That night, the fire blazed strong. Its light bathed the outlaws in a warm, energizing glow. They were content, joyous even. More than pleased with their success against such a superior force.

The rain stopped later in the afternoon, and the women immediately emerged from their individual huts bearing plates of food they'd prepared in celebration.

A veritable feast ensued. The night was filled with the noise of it.

Men sang ballads in deep baritones and downed ale after ale. Younger women danced and twirled in the radiant light, while the older women doled out a variety of offerings to please the palate, even some honey-basted cakes.

Later in the evening, their souls now satisfied, the ambiance began to soothe. They reclined in small groups, circling the fire, and the livelier songs dwindled into more nostalgic melodies that evoked reflections on all that was good in life.

Aidan studied their faces. Their happiness brought him true pleasure.

Normally, his mind would be consumed with concern and worry for these people, but tonight, only a twinge of it touched upon his thoughts, like a feather tickling the recesses of his mind.

He forced it away.

This night was a night to forget all hardship and celebrate what had been hard won.

Richard's men would return, but they wouldn't be back tonight.

At last, the lute's last tune reached its end.

Its final note faded from the air with an echoing twang.

A weighty, reflective silence followed.

Then, unexpectedly, Ysabella rose to her feet.

Flashes of firelight washed across her face in mystical patterns, as if she were a long-forgotten siren returned to renew her call.

Aidan could not help but notice the way the bonfire's glow warmed the colors of her skirt as it flowed over the curves of her hips. His eyes followed the slim line of her waist up to her strong shoulders and slender, graceful neck.

He was suddenly reminded of the day he'd heard her singing in the glades near the waterfall. The way she'd captivated his spirit with the sheer beauty resonating in her voice.

The firelight sparkled in her eyes, and just as he'd not expected her to rise up from among the rest, he was again caught off guard as she opened her mouth and let forth a powerful song.

When the sun rose high
And our way seemed lost
Among the trees of Winster

With bare feet a'thorned
And in hunger shorn
In Newhaven where we wander

There arose a one
Strong and tall in ways
Bereft of fief and manor

She drew out the words, singing them slowly, but with an underlying measured cadence, like one of the ancient ballads. Her voice lilted upward at the end of the first two lines of each verse, followed by a punctuated emphasis on the third. She alternated the last note of each stanza so that one would rise and the next would fall.

Her tone ran pure like crystalline water tumbling from a precipice, her voice strong and captivating. Everyone was rapt with attention for the clarity of it.

To allay our fears
And provide our bread
Aidan the Steadfast Hunter

Order to our lot
And shelter to the camp
Brought Aidan our true Leader

Her eyes stayed fastened on him as she sung, her face revealing no expression. She stood straight, stilled hands by her sides, not needing them to accentuate the song. The beauty of her tone and the light dancing across her body gave life to the words.

They sank deep into his soul, those words, and he sensed they were impacting the others as much as he. When she first mentioned his name, he reddened. He did not deserve to be glorified in such a way.

To support the queen
And promote her cause

AIDAN SONG

Was Aidan the Defender

While knights do plunder
And kings wage their war
One stays true above the fray

Fighting all corrupt
Traitors and king's men all
Aidan the Deliverer

Though her face shone like an angel's, he had to force his eyes to stay fixed on it, for he found them dropping repeatedly to the curves of her hips.

She was captivating him against his will. He yearned to let himself go with her flow.

Every time she sang his name, his face burned hotter, as if it were blasphemy against his own nature, yet as she went on, tingles ran up and down his spine in unwilling pleasure. Not pleasure for recognition in the eyes of others — but for the admiration clearly burning in hers.

The presence of the other villagers faded from his awareness as she drew his gaze ever more firmly.

When flashing swords struck fast
And arrows flew through men in vast number
There is one who stood to take them down
Aidan the Deliverer

He has saved our camp
Brought us peace once more
Aidan the Deliverer

Many a maid looks on
With hair loosed low
Yet, there be one who calls for him

May his days be long
May his nights be sweet
Among the trees of Winster

May his children bloom

And his heart be mine
Aidan the Deliverer

As her voice trailed away, the last clear notes echoing off the forest walls into the night, he found himself longing for more, not necessarily for more of that song, but for any song, just to hear more of that voice.

He overflowed with conflicting emotions. Fully embarrassed by the unexpected praise, he lowered his gaze to the ground while the rest of the village turned their attention to him, to see how he would respond.

Ysabella primly creased her skirt beneath her as she reseated herself on the log. The boldness of her offer had been crystal clear in those last verses. Bold maidens were not the norm, but even those usually made their advances in private. Ysabella had offered him her whole heart publicly, granting him the power to accept or destroy it, as he saw fit. An act of sheer bravery, a willingness to make herself vulnerable for the sake of love.

In the silence, he tried to process his thoughts. He could not settle his feelings for this woman. Even in the midst of her song, he felt Priscilla's ownership of his heart standing firm in defense. She held the key, and he didn't want to ask for its return, but Ysabella was *magnetic*. She also was beautiful and evoked in him a certain kind of animal attraction that bloomed into an overwhelming force whenever he heard her sing.

At last, when the moment had grown uncomfortable, Aidan stood to address them.

"Ysabella," he choked, clearing his voice when it broke unexpectedly, "That was truly beautiful, though I certainly do not deserve such praise."

He turned to the rest of them. "Her song sums up our struggle and has touched each one of our hearts. It is *our* struggle, and the credit goes to *all of you.*

"Thank you, Ysabella. Now, it's been quite a day and I'm going to retire."

The party continued lightly for another hour, but exhaustion from the day's events soon caught up with them. One by one, the villagers wandered back to their homes.

After all was quiet, and darkness had once again eclipsed the camp, Ysabella approached Aidan's hut.

With a hopeful spirit, she rapped on his door.

But he wasn't home.

He'd gone walking beneath the midnight moon.

Chapter 24

The rains resumed and continued throughout the week, washing away the ruts left in the mud by Richard's men dragging themselves away. In spite of the inclement weather, the outlaws continued to celebrate among themselves, though they were forced to do so separately, within their huts.

After that first night, though, Aidan's mood did not match theirs. The continual showers complemented the gloom in his heart very well.

The burden of his people's welfare lay upon him heavily — at least, he'd come to think of them as *his* people, though they were truly free.

On Sunday, at last the clouds parted to reveal a deep, rich blue overhead that had been hidden from their eyes for far too long.

Aidan was walking alone. He was passing through a field to the northeast of Becca's Well.

Wetness still dripped steadily from the tips of bright verdant leaves on the trees to his right and soaked his leggings wherever the moist overgrown grass brushed his calves. The sun warmed his front, and he knew it would soon evaporate all that remained of the rains into a dissipating mist.

Yet, his spirit would not rise with the stirring vapor.

In spite of Ysabella's song, he was no one's deliverer.

Yes, they had successfully beaten back Richard's attack. They had resisted a force much stronger than themselves and lived to tell the tale. But...a pervasive sense of doom circled nefariously.

These men and women had trusted their very lives into his hands . . . and they were *doomed.*

His uncle would never stop.

The hatred that pulsed through his Richard's heart was almost as necessary to its continued beating as his very blood.

There was no doubt Richard would hit them again, and much harder. If forty armed soldiers hadn't been enough, the next time it would be a hundred, or even two.

Aidan had humiliated his uncle. Richard wouldn't tolerate that.

He *couldn't* tolerate that.

Richard would spend his entire treasury if revenge demanded it.

Even if Aidan could somehow put a pinch on Richard's income so he couldn't employ so many mercenaries, it wouldn't stop the man.

Their little band was not about to upend all of England on its ear. There was an established order to the nobility and classes. The scandal of a group of outlaws besting a troop of trained soldiers and knights, while embarrassing to Richard, would also send a fearful tremor tingling down the back of every baron and earl who heard of it. Maybe even the king himself.

Such men might even loan their men to Richard free of charge just on principle. Common men could not rise up against their lords and be allowed to get away with it.

Aidan shook his head, lost in thought.

It seemed hopeless. No way out.

Honestly, the best protection for his people now would be to lead them to another forest, far away from Richard's reach. Yet, he knew few of them would go willingly.

Nor could he so easily sever his ties to Becca's Well. He'd stopped Walter, but Richard's abuses in Aidan's absence would only continue.

He knew the people of that town — he'd grown up with them. He could not bring himself to abandon them to the frivolous appetites of a monster. Yet, to stay most likely meant the destruction of the outlaws, with the people of Becca's Well no better off at the end of it.

In the distance, a faint voice calling his name interrupted his thoughts.

He lifted his gaze. A brown-clad monk emerged from the woodline. Aidan paused to allow the man to cross the field and catch up to him.

It turned out to be Brother Aelfric from St. Alban's. As the monk hustled toward him through the grass, Aidan noticed the bottom half of his brown tunic had turned black with the wet absorbed from the vegetation. He was out of breath but smiling.

Aidan wrapped his friend in a bear hug with joy.

"Aelfric! What brings you out this way?"

"Searching for you, Aidan."

"Why me?"

"The prior requires your presence at St. Alban's."

***

He tried every tactic he could, but there was no way for Aidan to get Aelfric to say another word about why he was being summoned in such a strange way. The brother remained tight-lipped the entire route back to the priory.

When they arrived, Aelfric led him through the front door and past the foyer. The chapter room, and in fact, the entire cloister, was empty. All the brethren were out in the fields working this afternoon.

Aidan followed Aelfric down the hall to the library, that same room where Prior Andrew had first revealed his sword to him.

Aidan didn't have it on him at the moment. Its absence left him feeling quite naked. In spite of the confidence Aidan had with the monks, Aelfric had still insisted he leave all his weapons outside the front door in accordance with custom.

It occurred to Aidan that this could be some elaborate trap on Richard's part to get him inside a building unarmed, but he trusted Aelfric.

Inside the library, they found Andrew seated at a writing desk. He had a scroll spread out on top of it and several bound books stacked along its edges.

Brother Geoffrey was also there, standing at the opposite side of the room from the shelves.

A third man, a stranger, stood beside the desk, examining the scroll with the prior. Though moderate amounts of daylight streamed through the small window behind them, the men had still lit a candle to better see what they were reading.

"Hello, Aidan," the stranger said.

The man clearly knew him, but Aidan had no idea who he was.

That he was also of a religious order was obvious by his humble attire. He hadn't been a member of St. Alban's while Aidan had lived here though, and his head was too grey, and his eyes were too wizened to be a novice. Which meant he had to belong to another monastery.

His face did seem a bit familiar though, and the longer Aidan stared, the more he realized he *did* know this man from somewhere, he just couldn't place him.

Then, the monk cracked a smile and recognition dawned.

"Brother Henri!"

"Yes, it is I. I'm surprised you remember me, Aidan. It has been a while."

"The last time you came to the manor . . . I couldn't have been more than fourteen."

Henri was prior of a monastery down Darley way. He was a godly man, full of kind words and acts of benevolence. Also sincerely humble, he required others to continually address him with the more common title of brother rather than that of an exalted prior, which was his by truth.

He was well-known among the people of the shire for being the best physician around. Some of the other physician-monks openly questioned his practices, for he was never known to prescribe bloodletting, as were most. Instead, he dealt in herbs and other medicines that proved quite effective on occasion, and when a sickness or injury was serious, it was Brother Henri most people called on for help.

In fact, though much of that fateful night remained shrouded in a hazy fog among his memories, Aidan did recall someone mentioning that Henri had been called to help his father, but they had turned him away at the gates once word spread that Lord William had already passed.

If only Henri had arrived sooner.

Would it have made a difference?

He would never know.

"I've heard of your exploits, Aidan." The fatherly monk smiled warmly.

Aidan feigned shock. "You and everyone else it seems."

"You mock, but your acts have buoyed the hearts of many."

Aidan apologized. "No, brother. I don't mean it that way. It's just that I am not deserving of the praise some would throw my way. I've done nothing but that which any other man would have done in my place."

"On the contrary, few would stand for those whom you have defended. You possess true nobility, Aidan, and I am heartened to see your humility is intact as well."

Aidan blushed and feinted a bow.

Henri continued, "Well, let's not beat around the bush. You know, your father was a great man . . ."

"Yes . . ."

Henri held up an open palm, cutting him off. "I was closer to your father than you were probably aware."

That actually *did* surprise him. As far as he knew, Henri had only visited their manor on a handful of occasions, and those had been to heal someone who was sick.

"Your father and I knew each other for many years. We were friends before I ever entered the Order of St. Benedict."

Aidan said nothing, puzzled, unsure where this was going.

"Over the past months, while my spirit has been lifted by news of your good deeds, my heart's also been broken by the knowledge of the tragedy that befell you. As I said . . . your father was a great man. His son never should have received such treatment."

Henri turned to the document on the desk.

"Your father *knew* what kind of a foe he had in your uncle, Aidan. He suspected much, though likely not enough."

"So, why did he not do something about it?" Aidan asked.

"You know many of the reasons, and I'm sure there are others neither one of us knows. Regardless, what I am here to tell you today is that your father left something very important in my possession. Something you will want to see."

Andrew picked up the opened scroll from the writing desk and handed it to Henri.

"I have verified the document," Andrew said to Aidan.

What could he have to verify?

"Aidan, this is your father's *real* will." Henri held it out to him.

The declaration shocked him.

His father's *will?*

"What do you mean?" He took the document and stared at it. "My father had no will, except for the forgery claimed by Richard."

"Unfortunately, the document in Richard's possession is no forgery. He extorted your father into signing it."

"Then, what is this?"

"This is the will your father signed *after that one*. He approached me several years ago and wrote out this will in front of myself and several other witnesses. He was afraid for his own safety, and for yours, and asked me to keep this final will a secret unless he met an untimely demise. If that ever happened, I was supposed to come forward and make sure you had this document in hand to make your claim on Falconer Manor."

Aidan was speechless.

He read over the vivid scrawls hurriedly. He knew the handwriting well. So familiar.

Henri continued, "It's fairly straight forward. It voids all previous wills and declares that all lands and goods pertaining to Falconer Manor belong to you as his son. It also specifically lays out that your uncle Richard has no rights of inheritance, just to be clear."

Aidan was flabbergasted. A trembling of hope rose up within him, vibrating against the bulwarks of assumed defeat.

Yet, still too much seemingly stood in his way. The nascent light was dampened by the surety of obstruction.

"Why . . . *why* did you not bring this to me before?"

Henri looked to the ground.

"*That*, I do regret. The night your father passed, Richard would not allow me into the keep. I didn't have the document with me then, and before I could return to my priory to fetch it, I was called away to France on an emergency to tend to several villages suffering from a veritable plague.

"I was six months on the continent. By the time I returned, your uncle's claim was firmly established, and he had the king's ear. Telling you the truth then would have only served to get you killed.

"Giving you the document too soon would have set you up to be squashed by Richard's strength. I hoped in time you might establish yourself and gain some support from other sides before I gave you the tool to take on one of the king's favorite co-conspirators."

As hard as it was to swallow, Aidan appreciated the wisdom in Henri's decision.

"And, I must say, you are your father's son," Henri said, "You've proven yourself quite well."

The news that he could legally claim the castle was an immense boon to his spirit. Yet, what Henri said about the king preferring Richard was still all too true.

Richard had made every effort to ingratiate himself to the usurper Stephen in order to solidify Stephen's support for Richard's own claim. Even with such a document as this, the idea that the king would rule in Aidan's favor was as far-fetched as Stephen voluntarily handing the crown to Queen Maud.

Even more so now that Aidan had used the outlaw band to help her cause so publicly.

"I don't see how this will help me in today's political environment," Aidan mused aloud, disappointed that even now he could not wrest victory from the talons of past defeat.

"You never know," Henri affirmed, placing a comforting hand on his back. "Time changes all things . . . and if you trust in God, all things are possible."

Chapter 25

May 3rd, 1138 AD

Rough, wooden slats battered Aidan's back as the cart rolled along, jostling and bumping with each stone and rut in the road. The smell of dusty wheat overwhelmed the senses. Dozens of sheaves of it prickled his face and threatened his eyes. He squinched them closed and clamped a dirty cloth over his nose and mouth and to keep from inhaling too much chaff.

On either side, Red and Eric were suffering just as much from the wagon's slow-moving progress as he was. None of them had the power to speed it up though. It would take what it took.

At long last, the cart halted.

Aidan heard a guard's rough barks followed by Ysabella's muffled voice.

They'd reached the castle gate.

"Buying's over for the day," gruffed a guard, "You'll have to turn around."

"Please sir," Ysabella pled, "It's not quite five o'clock and we must sell this wheat today. We need food."

"Buying's closed, I said!"

"Tell the scribe we'll give him the cart for free. We just need to eat."

The guard knew a good deal when he heard it. He disappeared behind the wall and returned a moment later.

"All right. Drive your cart inside and leave it in front of the keep. You'll be paid on your way out."

The cart lurched and rolled forward. A few minutes later, it stopped again. It rocked back and forth as Ysabella and another of the ladies from their camp dropped to the ground. Their voices grew fainter as they went to the scribe's buying table in the courtyard between the outer curtain wall and the keep.

After a minute, Aidan peeked out from under the sheaves of wheat.

The coast was clear.

He and the other two outlaws slipped from the wagon and touched their feet lightly on the crushed stone inside the gate. Stealthily, they made their way to the keep's front door which was open.

Aidan peered around the corner. Seeing no one, he went in and motioned for Red and Eric to follow.

They turned right and moved at a swift pace, following the passage that led to the right of the great hall, anxious to reach their destination without being detected.

So far, the halls were empty, as they'd been assured they would be.

Lilith, the runaway servant girl who had taken refuge at Priscilla's house after fleeing Walter, had gotten a message through to another servant by the name of Emma to be ready to receive Aidan and his men. Aidan suspected Emma was another of Walter's victims, but Lilith would not confirm that.

What she had confirmed was that Emma's quarters lay behind the seventh door on the right.

He wished it had been the first — it was a lot of hallway to traverse without being spotted. Aidan counted silently as they passed each door.

"Here it is," he whispered.

The men drew their swords and Aidan placed his hand on the door latch. They could easily be walking into an ambush if this girl were a traitor in disguise.

Behind the door, however, was no troop of knights steeled for battle, but merely a slender, petite girl in her early twenties seated upon a crude bed and wringing her hands nervously.

She looked up, startled.

"Oh . . ." was all she managed. Fear swam in her eyes. If Aidan's plan failed and her aid were discovered, her life would be as forfeit as theirs.

Aidan, Red, and Eric entered and shut the door swiftly behind them.

"Emma?" Aidan asked.

She nodded.

"I was told you'd be expecting us."

"Yes," She said softly. She stood and smoothed her skirt. "Please forgive me, I am nervous. Make yourself at home here. I must return to my duties before they notice I've gone." She went to the door.

She looked like a snowflake ready to disintegrate under the force of a melting heat. Aidan touched her shoulder as she laid her fingers upon the latch.

"Never fear. We *will* succeed, Emma."

"I know," She nodded again. "Don't worry. I'll not betray you. Richard usually retires to chambers at nine, and the rest of the castle is settled by eleven." With that, she exited and shut the door behind her.

They waited in her tiny room for several hours, reviewing the plan over and over in hushed tones.

At nine o'clock, Emma returned.

They gave her the bed to sit on, but now with four bodies, the closed quarters were starting to feel stuffy and downright claustrophobic.

At half past ten, they made their move. They wanted Richard to be soundly asleep, but not the rest of the castle.

Emma left the room with them.

"Here, you will need this." She dropped a large key into Eric's palm before disappearing down a dark passage that ran behind the great hall.

They had already forgone armor to avoid unwanted noise as they walked. Now, they stepped as lightly as if they were walking on eggshells and trying not to break them.

Most of Richard's men would be laid out for the night on the floor in the great hall, which was on the other side of the wall to their left. So, when they reached the opening to it, they peeled past it smoothly but stealthily.

The soldiers who were visible were laid out on rush mats, huddled as close to the hearth as they could get. Most of them were already asleep.

The three outlaws successfully escaped the detection of those few who were still stirring, and they breathed a sigh of relief.

Next, they reached the armory.

Eric used the key Emma gave him to lock it up tight. It was castle policy to keep that door unlocked at all times in case of an emergency such as the one Aidan was about to unleash.

Tonight, Richard's men would find their access to it blocked and have to resign themselves to whatever weapons they'd taken with them to bed.

The three of them swept up the steps to the second floor. Richard's chambers were situated right next to the upper end of the spiral stairwell.

Aidan tested the latch of his door.

Unlocked. As expected.

Good.

Wincing in anticipation, Aidan slowly pushed the door inward, sure a high-pitched complaint would sound from its worn hinges. This had been his father's bedroom before his death, and the door was famous for its horrendous squeals and moans.

Yet, it seemed Richard had made at least one improvement to the castle. He'd either commissioned new hinges, or had lubricated them, for the door slid open as silently as a fox passing through a field of rye.

As far as Aidan was concerned, it was the only good thing Richard had ever done. Ironic it would help him now.

The chamber's interior was dark except for two sickly candles near the oversized bed that flickered on their last legs before winking out. It was a dangerous thing to leave candles burning while asleep.

Richard lay on the bed, covered in blankets and breathing deep. The fire in his hearth had deteriorated to a mass of dull, orange coals that barely glowed.

The three outlaws surrounded the bed.

Aidan raised a hand and ticked off a count with his fingers. On three, Eric and Red each grabbed one of Richard's shoulders and pinned it against the pallet beneath him.

The usurper's eyes flicked open, wide with alarm.

Richard's mouth gaped. He would have yelled but Aidan stuffed the orifice with a rag and then covered it with his palm, careful not to block the nostrils so the man wouldn't suffocate.

His uncle rocked and struggled but couldn't overcome the strength of the three of them. Aidan and Red pushed him over onto one side without letting go of his arms. Red grabbed a wrist and wrenched it behind Richard's back. He bound it with thick cord to the other. Then, Aidan took another rag, rolled it up, looped it around Richard's mouth, and then tied it behind his head to hold the gag in.

Once he was secured, Aidan raised a foot and booted him in the back with his sole.

He rolled off the bed helplessly and tumbled to the floor with a painful grunt. Aidan wasn't worried about the noise. The wooden floor was so thick the thuds would not be heard below. As long as Richard couldn't scream to be heard in the hallway, they'd be fine.

"Hello, uncle," Aidan said.

Recognition melted his scared shock into unveiled fury. It was as if Aidan's voice had finally made the lines of his face coalesce clearly for his uncle in the dim light.

"Yes, I'm sure there's much you'd like to say to me, but there'll be time enough for that," Aidan said.

Aidan let his sword point harmlessly at the floor. Red moved to block the chamber door with his body.

"Understand if you try to escape or alert anyone to our presence, I'll run you through without a second thought. Wouldn't be smart to test me. Now, sit still and keep quiet."

They waited in silence until it became uncomfortable. Richard stabbed at them mercilessly with his eyes. Aidan ignored him unless he made motions like he was going to stand up. Then, Aidan would simply tense and raise his sword tip an inch and Richard would settle back down.

After fifteen minutes, they heard muffled sounds of alarm echoing faintly within the castle. Then, they could make out a few men shouting, "To arms! To Arms!" and doors banging open everywhere. Booted feet thundered up and down the halls.

The distraction had begun as planned.

Outside on the wall, Richard's rear guard had spotted a couple of outlaws with torches racing for the cluster of rocks where the entrance to the secret tunnel was.

"Halt!" they commanded. "Who goes there?"

The outlaws dropped their torches to the dirt and then fled back into the black. Suddenly, a stream of arrows flew up from the darkened forest and sailed toward the guards upon the wall. They ducked and scrambled for cover, one of them shouting "To arms!" over and over.

Knights and men-at-arms ran to join the battle on the rampart. A few remained inside to protect against a sneak attack from within, a security measure implemented after Aidan's previous invasion, but the majority went out onto the wall.

Inside Richard's chamber, the outlaws listened to the fading footsteps.

"Time to go," Aidan said.

They plucked Richard from the floor and cracked his door ajar. Seeing the hall was clear, they rushed him down to the library. Red and Aidan went inside with Richard. Aidan searched the old writing desk and found the key right where his father had always kept it. They locked the door behind them.

They would wait in here with Richard. If the rest of their plan failed, they would escape through the secret tunnel with Richard as a prisoner. It would not be ideal but was better than nothing.

Eric had already peeled away to run down the second-floor hallway on the south side of the castle. A total of four doors connected the keep's interior with the rampart walk outside, one for each of the cardinal directions. Right now, Emma and another servant she trusted should be locking one of them each. Aidan had asked her to take care of the ones facing west and north.

Eric's job was to get to the southern door as fast as he could. He reached it without incident and threw the bolt to lock it.

When the thirty plus warriors on the ramparts realized only a handful of bowmen in the forest were responsible for the barrage of arrows, suspicions of an ambush from within would dawn on them. Since all of them were clustered at the rear of the keep, they'd naturally rush for the western door first to get back inside.

When they found it locked, logic said they'd next race up the side ramparts and go for the northern and southern doors. Their last resort would be the eastern one in the front.

Eric had to reach it before they did. This was the only weakness in Aidan's plan.

It turned out he had plenty of time. Eric reached the eastern door and threw the bolt before the soldiers had even discovered the ruse.

Next, he flew down the nearest stairwell and reached the over-sized, double-paneled oak door covered in spiked iron studs that covered the main-level front entrance to the keep.

Though most of the enemy had gone out onto the ramparts, five soldiers had gone to wake Richard. Another handful remained downstairs in the great hall, lingering, waiting for instructions, but they couldn't see the front door from there.

Eric was in the clear.

He lifted the bolt arm, hauled the door open, and ran out into the night.

The two knights and three men-at-arms who had gone up to fetch Richard found his bed empty. Their next stop was the library.

Seeing it was locked from within, they began pounding its planks with their fists, yelling for Richard.

When he didn't respond, they began searching for some heavy object they could use to beat it down — a decision that would delay them significantly.

Eric made it to the gates in the outer wall. One of Richard's watchmen had ignored the commotion at the rear and remained at his post faithfully to protect against an ambush from the front. The instant he noticed Eric in the courtyard below, he cried out.

A shadowy bolt from an unseen bow sliced from the blackness behind the guard and embedded itself in his back. Before he could utter another syllable, his body toppled over the parapet and thudded to the ground.

His warning had done the job though.

Dozens of booted warriors stormed up the keep's ramparts. All Richard's men were making a mad dash forward to intercept the new threat.

Eric reached the gates, threw up the arm, and pulled them inward. Twenty outlaws dressed in dark colors poured through the opening, all armed with either sword or bow.

Up on the ramparts, Richard's men had now reached the front of the keep. They barked and tried to organize when they saw the intruders, but they were stuck up on the second-floor walk.

Eric and the other outlaws rushed for the front door underneath the soldiers, crossing the courtyard as fast as they could.

Panic was setting in. The soldiers began throwing themselves against the small, upper door Eric had locked earlier, trying to get back inside, but it wouldn't budge. Calls for order among them degenerated into shouts of frustration as the outlaws entered the heart of the castle, unimpeded.

Richard's men were universally armed with sword or mace — not a bow among them — so they were helpless to stop the infiltration from above. When the outlaws reached the entrance below them, frustration changed to desperation. The distance from the ramparts to the ground was at least fifteen feet, but one bold knight took the chance and flung himself over the edge.

He landed with such an impact that even amid the noise of it all, the distinct crack of bone as one of his legs snapped was audible. The man collapsed to his side, grasping his leg with both hands and rocking in pain. He didn't try to get up. Which was a wise decision because the outlaws would have just ended him.

Another man-at-arms inside the great hall, having heard the new cries of alarm, tried to shut the front door against the outlaws, but he was a few seconds too late. They plummeted into the door as he was swinging it shut.

Under their combined weight, it barreled open with enough force to fling the man across the floor on his back.

Once Eric's men were inside, they slammed the door behind them and laid the arm back in place.

Within minutes, they'd rounded up the fallen man, the others in the great hall, and the group of five trying to batter down the door to the library.

Those hadn't made much progress anyway.

They tied all of them up, and then Aidan and Red emerged from the library with the bound Richard in tow and descended to the great hall.

Emma had spread word among the castle servants about what was happening. Once the commotion had calmed, they began popping out of their quarters, smiles plastered across their faces — albeit nervous ones.

Chapter 26

Aidan kept moving. This was no time to relax.

He guessed the mercenaries on the walk would prove to be strategically uncreative, but the more time that passed with them stuck up there, the more likely they were to come up with some devious plan of escape.

Aidan ordered his archers to ascend the ramparts opposite them atop the outer curtain wall and form a line facing the soldiers. The height of the outer wall was slightly lower than the keep's walk, but not so much so they could not contain the soldiers from there.

Many of his archers were armed with the deadly crossbows that had been so effective in the forest the day Richard's men had attempted to invade their camp.

Once the archers were in place, Aidan went out to join them. He frog-marched Richard ahead of him, still bound and gagged with the tip of Aidan's sword resting neatly upon his uncle's upper back.

When they reached the center of wall above the front gate, Aidan halted and sheathed his sword, switching it for a dagger he now pressed into Richard's lower spine.

"Hear me!" Aidan called out, "My men are well-trained, and their arbalests will pierce the hardest mail."

On this cue, the keep's front door swung open. Eric, Red, and five other outlaws stepped out, forcing the soldiers they'd captured within the castle ahead of them. Those had all been disarmed and were bound at the wrists.

Eric and Red prodded their prisoners forward until they reached the outer gate. They opened it and passed through.

Red commanded them to keep walking until they were fifty feet beyond the wall. Three of Aidan's archers on top of the outer wall swiveled to hold these men in place under threat.

Then, three more outlaws emerged from the keep. These ran all the way through the outer gate and then returned with a long ladder on their shoulders. They set the ladder against the keep's wall, right near the end of the line of bunched-up warriors stuck on the walk.

The ladder didn't quite reach all the way, but its end was only a foot short, so the soldiers could drop over and get down with minor difficulty — once Aidan released them.

"You will not descend that ladder until my people are safely inside the keep," he called.

Below, Red, Eric, and the rest of his men, including the three who'd carried the ladder went back inside and bolted the front door behind them.

The castle was now empty of Richard's men.

Aidan untied the twisted cloth that covered Richard's mouth. His uncle promptly spit out the balled-up rag Aidan had first stuffed into it. He coughed and gagged and clawed at his tongue to remove the dry fuzz so he could refresh his spittle.

"Tell them to descend the ladder and leave through the gate," Aidan said to him, "Or you will die."

Richard hesitated, so Aidan pricked him with his dagger's blade. His uncle let out a growling whimper, a sound reminiscent of a wounded animal, but finally relented.

"Get down and go out or he'll kill me!" He cried.

His tone was desperate and weak, not at all the type to lend inspiration. The soldiers didn't move.

"Get down or you'll not be paid!" Aidan added.

At that, the mercenaries began to descend the ladder in single file and pass through the wall. They stopped about fifty feet away where the bound men already stood and waited to see what else would be said.

With all of Richard's men now outside the outer wall, Aidan's archers all turned to train their bows and arbalests that way.

Next, Red and Eric reemerged from the castle and bolted the outer gate in the wall against them. Several outlaws looped a rope under Richard's arms and around his chest and began lowering him down the wall outside the gate. When he was still about three feet off the ground, they let go of the rope, dumping him unceremoniously in a heap. Richard punctuated the fall with a heavy expulsion of air from his lungs.

Aidan stepped forward.

"In the morning, we will call each of you to approach this gate one by one. You will receive your pay after having taken a pledge of honor to leave Becca's Well forever. Of course, if you wish to set out tonight without being paid, you are welcome to do so."

He focused his gaze on Richard, who glared right back.

"*Uncle*, if you dare show your face in the morning, I'll shoot an arrow through it."

***

The knights and men-at-arms melted into the village. Neither Richard nor his men would be welcome within its homes and would have to spend the night exposed to the elements in the fields along the road.

Inside the castle, Aidan's men double-checked every entrance to the keep and made sure each was secure. They searched all the rooms for stragglers, and Aidan himself secured the entrance to the secret tunnel in the library with padlocks on both ends.

The servants' mood lightened instantly the moment Richard's mercenaries were locked outside the castle grounds. Aidan's take-over had been swift and effective, executed better than they could have ever imagined possible.

To a man (and woman), they were relieved to have Aidan in control. When he told them of his father's true will and his rightful claim to the manor, their smiles only grew wider.

Log after log was tossed into the hearth in the great hall, and the fire soon blazed bright. Kitchen maids hastily prepared food and brought it in wooden bowls, steaming and filled to the brim. The spirit of festivity resembled an early evening feast, though it was easily past one in the morning.

They were fatigued, but there remained much to do. Aidan's primary support till now had been from the outlaws, but he did not expect many of them would switch to life in the castle. Many lived in the forest not just by circumstance, but by preference.

Nevertheless, he needed men to defend the castle, so he hoped there were some among Richard's hires who were actually worthy and honorable in spite of their former employer.

He and Red spent the next several hours interviewing the servants, asking about the names and behavior of the various soldiers they'd just exiled. They created a master list of their names, making marks by each to indicate good reports or bad.

When finished, they were shocked to see that over fifty men had been in Richard's employ. Aidan had only estimated about twenty-five to thirty after the rout in the forest. He'd thought their numbers had seemed a little larger than expected, but it had been difficult to take an accurate tally in the dark.

Fifty was an extraordinary number. Given the salary of the average soldier, it would have required an exorbitant amount of silver to consistently support —

and given the current size of the barony, only through the oppressive techniques Richard had employed could such an army be possible.

In the end, from the servants' reports, Aidan discerned the large majority were indeed shiftless mercenaries who weren't worth the dirt on which they stood. Walter hadn't been the only rapacious savage roaming the halls. None of the younger servant girls had escaped their vicious attention, and even some of the older ones. The knowledge of this broke Aidan's heart. The spirits of these women would be a long time healing.

Stories of theft, humiliations, beatings, and even murder, both within the castle and in the town, haunted the air like dirty phantoms threatening to roost permanently in their collective minds. The outlaws were disgusted by the tales that heaped up without end.

On the other hand, there did seem to be a small core of decent individuals among them who had never participated in the sins of the others. In the morning, Aidan would seek those men out.

Stephan, the commoner Richard had made steward after John fled the castle, approached Aidan. He bowed respectfully before posing his question.

"Baron Falconer, what shall we do with Marge?"

The name rang a bell, but Aidan could not place it.

"Who is Marge?" he asked.

"She runs the tavern in town. Her father passed earlier this year."

He remembered now. She was the young tavern girl who had fed him months ago.

"What about her?"

"She is still in the stocks."

"The stocks? What in the world did Richard have her in the stocks for?"

"She is known to be a . . . .eh . . . a prostitute. Richard put her there to punish her."

"In the name of all that is good, how long has she been there?"

"Two days."

"Two days! And she's still out there?"

The man nodded.

Unbelievable. The stocks were located in the village, about a hundred feet outside the castle wall. She would have been out there, listening as the events of the night unfolded, and she had most definitely heard Aidan's speech, but he and his men had not seen her in the darkness.

"By all means, man, fetch her right away! Why are you just now telling me? Red, go with him. Make sure Richard's men have cleared out before you open that gate."

Fifteen minutes later, they returned with the young woman. Her face was drawn and pale. She walked with a stoop, pained by frozen muscles that had begun cramping within hours of being put in the device. With each step, agony flared up in her visage. She appeared sickly and fragile. Her hair was unkempt and dirty, and she stank of involuntary filth. Whatever vestiges of beauty he'd seen before were no longer visible in her mess.

Aidan commanded water to be brought and a comfortable chair. She drank thirstily, her cracked lips absorbing every drop. Sitting, at long last, proved a mixture of agony and relief.

"Marge, why were you in the stocks? I left you enough silver to last for months."

Her brow creased in puzzlement. Then, through cloudy eyes, a flicker of recognition gleamed. She remembered him.

"Yes, milord. You did. I gave up those ways, but Richard said once a whore, always a whore, and demanded I submit to his men. I refused, so he put me in the stocks."

Aidan's eyes welled with tears. He struggled to keep them from spilling over. Her words coalesced all of the tragedies he'd heard this night into a tight lump within his throat. He wouldn't be able to stand much more without breaking down.

He ordered the servants to comfort her, let her wash, and give her a fill of hot food and the most comfortable bed they could find. She struggled off with the steward.

By four in the morning, the most urgent tasks had been attended to, and it was time to get some sleep.

Aidan refused to lie in his uncle's bed until the coverings had been removed and the room purified of his spirit. Tonight, he would sleep on the stone floor in the great hall with everyone else.

Chapter 27

The next morning, they called the exiled soldiers by name, one by one, to approach the front gate still shut against them.

About ten of them had not believed Aidan's promise to pay their wages and had left during the night.

Sir Hugo, the last alive of the original knights who had betrayed his father, was among that group. The shrewd warrior had not been willing to accept charity from Aidan's hand, not that Aidan would have been willing to give it where he was concerned.

Had he come to the gate with the others, Aidan probably would have ordered him shot through.

Aidan hoped he'd seen the last of that serpent.

Richard had apparently left along with his right-hand man as there was no sign of him.

Of the rest, once a man had taken his vow to leave Becca's Well and Falconer Manor forever, Aidan tossed him a sack of silver pennies equaling one week's pay. Without exception, these did as they promised and left town on the road for London.

Of the twelve names the servants had cleared of dishonor, one had left the night before, two opted to take their pay and move on, and one more did not pass Aidan's secondary interview.

That left a total of eight men who would stay on, seven men-at-arms and one knight, Sir Alan of Cambridge. The servants universally affirmed that Sir Alan had neither condoned nor participated in the activities of the others. Once, he'd even come to the defense of a cook who was being threatened by an unruly man-at-arms.

Aidan questioned him as to why an honorable knight such as he would be in the service of someone like Richard. Alan responded that he had only been in Richard's service for a week and as each day passed, he'd become more and more aware of the nefarious nature of the castle's culture. He'd vowed to leave this very same day, but then Aidan had taken over.

Sir Alan refused Aidan's offer of payment, saying he did not want to profit from service to someone like Richard. He'd planned to leave without pay anyway.

However, he had heard of Aidan and his feats and offered to stay if Aidan would have him. Aidan took an immediate liking to the man.

Sir Alan proved to be the only knight worthy of staying though.

Which was not enough. The king required Falconer Manor to provide three knights in order to hold the barony, and Aidan probably needed at least one more than that to truly manage the manor's holdings effectively.

About midday, Marge limped into the great hall where Aidan was holding court. Her muscles were recovering, but slowly. Just having gotten a good night's sleep and some food in her belly, she already looked a bit restored, but it would be a while before the aches left her joints.

She bowed deeply and thanked Aidan profusely before taking leave to return to her tavern. A simple thank you would have been enough. He'd only acted decently. The way she gushed left him red with embarrassment.

Late in the afternoon, several of the outlaws' families reached the village, some dragging all their worldly possessions on a travois, others in oversized bundles hanging from the sides of packhorses.

When they neared the castle gate, Aidan saw that Ysabella was leading them.

She walked tall and proud, a few steps ahead of the rest of the pack. Aidan was impressed, but also more than a little anxious at the sight of her.

Most were women and children who'd come to join their husbands. A few were families led by men that Aidan had left behind to guard the camp in Newhaven Forest.

Aidan had sent a runner the previous night to let the camp know they'd succeeded in taking the castle. The fact they'd brought their belongings with them did his heart good. These were obviously ready to leave behind their outlaw ways and follow him.

Aidan gathered the men in the great room for a late lunch. The servants had prepared a feast, even larger than the night before.

He took turns asking each of his friends what they wanted to do.

Eric, Tom, and more than half of the other outlaws wished to settle on Aidan's lands. They knew how long he'd agonized over the loss of his family's heritage and were happy to see his triumph.

Some were motivated by friendship to stay close by his side, others by the security his leadership provided. Still others had longed for land as badly as Aidan had his and saw today as an opportunity to realize their dreams and enter a new life.

Aidan was overjoyed. He'd longed to regain his inheritance but had secretly worried that success might cost him his friends.

Frankly, now he had too much land and not enough workers to work it. Richard had so devastated the manor's economy with his policies that over half of the citizens of Becca's Well had fled to better and freer places.

Richard's heavy hand and high taxes might have ensured a high income for a year or two, but there was no doubt the manor would soon have been bankrupted.

All men possess a natural drive to preserve themselves.

From his father, Aidan had learned that a lord oppresses his people at his own risk. If they can find a way around your rules, or flee to a land of greener pastures, they will.

Lock them up so tightly they cannot escape, neither through flight nor creativity, and they will merely shut down, nearly as unproductive as if they weren't even there.

That had been Richard's future, though he'd been oblivious to it.

Richard would have eventually lost even more population, and those that stayed would have become indolent and useless to him. When that happens, a lord can take up the whip and squeeze out a little more work, but eventually a scarred back grows dulled to the blows. Richard had been driving himself into ruin.

Baron William had taught his son about human nature, and how a lighter hand can actually increase a lord's income. His father had ingrained these principles in Aidan over the years, along with a strong sense of decency.

His father had also taught him that a lord's prosperity ultimately depends on the prosperity of his towns, even more than the fruitfulness of his fields. When Aidan had questioned him regarding how such prosperity could be achieved, he'd explained the key was to ensure that more silver flowed into a town than went out. Your people had to be selling more than they were buying. It was as simple as that.

Simple it may be, but how exactly to achieve such a balance still puzzled Aidan, and the sudden importance of figuring it out pressed on him.

Regardless, the fact remained that Aidan needed men, and these before him were offering their service.

They inquired terms, initially wary he might want them to take vows of fealty and become serfs, but Aidan had no intention of that. He did not like the idea of serfdom and these people were his friends. To a man, he offered them free tenancy.

One by one, they presented themselves before him in the great hall, and he allotted them as generous holdings as each could likely tend. The fall and winter would allow them time to repair homes abandoned by others and to prepare their fields for planting in Spring.

Ysabella arrived at the great hall and presented herself before him on one knee with face inclined to the floor in humility.

His heart skipped a beat. He wasn't sure what he wanted her to say.

"I would ask land of you as well, milord," she said.

She'd shocked him once again. She seemed to have a knack for that.

"Ysabella! Do not kneel before me, and you certainly don't need to call me lord!"

She looked up at him but remained on one knee.

Actually, that she was here by herself should not have surprised him. In the forest, she'd lived alone, and for all he knew, she might very well be an orphan of sorts, though she'd quite the age (and figure) of an adult. He'd never heard mention of her parents. For some reason, he'd never thought to inquire either.

Her request was unusual and went against all custom. Women were rarely granted tenancy of land, especially young, unmarried women. It was believed they had neither the strength nor the influence to see the work done that would be necessary.

Waiting, her chest heaved with anticipation.

He stared in silence. Everyone's attention was riveted on the scene.

In the end, he gave in to the only decision he knew he could make. He awarded her one of the best acreages he had, right to the north of Becca's Well. The holding was well-watered, large and fertile, and she could live within the protection of the town.

Her eyes welled with tears, and she smiled.

"Thank you, milord," she sighed, relieved.

"Call me that again and I might take it back," he responded, grinning.

"Yes, mi . . ." she caught herself, got up laughing, and left the hall.

That girl truly vexed him. She was completely unpredictable. What kind of maiden was brazen enough not only to ask for land, but also to believe she could run it?

Red, Ranulf, and the remaining families were no less affectionate than those who desired to remain, but they said they wanted to return to their life in the forest. Red allowed they would stay on at the castle for a couple of weeks while Aidan established himself, but after that, they would return to camp.

"You will continue as an outlaw then, I suppose?" Aidan asked, fixing Red with his eyes.

"I will," his friend answered with a cocky grin. "An' I won't have to take any more orders from the likes of you!"

Aidan chuckled but remained serious. "Will you continue to operate under the principles I followed?"

Red nodded.

"Will you vow to never rob any man traveling to or from Becca's Well or Falconer Manor, or any nobleman who supports Queen Maud?"

"I will," he repeated.

"Good! Then, we part as friends."

They clasped each other's wrists and Aidan pulled Red into a bear hug. When they parted, Red grasped Aidan's forearms.

"Will you come to our defense if we are attacked?" he asked Aidan.

"Of course," Aidan smiled, "And I plan on calling you if I'm in need as well."

Red nodded.

Aidan requested Red bring half of the treasure they'd acquired in the forest to the castle so he could support his people here and told him to distribute as much of the rest to the outlying villages as they felt comfortable.

Two days after Aidan took the castle, John the Steward returned. He'd rushed back as soon as the news had reached him that Aidan was in control again.

Aidan could scarcely believe the hints of age he saw in the man now. A certain frailness gripped John's frame, and a wounded spirit lingered behind his eyes.

That pained Aidan, but he was overjoyed to see the man. John had been more than just a faithful servant to his father — he was a family friend.

Aidan embraced him heartily, stiffening involuntarily as the pads of his fingers sensed long, raised ridges running down the steward's back under his tunic.

Scars from Richard's whip.

Everyone in the castle remembered that scourging. The brutality of it had almost killed the steward. The day news of it had reached Aidan, he'd grieved.

"John, you've come home!"

"Yes, Sir Aidan."

Aidan glanced away. "I have no words for what you endured."

A wisp of a smile appeared on the smaller man's lips.

"What else can you expect from a donkey but a kick?" he said.

Aidan burst out laughing and soon everyone else joined in. The joke had done the trick and evaporated the emotional heaviness in the air. Perhaps John Steward wasn't as broken as his posture implied.

"I'd rather be working for you, young Aidan, than anywhere else — if you have room."

"By all that's good, John, we'd be blessed indeed to have you. I need people who understand Falconer Manor and its lands. When can you start?"

"I'm ready now, sire."

Aidan gave him his old quarters back. They were currently occupied by Stephan, the man Richard had named as chief steward in John's absence, but he'd only been a butler prior to John's flight and frankly, he'd never performed well in the job. He was not a natural leader and looked relieved when Aidan liberated him from the obligation.

Aidan asked John to undertake a survey of the lands as quickly as possible and to report back with how many tenancies had been abandoned since Richard's takeover. He also asked him to inventory the supplies within the castle. John set about these tasks with new enthusiasm.

Things were coming together well.

Growing up, Aidan had been haunted by lingering doubts as to whether he'd ever be able to fill his father's shoes. Today, the question was being answered, and he found himself filling the role naturally.

He'd watched his father rule the barony with a firm but understanding hand. In his father, he'd seen a combination of shrewdness, patience, wisdom, and a kind heart. Until now, he'd not realized just how much of those qualities he'd absorbed over the years through mere observation.

A few years ago, Aidan had been nothing more than a young hothead, concerned only with winning tourneys and becoming the best swordsman around. He even remembered foolishly longing for a chance to prove himself in a real battle.

The upheaval and hardships of the past two years had hardened him. They had also accelerated his maturity. The juvenile shell surrounding his core had broken away, revealing a steeliness needed by any true leader.

Much still remained to be done, but he was home now and confident of success — as long as he was given enough time to firm it up, that is.

Richard would not take the overthrow lying down. He would strike back as hard as he could. The only questions were how and when he would hit, and whether Aidan would be able to prepare sufficient defenses to thwart his uncle's coming attack.

He needed time.

Chapter 28

He got a week.

Early in the morning, a breathless servant informed him a party of riders was advancing through Becca's Well toward the castle, one of whom was Richard.

With him was an unknown nobleman who, from his attire, appeared to be very rich, which of course meant he probably held a powerful title too. There were also a large number of well-armed knights and other soldiers, some of whom rode powerful destriers.

Aidan sent orders to man the walls. He instructed his men to allow a small group of the riders to enter the gates, but most had to remain outside. Aidan would meet the smaller group in the great hall for parley.

Ten minutes later, Richard and five others stormed in bearing assumed rights Aidan did not intend to grant.

Arrogant indignation steamed from their pores with each step.

Aidan sat relaxed, legs crossed, in a high-backed chair in front of the hearth to greet them. Eric and Sir Alan stood to each side of him. (Red and Ranulf had already returned to the forest.)

Two of Aidan's men-at-arms guarded the rear exits. The rest moved in to block the front doors after Richard's group entered.

Tom and a line of archers silently filed onto the narrow second-floor balcony above and behind the visitors.

Richard was not yet aware of their presence. Barely contained fury boiled behind his venomous glare.

To Richard's right was a nobleman dressed in the most expensive finery Aidan had ever seen. He was clearly someone of high rank, but Aidan didn't recognize his face. The other four were knights. Those took a stand behind their leaders, ready to back up whatever play was made.

"Hello, uncle," Aidan said, "I didn't expect to see you again so soon. I thought I'd made myself quite clear that you were no longer welcome within these walls."

After his return, John Steward had shared with Aidan his belief that Richard had been involved in his father's death. Initially, all John had were suspicions, but those suspicions had been confirmed one evening by Richard's drunken bravado while jesting with Hugo and Walter. Slithering banter about poisons and innuendo alluding to William's favorite goblet had transformed John's cynicism into certain horror. The trio had been too drunk to even notice the steward listening.

Richard opened his mouth to respond, but the mysterious nobleman lifted a commanding hand to shush him.

"You are Aidan, son of William Falconer?" he asked.

"I am."

"Then you are accused of traitorously usurping your uncle's rightful place as lord of Falconer barony. How do you answer these charges?"

"You will have to forgive me, I didn't know this was a trial," Aidan answered lightly. He raked his eyes across each member of the visiting party. "I don't see a constable present though, nor a jury. And who might you be?"

The noble's eyes narrowed. "I am Ranulf de Gernon, Earl of Chester."

Aidan knew the name. He was indeed a wealthy and powerful ally for his uncle.

"I repeat, you have taken your uncle's castle unlawfully and I command you to hand it over and submit yourself to face charges," the earl continued.

"Well, Sir Ranulf de Gernon, while it is certainly a pleasure to make your acquaintance, you have no authority here. We are both tenants-in-chief to the king and equal to each other in title."

The Earl of Chester reddened.

The upstart had dared to speak back to him.

No one spoke to him that way without being punished.

"As for the claim of my uncle," Aidan continued, "he has no claim."

"Your father willed the barony to him. The document was recorded appropriately. If you leave without a fight, your uncle may be willing to let you go free. If you do not, we will have to take the matter to the king."

"That will is null. My father wrote a second will, a *later* will, which superseded the one my uncle claims. My father wrote it and signed it in the presence of several witnesses before his death. *That* document clearly leaves the entire barony to me, as is only customary among barons and their offspring."

"You lie!" Richard growled.

"Here it is if you wish to examine it." Aidan pulled a rolled-up scroll from within his tunic and offered it to the earl. Richard suddenly snatched the document from Aidan's hand and held it over a burning candle.

Aidan remained calm as the flame licked and then consumed the paper hungrily.

"Well, you *claimed* to have had a document proving your inheritance," Earl Ranulf snickered, "but that is clearly no longer the case."

"Not to worry," Aidan explained, pulling a second scroll from his tunic. "That was just one copy of several. As is this one. You many burn it as well if you like, but Brother Henri is on his way to London as we speak with one of the originals to register it with the king's scribes. As much as King Stephen may agree with your policies, he will not upset the rights of noblemen so frivolously."

"Brother Henri?" The earl asked. The name was known.

"Yes, my father signed his decree in front of Henri, and the monk will testify to that."

Richard and Ranulf glanced at each other, their faces paling considerably. This time, Ranulf took the copy of the will and actually read it.

With contempt, he tossed it to the floor and turned to Richard, growling, "Let's take it anyway. Right now." Hot anger returned the flush to his cheeks.

Aidan smiled. "Before you do anything rash, gentlemen, I advise you to check the gallery behind you."

The visitors turned as one and saw the archers lined up on the balcony. They'd silently notched their arrows and held their bows at the ready.

"I heard you were a coward who used cowardly measures," Ranulf spat.

"Yet your swords remain sheathed?" Aidan asked, "Seems to me only stubborn fools and the proud would call that which is effective a coward's tool."

The Earl of Chester's face burned an even brighter shade of crimson. "I will *not* be spoken to in this manner!" he sputtered.

"Tis my castle and I'll speak to you any way I please."

"Your *enfeoffment* from the king requires four knights pledged to service," Sir Ranulf hissed through gritted teeth. "I only see one here. I will report that to the king, and you will be stripped."

"I have enough knights. They are performing other duties today. Just be glad I'm not having you run through. There are witnesses who have informed me that my father was poisoned by my uncle's hand."

Richard paled, which was enough to clinch the truth in Aidan's mind. It was his turn to let anger flow, and the rage welled up from the depths of his heart, controlled only by sheer will, and then barely so.

Aidan rose and drew his long sword with a sweep of the hand. Sir Ranulf's knights laid their hands on their hilts, but Aidan had the tip of his blade resting at the base of Richard's throat before they could draw.

"Uncle, you are a *worm*. I should kill you where you stand." Aidan glared, unblinking. "You murdered my father and tried to cheat me out of my inheritance. Not to mention the rapacious plunder you inflicted on my people while I was in exile. Regardless, I will not start a war here today.

"Earl Ranulf, you've allied yourself with a snake, though perhaps you had not seen the scales beneath his skin until today. I advise you to forget me and separate yourself from this poor excuse for a man.

"Now, my men will escort you out. You will leave Becca's Well without incident or molestation of its people. If you do not, we will take retribution. If either of you ever returns, you shall not find me so accommodating."

Aidan's men moved out from the doors to prod the party from Chester back the way they'd come. Albeit reluctantly, both Richard and Ranulf de Gernon turned and marched out of the great hall.

***

Ranulf glared nails at Richard as they trotted their destriers down the central thoroughfare of Becca's Well.

"Did you poison Falconer?" he demanded.

Richard returned the stare, with equal venom, but did not reply.

"You did. You should have told me. I don't like being confronted with surprises and looking the fool as I did today."

"Now what?" Richard asked.

He hated the dependency he now had on this man. Yet, and the realization came with much resistance, Richard knew he must appease De Gernon at all costs.

"We will destroy him," Ranulf said, "I do not condone what you did, but what is past, is past. I will *never* tolerate being insulted the way I was today."

They reached the limit of the range of the archers Aidan had stationed on the curtain wall. Once they passed that invisible line, the earl commanded his party to stop.

They turned their mounts to face the castle. The earl could make out Aidan's figure standing above the gate amongst the archers, watching them leave.

"Fire that house," Sir Ranulf ordered his chief knight, pointing his sword at a house to his right.

The knight scampered off to the blacksmith shop and snatched a flaming stick from the coals. Ranulf pumped his arm, creating a vulgar gesture for Aidan's enjoyment that could be discerned even from that distance, while the knight ran to the house the earl had indicated and touched the fiery end of the stick to the thatch of its roof.

The citizens of Becca's Well had lined the main street to watch the retreat of Richard and the Earl of Chester. Seeing Ranulf's order being executed, they began to yell in protest, but his knights pulled their weapons.

Once Ranulf saw flames licking up the full height of the thatched roof and was confident the fire had taken root and would only grow, he issued the order to ride out at full gallop.

Aidan watched in frustration. He did not have the manpower to take on Ranulf de Gernon's thirty plus warriors directly.

Yet, before the party had ridden all the way out of sight, he was already issuing orders.

"Eric, gather everyone to the village. We must stop that fire. Tom, get to Red in the outlaw camp as fast as you can. Tell him what happened and ask him to intercept those men for me and kill as many as he safely can from the cover of the forest. Tell him to be sure and get the knight in the crimson tunic who set the fire."

By the time they were able to mobilize everyone, three houses were ablaze. The castle guard and the villagers formed human chains from the well to the burning structures. They vaulted bucket after sloshing bucket full of water onto the flames. Eventually, they succeeded in slowing its pace, but they were not going to be able to stop it.

The heat pressed back against them, a sweltering, taunting force.

Aidan stepped back to assess a better strategy and bumped into his friend Thomas Weaver, whose brow was soaked black with streaks of soot and sweat. Aidan imagined he must look no better.

He hadn't seen his friend since taking over the castle. They paused to shake hands and then jumped back into the fight.

Recognizing the futility of their efforts with the houses that were already burning, Thomas took off at a run and began organizing people to soak the neighboring houses that had not yet caught fire.

Aidan saw the wisdom in that. He grabbed Eric by the sleeve as he passed, and they began calling for the other half of the human fire-fighting chains to do the same.

From that point on, the three houses burned uncontrollably, but every time a spark flew up and threatened to light the next one over, they were able to douse it with a bucket full of water.

The fire could have easily consumed the whole village, but in the end only three homes sank into dark, ashen ruins. Thankfully, no one had been hurt. Still, three families had just lost everything they owned.

Aidan could only hope Red and the rest of the outlaws had been able to exact some amount of revenge from Ranulf de Gernon.

Chapter 29

The branches whipped at Aidan's face and tore at his clothes, but he didn't care.

He drove his heels into the courser's side again and again, pushing the mount ever faster.

Finally, the trees broke to reveal the cottage in the clearing ahead of him.

The morning light was bright and bold. It induced an ethereal glow about the house and its surroundings, as if Heaven itself had descended upon it.

Aidan swept into the yard.

She must have heard the thundering of hooves, or spied him through a window, because the front door opened before he could dismount.

Priscilla.

The delicate lines of her mouth dimpled with a welcoming smile.

Her flush lips parted to reveal glimmers of teeth as white as pearls glistening in the sun. As she stepped from the house, the morning glow spread to her flowing chestnut hair, transforming it into a handsome, honey brown.

She fled the door and rushed to him.

"I knew you would come," she said excitedly.

"You've heard then?" he asked.

She nodded. "You've done the impossible. God's favor is truly upon you."

Baron Nicholas emerged next. Lilith, the young servant girl they'd taken in after she'd fled the castle, stood behind him in the doorframe.

"What is the meaning of this?" Nicholas demanded, his tone gruff, loud, and punctuated.

Aidan broke his eyes from Priscilla to face the man, straightening in his saddle to sit taller.

"Nicholas, I inform you that I have now regained Falconer Manor and my father's title. I am a full baron, tenant-in-chief to the king, with rights to as much land. I have come to formally ask for your daughter's hand in marriage," he declared.

Priscilla squealed and clasped her hands together, glowing with elation.

"I have already given my answer on that subject. This will never be . . ."

Priscilla's face firmed in determination.

"Father!" She cried. "First, you said I could not be with him because he had nothing. Then, it was because he was an outlaw with no title. He received a knighthood, and still you refused because he had no land. Now, he's regained his lands and you still object? I will not have it, I tell you! I am going to marry him!"

"I will not be spoken to that way young lady . . ."

"I want to marry Aidan, Father. You cannot stand in my way forever."

Nicholas paled visibly. He knew how determined she could be when her mind was made up. The truth was he knew Aidan was a good man, and courageous and honorable as well. He came from a good family and the lands of Falconer Manor would provide for her well.

He knew his real resistance was because he didn't want to lose his daughter. Since her mother had died, Priscilla was all he had.

"And when is this wedding to take place, may I ask?"

"Within the week," Aidan said.

Nicholas sputtered. "A . . . a week? No, it cannot be. We don't even know if Richard will come back . . ."

"He's not coming back," Aidan said, "He's already made his move, and I've successfully fought him off twice now."

"But . . . but . . ." He looked around, as if wanting to grasp at any tiny reason that might happen to be floating by as to why they could not marry, but none was to be had.

"Enough, Father!" She declared. "I love you, but I am going with Aidan."

She swung up behind him onto the saddle and wrapped her arms around his waist. Before Nicholas could stammer another word, Aidan spurred his courser, and it leapt forward for the woods.

Nicholas was so shocked he couldn't even manage to think of what words to call out after them. Behind him, Lilith covered her mouth to mask a giggle.

The cottage disappeared behind the trees as Aidan rocketed away at full speed. Priscilla hugged him tight, pressing her cheek into his back and hunching low for protection from the branches that might try to rip her from him.

Once they were far enough away, Aidan slowed to a trot. They continued until the trees separated to allow for a bubbling brook and then dismounted.

Priscilla was free — *finally* free. At long last, her dreams were being realized. Her spirit felt as if it'd been borne up on the airy breeze, warmed by the blueness of the sky and its hearty sun above.

"I brought biscuits and honey," Aidan offered with a smile.

He withdrew a couple of small bundles from his saddle pack and opened them on a rock.

The brook's currents tumbled across its stones like a crystalline melody. She seated herself next to him, and they ate, relishing every bite like it was the first, next delicious moment of the rest of their lives.

The excitement naturally led them to discuss plans and the wedding.

"What shall we do now?" Aidan asked. "Are you coming with me to the castle?"

She considered the idea while staring at a large, mossy rock buried in the brook's bank.

"I will come with you today to make an announcement to your people, but then, I think I should go home," she said. "It would not be proper for me to live at the castle before we are wed. Plus, my father would only worry. I'll need to go home and console him."

"What if he locks you up?" Aidan asked, alarmed.

She smiled and touched his cheek. "Don't worry, father is not that way. He won't impose his will any further. We'll be married Saturday next — *God willing*, that is."

* * *

Ysabella dug her fingers into the moist soil and rooted out a small rock from one of her furrows. She'd hired several laborers to help with the ploughing, but since they'd begun so late in the season, she didn't know how strong their crop would grow before the harvest — no one did — but they were all giving it their best nevertheless.

Her laborers had missed many of these smaller rocks, so she toured her rows every day, filtering them out and pulling weeds. The weeds were especially stubborn. The fields Aidan gave her had been abandoned for several seasons, so nubs of grass had rooted themselves deeply in many places.

She straightened and wiped the sweat from her brow with a tanned forearm.

In the distance, a dazzling white horse and rider galloping across another field caught her attention.

Aidan!

Her joy upon seeing him evaporated as soon as she realized another woman rode behind him in the saddle, hugging his waist tightly.

Ysabella would give almost anything to be that woman.

But she knew who it was.

The one he always pined for. Priscilla Fontaigne.

She felt no anger. No jealousy. Just a deep, welling sadness.

She studied her hands. Streaks of mud coated her wrists and arms, and swaths of soil under her nails darkened their tips.

She'd been out of the forest for less than two weeks, and already her skin had tanned from the daily doses of sun she endured in the fields. Not at all like the delicate, creamy white of Priscilla's, the kind of pure tone desired by all noble men. If only she'd been born wealthy, perhaps Ysabella could have had that kind of skin too. But she hadn't, and so her lot was to bear the bronzed pigment of a commoner. She knew that.

She turned her hands over and stared at the chipped nails and roughened fingers, realizing they could never compete with the smooth, pampered digits she imagined must belong to Priscilla.

A tear spilled down her cheek. As they rode out of sight, she wiped at it with the back of her hand. A dull ache, like a rending deep within, enveloped her.

Ysabella brushed off the dirt and turned toward her small dwelling. She didn't feel like working any more today.

Chapter 30

The wedding was a feast for the eyes.

Priscilla had wanted an outdoor ceremony.

She said she'd rather have God's sky as her roof, so they held the ceremony in the churchyard. They'd pulled the church benches outside and lined them up in rows.

That morning, hundreds had arrived to celebrate with them. The seats had all been quickly taken, and now a thick crowd had formed behind them.

Flowered trellises and other decorations surrounded the yard. Everything, from the priest's podium to the ends of each row, was bathed in primrose and summer snowflake blossoms.

Her dress sparkled a blinding white in the warm light. Aidan felt it echoed the delicacy of the flowers perfectly. The bouquet in her arms and the crown of baby's breath in her hair topped off the vision.

He couldn't stop looking at her.

Light-headed with anticipation, he virtually floated through the whole affair, intoxicated with her presence and what it meant here and now.

Brother Henri had made the journey to perform the ceremony. Red and the outlaws had emerged from the forest to attend as well. They'd contributed as much as anybody to the spirit of joy permeating the air.

Once Priscilla's father had seen the futility of his objections, that he was going to lose his daughter one way or the other — one of those ways being worse for him than the other — he'd grudgingly relented and given his blessing.

Slowly, he was warming to Aidan, struggling to change his heart. In his eyes, a marriage was a marriage was a marriage. His time to object had been before the engagement. Once Aidan and Priscilla became one in God's eyes, his job would be to support them in whatever way he could.

He sat in the front row and even smiled at times, recognizing the clear happiness written across his daughter's face.

Ysabella stood apart from the crowd at the very back. She watched by a trellis with masked contentment. There was a moment when she caught Aidan's eye.

She had smiled, truly happy to see him happy. She just wished it were her standing before the priest and taking vows.

In the moment the priest pronounced them man and wife, the people of Becca's Well erupted. The festivities would last for days.

Aidan and Priscilla opened the castle gates and invited the public inside for a meal to be remembered. Raucous dancing and drink would flood the village for most of the week.

The fields could wait.

This people, unlike those of most other manors in England, truly loved the man they called lord and were elated by his joy. It seemed the beginning of great times for all.

***

A week later, John Steward returned from having completed a full survey of Falconer Manor.

A few days prior, Aidan had knighted both Eric and Tom, which meant he could now officially provide three of the four knights required by the king.

He knew Eric and Tom's combat skills weren't really on par with that of a true knight yet, but they would be soon. They'd never reach the level of a Sir Bart, but he was working with them every day and estimated they'd be ready to enter tourneys within six months or so.

He'd asked them to be present now, along with Sir Alan, for the recitation of Steward's findings.

Priscilla and Baron Nicholas were there too. Nicholas had been spending a good bit of time at the castle since Priscilla moved in. His stated reason was to help Aidan assess and plan, but Aidan thought a longing for his daughter's company was probably the larger motivating factor.

It didn't take Aidan long to realize that Nicholas possessed a masterful understanding of business and economics though. Were the baron's nose not glued to his books so much of the time, he could have easily used his knowledge to become very wealthy.

That day, the sun outside burned unusually hot, so they retreated to the great hall to enjoy the coolness radiating off its stone walls.

Aidan pulled his chair away from the great table and positioned two others by his side, one for Priscilla, and the other for her father who sat to her right. His knights stood on both sides of them.

He did not like the pretentious feel this arrangement created, but he'd received a relentless flow of petitioners over the previous days and had been

AIDAN SONG

forced to create the semblance of a court.

"So, what's the news, John?" Aidan asked.

The steward hesitated...

Then, he released his emotion with a sigh, "The manor is in quite a sorry state, I'm afraid. Throughout your lands, only 175 families remain."

"*What?*" Aidan gasped. "That cannot be. There were easily 500 to 700 in my father's day. I can't believe that many have fled to other lands."

"Nevertheless, tis true. More than two-thirds of the fields lie fallow. Of the seven villages, only 15 to 25 families still reside in each. In Becca's Well, only 30."

Aidan shook his head. He knew the numbers would be bad — plenty of the shops and homes in town were boarded up or just abandoned — but he had not expected them to be *so* low.

"What about my fields?" Aidan asked.

The manor was divided up into eight parts. Becca's Well and its surrounding fields were run directly by the castle and the crops they produced belonged to the baron. The shopkeepers, merchants, and other residents of the town paid rent to him for their homes or other buildings.

The other seven parts were seven smaller villages spread across the manor and their surrounding fields. Those sections were ruled by the knights of the manor who had taken an oath of fealty to the baron. Historically, there had always been enough land to support four knights.

In those villages, the knight held lands himself, and the rest of the land was held by either serfs or free tenants. Serfs worked their lands for free but had to spend one day out of seven working the knight's lands. Free tenants paid rent on their land, but did not have to work their lord's lands.

The knight's income came from receiving these rents and selling the crops from his lands. He would then owe a significant percent to his baron. Some of the fields around Becca's Well worked the same way, but those serfs or free tenants owed their service or rent directly to the baron instead of a knight.

Richard's hand had been far too heavy. He had revoked free-tenancy and forced all into serfdom, giving himself the right to flog runaways and to require *all* common men and women to labor on his lands at the expense of their own crops. Yet, he'd also demanded rents from all, as if they were still free tenants.

In England, men owed service or rent, but not both. Richard's had been an oppressive, double taxation. Not to mention forcing a free tenant into being a serf went against the laws of God and king.

And then, there was his uncle's greedy confiscation of crops and livestock. Essentially, Richard had tried to sweep the entirety of the manor's wealth into his own hands, while simultaneously driving the people into an abject dependency upon him. It was slavery. Their freedom had been extinguished, their labor belonged wholly to him, and in return, he gave them food to eat.

John continued, "Besides your outlaw friends who have settled around Becca's Well, I found only seven families still working the castle's fields."

Aidan sat back heavily in his chair.

"Unbelievable," he said, shaking his head.

"As you know, hundreds of sheep and other livestock are penned up behind the castle. They are what's left of the ones Richard commandeered from the people."

"Can we know from whom they were taken?"

"I have a full list, though some tried to exaggerate what they'd lost, but I took that into account. Unfortunately, Richard slaughtered much of the livestock to feed his small army and already sheared the sheep. Presumably, the fleeces are long since sold."

"Very well. Return those animals that are still alive to their owners immediately," Aidan commanded, "For those that were slaughtered or lost a fleece, pay the owners from the treasury the market rate for their loss."

Baron Nicholas smiled, pleased by the order. It was just. Perhaps he had underestimated this young man.

Priscilla beamed.

At Aidan's request, Red had brought half of what the outlaws had accumulated in silver, gold, and other treasure from the cave to the castle. It had amounted to a small fortune — *over four hundred pounds.*

That, together with the amount of silver Richard left behind, meant they had enough funds to support the castle for a good while, but with only 175 families left on the manor to produce income, Aidan would be losing money at a rapid rate every month.

Also, the manor had to provide four knights or Aidan's rights to his lands could be revoked by the king. Thankfully, the king was distracted by his battles with Maud, but nevertheless, Aidan had to retain at least four knights — and probably more than that. Four should be enough to satisfy the king, but he fully expected Richard and the Earl of Chester to return some day.

"Have you calculated our current losses, John?"

"I have." The steward unrolled a scroll of paper covered in hash marks and laid it on the table, pinning the corners with small wooden cups left from the previous meal. "Twelve of the original castle servants remain. The others ran away. You retained eight men-at-arms and, with the addition of Sir Eric and Sir Thomas, you have three knights."

"You can call me Tom," Tom interrupted.

John made a funny face, then went on, "If you continue with Richard's oppressive taxation, you'll run a surplus, but I'm afraid your populace cannot continue to support such heavy-handedness."

"That is not an option," Aidan confirmed.

"Well, if you return to normal rents and service terms, you'll run a deficit of three to four pounds per month, including estimated monthly expenses for the castle and keep. That will go up to five if you retain another household knight."

Aidan whistled. With such a low number of laborers, he would have to supplement his knight's income, and the loss John calculated was the equivalent of the monthly income of forty common laborers.

"What do you suggest?" Aidan asked.

"You have a lot of silver at your disposal and can continue to lose at that rate for several years, but the castle is in need of repairs. You've also made some bitter enemies, powerful ones, and defenses will need to be improved soon. Construction costs would consume your treasury at a much faster rate. Essentially, we need more people to return the manor to a functional state."

"How do you propose we accomplish that?"

The steward exhaled heavily and paused.

"I'm not sure," he said, "Most who left have resettled elsewhere and would not uproot again so easily. They may have even taken oaths of fealty to new lords."

Aidan turned to the others. "Ideas?"

Silence.

Finally, Priscilla's soft voice broke it.

"Dear . . . my father might have some wisdom to add on the subject. He has discussed such matters with me many times before."

"Sir Nicholas?" Aidan prompted him.

The lesser baron straightened.

Having antagonized Aidan so much prior to his marriage to Priscilla, Nicholas was now taking extra efforts to show Aidan the respect due his position.

"I have in fact studied various philosophies regarding these things over the years and have had the opportunity to employ some of their principles at my own manor, on a much smaller scale of course."

"And?" Aidan asked.

"If I may, Sir Aidan, ask you a question first?"

Aidan nodded.

"If you were told to endeavor on a project, be it working a field, or running the shop of a merchant, yet you knew you had no rights of ownership and after all your hard work, it could be taken away from you on a whim, how strong would your motivation be to work?"

Aidan thought long and hard about the answer.

"Your point is well taken. I would not be motivated but would do only what was required."

"Some might even be tempted to work just enough to survive? Now, imagine you also knew that if your crops failed, or if no customers came to your shop, you would still be required to pay the same in rent regardless."

"I think I would be quite discouraged. Yes, I have sympathy for such cases. My father was mercifully light-handed, and so shall I be."

"Yet, your people have no assurance of that. What if you change your mind when the treasury runs low? Or what if you are killed and someone like Richard takes over again? Why would they be able to trust they will always have mercy? Your own pressures might force you to pressure *them* in extreme circumstances."

"Then what do you suggest?"

"I have seen that men will work much harder for something that belongs to them than they will for someone else. If you free your people to build something up for themselves, you allow the full power of their resourcefulness and creativity to shine through. People will produce prosperity for you when it coincides with their own interest."

"But these people are poor and uneducated. Many might not . . ."

"They will. As you saw among the outlaws in the forest, and as you've seen all your life among the villagers, if you'll think about it."

He paused.

"I recommend eliminating serfdom and offering free tenancy to *all*."

Aidan and the others looked to each other, bewildered. What Nicholas proposed was unheard of.

"And what of my lands, and those of my knights? Who will work those lands?"

"I will get to that. First, for the free tenants, you should waive the requirement to pay rents and offer legal rights to their land so they cannot be evicted, unless they fail to fulfill the terms of their agreement with you."

"Untenable!" John Steward cried. "How will the manor survive without rents?"

"Instead of a fixed rent, they will pay a 12% fee on all income. You would do the same with the merchants in town. Charge no rent but collect 12% of what they earn."

"Impossible!" John exclaimed. "How will we know what they earn? Why wouldn't they lie?"

"Some might, most won't. You will have a general idea of what people are earning. The 12% is a much lighter burden than rents in most towns, so why would they lie if it could mean getting exiled from Becca's Well and having to pay more to another?"

"You are right to say the 12% is low," John interjected again, "Such a rate would only accelerate the loss Aidan is already facing every month!"

"Initially, yes. But you assume that more people will not come. If we send word out to the surrounding baronies that all who come to Becca's Well will be given land with no fixed rent and only an obligation to pay on actual income, I believe men will flock here in droves. As the residents of Falconer Manor increase, so will the income to the castle. Plus, people will work harder for land they feel is theirs. Their profit will be greater, and thus, so will your income."

"We cannot give people land, Nicholas," Aidan reasoned, "As you well know, it all belongs to the king."

"No . . . but you *can* give them certain rights. The same kind of fief rights you hold before the king."

"You're talking about creating hundreds and hundreds of little knights with small land holdings."

"Well, they would not have the title of knight, but essentially . . . yes."

The ideas were radical.

Yet, where a door would not have even cracked ajar before, desperate times allow for desperate measures to be given consideration. There was a certain logic to what Nicholas said . . . but such things were not customary . . .

"So, this could be viewed as restoring some of the freedoms England enjoyed before the Normans conquered?" Aidan pondered.

"You cannot do this!" John protested, "It would be economic suicide!"

"It doesn't hurt to try," Nicholas offered.

"Well, it *could*," Aidan countered. "I cannot give my word on something and then take it back."

"I understand, but I assure you my principle is sound."

"I do agree with John though," Aidan said. "12% is too low. 20% is still lower than the current rents. What do you say about that?"

"You are right, it is lower. It might be enough to make a difference, but it will not have nearly the impact on attracting people as my proposal would."

"And my land?" Aidan asked. "Who would work it?"

"Hire laborers for a penny a day, or even offer a little better than that to make sure you get the best workers . . . and then offer 10% of your profit at the end of the year to all who work the fields."

"Are you crazy, man?" John cried, his face twisted in presumed agony.

Priscilla scowled. "I assure you, John, my father is perfectly sane."

"My apologies, milady. I meant no offense. It's just . . . it's just . . ."

"I know," Aidan tried to calm him, "These ideas are untried and against all custom."

"Yes!"

"I can see how it might make the people work harder for me though," Aidan considered.

"More than that," Nicholas finished, "allow them and all your other tenants the freedom to choose their own crops, to grow whatever they want in their fields."

That suggestion was truly shocking.

"But . . . that would breed disaster! What if these people try to grow crops that are doomed to fail?"

"Some inevitably will. Some will continue with what their fathers knew. Others may try a new crop that yields much more profit than the typical wheat and barley. Thus, earning you more profit when they sell. Your income would be fixed if all you ever got was rent on the land, but if you earn a percent of the crop, you can do better."

"What do you think, men?" Aidan asked his knights.

Eric and Tom were doing their best to disguise their enthusiasm, afraid to assert it. They were not yet used to speaking with the authority a knight carried.

Sir Alan was more reluctant to accept the new ideas.

"Well, Nicholas, you never fail to birth controversy," Aidan said. "I'll need some time to think these things over."

Chapter 31

Later that evening, as the sun began to set behind the oaks to the west, Aidan and Priscilla strolled along the castle walk.

It looked like God had painted the sky with broad strokes of pink and orange. The rare light bathed her high cheeks in a healthy glow.

He couldn't imagine he would ever tire of her cultured beauty. He often stole glances her way whenever he could get away with it. Yet, in moments like this, she so captivating, he couldn't help but stare.

"What do you think I should do?" he asked.

"I think you'd do well to try what my father's ideas," she answered. "I've watched him administer his people over the years. The more he freed them to work for their own profit, the more diligent they were. And he has honestly prospered along with them."

"But your home is modest . . ."

"Believe me, he has a tidy sum saved up. He's just never been one to display wealth. He only splurges on books."

"It's just . . . it sounds so . . . *chaotic*."

"He's had his share of failures too, but whenever someone made a mistake, others were always there to step in and help . . . and those would usually do well enough to make up for the loss.

"On the other hand," she continued, "With your current system, what if everyone grows barley, but barley doesn't do well this year? If the barley market prices are low, you'll suffer a disaster. Surely, you saw such years while your father was alive?"

Aidan nodded.

"And with the number of fields in your barony," she continued, "if you tried to dictate to the people a wider variety of crops yourself, you'd be overwhelmed with the administrative task of managing it. I believe my father is right in saying it's better to let every man pursue his own interests."

Aidan hesitated.

She smiled. "You know I'm right."

"I guess I do . . . it's just . . ."

"Well, I'll be! Aidan Falconer!" She stopped to face him, setting her hands on her hips. "You are not *one bit* worried about chaos. You're worried what others will say, departing from tradition . . ."

"I am not!"

"Yes, you are."

He reddened, realizing she was right in that too.

"The Aidan I know is bold and daring and leads instead of following useless traditions. If you wish to be a great man, my husband, you must step out in faith and take a risk."

The look she gave him was piercing, electrifying even. It reached down into his heart of hearts and stirred something ferocious and determined, flooding his veins with new energy.

She was right — and he knew he'd chosen very well.

***

The crowd below hummed and murmured as people milled about in anticipation of what Aidan might have to say.

He'd sent messengers through all eight villages, summoning one and all to a mandatory assembly. Hundreds of people now stood in front of the castle's gate. Aidan and his knights stood on the wall above.

He leaned forward and gripped the edge of the battlement.

"Men and women of Falconer Manor!" he called.

As soon as Aidan began his address, the murmurs grew quiet, and the people turned to face him.

"We are gathered here to celebrate a new day! Today, we celebrate your liberation from the rule of Richard Falconer!"

The crowd roared with cheers of approbation. The revelry was short-lived, however.

In spite of their memories of his father, in spite of their joy at his marriage, Aidan remained an unknown in their minds. They had heard of his feats in the forest, but how would he rule them now that he was in charge? Was he more like his father or his uncle? Wild rumors of every ilk had floated from ear to ear, but of yet, there was nothing solid on which to build hope.

"We have prepared a feast for you!"

The gate swung open, and the castle servants filed out bearing large steaming plates overflowing with rich delicacies. The servants set the dishes on makeshift tables that were nothing more than long planks set atop casks and covered with cloth. These elongated tables lined both sides of the main thoroughfare. The procession was just the first of many the servants would make, for Aidan intended the party to last all day.

The townspeople had already broken ranks and were moving to the tables, unable to resist the rich aromas, but Aidan called out again, so they turned back to him.

"My uncle ruled you with a heavy hand," he continued. "He lived only for himself and his own greedy desires. His men ravaged your fortunes and violated your daughters. He unleashed a plague of unprecedented suffering upon this manor and its people . . . and the truth of that breaks my heart.

"But I stand here to assure you those days have finished!" His voice boomed, echoing across the grounds.

Raucous cheers rose up again at that.

"I have already given orders to have all the livestock and produce confiscated by Richard and still in possession of the castle, returned to their rightful owners. For that which was already consumed, we have paid and will continue to pay the fair market value for whatever was taken."

More cheers. Knowledge of Aidan's actions in this regard had already filtered out among them.

"Now, Richard eliminated free tenancy. He forced all of you into serfdom!"

A cacophony of discontented boos and hisses rolled through the people as they recalled the injustice.

"Yet, he still required the rents!"

The boos grew louder.

"As lord of Falconer Manor, I hereby declare that serfdom is now abolished on all lands under my control. All persons holding land are now free tenants!"

The hissing transformed into a surprised silence.

Had they heard him right?

Until now, the cheers and boos had accompanied Aidan's speech like a choreographed piece of expected theater. Now, he'd caught them off guard, and the reaction was genuine.

They'd expected change, but to eliminate serfdom for all was, frankly, unbelievable.

"And you will be given legal rights to pass your land on to your children, provided you abide with the terms of your fief, with no surety due."

Excited chatter spread quickly as they conferred with one another. No one was sure they'd just heard what they thought they'd heard. All manors had serfs. Free tenancy was much preferred to the semi-slave labor of serfdom. The concept of actually having rights to their land had gone right over their heads, so foreign was it to the common thinking.

"Furthermore, you shall no longer be required to pay fixed rents for your property, be it lands, houses, or merchant shops within the towns!"

Now the crowd was roaring, a jumbled mixture of happiness and unbelief. The elated cries were hard to distinguish from bewildered questions they were now shouting his way. They instinctively understood the castle would require income. What he was saying did not make sense.

Aidan held up his hands until they quieted.

"My uncle was reducing you to the point where you were just working for food. Normal rents for free tenants in other villages is usually about three parts of every ten of the normal yield of a field, and you must pay a minimum amount whether you have a bad year or not.

"I will only require you to pay 20% of whatever you *actually* earn in a year, bad year or no! Also, after this first harvest, you are free to plant whatever crops you think will do well with no punishment from the castle for failure. You may spread the word among your relatives that all newcomers to the manor who wish to settle on Falconer land shall receive the same treatment."

It took a minute for what he'd just said to fully sink in, but once it did, the eruption of joy was complete. People yelled and jumped up and down, embracing each other spontaneously. Husbands kissed their wives, and some young men took the opportunity to sneak a peck with a maiden who had caught their eye.

"Furthermore, the blacksmith, the fuller, and all other tradesmen are hereby free to practice their trade in Becca's Well without interference from the castle. Merchants may buy and sell whatever product they wish at the market with no transaction fee.

"This day, you are being given freedom. Freedom that is the right of every man. Use it well! Now enjoy the feast!"

Aidan turned and descended from the wall.

The servants were still emerging with the first run of steaming dishes, but when the crowd turned, the tables already looked full beyond capacity and the delicious odors of roasted lamb and hot bread saturated the air tantalizingly. Lutes and recorders appeared in the hands of several of the villagers and the music began.

It wasn't long before the dancing broke out too.

Chapter 32

June 1138 AD

Richard slumped in his chair and stared at the messenger gloomily. The Earl of Chester, on the other hand, sat stiffly in his throne-like seat, listening to each word with crisp intent.

". . . and he has sent messengers to villages all across Derbyshire, and to the north and southwest of Becca's Well, offering high wages to any laborer," the informant continued.

"Why to the north and southwest?" Richard interrupted.

"Because that's away from us and the Sheriff of Nottingham, you dolt!" The earl exclaimed. "This is absurd. Offering a crop share to common laborers and free tenancies without rents!" He snorted.

"We cannot let him get away with this," Richard snarled.

Ranulf dismissed the messenger with a wave.

"Let him get away with what?" he asked, "These policies are suicide for him. Even if it doesn't bankrupt the boy, it will assuredly weaken his treasury. He is young and foolish."

"We should destroy him now!" Richard pushed.

"Enough!" The earl slammed his fist on the arm of his chair.

The others in attendance stirred.

Richard blanched.

"You forget, I fight for my own interests, not yours!"

"Yes, Earl Ranulf, my apologies." Richard dipped his head in bowed submission.

"Never fear, I have not forgotten the boy's insolence, nor the assassination of my best man, Sir Reginald. We *will* have our vengeance. For now, though, King Stephen has summoned us to his side to aid his cause in battle. Before all else, we must answer that call.

"That will give Aidan's policies time to begin their crushing effect. And while we're with the king in his court, we will speak to him of a young, inexperienced baron who is running one of his formerly prosperous manors into the ground."

***

Aidan enfeoffed to Sir Alan the villages of Taddington and Brushfield, which were situated between Becca's Well and Chester. Since Alan was the most experienced of his knights, Aidan felt it was wise to place him over those regions because he would be the one to give Aidan early warning should the earl and Richard make any forays onto Falconer land.

He placed Eric over Pilsley and Edensor, and entrusted Flagun and Maneis to Tom. Half of Maneis belonged to a monastery located there, but there was enough land to the east of it to make up for the loss.

Conksbury was the last village to be allotted. Aidan held it in reserve for the fourth knight he knew he would need, but in the meantime Sir Alan would run it.

John Steward reported that since Aidan's announcement, families had begun trickling back into Becca's Well and the outlying villages, about five families to each, for a total of forty new families. The laborers working on Aidan's own land, however, had doubled.

With these changes, he now had no worries about being able to manage most of the cleared acres, as long as everyone was willing to work hard.

By all accounts, a new fervor had entered the people, and they were already making extra preparations for the planting season, being more thorough in the removal of rocks from fields and whatnot. He'd even heard reports of a few voluntarily making new cisterns to help with irrigation later.

Some mused about what kind of crops might be planted that could sell for more than the normal market rates for grain, but in the end, most opted for the standard winter wheat since time was short and it was a crop people knew. Wheat was always more profitable than barley and was usually chosen when the seed could be had.

Which was the next problem to overcome.

The people had no seed to sow.

Most of the wheat harvested earlier in the year had been consumed by Richard and his men or sold to other markets by him. Aidan had compensated the farmers for their loss, but the seed they normally would have retained was still missing.

He sent men to neighboring manors to purchase wagonloads of seed to be distributed among the various tenants of the manor. Those that could pay for it from what Aidan had just reimbursed them would do so, and those who could not, Aidan loaned the seed on promise of repayment once a harvest was had.

Those who had been denuded of sheep, or pigs, or other livestock, set about using Aidan's reimbursement to purchase lambs, kids, and piglets from neighboring towns to replenish what they'd lost. Being emboldened by promises of better profit, these risked to buy more livestock than they normally would have undertaken.

Ysabella opted for winter wheat as well and somehow managed to plant her entire strip, mostly with her own hands and the help of a single laborer, a lanky, but hard-working teenager by the name of Mark.

Tenants normally divided their holdings into three parts. One field for a winter crop, another for a spring crop, and the third was typically left fallow. The following year, the three fields would be rotated so that each field would have a turn to be fallow.

In their exuberance, some of the tenants were ignoring the fallow field rule and sowing two of their fields with wheat seed. While he understood their reasons — in fact, this was exactly the type of behavior Nicholas' theories were supposed to inspire — the practice disturbed him.

Leaving one field fallow every season gave the land a chance to rest. He knew from his education that land needed time to recover from multiple harvests. No one really understood why, but it was a traditional practice for a reason.

These peasants, however, did not have the benefit of his knowledge. For many, it was just a rule of their master to be obeyed. Now that the yoke had been thrown off, they dove in wholeheartedly.

In that respect, Nicholas' ideas had already proven true. The men and women of Becca's Well were leaping at the chance to make extra income, and they would realize it in the short term. It would take several harvests, though, to see if Aidan's concerns were valid.

A failure to let the fields rest might result in widespread crop failure several years from now, which would cripple the entire manor. Regardless, he had committed to non-interference, so he would let the course run as it may.

Still, once some had dared to break tradition in this way, others then scrambled to sow their fallow fields as well with whatever seed they could scrounge up before the planting season was finished, and Aidan's concerns only grew.

Chapter 33

"I heard John issued a new report today," Priscilla said.

Aidan rolled over in the bed to face his bride. She lay on her side atop the fine linens that had been in his family for years, her head propped up on one hand instead of nestling in her plush pillow. Those linens were beginning to show some wear, but her face eclipsed it from his awareness.

Her eyes were alert, ready to talk.

It hadn't taken long in their marriage for him to realize that she enjoyed hearing about the daily business of the manor even more than he.

"Yes, he did," Aidan replied.

"I heard there are fifty more families now than there were a month ago," she offered coyly.

"You did, did you?" He smiled.

She was always well-informed regarding the castle's affairs, often knowing things even before he did.

"Yes."

"Well, yes . . . there are."

"That's wonderful!" She beamed. "I also heard that with those additional workers, the projected income to the castle is enough you can retain a fourth knight and still lose less than predicted a month ago."

"That *is* what it looks like . . ."

"Well, aren't you excited? What a relief!"

"I suppose it is. It's just there's so much still to do."

"Don't you see, though? What matters is the number of people combined with how hard they work, not how much you take from each one. If you increase the amount each must pay, they won't work as hard. Nor would so many families be returning."

"Maybe . . . it's not clear yet. What if those are just people who are returning home simply because Richard is gone?"

Her brow creased and an exasperated puff of air escaped her lips. "I spoke with Eric and Alan, and they say there are many newcomers among them."

"Priscilla, I know how anxious you are to prove your father was right . . ."

"I think it's becoming rather clear that he was. The proof is already here. Surely you have to admit . . ."

"Yes, yes. All right, fine. Yes, it looks like he might be right, but it's still early, and we haven't yet seen if these people are going to make mistakes, or if they're going to begin questioning my authority."

"They will not do that."

"I don't know. It's all so . . . *chaotic*."

"You've said that before, but I'm afraid it's going to be that way for a while, my love." She brushed the back of her hand against his cheek. "Give it a chance."

"I will. I've given my word to let things work themselves out."

"Since the 20% rate is working out so well, what about lowering it further, maybe to 15%? I think that could bring in even more families."

"Oh!" he laughed "You're just going to keep pushing, aren't you?"

He grabbed her shoulders and planted a healthy, passionate kiss on her lips. He needed to shut her up before she talked him out of his entire inheritance.

***

With so many of the designated fallow fields being planted with winter wheat, the tenants themselves began sending word to relatives on other baronies seeking help since they'd doubled their own workload.

The common man's established wage throughout England was a penny per day. However, the demand for workers on Falconer Manor was so great that those who could afford to hire were having to offer more. A penny and a farthing per day seemed to be the amount needed to attract people away from other manors. Tenants who could not afford to pay their laborers up front were offering a portion of the profits once the harvested crop was sold.

The inflow of families accelerated, yet once many of the new arrivals learned of Aidan's offer of free tenancy on land of their own, they snatched the opportunity instead of working as laborers. There was still plenty of vacant land that had been abandoned during Richard's rule that needed managing. There were always some people though who that preferred the silver-on-the-spot being a laborer provided.

Aidan's best guess was that half the tenants were sticking to the old ways. Some of them refused to plant anything besides barley, declaring that was all they knew how to grow.

The other half pushed forward with whatever means they had. Some went all out, planting in every nook and cranny where they could find room. A few even sowed all three of their fields, sowing even their spring fields with winter wheat seed. To Aidan, this was clearly not wise, putting all your eggs in one basket.

A handful of men worked less than before, planting only half a field or so now that no fixed rent was required. The laziness of these men and their disdain for the welfare of their wives and children appalled Aidan, but he had to grit his teeth and bear it, once more remembering his vow of non-interference.

One group of enterprising young men began clearing trees from the forest to create a *new* field. The moment Aidan heard about it, he put a swift stop to the effort.

The forest belonged to the king, and they could not afford to antagonize him any more than they already had. The truth was nobody had seen the king's foresters for quite a while, but it was still a risk he wasn't willing to take.

By the end of the second month, the vibrant green of nascent wheat sprouts dotted fields everywhere and over a hundred more families had moved onto the manor. They now had close to 325 families and John Steward's newest calculations (revised for the third time) predicted a *surplus* at harvest.

Nicholas had been right.

As reluctant as Aidan had been to admit it, these strange policies were working. Almost all the immigrating families were newcomers who'd never before set foot on Falconer Manor in their lives.

At this rate, Aidan would definitely be able to support a fourth knight. He couldn't help but smile now when he walked by the hope-filled fields of Becca's Well, basking in the excitement that seemed to envelope everything and everyone.

One hot, clear day, Thomas Weaver came to visit.

The friends hadn't seen much of each other since Aidan had returned — both were very busy these days — but he was happy to see him looking so much happier than before.

"Thomas!" Aidan rose to embrace his friend, clapping him on the back.

"So good to see you, Aidan."

"How is your father?"

"Much better, thank you. Business is good again, not quite up to what it was before, but customers are returning."

"What is the mood of the merchants in town?"

"Encouraged, but wary."

"Good. Well, I hope to dispel their concern with time."

They talked for a while before Aidan brought the meeting to its point.

"So, what brings you out to see me? I imagine you came for a reason?"

"I did," Thomas nodded. "Many of the craftsmen and merchants are concerned about some upstarts who've arrived recently. A peddler pitched a tent at the end of the street yesterday and is selling bottles of what he claims is a healing potion. The fuller's wife bought one and woke up this morning vomiting. Of course, the peddler left during the night.

"Another has arrived to set up shop as a weaver. There isn't enough business to support the both of us. I've spoken with the others, and they want to form a town guild to regulate who can do business and who cannot."

Aidan fell quiet.

"Well, those are two different things though," he said at last. "A peddler selling poison as medicine is a man who needs to be brought to justice, not regulated in his business. We have no alderman, nor council of elders, do we?"

"No, Richard dissolved it."

"We must reestablish it. We need a council to help adjudicate civil matters and bind offenders over to face justice, as well as maintain law and order within the town. How would you feel about being alderman, Thomas?"

His friend sputtered. "*Me* . . . why me?"

"You are well-liked and known by all, as well as highly respected. You stuck around when others fled and refused to give into Richard's demands. Plus, I trust you."

"If it is your will, I will accept." Thomas bowed at the waist.

"Man, don't be so blasted formal. We're still friends."

"I'm sorry," Thomas chuckled, "It's just . . . you *are* different now, not the same wild one I grew up with — and you're a baron."

"I'm the same. Now, go and choose a few other men you trust to be on the council. You'll probably need at least seven.

"As for the new weaver in town," Aidan continued, "I cannot help in that matter. You will just have to suffer with the competition. My policy across the manor is freedom for all to seek prosperity as they may. We'll have no guilds, nor will we run others out of town for practicing their legitimate trade."

"But there isn't enough business to go around . . ."

"Our population continues to grow. Plus, you and your father are good weavers. If this other man is a poor one, the people will come to you instead, and you may even be able to charge higher prices. If he turns out to be as good as you, you'll just have to find a way to do a better job than he and win the people's business."

"I don't know, Aidan . . ."

"Give it a chance, Thomas. Embrace it for a while. Let's see how it goes."

"Very well," Thomas grimaced, "but that isn't the only concerning matter. There are rumors of rogue soldiers roaming the highways and forests, plundering wherever they can. Will's lad spotted a group of them a few miles from here last week. The townspeople are getting worried."

He had Aidan's full attention now.

"What?" Aidan's brow creased deeply, "Whose men are they?"

"We think they're coming from the north, men left with nothing after David's raids."

"I mean, are they Maud's men, or are they with Stephen?"

"No one knows. They don't seem to be with *anybody*. They're like vagabonds with armor."

"How do we know it wasn't a forward scouting party for an attack?"

"We don't for sure, but their behavior didn't seem like a disciplined band. Still, I thought you should know."

"Thank you. I'll look into it."

Chapter 34

A few days later, Aidan, Alan, and John Steward were in the great hall discussing the castle's readiness to resist an attack. It was time to prioritize the improvements to fix the weaknesses that had been uncovered in the Steward's survey. Alan had just made a point about the primary importance of the gatehouse when they heard a commotion erupt in the front of the keep.

Aidan laid down the parchment he was holding as they all looked up to see what was happening.

One of Aidan's servants entered the room first, followed by two strangers, both of them attired in the vestments of a knight.

The strangers had been arguing with each other in the passageway but fell silent the moment they reached the great hall. The servant introduced them.

"Sir Aidan, may I present Sir Guy and Sir William, both knights of the realm."

The knights bowed courteously at the waist.

"To what do I owe this honor, gentlemen?" Aidan asked.

Sir Guy was a tall, broad-shouldered man with a long, sharp nose and narrow face. Everything about him shouted aggression, from the thick, red scar that ran under his jaw line to his wide stance.

Stepping forward, he spoke first.

"I heard a man in Derby speak of your need for a knight and I have come to humbly offer my services. It would indeed be an honor to serve you, Lord Aidan, and I think you will find my abilities to be exemplary." Sir Guy flourished his hand with a twirl of fingers and bowed again.

"And you, Sir William?"

William bowed a second time as well, but with a much simpler form. "I too had heard of your offer for employment, Baron, and am here to offer my services."

"Are the two of you friends?"

"Not hardly!" Guy exclaimed. "I first laid eyes on this man outside the wall of this very castle."

"What experience do you have, Sir Guy?"

"I've fought to the death in battle many times, and I *always* emerge victorious. Both in single combat and against larger numbers. I've also been entrusted with leading a charge into hostilities on several occasions."

"Who did you fight for, Maud or Stephen?"

Guy hesitated. "For Maud, of course, milord."

"Then why are you here? To the best of my knowledge, her fight is not finished. Or is Stephen vanquished and I had not heard of it?"

Guy hesitated once more. "Milord, my master was killed recently, and his tenancy dissolved for lack of an heir. I seek a new patron."

"And you, Sir William? What experience do you have?"

William was shorter than his competitor, but about the same height as Aidan. His hair gleamed raven black, was neatly clipped, and swept back and to the right. His face was squarish, handsome and unmarked from battle or any other kind of scar.

"Before the recent upheavals, I served my master faithfully and administered his entire estate. I increased his productivity two-fold in five years."

"What do you mean? You did the job of the steward?"

"I did. The actual steward proved unfit, and my lord recognized my talents."

"With whom was your barony affiliated?"

"King Stephen."

Aidan scowled. "And did your baron never send you into battle? Have you no combat experience?"

"I do. I fought in King Stephen's army against David in the north for several years with excellence." He glanced at Sir Guy, who stared stoically forward. "I *also* overcame many obstacles."

"With King Stephen," Aidan's scowl deepened. "And how do you come to be here?"

"I asked my liege to release me from my vow of fealty."

"Why?"

"Many reasons. I no longer felt I could offer him honest service."

"And he agreed?"

"He did."

Aidan pondered this admission. So far, he had already turned away five other men who had come seeking the tenancy, not perceiving them to be up to the task. Now, he'd received two in one day, both of whom seemed more than competent for the job.

"Well, gentlemen, for the time being, my problem is that I can only retain one knight," Aidan said.

Sir Guy's eyebrows turned down. "I assure you, sire, I am more than capable, certainly more so than this pretender." He spat the last word at William.

Aidan stood.

"Here is my decree. Tomorrow at noon, we will decide the matter through combat. You will fight each other in the courtyard and the winner shall become a knight of Falconer Manor."

***

The hot sun beat down mercilessly as the two warriors faced each other. A crowd from Becca's Well had formed to watch. The event was an entertaining respite from the day's labor.

Sir Guy catered to their sense of excitement, alternately glaring at William, then turning back to the crowd and flapping his arms up and down, urging them to get louder and cheer for him. They generally obliged, enjoying the sport.

For Sir William's part, he remained passive. He ignored the raucous bunch, focusing his attention only on Guy. His expression revealed nothing, neither intensity, nor fear.

Both knights wore full mail, but their scabbards were empty. Along with Sir Alan, Aidan entered the circle holding two wooden swords. He handed one to each man and then announced the rules.

"This is *not* a fight to death. You will not draw blood or otherwise intentionally harm the other. In that spirit, we have replaced your weapons with sparring arms. Your personal arms will be returned to you at the end of the match.

"Sir Alan will administer as referee. I will decide the winner. The loser shall collect his things and retire from the manor peaceably. Any questions?"

They shook their heads.

"Begin!" Aidan shouted.

He stepped back and left the duel for Alan to manage.

Guy's stance was aggressive and forward moving right from the start, while William was cautious, but not timid.

Guy feinted to William's right and then shifted to strike for his lower body. William was not caught off guard though, and easily flipped his blade back to parry the swing.

Next, Guy feinted with a strong sweep at William's legs, but switched in mid-movement to come back up for a strike at his head. The attack was a tricky one and required a masterful control of one's blade, not to mention tremendous strength in the forearm and shoulder. Guy's arm muscles rippled with the effort.

For any opponent, the move was difficult to counter. Not expecting a change of direction, or not knowing in which to direction to expect the change, a man would usually first try to block low and then be unable to recover in time to save his neck.

William, however, did not even try for the low block. Instead, he hopped up and back to avoid the leg strike and raised his blade in expectation of a head attack, blocking Guy's swing with seeming effortlessness.

Guy moved in to close the distance, but William had already rocked forward on the balls of his feet and stabbed for Guy's mid-section. He struck home and Guy gasped for breath as the air was partially driven from his lungs.

William had landed the first blow.

Guy retreated to gather himself and fill his lungs again. He knew he had underestimated his opponent.

The two circled each other warily.

Guy roared, and the anger boiling in his blood rose to redden his face. He ran full speed at William and rained down blow after blow in rapid succession. The sheer force of the onslaught nearly drove William from his feet, but he managed to remain standing, barely keeping up with the rapidity of it.

Blades met each other high and then low, and on every side. The dance went on for several minutes with Guy not relenting for even a second between strikes. William had no time to advance an attack of his own and was barely, yet artfully, fending off each thrust. He was forced to lean back much of the time, pressed to it by Guy's aggressiveness, but over and over he somehow found an upright position again.

At last, Guy broke for a rest, and both men heaved, trying to catch their breath, still circling.

Guy roared and rushed William again. In the instant before he reached him, Guy suddenly scooped some dust from the ground and flung it into William's eyes, blinding him.

William stumbled back and thrust his blade up to fend off Guy. He was forced to hold it with one hand as he desperately sought to clear his eyes with other. Guy pressed in, planted a foot behind William's heel and barreled into the other knight with all his weight. William flew back and landed hard in the dirt.

Guy conked him on the helmet with a severe blow and then stabbed at his chest. In a real battle, William would have been deader than dead.

Slowly, William stood, scratching at his eyes. Guy half-turned, awaiting Aidan's pronouncement.

"Bring him some water," Aidan called to a servant.

The servant fetched a cup and brought it to William who immediately began flushing out his eyes. He shook his head to rid himself of the fogginess brought on by Guy's helmet blow.

"Continue," Aidan said.

William wiped his eyes once more, threw the cup to the ground and faced Guy. A spark of anger could be seen simmering beneath his impassive surface now.

Guy shot an impertinent, dissatisfied glance Aidan's way. Grim-faced, he'd expected a clear kill to have won him the contest. Yet, Aidan was having them continue. Very well, he would just have to "kill" William again, and again, and as many times as needed until the victory was his.

He rushed William a third time, who readied himself. Before reaching him, Guy stopped short and bounced low, scooping something up again. William raised an arm to protect his eyes. Instead of dirt, Guy flung a sharp rock.

It bounced off William's helmet with a resounding clang. Several times, Guy bounced up and down as he circled William like some monkey from the wilds of Africa, slinging rocks at withering speeds. One struck William's chest, another his neck, that one drawing blood.

William was fed up.

When Guy bounced down to snatch the next rock from the soil, it was William's turn to rush him. Right before William reached striking distance, Guy leapt to the side and brought his blade down in a wide arc at William's head. The rock-throwing had just been a ruse to goad William into a reckless attack.

Yet, Guy's weapon only found air as William dropped and rolled. As he came up, he swung for Guy's legs. His wooden blade struck home solidly on Guy's knee.

Guy yelped with pain and hopped back. He had to limp around for a full minute before he recovered enough to walk normally.

They launched into each other for another round and then came apart again.

Sir Guy ran at William once more, but this time, when he was still six feet away, he planted his sword in the ground and used it like a pole vault, driving the soles of both his feet into William's chest.

William flew backward through the air and slid across the dirt, his mail scraping rocks. He rocked from side to side in obvious pain.

After a few moments, William finally caught his breath and struggled back to his feet.

Guy repeated the trick, launching himself once more through the air like a human missile. William expected it this time though and deftly stepped to the side at the last second.

With a thunderous smack, he landed a solid blow to Guy's back.

It was now Guy's turn to arch with pain, straining to reach his spine in a futile effort to alleviate the agony.

Furious, he cried out and went for William again.

"Enough!" Aidan yelled.

The two men stopped in their tracks and turned to face him.

"I declare Sir William the winner. He will become my vassal."

"*What?*" Guy roared. "I clearly defeated the cur! This is an outrage!"

"I have made my decision," Aidan replied.

But Guy was not about to be shut down so easily. "If you think this puny excuse for a knight won this contest, then you clearly know much less about true combat than I presumed, *Sir* Aidan!"

"Really?" Aidan looked amused. "Would you like to have a go at it with me then?"

Guy was clearly taken off guard by the suggestion, but his eyes showed he relished the opportunity.

"Yes!" he declared.

"William?" Aidan held out his open palm. William tossed his wooden sword through the air and Aidan caught it.

Aidan hefted it back and forth to adjust to its weight and took a few practice swings. The sparring tool felt so light in his hands. Every afternoon, he practiced for hours with his long broadsword. That blade was so heavy, it made this piece of wood feel like a feather.

He stormed Guy, a determined ferocity flooding his expression. Guy raised his weapon to defend, but barely got the chance.

Aidan's blows were like lighting. His arms moved in a blur, thrusting, twirling, blocking, and stabbing. He struck Guy in the neck and then the side. The next one slapped Guy in the head, dizzying him.

Guy was helpless to fend him off. The strikes were just too quick. Aidan's blade was moving so fast, he couldn't even see well enough to know for sure where it was at any moment. In and out, left then right, then right again, unpredictable. He could only manage to block one strike, two if he were lucky, before another would land home, and the blows did not descend lightly. They hurt.

Finally, Aidan thrust the tip of his blade into Guy's stomach and pushed him off his feet. The knight landed on his rump in the dust.

He had not landed a single blow of his own, and the entire battle had taken less than a minute.

The crowd stood in awed silence.

"Now, go!" Aidan said firmly, the tip of his wooden blade pointing down the road out of Becca's Well. "I have made my decision."

Chapter 35

Aidan interviewed William extensively for the rest of the day. The knight not only had a strong understanding of business, but he knew castle defense. He'd been placed in charge of fortifying a castle before, and Aidan was impressed by what he described he'd implemented. Even more importantly, he'd done it inexpensively.

Aidan enfeoffed Conksbury, his last village, and the lands surrounding it to William. He turned over to him the list of improvements to the castle's defenses recommended by John Steward and Sir Alan and put him in charge of the project, with permission to add his own improvements as he saw fit.

William took up the challenge with relish.

But he hesitated.

"Sire, may I ask a question?"

Aidan nodded.

"Why did you choose me over Guy? He clearly landed more killer blows than I did."

"I didn't like his style," Aidan replied.

"What do you mean?"

"Guy is bold and aggressive. Obviously well-trained, but his assaults relied on brute strength. And he was prone to repeat the same attack several times in a row before changing tactics.

"You, on the other hand, while not as strong and less experienced, showed masterful control over your body. I could see you put thought into your moves and correctly anticipated what he would do before he did it several times. You also learned quickly and never fell for the same tactic twice.

"A skilled, but measured thinker is always more valuable than someone who just plows straight in."

"Of course, in battle, anything goes," Aidan said, the beginning of a smile cracking his lips "but if you're trying to impress a lord with your combat skills, throwing dirt and rocks is not the best way to go about it. Don't you agree?"

"Yes, milord." William grinned.

The decision had puzzled him, but now he understood. Honestly, he'd not expected so much thought to have gone into it.

"No worry," Aidan said, "With a little training, you'll be better than Guy ever was. Plus, I already feel I can trust you, which is more important."

William nodded, humbled but pleased. He bowed at the waist and took his leave.

***

Three days later, he and Aidan toured the battlements.

"John and Alan's recommendations were sound," William said, "but I think we need to go beyond them. In addition to strengthening the walls, there are other things we should do."

"Such as?"

"Build up the ramparts here until they're chest high. We should also stock up on arbalests."

"Arbalests are expensive," Aidan said.

"Yes, but they're also effective."

Aidan didn't disagree.

William paused as they reached the front of the keep and turned to look over the gate and the town.

"We should also tear down that entire gate and re-build it," he continued.

"Why?"

"You need a full gatehouse. As it stands, one battering ram manned by enough soldiers would push right through it."

"It's the common design . . ."

"Yes, but there are better ones. We need to thicken its walls and alter the entrance tunnel. Instead of a straight path through the wall, we need to have it make a couple of sharp turns. Then, we can put barred oaken gates on both sides of the wall, not just one. That way, if attackers have a battering ram, they may get through the first door, but there would be no physical way to get its length all the way into the tunnel to use it on the second because of the turns."

It was an excellent idea. Why hadn't anybody done such a thing before?

"How did you think of that?" Aidan asked.

"I've heard crusaders speak about such a design. It's more common in the east."

"What else?"

"Well, you need at least one portcullis, but two would be better."

Aidan nodded.

"I recommend building a secondary wall around the town. Becca's Well is vulnerable."

Aidan whistled. *"That* would be a huge undertaking," he said.

"If there's a way to make it happen, I really think we should. During an attack, the villagers may not have enough time to get into the castle. Plus, the extended access to rations and supplies could help during a siege."

"Very good points."

"And the secret tunnel that leads from the field behind the castle to your study . . . from what you've told me, we cannot assume Richard is ignorant of it now."

"I don't wish to close it off. It's proven too useful."

"Then, perhaps we could extend it so the new entrance lies in the woods where no one will find it."

"But that is hundreds of feet away."

"It can be done. We'll fill in the old entrance and remove the stones around it. If Richard came looking for it, he'd just think we'd closed the tunnel up."

"It won't do us much good if everyone knows what we're doing. The secret won't be much of a secret."

"We could form a dedicated crew to excavate only at night. There would naturally be stockpiles of stones for the new town wall in the fields. We could borrow a few each night to create the underground passage in stages. Specifically, you should order large narrow slabs from the quarry to be stockpiled.

"Every night, a crew could dig out a section of the tunnel, drop three slabs into the hole, two uprights for walls and one on top to form the ceiling. Seal the cracks between the sections with mortar and then cover it back up the same night with dirt. Smooth it out and no one would be the wiser come morning. During the night, we'd post guards at a distance encircling the crew to prevent discovery by accidental wanderers."

"That might actually work," Aidan considered.

"It would be slow, but in the morning, all anyone would see is some disturbed dirt that's been tamped back down. Since most of the distance will be under that fallow field over there, it wouldn't even draw that much attention."

"This is all going to cost a lot of money."

"I know. That's why I need your approval."

"How long will it take?" Aidan scanned the fields and the town, trying to imagine what the new developments would look like once in place.

"The new gatehouse and the tunnel can be done within six months if we have enough men. If done right, the city wall would require a minimum of several years, and it would definitely be the most expensive of the projects."

Aidan considered his options.

It might break his treasury, but it was his duty to protect the people of Becca's Well, and there was no doubt Richard would return some day.

He turned to the knight.

"We'll find a way. Do it."

***

During Richard's rule, his uncle had established a quarry to the south and had already begun some garish improvements to the castle — at least what the man had considered improvements.

Part of the repairs Aidan needed to make involved deconstructing some ugly outcroppings Richard had made and filling in the gaps their absence would leave. Aidan wasn't sure what his uncle's building plans had been, but any inherent rhyme or reason to them was not apparent.

Regardless, an already existing quarry was a major boon, and the stones it produced were of high quality. Now, Aidan only needed to hire builders and laborers to cut and transport the rock.

Nevertheless, the process would be a long one. Before they could even start, they'd have to dig a ditch for the foundation of the new wall. Later, they'd need scaffolding.

What Aidan really needed was a master builder.

After the following Sabbath, he sent runners into neighboring lands again, this time announcing his need for laborers and builders. Soon, a stream of them began to arrive. Many of these newcomers threw up hastily-built huts outside the developed areas of Becca's Well. This created new rows of muddy lanes that would also have to be encircled.

It wasn't long before the work on the wall and the other improvements advised by Sir William began.

Aidan really wanted to extend the new wall a good way outside the current borders of Becca's Well, which meant it would encompass a lot of empty land. He'd already seen how well Nicholas' radical economic policies were working and had faith the town would grow to be much bigger than it was now.

Among the newcomers were a lot of men calling themselves builders, but only a few seemed to have any actual experience working on large stone projects such as this.

One stood out though. A man by the name of Peter who'd built stone houses in London and had worked on a castle in Essex.

Peter was a bit gruff in manner, but Aidan thought he detected some leadership abilities in him, so he appointed him as master builder. Still, Peter could bear some watching and Aidan would do well to keep his eyes open in case a better candidate came around.

Six months after Aidan reclaimed the castle, the winter winds began flowing in from the north. Another month after that, the construction, which had barely shown any progress yet, was forced to halt. Mortar does not set well in cold temperatures.

Still, as long as they were able, men continued to work the quarry at a feverish pace, storing up hewn stones in preparation for spring. Those that weren't doing that were building more permanent homes for the newcomers.

These winter laborers were extremely grateful for the work Aidan was providing. As field hands, they would have earned nothing over the winter months, but now they were receiving daily wages on top of what they would get at the harvest.

Aidan's main concern continued to be his treasury.

Funding these projects was draining it fast. While the laborers would pay him 20% back out of their salaries, they were otherwise solely a drain on the funds. He needed to increase the manor's population further than he already had, and fast. Three hundred families could not support this level of industry long term.

Priscilla's words and gentle pressures to further lower the tax rate had finally nestled themselves deep enough into his thinking that he gave in and concurred. He knew she was probably right, and he silently blessed the stubborn woman for her persistence.

Across the manor, he announced that the new tax rate owed to the castle in the spring would drop to 15%. Crops already planted would be subject the original 20% rate, but anything after that would be taxed at the lower rate. Including anyone new moving onto the manor's lands. Aidan encouraged all villagers to send word to others outside the manor about the change.

The development sent tremors of excitement across his lands and those of his neighbors. The idea of a lord voluntarily lowering taxes on his people, and in the middle of a great construction project no less, was unheard of.

As far as Aidan was concerned, even if time proved him wrong and the whole project failed, the admiring glances Priscilla kept shooting his way were enough to make it all worth it. Especially the ones he caught when she thought he wasn't watching. Admiration from a vibrant woman like her lifted his soul like nothing else. He reveled in it.

The winter months settled in, and the farmers withdrew into their homes as if hibernating while his knights firmed up their grasp over their own demesnes. Aidan and Priscilla spent the dormant season in front of the castle's different hearths, studying her books, playing games, and sneaking private kisses by the fire.

He'd become a much better reader since they'd married. The variety of her tomes was a testament to her father's library. From volumes on foreign languages to histories and philosophies, he tasted it all under her warm instruction — and enjoyed it.

He began to understand the wisdom of what she and Nicholas had been saying about the manor's business. He knew his own father had instinctively understood and agreed with many of these principles, though he'd not gotten them from books but his own mind, and Aidan knew his father would have been proud to see how much progress they'd made in just a few months. He just hoped Spring would bear out the wisdom of his intentions.

Chapter 36

All of England was falling into chaos.

Reports of errant knights wandering the countryside in search of plunder became frequent enough to represent a serious threat. The ongoing civil war between Stephen and Maud had wrought so much destruction and loss of life, the news of it was endless.

Maud herself had not yet invaded, but rebellions by sympathetic barons had risen up in the southwest and in Kent. Stephen had essentially lost control of Wales and was desperately trying to come to peace terms with David of Scotland after winning the Battle of the Standard the previous August.

Castles had been sieged and crops burned before they could be harvested. Every earl and baron was expected to choose sides, and even those reluctant holdouts for neutrality were being sucked in against their will.

These roving bands of knights and men-at-arms were deserters, or men who had lost their lord in battle, and they roamed the land like armed locusts in search of food, gold, and women for the taking. Their number was growing at an alarming pace.

It was soon evident the king's justice had been suspended.

King Stephen was fully distracted and had no time for civil matters. Maud was still in Normandy and had no recognized authority to deal with legal issues anyway.

Law and Order had been chased from the land, so what a neighbor could take from his neighbor was his to keep.

This included entire baronies.

Aidan considered himself quite lucky that Richard and the Earl of Chester were also distracted by their quest to aid King Stephen. This would be a ripe time for his uncle to take what he wanted by force without fear of facing consequences. Rumors abounded of others doing just that across the realm. Only circumstances seemed to be preventing it.

Regardless, the vagabond soldiers were becoming a regular danger to the people of his lands.

After a third attack in less than two weeks, Aidan ordered his knights to organize armed militias from among each their villages. Every village militia would be commanded by the knight himself and would receive some combat training for at least an hour every day.

Two or three militiamen would patrol their village's perimeters night and day, changing watch every four hours. If invaders were detected, the patrols would immediately alert the rest of the village, which Aidan hoped could respond with swift enough force to dissuade a small group.

From his time with the outlaws, Aidan was blessed in that he still had a *lot* of extra hauberks, shields, and weapons. So, he ordered them distributed to whichever villagers seemed the most skilled.

Becca's Well had two blacksmiths now. He commissioned them to fabricate hundreds of extra swords and dozens of crossbows. Soon, both smiths were essentially working full time for the barony.

He placed Becca's Well's militia under the direction of his friend, and now alderman, Thomas Weaver. Thomas flourished in the role. Aidan and William personally trained him daily, and whatever he learned he then passed on to the rest of his men.

Thomas' militia was much larger than those of the other outlying villages, so Aidan ordered at least three or four patrols of them to be wandering the lands around the castle at all times.

Only one professional bowyer lived in town, but another man who used to fabricate bows while in service to King Henry a decade prior had arrived looking for work.

A good bowyer could make an English longbow in as little as two hours. Aidan commissioned both men to produce as many bows as they could, as fast as they could.

Alan discovered a couple of fletchers residing in Pilsley, and Aidan paid them to do the same with arrows. Of course, Aidan would need a lot more arrows than bows, but both the fletchers took on apprentices, so they seemed to be keeping up. The middle of winter was a good time to focus on armament while the quarry and fields were idle.

In February, Aidan hired a fifth knight, a man by the name of Adelard. He hoped he wasn't getting too far ahead of himself, but he felt a pressing need to build in every direction.

Large construction projects, a build-up of arms, and now *five* knights were causing his treasury to hemorrhage money.

John Steward wouldn't have his new income predictions ready until late March, but more families were streaming onto his lands all the time, even during the worst of the winter months, so Aidan held on to hope.

Sir Adelard turned out to be competent, but not quite the leader William was, so Aidan gave him charge of Conksbury village and freed William up to fully supervise the construction projects and the militia in Becca's Well (which had developed quite well under Thomas' watch).

By the time the first spring sprouts of green were peeking through the deadened soil, Aidan was starting to feel somewhat prepared.

If Richard would stay away for another year, he might actually be ready to face him.

***

A peal of thunder reverberated through the keep's stone walls.

The vibrations rattled everything from the candlesticks on the table to the tapestry hooks on the walls.

To Aidan, it felt like a shiver reaching into the depths of his bones as he huddled close to the fire trying to absorb more of its warmth. The rainstorm had rolled in just an hour before, but temperatures had dropped fast. It seemed the chilled air was grasping at March in a desperate attempt to pull it back into winter.

Priscilla sat in a plush chair across from him. She had a rich blue dress spread across her lap and was darting a needle in and out of one of its seams to repair a small tear. She insisted on keeping herself busy with such tasks rather than relying on servants to do it all.

"Where is everyone?" Aidan asked.

"I think the servants are down in the undercroft. They were worried the dry goods would get wet with all the rains. John has a plan to get them up off the ground."

Aidan grunted. This spring had been very wet. Over the past month, it had rained more days than it hadn't, and the fields were becoming unmanageable morasses. Everything seemed permanently soaked.

"I should be down there with them," he mumbled, not wanting to leave the warmth of the fire. He'd had a headache too for the past couple of hours, probably also related to the storm. Whenever a bad one came in, he felt the pressure in his head.

He'd go in a minute. Just a little more time by the fire.

A sharp knocking sounded from the front of the keep. It repeated several times.

"Where is the porter?" Aidan demanded.

Priscilla looped her needle down into the fabric again. "I imagine he's down with the other servants," she said, "I believe you may have to get it yourself, dear."

Aidan cursed and stood.

She shot him a disapproving look. He ignored her and left the great hall. He'd been cursing his own lethargy more than anything anyway.

The door's iron latch was cold to the touch. He tugged on the oaken portal. It swung open to reveal a young child, a girl of about seven with strands of wet, stringy blonde hair clinging to her face.

The panic in her eyes was evident.

"Come quick, sire! Please! Pa's hurt! Help! The sheep!"

The words were clipped, rushed, mustered only with difficulty as the girl was out of breath from running. As soon as she'd finished her plea, she sped off, disappearing into the downpour.

Aidan turned to let Priscilla know he was going out to see what was the matter, but she was already standing by his side.

"Go," she said.

Aidan ran out into the rain to see where the little girl had gone. He sensed Priscilla was right behind him.

He spied the child's blurred form ahead. She was running toward the river. Surely not the safest place for a young girl to be in this storm. He raced to catch up faster, hoping to intercept her.

He arrived at the riverbank right after she did and immediately saw the problem.

Her father lay in the mud, his head cradled in her mother's lap. More scared children of various ages stood helpless nearby. A dripping of blood flowed from the back of the man's head and mixed with rivulets of water below.

A loud bleating expanded Aidan's view of the scene.

A small herd of sheep was clustered on a small grassy island in the middle of the river.

Although it would not have been an island even an hour ago.

The river was violent and swollen way beyond its normal shores. The sheep had probably been grazing on a small knoll but had been cut off when the waters rose from the storm.

"What happened?" Aidan asked the woman cradling her husband's head. Priscilla came up behind him.

"My man slipped in the mud . . . hit his head on a rock . . ." she gasped, oblivious to the sheets of water pouring down over them both.

Aidan kneeled beside him. "Is he alright?"

The shepherd stirred. He was conscious, but groggy. His wife looked to Aidan with pleading eyes. "I think he's okay, sire . . . but our sheep!"

He glanced at the newly created shoreline and could see it visibly creeping toward them one inch at a time. The flooding had not yet crested. This family's livelihood was in danger.

He assessed the dark, swirling currents and estimated the water between himself and the sheep wouldn't be more than two to three feet in depth, but it was easily fifteen feet across.

"Go, Aidan," Priscilla urged, also kneeling beside the man. "I'll watch them."

Her voice spurred him on.

"Get them back from the river!" he said.

He plunged into the cold water, feeling its sharp fingers envelop his calves and then his thighs as he pushed through. When it reached his waist, he cringed involuntarily from the chill.

Then, he was emerging again onto the small knoll. He approached the sheep, but the rising waters had them scared and irrationally nervous about him. They didn't have anywhere to go though — the newly created island was tiny — so corralling them wouldn't be impossible.

He was evaluating the best method for getting them all across when he heard Priscilla screaming his name from the shore.

He glanced up and saw she'd gone pale with fear. She was desperately pointing further up the river.

Then, he heard the roar.

He followed the line of her finger upstream and saw it.

An enormous roiling head of water was rushing down the river and sweeping away everything in its path.

As it would him.

Now, the little girl began screaming at the top of her lungs.

No time.

Hastily, he grabbed for the sheep closest to him, which happened to be one of the smaller ones, and hefted it up into his arms.

He was only going to be able to save one.

If any.

He drove his legs back into the cold water, his eyes fixed with determination on the safety of the shore, only breaking his gaze periodically to glance back at the oncoming head of water.

He trudged through for what seemed an eternity. It felt like the water was pulling on his legs, tugging him back, conspiring to hold onto him just long enough to kill him.

The small sheep bleated over and over, terrified by the panic it sensed, even if ignorant of the reason.

The head of water churned forward. For every inch he moved toward safety, it seemed to gain a foot. He glanced to the side and realized the flash flood could easily be eight feet high.

It was threatening to dash him and the little sheep against every rock and tree trunk downstream. They'd be lucky to find his broken body.

He was almost there, but it was upon him.

He heaved the sheep into the air, casting it as far from the river as he could, and ran as fast as the current would let him.

The sheep landed on dry ground on its side with a loud grunt that sounded totally unlike a sheep. He saw it scramble to its feet and scamper off.

He himself had just stepped onto dry ground when the head of water roared through, and he was not far enough in to escape its wrath. In a matter of seconds, the river swelled past its current banks and swept his feet out from under him.

He fell forward. His hands grasped for a hold. His fingers finally found some mud outside the water line and dug in. The current dragged his legs around and yanked him downstream, uprooting his fragile anchors and spinning him around.

Just when he thought he was about to be carried away hopelessly, his hands found a submerged rock. He grabbed it and held on with everything he had. The effort proved enough to stop him, but only because he wasn't yet in the middle of the main current.

At last, the water subsided, and he dragged himself to dry ground. He rolled onto his back and stared at the dark, grey clouds overhead.

Somewhere, outside of his view, a sheep bleated.

Aidan and Priscilla slowly walked back to the keep together.

The afternoon's torrent had finally stopped, not that their soaked clothes knew any difference. Aidan kept wanting to pick at the sodden fabric and pull its cold touch away from his clammy skin. Leather was especially uncomfortable when wet.

"If that woman had kissed your cheek any more times, I was going to get jealous," Priscilla quipped.

"She was just thankful."

"Oh, I know. You did a wonderful thing, my husband. Very few lords of this realm would risk their necks for one of their subject's sheep!"

"It's too bad I couldn't save the rest."

He'd saved the one, but the flash flood had carried the rest of the flock away and drowned them. The man had recovered from the blow to his head and Aidan had helped him search for the bodies, but they'd only found a couple of the wooly corpses scattered downstream. The rest were long gone.

The rich smell of moist earth filled their nostrils. All the recent rains had frustrated the people's efforts to begin their spring planting in still vacant fields, but most had persevered through anyway. Almost all the fields were tilled now, and many had seed in the ground already.

Aidan had never heard of anything like it. Under normal circumstances, serfs would have remained indoors until the rains let up and simply delayed their sowing a few weeks. Of course, whenever that happened, the result was a diminished crop at harvest time, though serfs usually didn't care.

Having a profit motive was proving to be a powerful tool for overcoming harsh circumstances.

"What are those men doing?" Priscilla asked.

He looked up and saw a group of men hastily piling dirt with wooden shovels into an elongated berm. The field it bordered was sprinkled with thousands of bright green dots that represented new plants which had just broken the surface.

"I think they're trying to keep run-off out of their field. They don't want the rains to carry away the new shoots."

"Is that normal?" she asked.

He thought he detected a touch of mischief in her voice.

He glanced at her.

"No, it's not," he answered, smiling.

Chapter 37

Eventually, the rains abated and work everywhere reignited in earnest. Becca's Well was filled with the ringing of blacksmiths' hammers that clanged almost non-stop. The quarry also revved back up. Day by day, the new town wall's length inched forward.

The remaining fallow fields that had not been planted previously were now combed with neat rows of seed.

Aidan's worry returned. Normally, one-third of all the fields should have remained fallow to rest. This year, very few fields were left untouched.

And he was concerned about the treasury too.

Finally, late in March, Aidan was happy to learn John Steward had finished his newest financial predictions that took into account all the recent changes on the manor.

"I'm sorry for the delay, milord. It has been difficult to keep up with everything that has been happening," John said. "There are almost *five hundred* families living and working on Falconer lands now. A hundred and thirty of them arrived just within the past two months. Most of those told me freedom or low taxes was their main reason for coming."

Aidan's mouth fell open.

He couldn't help it.

Honestly, he was at a loss for words. He'd never dreamed of such an outcome, especially not in such a short time, even less so in the middle of winter.

"That is . . . nothing short of *amazing*," he managed, enjoying the deep elation he felt bubbling up.

"It truly is, sire."

"And how will that impact the castle's funds?"

"Well, by lowering the rental rate, you have sacrificed four pounds of income per month to the castle."

A thick queasiness suddenly gripped his stomach. Four pounds was a good bit of money. For that amount, he could have hired forty more workers to work on the wall.

"But you gained a little more than that in future revenue with the arrival of the new families."

"I guess that's a relief. So, it's a wash? We'll break even?"

"It's early sir. These arrived in the harsher months. I have to believe more are yet to come because of your announcement. Your current income is going to be over 15 pounds per month, and, at the rate we're going, I expect it will go higher before the year is over."

The queasiness fled and a broad smile broke out on his face.

"You're kidding! That much?"

"Well, it's still not a lot. That's on the low end of what a baron will typically earn, and it's certainly not enough to support the massive projects you've undertaken."

"Not a lot, *my foot*," Aidan laughed. "I do believe that's more than my father took in most years, and that was with the normal rents and obligatory service."

"I have to admit, sire . . . Lady Priscilla and her father do seem to have been on the right side of things. I humbly retract my skepticism and wish to formally offer my support for their methods."

Aidan guffawed at that. "That is certainly a fancy way of saying you were wrong, and they were right."

"That's about the sum of it."

"Well, I'll pass on your apology and good news to them. In the meantime, keep up the good work."

April 1139 AD

By mid-Spring, the bowyers and fletchers had made enough longbows and arrows to fill two small rooms in the keep. The next hundreds would be loaded onto wagons and sent to Red in the outlaw camp. Red had agreed to conceal them in the cave there until a day when they might be needed.

The swords and more complex armaments were slower in the making and all of those went out to the militias for immediate use. The castle's front gate was now fully disassembled, and its new foundation was almost finished.

The city wall, however, was off to a much slower start than Aidan wanted. Too little seemed to have been done, though hewn stones were building up back in the quarry. William promised he would shift some of the quarry workers to help with the construction in town to balance out the process better. Aidan hoped it would make enough of a difference.

In a dramatic turn of events nationally, King Stephen, in order to achieve peace with David of Scotland, had ceded all of the Earl of Chester's northern lands to David's son Henry.

Reports were that Earl Ranulf was beyond furious over it. Some said he might even break with Stephen over the treaty and throw his support to Maud.

That was all good news to Aidan. A division between Ranulf and the king would only help him and weaken his uncle. It was a critical development that would give him more time to fortify.

***

Today's ash-colored sky was the type that tended to elicit a certain melancholic yearning in the hearts of its subjects; a day that bore breezes laden with promises of rain that never materialized. Yet, the moist afternoon air lay cool on the tongue, easing the stress of any soul that breathed it in.

Aidan stepped from his study and arched his back, stretching his muscles to their limit. He'd been sitting for several long hours, poring over the financial records.

It was getting old. He was tired of looking at papers. He needed something different.

A sound caught his attention.

He paused.

A faint, but captivating melody echoed through the keep. Not a voice, but some type of musical instrument. The notes were slow and drawn out, and for a stringed instrument, the resonance was surprisingly clear.

Aidan followed the lofty tune through the halls, seeking its source.

Its strength grew.

Who could be playing?

The wistful music wove tales of rainy glens and lost loves and other sad stories without a single voiced word of accompaniment. Notes rose and fell, pulling slowly upon the heart's longings as it flowed.

The musician had to be in the great hall, whoever it was.

There, he found Priscilla perched upon a wooden stool in front of the blazing hearth. She held a strange looking lute under her chin. Instead of plucking its strings, she was drawing what looked like a smallish bow across them. The patient hand that held the bow arched alternately up, then down with each sorrowful note.

The song was truly magnificent. It was as if she were somehow transporting the loneliness of mist-laden fields right through the castle walls. The emotions her instrument provoked were as opposing a mixture as the cold stones that cooled one side of her body while the heat from the fire warmed the other.

After a minute, the bow slid to a halt, and she lowered the strange lute.

"Priscilla," he said softly, walking toward her.

"Aidan! I didn't know you were there."

"And I didn't know you played so well! That was beautiful. What is that instrument?"

"It's my *vielle*. Father sent it over this morning. I told you I played, remember?"

He did remember, but he'd not understood what a *vielle* was, nor had he really grasped the level of her talent. "That was beautiful," he repeated, and she blushed.

He reached into his pocket and withdrew a small leather pouch. It held something he'd wanted to give her for quite a while but had been waiting for the right opportunity.

He held it out to her.

Cocking a speculative eyebrow, she took the pouch and opened it.

Inside was a gleaming, golden cross with a small sapphire embedded in its center. Eight more blue gems were distributed among the tips of its four branches.

The goldwork was delicate. The tiny rims holding the gems in place on the branches had the appearance of miniature crowns. The inner ends of the four branches, where they connected with the center, were formed into small hearts surrounding a fleur-de-lis.

The thin chain that bore it was not leather, but consisted of tiny, golden links interrupted regularly by yellow topaz and more small sapphires. Where the cross met the chain, two more sapphires had been embedded side by side. Up the chain and to the left from the double blue gems was a topaz, but on the right side was a single violet amethyst. It was the only purple gem on the whole piece, and it had struck Aidan as odd.

In fact, the whole cross had stood out to him as a special item from the first day he'd seen it. It had been among the loot they'd recovered from a traveling knight they'd accosted while Aidan was still with the outlaws.

He'd kept it for all these months, waiting for the right time to give it to her. He'd been tempted to do it the day she rode off with him away from her father's house, and again on their wedding day, but for some reason had not either time. However, today, after hearing her song, he found he could not bear the thought of her not having it for another minute.

She gasped.

"This is . . . it's beautiful, Aidan."

She turned it over several times, examining the facets. "I've never seen anything like it. It must be a very expensive piece. Wherever did you get it?"

"Oh . . . you don't want to know."

"All right," She laughed.

She rose and gave him a pressing kiss that warmed him through and through.

He longed to taker her in an embrace and remove her upstairs.

So, he did just that.

Chapter 38

Priscilla stepped around a mud puddle in the courtyard and laid her hand in Aidan's. Her delicate fingers were cool to the touch.

She placed her foot on the small step so Aidan could boost her up into the wagon, but he stopped short. Something unusual had caught his eye.

A man was in the stocks.

A peasant whose head drooped toward the ground in either shame or an unsuccessful attempt at sleep.

Aidan turned to the guard by the gate. "Who put that man in the stocks?"

He knew *he* had not issued any such disciplinary action and no one else would dare assume such authority, or so he had believed.

The man-at-arms snapped to attention and bobbed his head. "It was Father Osbert, sire."

"The priest? On what grounds?"

"I do not know."

There was one way to find out. He strode purposefully toward the stone-built church across the plaza separating the castle from the town. Priscilla followed him.

They entered the darkened sanctuary and found Osbert sweeping the front of the church. When he saw the baron, the brown-robed priest rose up and folded his arms across his chest, entwining his hands in the opposite sleeves as he poised to greet.

He was a slim, narrow-faced man with a long, hatchet-shaped nose to match. All bone, no muscle.

"Sir Aidan and Lady Priscilla, to what do I owe the pleasure?"

"You put a man in the stocks. Why?"

"He was caught in possession of the sacred Scriptures translated into English."

"That is not a crime."

"Of course, it is! The church prohibits the translation of Scripture into the crasser languages of the people."

Aidan gritted his teeth. "Has the church officially banned it now? I had not heard. Even if it had, that would not make it a crime then, would it?"

"Of course, the church has . . ."

"When? Which council?"

"There have been . . ."

"And what is the 'church' so afraid of, pray tell? I've read the Gospels myself and they are full of truth."

The priest gasped audibly. "You would flaunt the authority of the church so . . ."

"God gives authority to every believer, Father Osbert," Priscilla stepped in. "His Word is for all His children."

"I'll not be lectured by a woman," he sputtered.

Aidan stepped forward aggressively, fuming. "You will not speak to Lady Priscilla that way, priest!" He stabbed his finger at the cleric. "She is the lady of this barony, and you will respect her. And I warrant she knows more about the Scriptures than you'll ever manage."

Osbert shut his mouth and reddened, chastened and embarrassed by his lapse of protocol.

"The next time you think to lock somebody in the stocks, Osbert, you'd better check with me first," Aidan said.

"What are you going to do?"

But Aidan had already turned with his lady in tow and was storming back toward the castle. The priest carried after them shouting and fussing, vainly trying to get Aidan to stop. Aidan ignored the man the entire way. Once they reached the courtyard, Aidan addressed the guards.

"Release that man!" he commanded, pointing to the peasant.

"What?" cried Osbert. "How dare you supersede the judgment of the church!"

"It is not the church who put that man in the stocks, Osbert, just you. And I'll supersede your judgment any day of the week."

The guards released the catch and the peasant straightened awkwardly, rubbing the life back into his wrists and neck.

"Sir Aidan, you have no right! I will see . . ."

Aidan had had enough. His face hardened against the priest.

"Put this man in his place!" he ordered.

"What?" Osbert cried.

The men-at-arms hesitated.

"Now!" Aidan called.

The two guards each grabbed Osbert by an arm and dragged him across the grass, his limp feet kicking fruitlessly in an effort to stop their progress. They forced his neck into the slot and locked the bar down over it and his hands.

"Blasphemy! The bishop will hear of this!" He screamed, full of bluster and spewing.

"Blasphemy? Not hardly. You will be free to tell the bishop whatever you want, after you've gotten out that is, and that won't happen until you've repented. Now shut your trap or I'll have you gagged."

The priest saw his threats were having no effect and he feared the gag, so he shut up and resigned himself to trying to kill Aidan with his eyes.

Aidan and Priscilla mounted the carriage and the driver rolled out the gate and through the town, leaving the fuming cleric behind.

"Will he be all right?" Priscilla asked.

"He'll be fine. He'll calm down after a while."

"He'll never forgive you, though. That was a bit much don't you think? Punishing a priest? We don't really need a problem with the church, do we?"

"Why, my dear," he replied, cocking a smile her way, "and here I was so sure you would approve."

She laughed. "I do, I do. It was just so unexpected. I know *he* was caught off guard, that's for sure. It needed to be done, but no one's ever dared."

"It'll be all right. I'll make a stop along the way that will help. In the meantime, should we ask your father to come out and recite Scripture to him while he's in the stocks?"

She laughed even harder.

"That's probably a bit much," she said.

***

St. Alban's looked as it always did. Its small frontage gave the appearance of a simple, forest cottage enveloped by vines and shrubbery. Its door, however, led to a sprawling monastery complex that a first-time visitor would never expect lay beyond it.

Most of the monks were out in the fields, which was not a surprise for this time of day, but Aidan found Prior Andrew inside.

"Well, well," the prior said, smiling broadly, "This must be the lovely Lady Priscilla I've heard so much about."

Priscilla curtseyed.

"It is," Aidan beamed.

"Very good! It's a pleasure to make your acquaintance, madame. You must be quite the woman to be willing to take this one on."

She laughed, "I try to keep him in line, but it's a job."

Aidan mocked a grimace but laughed with her.

"So, Aidan, to what do I owe this pleasure?" Andrew asked.

Aidan explained about what had just happened with Osbert.

The prior's face darkened and then lightened again several times during the telling.

"Aidan, Aidan . . . what you have done? I don't know what to say…but I *do* know that Osbert. He's a cruel and legalistic man, not one who should be a priest to be sure, but nevertheless he is a man of the cloth. This will be construed as an attack upon the church." He shook his head.

"He put a man in the stocks for reading the Scriptures!"

"I know, but as *you* well know, there are many in the church who do not want the common people reading God's Word."

"It was here in St. Alban's where I first learned to appreciate the Gospels. Surely, you would want others to read them as well."

"The bishop will not take kindly to your action, Aidan. You have stepped into his realm of authority."

"Most of the bishops have sided with Queen Maud against Stephen. They will know of my support for her."

"But yours hasn't. Roger de Clinton is a staunch ally of Stephen's."

Aidan was firm. "I will cross that bridge when I get to it. For now, I have done what I have done."

Andrew closed his mouth and crossed his arms across his belly. What Aidan said was true. What was done, was done.

"And I assume you are here to ask me for something? Otherwise, you would not be bringing this to my attention."

"I would like to ask you to send either Brother Aelfric or Brother Geoffrey to conduct services at the church in Becca's Well. I plan to run Osbert out of town."

Priscilla gasped. He hadn't shared that part of the plan with her. Andrew's eyebrows shot up in surprise.

"What you are asking . . . this is not done."

"I know, prior. But I trust you and I trust them. I do not trust Osbert. Shouldn't God's house be attended by someone who is actually His man?"

The prior considered this and then nodded once. "It's hard to argue with logic so basic. I'll send someone."

"Thank you, prior."

Chapter 39

In May, Eric and Tom asked Aidan if he would allow them to hold weekly markets in their enfeoffed villages. They explained their people were actually the ones behind the request because traveling back and forth to Becca's Well took an entire day.

Becca's Well held the only charter from the king allowing a Market Day, so Aidan didn't technically have the legal right to say yes.

Currently, the people from the barony's outlying villages had to travel to Becca's Well every week to purchase produce and whatever else they might need that they couldn't provide for themselves.

This was normal practice across England. A market town was the town most closely associated with the castle, and the market was intended to guarantee increased income for the overlord.

At the time Aidan had taken over the manor, there'd only been about 80 to 100 people remaining in each of their villages, which wasn't even close to enough to support a market.

Since then, two things had changed though. First, the population of most of the lesser villages had grown to over 200 people each. A few even had more than 300.

Second, Aidan had introduced economic freedom to his people in many ways, and now they were seeing no reason why those economic freedoms shouldn't carry forward to other areas too.

Aidan found himself wanting to agree. Why shouldn't villagers be able to buy the vegetables or cloth they wanted in their own village instead of traveling all day to Becca's Well once a week for the same privilege?

Nicholas pointed out to him that if such markets were allowed to pop up spontaneously with respect to the demand of their respective populations, those markets would likely be much smaller than the one in Becca's Well, but they still could have the effect of driving prices down across the board. The merchants in Becca's Well would be hard pressed to ask a higher price for an item if word got around that it could be acquired in a nearby village for less.

Thomas Weaver, representing the merchants of Becca's Well, passionately disagreed.

He claimed that at least half of the business done in Becca's Well each week came from these outlying villagers.

He argued that if Aidan approved Eric and Tom's proposal, it could bankrupt his merchants closer to home.

"Many of us would have to close our shops," Thomas concluded.

Aidan could see his friend was truly frightened by the concept.

"We expect more people to immigrate to Becca's Well over the next few months," Aidan offered. "Even if you were to lose significant business temporarily, you'd probably regain it soon just from that."

"Plus," Nicholas countered, "What you're saying is that we should prevent some people from the opportunity to prosper in order to protect the incomes of certain others. Where is the justice in that?"

"Tis no justice if we all go broke," Thomas answered testily, resigning himself to the way he saw the decision was going.

Nicholas softened his voice. "I'd think some of your merchants might be inspired to send apprentices to the outlying villages on a rotating basis. That might actually end up earning more for you that way."

The new idea caused Thomas' face to brighten a bit.

"Eric, Tom, consider your request approved," Aidan said. "Now, if you'll excuse me, gentlemen, I'd like to have a word with Thomas alone."

The others left the room.

Aidan laid his arm across Thomas' shoulders as he escorted his friend toward the front of the keep.

"Aidan, you should know, some of the merchants have been murmuring about going to the king over this."

Aidan dropped his arm and stopped. Market towns were chartered by the king himself, and no village or town was supposed to operate one without the king's approval.

"Then, I suggest you remind them of the prosperity I have brought them so far with my policies," Aidan said. "If they bring the king into this, they will find themselves much poorer, for many things will stop. Anyway, the king is currently distracted and does not have time for these matters. Please convey to them some of Nicholas' ideas and ask them to trust me for a little while to see how it goes."

Thomas nodded.

***

Brother Geoffrey arrived to take over the parish church.

At first, he acted quite timid, hesitant to take charge, mostly because of the unconventional manner in which he'd come into the responsibility. Yet, deep down, he was secretly happy for the opportunity to lead something outside the priory. Prior Andrew was a good prior, but there could only be one of those in a monastery, so there wasn't much room for aspiring leaders like Geoffrey to grow.

To say that Father Osbert had not wanted to leave under Aidan's orders would be a significant understatement.

As much as Geoffrey was excited by the new venture, so was Osbert loathe to give up his place. Of course, his rebellion against it was exacerbated by Aidan's lack of authority to make such a change.

It didn't matter though. Aidan made it clear to Osbert that if he did not clear out on his own, he would be hog-tied and dragged out of town behind a horse. Osbert didn't need to wait to see if Aidan was serious — he knew he was — so he decided to retain his dignity and leave, but there was no doubt he'd be taking the matter straight to the bishop.

Many from Becca's Well had already brought Geoffrey chickens and vegetables and even baked pies to welcome him. Eating so well was not something he'd expected when he left the priory, but he intended to enjoy it as long as it lasted!

This particular morning, he'd decided to sweep out the chancel (the area around the altar). It had been only a short while since Osbert left, but dust had already begun to build up.

He was about halfway done when Aidan's cheerful voice interrupted his cleaning.

"So good to see you here, Geoffrey!" he called.

The monk turned with a smile. They embraced. "Happy to serve," he replied.

"Did Osbert leave you a mess?" Aidan asked.

"It's not so bad. Osbert seems to have been an orderly man if nothing else. Just normal cleaning."

"Listen, I need to ask you a favor."

"Name it."

"Would you be willing to teach some of the people to read?"

The minister didn't immediately respond.

He liked the idea. Parish priests often spent time educating peasants who showed an interest in learning. What was not customary was for a lord to request it.

"Why?"

"Well . . . because I want them to be able to read the Scriptures like I did at the priory when you sheltered me."

Geoffrey squeezed his eyes shut.

He'd been afraid this was where Aidan was going. Back then, he hadn't even been sure it was a good idea to let any layman read the Gospels in English, even a noble.

While the church had not explicitly prohibited translations of Scripture in the common man's tongue, most clerics frowned upon it severely, afraid of false doctrines that might arise from the uneducated reader or a bad translation.

Still, he sympathized with Aidan's heart. He knew the words were life.

"Do you realize the magnitude of what you're asking?"

"Yes," Aidan nodded. "Priscilla agrees with me. She feels just as strongly. How can we withhold God's Word from the people?"

"Educating people has a way of giving them a mind of their own . . ."

"I know, and that can only help Falconer manor, can't it?" Aidan smiled. "Better minds birth better ideas."

"Very well. I'll do it. But if the bishop comes looking for me, I'm sending him straight over to the castle to see *you*."

"Fair enough!"

***

As the summer waxed hot, Alan and Adelard approached Aidan with a new idea.

Within a few months, they'd realized, so many crops had been planted, there wouldn't be anywhere near enough traveling merchants visiting Becca's Well to buy it all, nor enough wagons to transport it to other market towns.

When the spring crops were ready for harvest, an inability to transport them could mean a huge failure for the barony as foodstuffs rotted on the side of the road.

The two knights wanted to go into the wagon business together. But they needed Aidan to fund the venture.

He saw their point. As it was, Aidan already needed more carts than currently existed just to move rock from the quarry to the castle's many building projects.

They asked if he could loan them the money to build the extra wagons needed. They planned to construct an entire fleet of them and promised to operate the carts free of charge to the castle for help with construction projects as long as they weren't needed for transporting crops.

At harvest time, Alan and Adelard would then rent out the wagons and drivers to tenants so they could move their crops to markets in other towns where they could get better prices. They also promised Aidan to pay off the loan in full with interest after the winter wheat came in.

So, Aidan would gain the free use of the carts for his building projects ongoing, plus interest on the loan.

It sounded like a good idea, so Aidan agreed.

The state of chaos across England had reached such a level the king's justice could not be appealed to for any matter. His enforcement of the royal laws had virtually ended. The number of corrupted soldiers plundering and ravaging the countryside everywhere had become dramatic. Women were raped, silver stolen, houses burned, and peasants were tortured.

Yet, Aidan's organized militias held up well against attempted forays on Falconer lands. The errant warriors expected easy pickings from an unarmed citizenry as they found elsewhere. Instead, in the territory under Aidan's control, they encountered a people not only armed but having some actual combat training.

The amateurish levels of resistance his people were able to present proved to be enough to send the brigands scampering away in search of safer targets. Word soon got out that Falconer Manor was a place best avoided by outlaw types, and the attacks diminished, though they never quite ceased entirely.

Thus, Aidan's barony became an oasis of law and order amidst the chaos. Which, unbelievably, could not have come at a better time for Aidan.

As John Steward predicted, more and more families streamed onto the manor throughout the summer, but now the incentive to immigrate was not only financial in nature, but a matter of safety. The number of newcomers had peaked so fast the space available for them had almost run out.

Alan called for a council, so Aidan summoned the other knights.

"I've run out of fields to offer these people," Alan said. "Five more families showed up in Pilsley, and I don't have anywhere to put them."

"I'm facing the same shortly," Eric agreed. "I only have three unoccupied fields left. Those will be gone in a few days."

Aidan frowned. "Tom?"

"I ran out of room last week," Tom admitted.

"The people in Becca's Well are asking for permission to clear more land from the forest," William said. "I think it's the only option. We only need so many blacksmiths and fullers."

Aidan's frown deepened. The king's forests were never to be touched, and all forests were the king's forests. Violating them carried the death penalty in most cases. The king normally maintained a small army of foresters wandering his realm to ensure the sanctity of the forest law remained inviolate . . . but then again Stephen was distracted . . . *and it had been quite a while since anyone had even seen a forester.*

Plus, death was a punishment meted out to peasants who poached deer, not knights and barons who ruled decent-sized baronies. If called to account, and in today's environment that looked less and less likely every day, the most one of his position could be expected to face would be loss of land or title.

Which was the risk he already faced for supporting Maud. On the other hand, the possibility of being attacked by Richard and a vengeful Earl of Chester was much more real and certain, *one that he would only overcome through growth.* Growth that would not be possible to continue without doing something radical.

"Do it," he said.

They hesitated, looking at each other questioningly.

"My apologies, sire. Do *what* exactly?" Adelard asked. "Allow them to clear a few fields? How many acres? Surely if we are to do this, we must do it on a small scale."

Aidan shook his head. "Tell everyone they are allowed to clear all they want, provided they can man it. I've already openly declared myself an enemy of this king and angered one of his favorite bishops. Clearing forest won't make my position any worse. Stephen has more important things to worry about than whether or not my peasants are clearing land. He never hunts this far north anyway, and sufficient hunting ground is all he would care about."

Several of the knights paled.

"Are you sure, milord?"

"Absolutely. There will be no repercussions, and if there are, they will fall on me alone."

"But after the war, if the most unfortunate happened and Stephen were to overcome Maud, wouldn't this hurt your chances to be forgiven past alliances?"

"If Stephen wins and he still wants my support badly enough to forgive me for supporting Maud, whether or not I cut down some trees won't factor into it."

They nodded and affirmed they would carry out his instructions.

"However, tell your tenants I want them to obey the fallow field rule from here on out. One third of all fields need to be left fallow each year to ensure fertility."

They nodded and started to leave, but Aidan stayed them.

"You've yet to hear the good news!" he said. "I've been looking over John's latest projections, and they're so good I've decided I can afford to pay each of you a shilling a day now."

A shilling was equal to twelve pennies, which was twelve times more per day than the average laborer.

"Why . . . *that's over a pound a month!*" Eric exclaimed.

"Your responsibilities are increasing by the day," Aidan continued, "It's a lot to keep up with. You've worked hard and deserve it for a job well done. Of course, you'll still receive your portion of the profit made from the lands under your care as well."

"I'd say *that* calls for a celebration!" said William.

Of everyone, Eric and Tom were the most elated. Just a year ago, they never could have imagined a pair of young outlaws like them, most assuredly destined for nothing more than a noose hanging from a tree, would end up knighted and serving one of the kindest noblemen in England — and growing rich in the process.

Aidan may not have enjoyed it at the time, but Eric and Tom blessed that day when they'd first helped Red rob him in the forest.

Destiny was a tricky thing.

Chapter 40

Switching feet, Fulke huffed hot breath into his cupped hands and stamped the ground in an attempt to keep his blood flowing. This morning had been a typical sweltering, mid-summer morning, but colder, northern winds had blown in all afternoon. By nightfall, the climate felt more like late autumn. Perhaps if he'd known to dress warmer tonight, the temperature would have been tolerable. For heaven's sake, he could almost see his breath.

This job was a miserable business anyway, no matter the weather. Standing guard over the tunnel extension just to keep it a secret? He'd signed onto Falconer Manor eight months ago as a man-at-arms, but for seven of those months, he'd done nothing but stand out here in the dark — often in the *cold* — with nothing to cure his boredom. Frankly, the routine was getting old.

His wife had pressed him to uproot their family from Wirksworth when they'd heard about the new opportunities and unusual baron in Becca's Well. She'd pestered him and pestered him until he finally agreed, so here they were.

He had to admit, though, the pay was *really* good, especially for his line of work. He just hadn't known he'd be staring at black nothingness all night every night and stomping his feet to keep his toes from freezing off.

Once summer arrived, it had gotten better . . . but then a night like tonight happens. Thankfully, the progress on Aidan's tunnel was going fast, so maybe this would be over soon.

The reason *he* was blessed every single night with this exceptionally unpleasant job instead of rotating with other men-at-arms was because of the blasted secrecy surrounding the project. Only he and a few other guards had been entrusted with knowledge of its existence and were sworn to silence. The baron didn't want any more guards involved than had to be.

All anyone else knew was that the tunnel's secret entrance had been filled in months ago. So, as far as the villagers were concerned, the tunnel was gone.

And they'd been successful in keeping the matter quiet so far. The diggers shoveled quietly each night. They didn't speak and used a single torch for light. They surrounded the work area with black curtains on poles as tall as a man to block the torchlight from being seen from a distance.

Even knowing what was going on, Fulke could barely make out their sounds from his post. Not to mention Sir Aidan was paying them double what he paid his other men-at-arms, which tended to keep lips glued shut even more solidly than a vow.

The extra pay went a long way toward making him forget about his numb toes.

He flexed his fingers around the bladed pike in his hand, otherwise known as a halberd. It was the weapon he felt most comfortable with, having been trained with it since a boy, and he felt it suited him best in this role.

Fulke blinked several times to clear the cold moisture building up in the corners of his eyes. The crispness of the dewy night air was fresh in his lungs, and the sky was clear. The stars overhead gleamed like tiny, glittering crystals against the black.

All was still.

The cool weather had the effect of stifling much of the activity of the cicadas and other chirping insects. If not for that, he might never have heard the unusual scraping sound.

He peered into the darkness, straining to see what had caused it, but there wasn't enough light.

Somewhere on his left, something had scuffed against a rock, as if someone were trying to slip stealthily toward him but had mis-stepped. He moved forward into the dark.

Still, he saw nothing.

Nor did he hear another sound.

Yet, he could not take a chance. The clandestine nature of the tunnel was vital to the survival of everyone on the manor.

"Halt! Who goes there?" he cried out, fishing for a reply.

His verbal line got a solid tug.

Whoever it was abandoned all efforts to remain undetected. Rapid footsteps erupted from the field to his left. The runner sounded like he was about forty feet away and headed for the road. They would reach it just ahead of where Fulke was stationed, so he snatched his pike with a firm grip and burst into a sprint to intercept the intruder.

His gut twisted when he realized the man might get away. The runner was fast — just as fast as Fulke, if not faster — and he'd gotten a head start. His faint shadow flowed out onto the road twenty feet ahead of him.

Then, the fleeing man's form sped up the darkened path. To Fulke's great frustration, he saw he wasn't going to be able to close the gap. In fact, the intruder was already distancing himself. And Fulke knew he couldn't keep up his current pace for long.

So, he stopped short, planted his feet firmly, and flipped his halberd around in his hand. His shoulder muscles strained with tension as he pulled back, pouring energy into the missile. Then, he launched the halberd like a spear, blunt end first.

The shaft sailed through the air and landed exactly where intended, right in the center of the intruder's back.

The darkened form cried out, stumbled, and then collapsed to the ground, writhing under unexpected pain.

Fulke was upon him before he could recover.

He grabbed the man's shoulder and flipped him over.

Nothing more than a peasant from Becca's Well. His face was twisted in pain, but Fulke still recognized him. He didn't know the man's name, but he'd seen him around.

He yanked the peasant roughly to his feet and marched him toward the castle.

***

Aidan awoke to the sound of someone hammering on his door.

If looks could kill, the messenger would have fallen over dead as soon as Aidan opened it. As it was, he certainly repented of the manner he'd chosen to get Aidan's attention.

After hearing the reason for the interruption, Aidan met with his men in the great hall, bleary-eyed, still unhappy his sleep had been cut short so rudely.

They thrust the boy, because that is what he was really was, a boy, to the floor at Aidan's feet.

The lad was tall and lanky, with toned, stretched-out muscles that implied he already had several years of hard work under his belt, though he couldn't be more than fifteen years old.

"We caught him snooping out in Fallow Field, sire." The man-at-arms said.

"Look at me, boy," Aidan commanded.

The young man turned his dirty face up to meet Aidan's gaze.

"I know you from somewhere. What is your name?"

"Mark, sire. I work as a laborer on Ysabella's fields."

The recognition clicked. "Ah yes. I knew I'd seen you before," Aidan said. "What were you doing wandering the fields this late at night?"

"I . . . uh . . . I don't know, milord. I could not sleep. I went for a walk. I saw nothing, I promise."

"Tis not true!" Fulke interjected. "He was coming *from* the . . . eh . . . the project, not going toward it. He had to see."

"He would not have mentioned seeing nothing if, indeed, he'd seen nothing," Aidan confirmed. "Don't lie to me again, boy, or I'll have your tongue out. Now, what did you see?"

Mark shriveled under his stare and mumbled a response so low he could barely be understood. "That they are building a tunnel . . ."

Aidan expelled his breath and sat down.

"Do you work for my uncle?" He asked.

"No, Sir Aidan! I swear it!"

"Then why would you go roaming around in the middle of the night like that, right where we're working?"

"A month ago, I heard tale of sentries stationed in the fields at night, but no one knew why. I don't sleep well sometimes . . . and . . . I . . . I get bored . . . so I started sneaking over to see what they were doing." He straightened and grew excited. "But, I swear, sire, I was just curious! I have not told a soul, nor will I!"

"On how many different nights did you go out?"

"For a couple of weeks," the boy mumbled, barely intelligible once more.

"A couple of weeks! And this is the first night they caught you? Doesn't say much for our sentries, does it?" Aidan glared at the soldiers.

"I'm very quiet, milord, don't blame them!" he squealed.

"I will blame them if I want to, boy! You will hold your tongue. Now be quiet while I figure out what to do with you."

After an awkward minute, Aidan said, "You will take a vow of silence before Brother Geoffrey. The safety of this entire village depends on you keeping your mouth shut."

"Yes, sire." He bobbed his head.

"And you will have to join the castle guard where we can keep an eye on you."

The young man's eyes lit up, but he hesitated. It would mean greater pay for him, but Ysabella was in need of his help.

"Don't worry about Ysabella," Aidan said, as if reading his mind, "She'll find someone else to lend a hand. And you Fulke," he pointed at the man-at-arms, "I'm charging you and your men with training this lad well. He's your responsibility."

"Yes, sire."

"You guards *will* do your jobs better from here on out, do you hear me? We cannot afford any more leaks."

"Yes, sire."

"And figure out where that rumor about the sentries came from."

"Yes, sire."

They bowed and marched the boy back out of the hall to see if he could be made into a man.

Chapter 41

Ysabella stood and arched her back against the aching muscles in the small of her spine. She'd been bent over too long.

She surveyed her fields, dusting her hands on the sides of her hunter green skirt. The idea she would ever have her own land to work was something she never could have imagined a few years ago. Living meagerly in a woodsman's hovel among the outlaws, she'd considered herself lucky to not have been forced into selling her body for survival.

She smiled at the sight of the neatly plowed rows before her. Seed in the ground. A sure and bountiful harvest. *Her own land.*

She was finally safe.

Her laborer, Mark, had not shown up for work this morning, which had irritated her, but it wouldn't be the first time. He'd asked her for an advance on his pay a few days ago, and she'd foolishly given him a few pennies. Now he'd likely gone off and sloshed himself with ale. She'd be lucky to get a good day's work out of him when he finally got around to finding his way to her fields.

He was too young and too immature to handle life's responsibilities yet, but her heart went out to him. Being an orphan as she was, she tended to give him considerable leeway on that cause alone.

A hint of movement just inside the forest line momentarily caught her eye. A glimpse of unnatural lines peeking through the leaves.

She peered closer, trying to make out the shape.

It was big, whatever it was.

A deer maybe?

The shadows and the distance made it difficult to identify.

Suddenly, a glint of light flashing off metal made her heart lurch. Then, the spot of metal became the full form of a mail-clad solider as he emerged from the woods into the sunlight.

She retreated instinctively. She hadn't seen of any of the town's militiamen yet this morning.

She was alone. The man had seen her. And he was advancing.

She whipped around and ran to flee back to her house, but almost tripped over herself in shock as she saw a second soldier stood between her and the cottage, not more than thirty feet away.

This one was close enough she could make out the details of his face. Its lines were smeared with dirt and cruelty. A nasty leer lurked in his eyes.

She knew what that look meant. She screamed.

She didn't stop running but made a mad attempt to curve her course away from him. He lurched forward to intercept her.

In a matter of seconds, he'd seized both her upper arms in his roughened claws. Pain shot through her shoulders as she struggled against his clear and vulgar intentions.

Out of the corner of her eye, she could still see the first soldier. He'd also broken into a run toward her.

She darted a desperate glance his way, but any fleeting hope he might actually be coming to her rescue evaporated. The vicious avarice for flesh flamed just as brightly in his eyes as in those of his companion.

Her captor laughed and shook her. She was helpless to keep her head from bobbling about. She pushed and pulled and strained for freedom, but to no avail.

Terrible dread like an inevitable flood overwhelmed her.

He slapped her across the side of the face hard enough to knock her down. The sharp echo of it cracked the morning air.

She stayed afoot only because he would not let her fall. His tight grip was a rude, hurtful intrusion under her arms. Hot, salty tears spilt down her cheeks in spite of herself. She didn't want to give him the satisfaction, but she couldn't help it.

When his partner arrived, the soldier holding her cast her to the ground and pounced with his full weight to pin her flat before she could scramble away.

The back of her head struck a small rock. Slivers of piercing pain raced through her skull, dazing her.

To her horror, she realized the ghoul intended to take her right here in the field. He was scratching at her skirts while his friend leered on with an evil grin, impatient for his turn.

In desperation, Ysabella renewed her efforts to escape with vigor — and she did *almost* break free — but the man straddling her reared back and raised his fist to pummel her full on in the face.

In the split second before he could release his blow's power, a solid, wet thud sounded, punctuated by the tip of an arrowhead suddenly protruding from his chest.

He grunted, gasped, and then collapsed upon her limply.

Dead.

Revolted, she rolled his body off her to the side and jumped to her feet.

The other soldier's mouth fell open in surprise. He managed to turn his head toward the direction from which the arrow had come before a second bolt passed through his neck.

He, too, spilled to the ground lifeless.

Still bound by the horror of the moment, Ysabella rashly scrubbed at her arms to rid herself of the taint of their touch.

A rider bearing an empty bow was speeding toward her at full gallop.

She struggled to process what had just happened, as stunned by the sudden turn of events as she was by the initial attack.

Then, she realized the rider was Aidan.

Her heart leapt and swelled with something entirely opposite of what she'd felt when she'd first seen the rogue soldiers.

Aidan's tall form bounced rhythmically as he cantered to a stop.

With a deep exhalation of breath that carried away her fears, her spirit melted.

Adrenaline was still rushing through her though, making her fingers tingle and shake. Swooning might actually prove to be a nice relief from her current upheaval of emotions.

Aidan had been on his way to let Ysabella know he'd conscripted her laborer, Mark, when he'd spotted the brigands.

Immediately, he'd spurred his mount into a full charge. His response had been so natural and focused by his anger that he hadn't even had to think about his shots as the missiles hummed from his bow.

He only regretted not being able to stop them before they'd caused her so much distress.

Now, he found himself staring, unable to tear his eyes from her.

Something about their sudden coming together, the excitement, the way her chest heaved breathlessly from the mingling of fear and exertion — it all fascinated him.

The top hem of her skirt clung to her narrow waist. Its folds flowed voluptuously over her other, rounder curves. The strong line of her jaw seemed so sleek, so true; it was as if the very essence of her physical nature was screaming for his attention without her even uttering a word.

He'd never denied that she was beautiful, nor that he cared for her, but his heart was not free to wander — and he would not release it.

With a willful effort, he tore his gaze away and glanced around, as if searching for more threats, giving his emotions time to calm, though he already knew no one else was in the field.

"Aidan . . ." She breathed.

"Are you all right?" he asked, still not looking at her.

"Yes, I'm fine." She'd noticed the flicker behind his eyes, the way he'd stared at her. The knowledge her form had pleased him elated her, but that was tempered by reluctance and guilt. He was a married man, and she genuinely liked Lady Priscilla. She had no intention of provoking him now, nor would he ever fail to uphold his vows, she knew, but the knowledge he found her desirable still made her happy.

"How did you know?" she asked.

"I didn't. I was coming to tell you I drafted Mark into the castle guard."

"Oh."

Aidan surveyed the bodies on the ground. "I'll send someone to collect them for burial. You'll need someone else to help you in your fields, won't you?"

"Oh . . . yes . . . but don't worry about me. I'll manage," she said demurely.

"Very well." Aidan reined his horse around to return to the castle.

"Aidan?"

"Yes?"

"Thank you."

He nodded, shot her a sincere, but regulated smile, and then rode off.

***

Late that afternoon, the mood inside the castle was not pleasant.

On his way back from speaking with Ysabella, Aidan had stopped in town to inform Thomas of the attack. From there, word had spread quickly through Becca's Well and circulated among the castle guards and servants. When the news reached Priscilla's ears, her pretty and normally unlined face darkened into a vibrant anger.

She surged into the great hall with a barely veiled fury and interrupted Aidan's meeting with a merchant from a neighboring manor. Seeing the unusual tempest brewing in her, Aidan immediately excused himself and escorted her to another room.

"Do you mean to shame me, *Sir* Aidan? How dare you?" she demanded.

"Priscilla, what in the world are you talking about?" He was genuinely flabbergasted, trying to understand the source of her wrath. He'd never seen her like this.

"I heard about your exploits this morning," she spat with contempt.

"And?" His eyebrows arched upward along with his level of confusion. She could only be talking about the rogue soldiers. He thought he'd performed quite heroically. So, why was she mad?

"I heard how you delivered that *Ysabella*. What *exactly* were you doing out there in that field alone with her?"

"N…nothing," he stuttered, not expecting this line of attack. "I hadn't even arrived when those men assaulted her. I saw it from a distance and rode in."

"But you were on your way to see her."

"Yes."

"I repeat, *why* exactly were you going to see her?"

"I went to tell her that we'd recruited her laborer into the castle guard and she'd have to find other help."

"*You* went to tell her that? *You* have time to take care of menial messages like that? Why didn't you send someone else?"

"Because I know her . . . from my time in the forest. She's a friend."

"See! I *know* that you know her from the forest. I heard how she threw herself at you . . ."

"Priscilla . . . darling, it's not like that . . ."

"Oh, really? She did not throw herself at you?"

He was losing ground fast in a battle he hadn't known was coming and was now scrambling for any kind of foothold.

"Well, yes, but if you know that, then you also know that I did not respond. I saved myself for you."

She seemed a bit mollified by that, but not completely.

"It's true. I could have been with her in the forest, in fact she was not the only one, but my heart was always yours. Even when we were apart, my heart has always belonged to you."

Her eyes flicked with uncertainty — an unusual state for her.

"So . . . maybe now you regret not taking advantage of the opportunity to bed her when you had it?" She cocked an eyebrow.

"No, I . . ."

"Are you sure? She *is* a beautiful woman. I've seen her."

"No, I . . ."

"Don't you lie to me! I know how the village men look at her."

"Priscilla," he sputtered, "this is not like you! What's the matter?"

She lowered her eyes and pursed her lips. When she spoke again, it was with a firm and resolved tone.

"Aidan, you may not *intend* to be entrapped by her, but I guarantee her feelings toward you have not changed. I do not wish to ever, and I mean *ever*, hear that you have been alone in the fields with her again. Is that clear enough?"

"Would you have preferred it if I'd not been there, and she'd been killed?" He asked, incredulous.

"Send one of your knights next time. Let someone else save her."

With that, she stormed from the room, leaving him dazed by the sudden whirlwind of unexpected emotion.

A couple of days filled with cold shoulders and fiery eyes passed before she warmed to him again, but by then, Aidan had gotten the message loud and clear.

Chapter 42

Richard swept a splatter of muck from his cheek with the tips of his fingers. A few years ago, he would have experienced a mild disgust for having been sullied, but now the grit upon his skin sent a flood of elation through him. Not because he enjoyed being dirty, but because he'd gained it through battle.

He noted with relish mud splatters also covered his once-white tunic . . . and thick crimson blood dripped slowly from his blade.

English blood.

Which didn't bother him at all.

He scraped the sword's edge across the grass at his feet to clean it before returning it to its scabbard.

"You're a *mess!*"

The Earl of Chester looked down on him with distaste from high on his destrier. Richard turned to face him and cocked an eyebrow.

"I guess the real question is why you are not?" He responded.

The earl jerked his head back as if he'd been slapped. A snarl formed on his lips, revealing his severe displeasure with the remark.

Earl Ranulf was not the biggest fan of King Stephen at the moment, not since the royal had given away his northern holdings with the same ease as one giving a piece of buttered bread to a child. Until Stephen restored his lands, Ranulf would provide knights as required, but he would not personally lead them into battle. They would fight, but he would remain behind the lines. He wasn't about to put his own life at risk for such a faithless sovereign.

Richard knew all this, but for him, the ongoing strife between Stephen and Maud had provided too rich an opportunity for a man to throw himself into the thick of it. Richard enjoyed the grime, sweat, and coppery smell of blood far too much to sit passively on the sidelines.

He only regretted that it was the blood of some random Englishman he was wiping on the grass instead of young Aidan's.

Nevertheless, though he held a growing disdain for Ranulf's unwillingness to dirty his hands, Richard knew better than to insult or anger the earl. Chester was his strongest ally and support. He should be working to curry that favor, not spit on it.

His patience was simply running thin. He itched to throw his reins back over what was rightfully his, to punish his young upstart of a nephew. And he was frustrated by how slowly Ranulf seemed to be moving toward aiding him in a more solid way.

He straightened and bowed formally at the waist.

"I do apologize. It was the heat of battle still burning in my veins that spoke just now. You deserve no rebuke."

The earl seemed mollified. "You'd do well to remember my grace and provision, Sir Richard. You have few friends aside from me."

That statement irked him, as Ranulf knew it would. He was twisting the dagger.

Richard knew other nobles indeed were sympathetic to his claim. Many felt threatened by the rumors of Aidan's unconventional methods and blatant disrespect for tradition. Ranulf was simply the most powerful of them, his best option to reclaim it, so Richard had tied his banner to the earl's mast.

Maybe he'd be wise to consider other options though.

A year prior, at the Battle of the Standard, Robert de Ferrers had been instrumental in achieving the victory for Stephen. In appreciation, the king had created a brand-new earldom for him and named him Robert the 1st Earl of Derby.

Of all the nobles irked by Aidan, he'd heard that the new Earl of Derby was the most concerned over the happenings at Becca's Well. Sir Robert was not only a close neighbor to the Falconer barony, but he was also a firm supporter of Stephen, not a waverer like Ranulf.

Richard decided to be sure to make the man's acquaintance at the first opportunity.

"That is true, and please, *do* know that I am *ever* grateful for your support, Ranulf. Yet, you would also do well to remember what a threat my nephew is to your own holdings. You, along with all the other neighboring baronies, have lost many paying tenants. Men who have moved to Falconer Manor because of the usurper's foolish policies. As long as he continues in his charge, you risk failed crops and a peasantry demanding higher pay.

"You know the tales of his growing armory. Do you think that is for defense alone? How long will it be before he casts his greedy eyes upon other lands? Or incites your peasants to revolt? I am your only hope for a claimant you can trust who can remove this thorn from your side."

Ranulf's eyes narrowed. He tolerated no one speaking to him in such a forthright manner, yet he could not deny the truth of Richard's words, so he tamped his anger back into place.

He glanced away. "I know you grow impatient, Richard," he admitted.

"How long must we wait?" Richard asked.

"The day draws near. My forces are still mobilized. We only await a break in this long stream of skirmishes so Stephen can release us from our duty long enough to act decisively. We are not the only ones — others also grow restless to get back to their lands. Maud's men can be no different."

"May justice come swiftly then," Richard bowed once more to top off his efforts at mollification.

The Earl of Chester glared down at him.

"Justice? There is no justice. Only power."

Chapter 43

Late August 1139 AD – Becca's Well

Almost a year and a half had passed since Aidan reclaimed his family's manor. Some of his people affectionately referred to his changes as "Aidan's Foolishness."

But he was elated.

The summer harvest was coming in, and yields were so much higher than expected. According to John, over 700 families resided on Falconer lands now, which meant over 3,000 people, including children. Far more than the manor had ever held before!

They were immigrating from other baronies, sometimes even when they weren't legally allowed to leave. The draw of Aidan's lenient policies were proving too much for many to resist.

When the rest of England had descended into lawlessness, why wouldn't a man risk flaunting authority for a chance at prosperity, and even security, somewhere else?

His tenants had first reaped the winter wheat they'd planted the previous Fall, then the barley sowed in Spring, and now the other Summer crops.

This last harvest was unprecedented.

Why? Because a record number of tenants had worked the lands, and those had worked harder and longer and tended more fields per man than ever before, not to mention the plentiful rains earlier in the year that had boosted growth.

Needless to say, John Steward's projections of Aidan's expected revenue had been significantly underestimated.

Rents were about to be paid. It looked like they would be filling the treasury back up much more than Aidan could have hoped. Still not quite enough to make up for his expenditures on all the building projects, but it was a good start.

Alan and Adelard had been right about there being a shortage of wagons at harvest time, and they'd not only made a pretty penny from wagon rentals, but Aidan had also protected his income and that of his people in the process.

Without enough wagons to export the crops, the local market in Becca's Well would have been flooded with an oversupply of goods, and prices would have hit rock bottom. And even then, given how much was being harvested, much of the crop would have remained unsold and rotted.

Without giving his knights the freedom to experiment and try new ventures, it could have all fallen in on itself.

On the town side, the merchants' fears had also proven unfounded. With all the new families immigrating to the manor, and the news of Aidan's policies spreading to other regions, the weekly market in Becca's Well was booming in spite of the additional markets that had sprouted up in its surrounding villages — and those were also off to a good start.

For Aidan, the best part was that he earned a percent of the profits of all the markets, not just the one.

Trees had fallen all summer long as newcomers kept opening up new fields. Aidan used a lot of the timber for his building projects and sold the rest to locals for the construction of new homes and merchant shops.

The money he received from those sales he kept separate from the rest of the treasury just in case the king ever demanded an accounting of what had been done with his trees. Should that happen, Aidan could turn the proceeds over to him without even blinking an eye.

All his knights were prospering. His men-at-arms and the castle servants seemed content as well. He paid better than neighboring baronies, and his lands were at peace. Wandering knights recently orphaned from their lords regularly appealed to become his vassals, but for the time being, he refused all, as he couldn't afford to take on more dependents yet.

Still, he made note of the names of several who impressed him, men of quality who had never participated in the raids plaguing England. He might call on them later.

They kept hearing about earls and barons who were torturing their peasants to force them into serfdom, or to reveal what little worldly wealth they might have managed to stash away under floorboards or in holes in the ground.

Such stories tore at him. This was the one duty of a lord — to protect his vassals from harm.

To torture them just to extract a few pennies, or to steal a freeman's wife was anathema to everything Aidan's father had taught him to hold dear.

On Falconer Manor, though, even random raids by wandering soldiers were on the decrease due to Aidan's militias. Word had gotten out that his tenants were armed.

His only frustration remained the slow pace of the city wall. The castle's improvements were just about finished, but there were simply not enough laborers to move the wall along faster.

All the newcomers wanted to plant crops.

He'd made the idea of managing fields too attractive. Aidan realized he was going to have to significantly increase the builders' and quarry workers' pay if he wanted to accelerate things. He hadn't done so yet because he'd been afraid of draining the treasury too quickly (and it was drained), but the unexpected boom in income now that the crops were in helped.

Still, he was going to need a *lot* more money if they were to finish it. A wall around the village was a much larger, much more expensive undertaking than the castle gate. It could take years to fund it at current levels. He'd just have to find a way to press forward until the pennies dried up.

Unfortunately, they were drawing close to winter, and he didn't know how much more building they could get done before temperatures dropped below the level where mortar would set well.

Regardless, who could deny Nicholas' proposals had been successful? Priscilla beamed with pride for her father, and for Aidan being brave enough to implement his radical ideas.

Aidan only hoped he would have enough time to fully establish himself before his enemies reared their formidable heads once more — and that King Stephen would not be among them — but if he was, that Maud would win her struggle.

***

Chester, England

The porter trembled as he announced the visitor to the Earl of Chester. A day prior, he'd mispronounced a baron's name during his introduction to the court, and his lord's spiked glances toward him had been feral ever since.

He steeled himself and puffed his chest in a manner as regal as he could muster.

"Baron John de Bayeux, sire."

Ranulf dismissed the servant with a flip of the hand and stood to greet the nobleman.

John de Bayeux was a baron with moderate holdings up in the hills to the northwest of Derby. He resided in Pilsbury Castle, a sturdy motte and bailey fortification.

"Greetings, John."

"And to you, Sir Ranulf." In a land where many nobles did not bother with personal grooming, Bayeux always made a point to maintain a highly polished appearance, and he dressed in finery beyond his probable means. His jet-black hair was streaked with grey and swept back in a voluminous coiffure. A crisp, triangular nose gave his face a sharp appearance, and his eyes were beady and black, yet glistened with alertness.

"To what do I owe the pleasure?"

"I come to speak with you regarding Aidan Falconer. I understand his uncle resides here in Chester?"

"You have heard correctly."

"As you know, his father, William, was always an odd duck, but at least he was a reasonable man. Young Aidan has become a veritable thorn in my side of late."

"Really? In what way?" Ranulf asked, feigning ignorance of the coming complaint.

In England, the title of earl was not held onto by the faint of heart, but by those determined to keep it through guile and cunning. Over the years, he'd become a master of manipulating men for his purposes and had learned to recognize an opportunity when one presented itself.

He knew that if you let a man think himself the author of an idea, you could achieve true commitment to its pursuit. So, with Bayeux, he played dumb.

"He's stealing my people," Bayeux blurted before forcibly calming himself.

The outburst was uncharacteristic enough to demonstrate his level of frustration.

"Serfs, free tenants, merchants, I'm losing them by the dozens. And those who remain are demanding higher wages because they hear what he is paying."

"Yes," Ranulf agreed, "I've lost a good number as well, though probably not nearly as many as you, given that your manor is closer. I'm surprised he has enough fields to feed them all."

"Have you not heard? He allows them to clear the king's forest. He's making *new* fields! If he continues at this pace, he'll overtake even Chester in power within a few years."

Ranulf experienced a twinge of anger at the comment, for he feared the same, but was loathe to admit it, and definitely did not appreciate someone voicing it out loud.

"I *am* shocked by the lad's boldness. Under normal circumstances, he wouldn't dare, but he must know how distracted the king is."

Bayeux nodded firmly.

"Surely you can ensure the return of your serfs easily enough, though," Ranulf added.

Bayeux shook his head. "The Sheriff of Nottingham is as distracted as the king, if not more so. On top of supplying troops for his majesty, he has outlaw problems of his own."

"Yes . . . I'd heard. But why do you tell *me* these things? Your fealty is to the Robert de Ferrers, is it not? Why doesn't *he* do something?"

"As you know, Falconer holds his lands directly from the king. The Earl of Derby has no authority. Only the sheriff could intervene."

"So, what do you propose we do about the situation?"

John pursed his lips and squinted, gauging the earl for receptiveness, but perceiving treachery lingering behind the other's eyes, he decided to venture it.

"If the king is too distracted to enforce the law of his forests, then I'd bet he's also too distracted to care if some of his noblemen laid siege to another, especially if the aggressors were his allies and the defenders were known to be supporters of Maud."

"You propose an alliance?" Ranulf cocked an eyebrow and grinned.

"Yes. I cannot defeat the boy by myself — he has become too strong already. Milord Robert de Ferrers is willing to commit resources if you join us. He is utterly faithful to Stephen and only has distaste for those who are not. If we were to combine the force of Derby with that of Chester, he could not prevail against the both of us."

The earl smiled greedily. "I think this plan is worthy of further discussion."

***

The ground trembled.

The sensation of instability under his feet was terrifying.

The rumble of hooves grew louder and louder until it resembled thunder.

Foggy tendrils of mist parted to reveal the pumping necks and heads of hundreds of stallions straining under their riders, muscles rippling with the effort, nostrils flaring, storming straight for him, eyes wide with the relentless power of their rush.

Piercing the thunderous cloud of hooves stabbing and slicing the soil were the sporadic cries of the warriors driving them, forceful calls for blood, their eyes flush with a determination to destroy.

They were almost upon him. Their blades rang with metallic scrapes as

they whipped them from their scabbards.
    The smoke . . .

Aidan awoke with a start.

He felt damp. His forehead was dripping with sweat. His bedclothes were moist.

Sunlight streamed through the small window in their bedchamber. Its light was strong enough Aidan knew the morning had begun.

Priscilla was gone from the bed. She'd probably left him to slumber in peace as she started her daily routine.

He threw on his tunic and went downstairs. With set jaw, he ignored the greetings of those he passed in the halls and exited the keep. He passed through the gatehouse and crossed the yard to the stone church. Geoffrey wasn't immediately visible, but he emerged when Aidan called his name.

"I've had a dream, Geoffrey." Aidan breathed.

The monk couldn't remember seeing Aidan so unnerved.

"Tell me about it," he said.

So, Aidan did. He told him of the storming horses, how they'd been obscured by a mist until they were almost upon him. He described the army and the fierceness of the warriors.

"What do you think it could mean?" He asked.

"What do *you* think it means?" Geoffrey countered.

"I don't know . . . I thought it might be a warning that we were going to be attacked."

"If I told you it meant something different, would you believe it?"

Aidan considered it.

"No," he finally said.

"Then, there you have it," Geoffrey replied. "God has already given you the meaning along with the dream. He's told you what it means in your heart."

Aidan clenched his teeth. "Then, I should take it seriously."

"I would."

Aidan began to pace.

"When will it happen? How can I be sure it will happen?"

"If it was strong enough to make you rush over here half-dressed, I'd say you should take it very seriously. As to when . . . I have no idea."

Aidan stopped and stared at him . . . then began pacing again in concent-rated silence.

"Do you remember anything else?" Geoffrey asked. "Any details that might help?"

Aidan thought hard. "Their shields . . . some bore red shields with a white lion. Others had silver covered in black horseshoes." He grimaced.

"What's the matter?" Geoffrey asked. "Do you know them?"

"I've never seen the silver shield before, but the red is the coat of arms of Ranulf of Chester."

"Ah."

Aidan paced for a minute more, then muttered a half-conscious thanks under his breath and returned to the castle.

Chapter 44

In the end, there just wasn't enough time.

When the invasion came, the city wall still wasn't finished, though it wasn't for a lack of trying. The villagers had worked with a fury. Aidan had even seen a pregnant woman carrying a baby in one arm and a pail of water for the workers in the other.

They all knew what was at risk.

Everything.

The day the attackers arrived, several gaps of a couple hundred feet remained, far too large for them to defend. At least the castle's gatehouse had been finished, so only Becca's Well itself was unprotected.

But it meant the people had to abandon their homes and take refuge within the castle walls. Their fields were vulnerable too, but there was no helping that. Not even if the city wall had been complete.

Thankfully, the tunnel had been completed and its entrance/exit disguised. If anyone needed to escape, Aidan was grateful to know they could.

As soon as the outlaws had spotted the army marching through New Haven Forest, Red had sent messengers to alert Aidan. They reported hundreds of soldiers: a variety of knights, men-at-arms, and bowmen.

Unfortunately, the army the outlaws had seen had only been one part of the enemy's forces: those under the banner of the Earl of Derby.

Sentries outside Flagun had spied the Earl of Chester's men coming in from the west. Tom's report was that Chester's regiment was at least several thousand strong. It had been all Tom and Eric could do to move their people into the safety of the castle ahead of the invaders.

Aidan's vivid dream had given them sufficient warning to store up plenty of food and other supplies in the undercroft. Otherwise, he wasn't sure how they could have hoped to feed all these people during a siege of any length.

All of Aidan's knights were here, many of the merchants, and most of the free tenants, but not everyone on Falconer Manor had retreated to the castle. Some of the newcomers did not have the experience to know the stark difference between Aidan and Richard. While grateful for Aidan's liberal policies, they were not convinced that *who* occupied the castle was that crucial.

Also, some of the merchants and tenants had remained outside to try and protect their goods or their crops from the invading forces. Only time would tell how they would fare.

Chester's bright red banner became visible first. Next came the muted silver of Derby covered in black horseshoes. He recognized it as the second blazon he'd seen in his dream.

He grunted at the sight of the third, the bold Falconer blue bearing a white falcon with a red heart in its center. His uncle had no right to those colors.

There was a fourth banner as well, one he did not immediately recognize. It was similar to the Earl of Chester's in that it was scarlet red with a lion. Yet, while Chester's was a white lion rampant (meaning it was rearing back on its hind feet), this was a golden lion on all fours. This unknown banner also sported the letters "B" and "X" written in gold in the upper corners.

Aidan turned to his knights on the wall. "Whose banner is that? Does anyone recognize it?"

Alan spoke up, "I believe that is the Bayeux blazon. Most likely John de Bayeux."

"Yes, it is," Tom confirmed. "He's paid me several visits to complain about your policies, Aidan."

"I see."

Aidan watched in frustrated detachment as the soldiers swarmed the town and began setting up camp. It looked like it was going be a long siege.

Their cavalrymen staked their horses to the north and threw up a hastily built corral. Other soldiers poured through the town' tiny streets and paths, first surrounding and then searching the houses.

Aidan winced as a baker was pulled from his home and slapped around for protesting when Chester's men began looting his goods.

The invaders maintained a healthy distance from the castle wall though, always wary of Aidan's archers. The noblemen pitched their colored tents to the northeast, right next to Ysabella's fields.

"How many do you think there are?" Aidan asked. A nervous tension gripped his stomach.

"At least two thousand," Eric muttered in a muted voice.

The others nodded in silent agreement.

It was an insurmountable number.

Their only hope was to keep them outside the gates.

Aidan began issuing orders.

"Alan, triple the guard on the walls, and keep it that way at all times. Any unusual activity by the enemy, especially by Chester, is to be reported to me immediately. He's our real enemy here. Richard is powerless without him."

Alan nodded and moved off to reorganize the guard.

"Eric, find me two volunteers to be our spies. Have them sneak out through the tunnel tonight and mingle with the townspeople tomorrow as if they had always been there. We need to know what the earl's plans are."

"Yes, Aidan."

"And Eric? Make *sure* they are solid and loyal. Anyone who would switch sides out of fear will get us all killed."

***

"I've got some bad news." John Steward's face was grim.

Aidan laid down his quill pen. He'd been writing letters to some of the southwestern barons who were sympathetic to Maud in the hopes they might come to his rescue. If he could just get a messenger out . . .

"What is it, John?"

"Our water is running out."

"Our water . . . *what do you mean?*"

"It's the well. The water level's dropping too fast. It seems the well was originally dug deep enough to serve the castle but isn't going to be able to provide long term for the hundreds of people we have in here now."

The siege had barely begun, and they would soon be without water. It was a disaster. Aidan leaned back in his chair and ran his fingers through his hair.

"How did we overlook *that*?" he asked with clenched jaw.

"Clearly an oversight, milord."

"I'd say quite a bad one."

John nodded, blushing.

"What should we do?" he asked.

"Man, I'm thinking!" Aidan slammed his fist on the desk.

They'd stored enough food to last for a few months. Their hope had been that Chester would be called off to aid Stephen again before they ran out.

Now, Aidan held out a smaller hope for aid from another baron, but that would take weeks, if not more than a month, if it were even a possibility.

It was all moot if they ran out of water though. They could only last a couple of days once that happened.

"How soon?" Aidan asked.

"A week? Maybe more?"

"Summon all my knights. We must confer."

Aidan resumed his letter writing, but now he scribbled faster.

Later that day, Aiden went to his chambers to find Priscilla. He found her sitting on the edge of their bed, looking down at the floor.

"How are you, darling? John said you were ill."

She looked pale and unsure whether she wanted to get up or lie down. It didn't take but a glance to realize she was not herself.

She nodded. "I've felt better."

Aidan moved to the bed and laid some pillows along the wall at its head. Then, he eased her back until she could sit up while leaning against them.

"He said you'd been sick several times."

"Please don't worry about me. You've got enough to contend with."

"Holding this castle is worthless if you die from the siege."

Priscilla smiled up at him and took his hand in hers.

"It's not the siege, Aidan. You're going to be a father."

Chapter 45

At sunset, Aidan, William, and Eric stood upon the ramparts. They were studying the forces aligned against them.

"There are so many," William breathed. "I've never heard of such a force loosed upon a barony as small as ours before."

The soldiers milled around Becca's Wells like oversized ants. They filled its streets, went in and out of its houses, and blanketed the surrounding fields.

Any townspeople who'd been able to flee had already done so.

"It's out of spite they've come like this," Aidan replied, "Hatred leads this excess." He turned to the east. "Will the gates hold?"

William nodded, "The new design will stop them from being able to batter it down.

"What do you think they'll try then?"

"Time is against them just as it is us. They'll probably try to tunnel under the walls. It's what I would do."

"Look," Eric cried.

They followed his finger, which was pointing eastward.

A new band of soldiers emerged from the forest road. They were about three hundred strong and bore a detailed green, white, and red banner. Not a huge group, one that Aidan could have hoped to prevail against by itself, but when added to the thousands already surrounding them, it felt like another crippling punch to the stomach.

"That's the banner of the Sheriff of Nottingham," William said.

"Yes," Aidan agreed with the assessment. "His daughter Margaret is the Lady of Derby, so that alliance does not surprise me. I'm sure he hates me on his own just for how many of his men we robbed in the forest."

"But why so few then? He's one of the most powerful lords in England."

"His forces are probably occupied elsewhere in support of Stephen. This may be a token show of support. Of course, more could show up tomorrow . . ."

An hour later, night had descended fully. The enormous hearth in the great hall was cold and dark. The servants were saving what firewood they had for cooking fires and the coming colder months.

Without its blazing light, the hall took on an ethereal feel, encased in darkness that was pierced by only a few candles whose small glows were enough to light the table and every face sitting at it, but left the blackness behind each of them intact.

"You've all heard the news about the well?"

He'd gathered all the knights and John Steward. Each of them nodded grimly. There was nothing to say. The situation was serious.

For the regular people, surrendering would mean returning to slavery under Richard. For Aidan's knights, it would mean swearing fealty to Richard or imprisonment. For Aidan himself, it meant at least imprisonment if not probable execution for treason. You didn't expend the resources on that number of soldiers without exacting some kind of retribution.

Priscilla would be left destitute. Even Nicholas Fontaigne might lose his lands.

The consequences of throwing open the gates to Chester's armies would be terrible.

Aidan could escape with his men through the tunnel and rejoin Red's band in the woods, but the thought of starting over after so much had been accomplished was hard to stomach. So was the risk of leaving the people of Becca's Well at Richard's mercy after he retook the castle.

"I don't suppose the sky gave any sign of coming rain that we could collect?"

"No," Adelard said. "The weather is dry."

"How many fighting men do we have inside?"

William answered this time. "In addition to the six of us, you have twenty men-at-arms plus the militias."

"How many militiamen are inside the castle?"

"Perhaps close to a hundred, mostly from Becca's Well. The rest stayed in the outlying villages to protect them from roving bands."

"Very well." Aidan stood. He rested his hands on the table and leaned into the light. "We must take the fight to them. There is no other choice."

"What do you propose?" Alan asked.

"Tom, are you sure that was John de Bayeux's banner you saw out there?" Aidan asked.

"Yes, I know the man and his blazon well. His lands are right next to my villages."

Aidan smiled. "Well, John de Bayeux is an enemy I did not know I had. Yet, he has come to declare war upon us, so, as far as I'm concerned, all that he has is now fair game too. And if he is here with his men, then his castle stands undefended."

***

The following night, at midnight, twenty dark forms emerged from the ground in the forest like wolverines from their den. Their exit was hidden by a cluster of rocks placed strategically there for that very purpose.

Aidan glanced back at Falconer castle. It was quiet.

Nothing looked out of place — nor would it to the mass of soldiers camped in a semi-circular formation several hundred feet back from the ramparts. Their campfires were already dimming, which meant the invaders had settled down for the night.

"I'm glad we finished this tunnel," Eric whispered.

Aidan raised a finger to his lips.

They were not yet in the clear.

Richard might have been fooled by their extending the tunnel hundreds of feet into the forest line — or he might not. His men could easily be stationed nearby at that very moment, ready to pounce.

They tiptoed westward through the woods, away from Chester's troops.

Each twig snap in the crisp night air froze them in place as they listened intently for any sign of an ambush.

After what seemed an eternity, Aidan finally waved them forward. Collectively, the men breathed a sigh of relief and picked up the pace. They'd successfully escaped the castle with Richard, the earls, and the sheriff none the wiser.

They marched all night and passed through Flagun and Maneis a few hours before dawn.

Being Tom's villages, he gave rousing speeches to his people. Half of those militias joined their band, which swelled their number by forty more men.

They reached the outskirts of Pilsbury Castle around eight in the morning, yet remained hidden in the woods while they canvassed the fortifications.

The Bayeux manor's morning activity was quite sleepy. Probably because most of the guards were busy off-site besieging the Falconer keep.

Its castle consisted of wooden palisades that encircled three hills, all with steep sides, and a keep. The square, stone keep was perched atop the third and tallest of the hills, which was to the north and west of the other two. The other hills were covered in stables and small houses that belonged to the workmen and guards.

To get into the castle, one had to ascend a ramp from the southwest up to the southern mound where the stables were. From there, a drawbridge connected the southern mound with the northern mound where the keep was. If invaders successfully breached the first gate and entered the first bailey, this drawbridge could be raised to completely block entrance to the keep's hill. The sides of that hill were so steep, attackers would suffer heavy casualties climbing it — if they could even manage to scale it.

A second bridge connected the southern and eastern mounds, but there was no reason from them to go over there. No bridge connected that mound with the fortified keep.

Strangely, there was a large hill overlooking the entire fortification to the east that had not been used. Usually, barons built their castles at the high point of an area, yet this one was down in the valley. Probably to be closer to the River Dove since the castle was right next to it.

It was not a significant castle by any means — it had no stone curtain walls, only wooden palisades — but the depth of the ditches around the mounds combined with the drawbridge made it a difficult fortress to breach.

Unless you used subterfuge.

At Aidan's command, the men pulled tunics from their packs bearing the Bayeux coat of arms. The day before, Aidan had marshaled Thomas Weaver and all the spinsters in the castle to hastily create tunics emblazoned with the scarlet shield and the gold lion.

Aidan and his knights threw the tunics over their heads while some of the men-at-arms tied cords or red and gold to their mail to identify themselves as Bayeux men. The militia needed no enhancement.

For the mission to be a success, they had to breach all the way into the keep's bailey without the drawbridge being raised. Detection of their ruse too early in the game would blow all chances of taking it.

"Secure the steward first, then the Bayeux family," Aidan ordered, "Do not harm the women or children, but you may dispatch any guards who fail lay down arms."

Aidan's militia remained in the trees for the time being, but the rest of them left the woods and then walked up the road toward the southwest entrance that led up to the lower bailey.

They intentionally moved feigning confidence of familiarity and purpose so as to appear more authentically to be a group of Bayeux men, perhaps returning home from the siege.

The distinct odor of wood smoke from a dozen different breakfast fires filled the cool morning air. As they climbed the ramp, the snorts of the horses in the stables became audible. One of them suddenly whinnied sharply, sending a flash of fear through Aidan that they'd been discovered, but it was nothing.

That there were no watchmen upon the wall was a very good sign. Most of the guards had gone with Bayeux, and those that stayed were not on alert. Bayeux had no reason to fear. He had no enemies and felt protected by his relationship with the powerful Earl of Derby. He never could have expected the enemy he'd just made in Aidan to react so swiftly.

One guard was posted at the lower gate. He saluted and they returned it with a muted greeting mumbled so badly it could not be understood. Aidan and his men had put on their helms, and the nose guards made it difficult to identify a man unless he took it off.

As the first of their group passed through the gate, William turned back toward the guard. Bayeux's man showed no alarm until William wrapped his forearm around his throat. By then, though, it was too late to yell. William pressed until he fell unconscious.

They dragged the man inside the gatehouse, and Tom took his place. No one else was around to have seen the switch, so they continued on.

They silently took out the guard by the drawbridge manning the second gate and replaced him with two men-at-arms. Then, the rest of them moved on to the keep.

A pair of scullery maids going the other way shot them curious glances as they passed. Aidan risked a look back and saw them craning their necks around, staring at his men's backs. One of them trotted off to speak with a hostler who had emerged from the stables behind them. She started pointing their way.

"I think we've been discovered boys," Aidan said. "Let's hurry it up."

This keep was different from the Falconer keep in that here the entire ground level consisted of undercrofts dedicated to storage of goods. The living quarters actually began on the second floor and could only be accessed by an external wooden staircase that could be pulled up during an attack as a third layer of defense. Most castles were like that, and Falconer Manor was actually the unusual one in that it was not constructed this way.

Aidan had already made it past the first two defensive measures, but they still had to get to the top of that staircase before anyone figured out who they really were. If it was pulled up before they got inside, their chances of bringing the keep swiftly under their control would become impossible — and the scullery maids had seemed to realize he and his men didn't belong.

Thankfully, the hostler lacked the confidence to take on an armed band like theirs, so instead of calling out, he just hurried to catch up to them.

Aidan's group was at the top of the stairs before the hostler had finished crossing the yard. As his knights and men-at-arms poured into the stone keep,

Aidan turned and waved at unseen eyes he knew were peering out at him from the forest. The militia would now charge down the hill and join Tom and his other men at the gates.

Meanwhile, Aidan's men inside would secure the steward and the Bayeux family.

The hostler climbed the stairs and faced Aidan. He was a slim man with short brown hair and the thick muscles of someone who manages horses on a daily basis. He asked Aidan his name.

Aidan explained who he was and that they were taking over the castle.

"Oh" was all he said in response.

Then, he turned around and went back down to his stables. He apparently didn't care enough about who ran the castle to risk his life.

The militia were still about a hundred yards from the gate when a couple of Bayeux's watchmen emerged onto the top of a stone tower inserted in the middle of the upper palisade. They saw the militia and immediately cried out the alarm.

The watchmen raced for the drawbridge to raise it because they'd already realized they'd never reach the lower gate before the invaders did. It would be the two of them against his two men-at-arms.

Aidan whistled into the keep's interior for help and then raced down the stairs two by two. Bayeux's guards saw him, but because of his blazon thought he was one of them responding to the call of alarm.

Aidan took them out before they even reached his men. One he knocked unconscious with a hard slap of the sword to the man's helm. The other Aidan plowed into, shoving him across the fallen form of his comrade. He flailed and tumbled backward. Aidan disarmed him swiftly before he could regain his bearings and then knocked him out.

He reclimbed the stairs and reached the top just as Eric popped his head out.

"The steward is secured, as well as the family. None hurt. Three guards inside also subdued."

"Very good," Aidan replied.

He turned to survey the courtyard and exhaled with relief as he saw his militia pouring into the lower bailey. Two more of Bayeux's men stepped from a house down there, but they were no match for the forty men that soon overwhelmed them.

Pilsbury Castle was his.

Chapter 46

Richard glared at the fortress that should be his but wasn't.

He had not anticipated the new gatehouse, nor the partially built city wall.

His nephew had been busy.

In fact, if Chester had delayed much longer, that city wall would have been completed, and their siege would have been that much harder.

He turned back to the nobles gathered under the Chester tent. The earl had drawn a crude layout of Falconer Manor in the dirt with a stick and was pointing out potential weaknesses. Robert de Ferrers (Earl of Derby) and John de Bayeux listened closely.

To the left of Derby stood the Sheriff of Nottingham's representative, Sir Grunnald, who bore a nasty, round scar on his sword hand from Aidan's arrow and a malignant sneer that showed he'd not forgotten it.

Grunnald wasn't paying attention as intently as the others. He just wanted a chance for revenge; he didn't care about the details of how.

With him was another knight by the name of Guy, a skilled, but brash ape of a fellow who also bore some kind of grudge against young Falconer. Richard had to hand it to his nephew — the boy made enemies like no one else.

Sir Hugo stood at Richard's right hand. Truly, he'd never left it. He was and always had been Richard's closest ally. The knight didn't have the connections to become a lord himself, and the conniving revolutions that turned in his mind closely resembled Richard's own. Men as ambitious as they could not be considered friends, but their alliance would remain strong as long as it strategically benefitted them both.

Hugo spoke up.

"Aidan's weakness is in his people," he interjected.

Earl Ranulf winced at the unsolicited interruption but overlooked it as his desire to conquer dampened his demand for protocol.

"What do you mean?" he asked.

"The castle walls are strong," Hugo continued. "Tunneling under them could take weeks. Weeks we may not have."

Ranulf nodded. "And what would you suggest?"

"Aidan's weakness is his love for his people. Burn one of his villages, Pilsley or Edensor. Take the people captive and bring them here. Then, execute them, one per hour until the boy surrenders."

The earls blanched at the crudeness of the suggestion.

Still, they silently considered the idea rather than reject it. Chivalry could be suspended when pride was at stake and time was limited.

"What say you, Grunnald?" Hugo called. "Tell me of your encounter with Aidan in the forest. Is he weak-hearted?"

Grunnald straightened and narrowed his eyes. "Yes, the whelp cares for serfs as if they weren't dogs designed to serve their betters. He assaulted the sheriff's men just because of those curs in Wellsey — and gave me this nice souvenir to remember him with." He grunted, holding up his hand. "Hugo's plan may work. The boy's weak."

Just then, one of Chester's men-at-arms ducked into the tent.

"A rider comes with news, sire," he panted. "Pilsbury Castle has been taken."

"*What?*" cried John de Bayeux. "*What do you mean?* Who's taken it?"

"It was Aidan Falconer."

The blood drained from Bayeux's face. The Earl of Derby cursed.

"*How?*" Ranulf demanded, his face turning crimson. "How is that possible if we just saw the boy on the wall this very morning?"

"It happened two days ago. His knights hold it now and have buttoned it up."

Bayeux paled further. "And my family?"

"Your man says they are fine. Falconer says he will hold them hostage as long as you maintain hostilities."

"How could he sneak out of the castle without us knowing?" Ranulf grumbled through gritted teeth.

"I told you there was a secret tunnel," Richard said, "It's how Aidan snuck into the castle while I held it. But he's moved the entrance somewhere."

Ranulf barked orders at the man-at-arms. "I want every townsman still in this village rounded up immediately. Do what you have to until somebody tell us where that tunnel is."

The soldier turned heels and left.

"I must go home," Bayeux declared.

"What are you going to do there?" Hugo sneered. "Your fight's with the man inside that castle in front of you."

Bayeux blushed. "Perhaps . . ."

"I just want to kill Aidan Falconer," Grunnald interrupted, "I don't care where we do it."

***

Bayeux rode off with his men and a contingent of Derby's to assess the situation at his manor. Meanwhile, Chester, Derby and Richard approached the castle on horseback under a white flag to parley.

Aidan didn't trust them enough to leave the security of the castle, so he and his party addressed them from the wall by the gate.

The Earl of Chester trotted to the forefront of the group.

"Aidan Falconer, you have allied yourself with the pretender Maud and you have violated the king's peace and forced your uncle from his home. You have assaulted the Sheriff of Nottingham's men and now you've laid siege to one of the vassals of the Earl of Derby. We demand you surrender this castle immediately and submit yourself to justice."

"The king's *peace*?" Aidan laughed. "That's pretty rich. The justice part isn't even worth commenting on.

"You've made your demands, now hear mine. Vacate Falconer Manor or we will take action against you. Bayeux has already lost Pilsbury, and while he may earn his family back, he won't be ruling that castle again."

The Earl of Chester remained calm. He'd grown used to the fact that this upstart had no respect for his betters. He would soon receive his due. So, his insults would land upon hardened skin this time around.

"And who holds Pilsbury now?" Chester asked.

"Perhaps I do?" Aidan replied. "Why don't you run over there and check?"

A few of Ranulf's men-at-arms snickered.

Ranulf shot them a glare and then waved his sword in a circle above his head to signal to fall back.

"There's no use reasoning with this dog," he snarled.

They rode away and melted into the massive camp.

***

That night, cries in the halls and an urgent pounding on their door awakened Aidan and Priscilla. Aidan threw it open to see a servant bearing a burning rushlight.

"Sire, the gate is on fire!" the servant panted.

"What? How?"

"I don't know, sire! No one seems to know anything!"

"Calm down," Aidan demanded firmly.

He barked out more orders and searched for his clothes hurriedly. Priscilla was already half-dressed. She shot him a nervous glance as he threw his tunic over his head and grabbed his sword.

He paused.

"It'll be all right," he said firmly, then went out the door.

Soldiers and servants were running every which way with no order to their steps. He knew he needed to assume control or panic would rule.

Aidan slipped out the door onto the castle walk. He found William and Alan already at the front. Alan was calling for the archers to form a line on top of the outer wall.

"What happened?' Aidan asked.

"They snuck up in the dark," William said, "and covered the outer gate in pitch. Shot flaming arrows into it and set it ablaze."

Guards were hauling buckets of water up on ropes from the inner courtyard to pour down onto the fire from above the gatehouse. Eric and Tom soon joined the archers to help organize them so they could provide cover for the firefighters.

Chester's men were backing out of range again now.

"What are they trying to do?" Aidan asked.

"I'm not sure," William said. "The fire won't get them through both gates. Even if they somehow find a way inside to get at the second gate, there's still the portcullis to deal with in the center of the gatehouse, and our men will rain down wrath upon anybody inside the gatehouse who is trying to breach the second gate."

"I wonder if they have some plan for the portcullis," Aidan said. "We need to triple the guard and keep the archers alert up here. We can't let them get that close again."

The fire burned on stubbornly. The gate had been thoroughly soaked with pitch and was going to be difficult to put out. The danger was that the heat from it could crack the mortar between the stones surrounding the outer gate. That could weaken the gatehouse and cause the front end of it to fall in.

"What would happen with the portcullis if they tunneled under it?"

"It could cause all kinds of issues. It might drop further and pull some stones down with it . . . but if they did that, why wouldn't they just tunnel all the way past the second gate?"

"True. Doesn't make a lot of sense."

"Plus, that would take far too long."

"You're right."

Aidan watched as bucket after bucket rose up the wall and was poured down the front of the gatehouse. The soldiers had a regular chain going now. They might even be making a dent in the fire, but it was still hard to tell. The glow of it didn't seem any dimmer.

"William . . ." Aidan said, ". . . Chester must know we're low on water. He's making us waste it. Someone's been talking."

Now that the men were working together, Alan returned and joined Aidan and William. Aidan explained his fear that someone had turned traitor and that their attackers knew of their water problem.

The situation was grave. This morning, they'd told him there was likely only three or four days-worth of water left in the well for all the people. The effort to put out this fire could easily drop that estimate by a day or more.

They could sneak people out of the tunnel in small groups at night to reduce their demand for water, but every time they did that it would risk their enemy discovering their secret.

"That's it," Aidan decided. "I'm done hiding in this castle. William, gather all the fighting men who don't use a bow. We're leaving tonight."

He turned to Alan. "I want you to send your fastest runner to Red's camp. Ask him to attack Chester's troops from the woods at dawn."

"If he can't," Aidan muttered to himself after they'd left, "I'm not sure how much hope we have."

The fire was still burning.

Chapter 47

Baron John de Bayeux squinted in the sunlight.
Pilsbury castle looked the same as it always did — except for its gate.
It was midday, and the gate was shut.

His men's horses clopped around nervously behind him. The beasts seemed to sense the tension.

Seeing no archers on the wall, Bayeux turned and waved his small force forward. Twenty men was all he'd brought to the siege of Falconer Manor. It wasn't a lot, but it was all he could afford with the size of his fief.

They rode to the gate and stopped. As they neared, an unfamiliar guard popped up on one of the towers in the palisade.

"Open up in the name of John de Bayeux," the baron cried out.

The guard disappeared. A few minutes later, a firmer, stronger face appeared in the tower flanked by two others.

Bayeux tried to manage the conflicting emotions of anger, embarrassment, and anxiety that roiled within.

"Who are you?" he called. "I demand you open this gate immediately."

"I am Sir Eric," the knight responded, "And this is Sir Thomas du Bois. We have taken your castle in the name of Aidan Falconer whom you have besieged."

"I have obviously left the siege! Now return to me my manor or answer to the Earl of Derby who holds these lands from the king."

Eric laughed. "You may leave the siege all you want — and go again! This castle shall not be returned to you, not now and not twenty years from now. You declared yourself an enemy of Falconer and he is treating you as such. As for the Earl of Derby . . . is not Sir Aidan already suffering his full wrath? Why should this little castle make any difference?"

The baron's face burned red.

"And my family?" He asked through gritted teeth. He had no hope of taking his manor back with just twenty men.

"If you will take your men back to the woodline, we shall open the gate and release your family to you. We'll even give them horses."

"Why, you impertinent cur!" he growled.

"Now, now," Eric called, "If you get nasty, we'll keep the horses."

***

It remained to be seen what the Earl of Chester had planned for this day, but Aidan didn't intend to wait to find out.

He and his men slipped out in the dead of night and infiltrated the deadened, empty houses throughout Becca's Well. An invisible line had been drawn through the middle of the town, a line that roughly indicated the range limit of the castle archers. The invaders' camp began right outside that range, so every home between that point and the castle was currently abandoned.

Long before the sun rose, Chester's forces were milling about. Then, they began lining up in formation at the mouth of the village's main street. The earl was planning some kind of demonstration of force today.

He, his knights and the other nobles huddled in the center of the street, conferring. They were surrounded by at least two hundred men-at-arms.

A healthy group of enemy archers had also formed up behind them. Apparently, not seeing Aidan's archers on the wall, they intended to move in toward the castle. For what purpose, Aidan didn't know, but it seemed Chester's bowmen would be ready if any defenders did show up.

The enemy still had thousands of others that could flow around the town, or fill in behind the first group, but this main street was only wide enough for ten to fifteen men at a time.

It severely restricted the number of soldiers that could approach at once – which was why Aidan had chosen it for his showdown. Reinforcements could not come to aid Chester's troops directly but would have to circle around or filter through the side alleys to reach them.

"Fall in!" the Earl of Chester barked.

His men formed into thick lines.

Aidan sent up a prayer to thank God that Ranulf had decided to form up this morning. It only helped his plan.

Still, two hundred was more men than Aidan had at his disposal. It would be all he could do to handle them, and he was willfully ignoring the thousands outside the village that would serve as Chester's reserves.

The loyalty of Aidan's men amazed him — their courage and willingness to follow him into what could turn out to be just an elaborate suicide mission was nothing short of incredible.

The sun had been peeking through the trees for ten minutes now. The men inside the darkened house alongside Aidan grew restless. He imagined his men on the opposite side of the empty street were becoming just as nervous.

Red was late.

Where was he?

The first streams of clear sunlight now gleamed over the tops of the trees. Dawn had passed.

The earl raised his sword and pointed it to the sky.

"Forward!" he commanded.

The invaders spurred their horses and trotted forward, their eyes scanning the castle walls for signs of archers. Very soon, they would cross that invisible line and enter the castle's range.

Richard and Chester were at the center of the mass of soldiers, but they'd placed several lines of men-at-arms in front of them in case Aidan's bowmen did make an appearance. The earl's archers at the rear had already nocked arrows and pulled their bows taut.

As they moved in, they remained completely unaware of the many eyes watching their advance from within the houses on either side of them.

Then, it came without warning.

No battle cry or resounding trumpet. Just the silent sailing of a hundred missiles sliding up into the air from the forest and arcing high before turning down again. The stealth barrage decimated the earl's rear lines as dozens upon dozens of arrows embedded themselves in the archers' backs.

Red!

The unexpected wails of agony suddenly erupting from the archers at the back alerted Chester's men they were under assault. After the initial volley was spent, the forest outlaws' bolts then streamed in like intermittent drops of a whispering rain of death.

Since Chester's archers had already had their weapons nocked and ready, some of them accidentally released their strings the moment they were struck, and some of those arrows in turn buried themselves in the backs of fellow men-at-arms to their front.

Chaos set in.

The archer lines pushed forward madly to get away from the ambushers in the woods. This pressed Chester's formation closer and closer to the castle than was comfortable. The earl struggled to restore order. By the time he did, his core group was centered right between Aidan's hidden pincers.

Aidan let loose a deep cry from the depth of his lungs and launched the second prong of the assault. His men poured from the houses lining both sides of the street, sharpened blades swinging and slicing through mail.

The flanks of Chester's formation, all men-at-arms, instinctively retreated away from the unexpected side attacks.

As a result, Chester's best fighters, his knights, were locked in the center and pressed so tightly they were having trouble just finding room enough to draw their swords, much less a way to enter the fray. Aidan had turned the earl's attempt to protect himself into a severe handicap.

The formation condensed into a huddled mob pressed from the rear by the outlaw archers and by Aidan's men on the sides. The only avenue of escape was forward, toward the castle, so the mass of men naturally began to flow in that direction.

Then, about forty of Aidan's archers, who'd been hiding out of sight within the castle, popped up on the wall and unleashed their own barrage down upon the earl's men.

Now, panic set in. Chester's men were in a kill box.

They enemy men-at-arms were so busy looking for a way to escape the death trap, their hearts could not fiercely engage to defend. One by one, they began to fall.

Aidan saw the Earl of Derby at the far end of the road trying to rally men to come to Chester's aid, but as soon as he reached the mouth of the main thoroughfare, outlaw arrows descended in force. He was forced to retreat back and regroup without rendering any help. It became clear no reinforcements could come in from the east.

Slowly, Chester ranks were disintegrating. The men-at-arms were all falling or running away. After a few minutes, only Ranulf, Richard, and their knights remained on their feet in the center.

Aidan realized that Sir Grunnald, Nottingham's top knight, stood among them. That didn't surprise him, though he hadn't officially known the man was here. What did surprise him was the presence of Sir Guy next to him...and the hatred in that brute's eyes. If simply rejecting Guy for employment had been enough to turn the man into such an enemy, then Aidan had obviously done well by choosing William instead.

The enemy knights were making every effort to keep themselves out of range of the castle, still on the wrong side of that invisible line. Yet, they were also just out of range of the outlaw archers in forest, which meant they were in no man's land. They couldn't move forward or retreat without being skewered.

The only way of escape was through Aidan's men and into the side streets. That was also the only way of approach for reinforcements.

Urgent shouts bellowing in the distance indicated those weren't too far off. The Earl of Derby was rallying men.

Now that they'd eliminated most of the men in Chester's core group, Aidan ordered most of his forces into the alleys to fend off the coming reinforcements, though he specifically called for William, Alan, and Adelard to stay by his side.

The side streets were much tighter, and there would only be room enough for a man or two to fight at a time. So, intercepting Derby's reinforcements there before they reached the main thoroughfare where Aidan was could effectively reduce Derby's advantage of numbers and block him.

William launched into one knight while a second engaged Alan. Adelard tore into the last remaining group of men-at-arms and dispatched two of them with ease.

Grunnald, Guy, and two other knights moved in on Aidan together. The two unknowns reached him first. Aidan dispatched them neatly with two simple downward slices of his blade. They had not expected its extra length.

How he absolutely loved his sword. He was constantly sending mental thanks to Andrew for it, though he doubted the prior had a full idea of what a truly special gift he'd given him.

Grunnald and Guy stepped over their fallen comrades and barreled into Aidan. Both were aggressive fighters. The force of their combined weight flung Aidan from his feet. He landed heavily on his back. The fall expelled the air from his lungs with a grunt.

Suddenly, his vision was filled with snarling faces and descending blades.

He rolled to the side. Their swords bit dirt. His roll carried him toward Guy and away from Grunnald. From the fall, he was struggling to breathe normally, but as he leapt back to his feet, he managed to make a sweep for Guy's legs. The tip of his weapon slit the knight's calf.

Guy roared with anger and pain.

Aidan stood.

Then, out of nowhere, an arrow plunged solidly into the chest.

Even though it clinked harmlessly off his mail, the blow stunned him psychologically. He glanced up to see one of Chester's archers had climbed up on a roof. From such a close range, the arrow should have easily pierced his armor. He really didn't understand why it hadn't.

Guy was momentarily sidelined by his wound. He was crouching and gripping his leg, possibly crippled. It depended on how deep Aidan's cut had gone.

Grunnald had circled and launched a new attack just as a distracted Aidan brought his eyes back to the battle before him. At the last second, Aidan's blade somehow came up and parried. He met Grunnald's blows one after the other, first high, then low, but lethargically, with a sapped energy.

From the corner of his eye, he saw the enemy archer tumble from the roof, mortally wounded. One of Aidan's bowmen had seen him and taken him out.

Grunnald's onslaught was relentless. He pushed Aidan back on his heels farther and farther with each successive strike. Aidan's parries felt half-hearted, detached.

Then, he saw Hugo.

Richard's right-hand man had emerged from an alley about forty feet behind Grunnald. When Hugo saw the predicament Aidan was in, he shouted triumphantly and raced to join the fight.

Adelard had just finished off his opponents, so he went to intercept Hugo. They exchanged a few parries, but then Hugo thrust his blade into Adelard's thigh. He followed it up with a powerful blow to Adelard's side that was strong enough to split the mail and hit flesh. Adelard went down.

Hugo ran toward Aidan again, who was still fending off Grunnald. William was busy fighting a new group of men-at-arms that had come out of another alley and Alan was still dealing with his attackers.

In just a moment, it would be *three* experienced, aggressive knights against Aidan by himself. He wasn't sure Sir Bart himself could have handled those odds. Thankfully, Richard and Chester were occupied with Aidan's men on the other side of the street, or it would have been five against one.

Guy finally let go of his calf, swept something up from the road, and hurled it. A bloody rock sailed through the air and plummeted into Aidan's helm with a resounding clang. The terrible echo reverberated through his mind loudly enough to drive a blacksmith mad.

It was the same tactic he'd seen Guy unleash against William the day they'd sparred in front of him. The buffoon was just as unoriginal now as he was then.

Something about the sharp clang of the rock, the blunt force of it against his head, stirred Aidan's wrath.

He realized the archer on the roof had intimidated him with the near fatal blow to his chest. Sudden awareness of his mortality had momentarily turned him timid.

Renewed passion swelled his heart of hearts and blazed into a controlled fury. Right here, right now, he was going to eliminate his enemies. If he failed, Priscilla would be at risk. So would his unborn child. His son or daughter would never live in peace as long as Richard was alive.

The knowledge of that steeled him like never before.

He should not be allowing Grunnald to dictate to him the terms of this fight. That's what Bart would have told him.

Grunnald was even leering at him. In his eyes, Aidan could see he was sure he was about to finish Aidan off — and with reason, given the weakness of Aidan's defense so far. A few more swings and Aidan would be his.

Ready to rejoin the fight, Guy was about to launch a sweeping blow of his own. Hugo had closed the distance and was only ten feet away now. He'd be on Aidan in a matter of seconds.

Aidan released the fury pent up inside and let it flow into his arms and then the rest of his body. He stepped back, replanted his feet, and parried Grunnald's next thrust with little effort. Then, he flicked his blade around and turned the movement into a double strike back at Grunnald, the first aggressive move he'd made in several minutes.

The velocity and skill of the switched direction transformed Grunnald's confident snarl into open-mouthed surprise.

Smoothly, Aidan pulled his arm back from Grunnald and thrust it forward at Guy. Sir Guy had raised his sword high in order to slice down at Aidan's neck, but the tip of Aidan's blade bit through his mail and entered his stomach before he could. Guy's expression also melted to shock. Instead of finishing the strike, he collapsed to the dirt and moaned.

Aidan withdrew his blade and tossed it deftly into his left hand, which was already primed for an awesome blow.

He swung for Grunnald's neck. It sliced deeply enough to almost separate the man's head from his shoulders. Grunnald's lifeless body toppled over. Its head still bore the surprised expression.

Aidan readied himself again.

Hugo faltered as he saw the two powerful knights dispatched so cleanly in front of him. He nearly tripped over himself and Guy's sprawled form trying to stay out of Aidan's reach.

Aidan slung his sword out and the tip of it came to a stop an inch away from Hugo's throat.

Hugo backpedaled as Aidan lunged.

His blade found air. He readied himself again.

Richard's man glanced at the near headless Grunnald and the twice-wounded Guy. He swept his eyes across the rest of the carnage littering the streets of Becca's Well.

Aidan saw uncertainty flicker. He was a ruthless man, but never exposed himself to undue risk. For a moment, Aidan thought he would just turn and run.

The main thoroughfare of Becca's Well was now mostly empty, yet the cries of fresh warriors rushing to the fight was growing from all sides.

Hugo's expression narrowed.

"No," he sneered, "Let's end it *now*."

He launched himself forward and parried Aidan's blade. Unlike the others, he expected its unusual length.

Aidan was quick to recover though and more determined than ever.

The exchange of blades that ensued between them was like an artful dance. Steel flashed and twirled faster than the eye could follow.

It became clear that Aidan was the better fighter, and both men knew it. Yet, his prowess was not quite sufficient to finish Hugo off. The man was as cunning in his ability to escape as he was aggressive in his attacks. Every time Aidan pushed him back on his heels, Hugo was somehow able to find a way to put some distance between them and reset himself.

The rings of their intersecting weapons were soon drowned out by the roar of shouts coming from the side streets.

Aidan glanced back.

His archers were still in formation on the castle wall, and the gates had been opened. Men stood outside the burned-out gate waving for Aidan's men to run inside for safety. This had been the pre-arranged plan.

Hugo took advantage of the momentary distraction and thrust forward for Aidan's throat. Aidan parried and knocked Hugo's sword low, pinning it to the ground.

Suddenly, soldiers poured out from all sides into the main road. The first of them were Aidan's surviving soldiers and militia fleeing in full retreat. They were followed by endless streams of the enemy. Chester's archers suddenly appeared at the far end of the street again, ignoring the outlaws in the woods who kept peppering them with arrows.

The town now boiled with war.

Aidan planted his sword in the dirt and pole vaulted himself into Hugo. Both his boots pounded Hugo's chest and sent him flying back. The knight skidded across the dirt and gasped for breath, clearly in severe pain.

"Fall back!" Aidan called "Fall back!"

William and Alan ran to Adelard and helped him to his feet. They each threw one of his arms over their shoulders and carried him as fast as they could toward the castle. Aidan and some of his men-at-arms fell in behind them to fend off the attackers while the wounded and the militia reached safety.

Chester's archers unleashed a barrage into the sky. Two men-at-arms went down on either side of Aidan, but the rest fell harmlessly to the dirt.

Then, Aidan's archers let loose from the wall and Chester's foot soldiers were forced to fall back to a safer range.

Out of danger from the swordsmen, their only threat now was the enemy archers. Aidan and his men turned and raced as fast as they could for the castle.

After a minute, the last of them passed through the gatehouse. The solid thunk of the portcullis hitting the ground and the thud of the thick, wooden arm being laid in place behind the gatehouse's second door were most welcome sounds.

Aidan was covered in blood. He checked himself for injuries.

First his torso, then his arms and legs.

None of it was his.

Chapter 48

From the castle walk, they surveyed the enemy camp anew.

Chester's troops were stirring, but they weren't leaving.

The ploy hadn't worked.

It had all unfolded just as they'd wanted — Aidan had never intended to overcome *all* of the earl's coalition forces — no, his intent had been to cost those besieging him something. It was one thing to sit in a comfortable camp waiting for someone to starve, it was another to lose men. Losses made nobles reevaluate whether or not their target was worth the effort, and Aidan's barony was truly not large enough to warrant such an expenditure of silver and life. He'd hoped to weaken the enemy's will enough to make them pull out.

They surely *had* made an impression. From the bodies being dragged away, Aidan calculated almost two hundred of the enemy had fallen, plus some important fighters like Grunnald. Guy had been wounded along with many others. He'd seen the uncertainty in Hugo's eyes.

Yet, the Earl of Chester was a stubborn and vindictive man. He would not allow Aidan a victory even if it meant losing all of his men — and Aidan had no hope of vanquishing the thousand plus arrayed against them.

He clenched his jaws.

Torch bearers were riding out from Ranulf's camp. They set every house they could safely reach on fire.

Groans and sobs arose from the people on the walk as flames began licking the walls and roofs of their homes. Within a few hours, every house in Becca's Well would be reduced to simmering ashes.

The earl did not intend for Aidan to be able to repeat that morning's strategy.

Next, the invaders began setting fire to the fields around Becca's Well.

To Aidan, the feeling of helplessness was overwhelming.

Later in the day, seven small bands of men-at-arms rode off in different directions.

Aidan hung his head.

He knew where they were going. To set fire to his outlying villages.

It would be a massacre. Those people had no walls to hide behind. They'd be defenseless against professional soldiers. And there would be no crops left anywhere on Falconer Manor. Even if they somehow survived this siege, they'd all be destitute.

Unfortunately, Aidan no longer had confidence that if he surrendered, his people or his knights would be spared. With the way Chester was comporting himself, they would likely be surrendering themselves to be slaughtered.

That night, he, William, Alan, and Thomas Weaver conferred in the great hall. Adelard was laid up in one of the servants' quarters. He wouldn't be walking again for a while.

"They know we're out of water, Aidan," Thomas said, "They've burned our crops. What can we do but surrender and plead for mercy?"

"We could sneak out tonight," William offered, "Join Eric and Tom in Pilsbury."

"Chester and Derby would just uproot and besiege us there. And Pilsbury's defenses are weaker than ours here," Aidan said, "No, we have but one option. We must sneak out, yes, but only to assassinate Earl Ranulf in his camp while he sleeps . . . and Richard too, if we can get to him."

"No, Aidan," Alan protested, "Such a tactic is dishonorable. It would be better to die than suffer such an affront to our reputations."

"Aidan," Thomas said, "Think about what you are suggesting. The Earl of Chester is one of the most powerful men in all of England. If you kill him, you'd surely bring down the wrath of the king himself upon you."

"What hope do I have with him alive?" Aidan asked. "As to dishonor, is it more honorable to be hanged for treason? Choose for yourself, Alan, but I will be a father soon, and I will fight however I must to preserve the manor for the future."

The news took them all by surprise.

"Yes, you heard me right. Lady Priscilla is with child. All the more reason I must fight."

Thomas laid an arm around his friend's shoulders but could think of nothing to say other than a weak, "Congratulations, Aidan."

William grunted and muttered a similar sentiment. Normally, they would have been elated for him, but under the circumstances, the news just added more pressure to the stress they already felt.

Alan shook his head. "I'll fight to the death by your side, Aidan, but I'll not be party to an assassination plot. If you insist, I must leave your service."

***

Milo led a band of twenty men-at-arms down the forest road.

He'd served the Earl of Chester for five years, always with the hope of being made knight someday, but he was nearly thirty-five now, so that was looking less and less possible each passing year.

Still, opportunities like these gave him a chance to shine and make the earl take notice. That the earl had entrusted him with leading one of the seven bands he'd sent out on these raids said a lot.

All Milo had to do was make sure they completed their mission well.

His target was a place named Flagun.

As they neared the small village, he began noticing dozens of small openings in the hillsides that could only be mine shafts. He'd heard mining was one of these people's main occupations. Maybe they had some gold.

Another hundred feet and the hovels these serfs called houses came into view.

Milo rallied his men and spurred his mount. Soon, the entire band was racing toward the helpless village at full speed.

It was odd though. The place seemed deserted.

Which disappointed him. He'd been hoping for a fight.

No resistance meant no opportunity to display his prowess and garner the earl's notice.

No matter. They'd burn the huts and the crops and be on their way. A mission swiftly accomplished could also be appreciated.

The first sign something was wrong was when one of his front men lost his grip on his torch and dropped it to the dirt. Then, his limp body unexpectedly slipped from his saddle. That was when Milo noticed the arrow protruding from his back.

Yet, before he could shout a warning, three more of his men went down on the right. Some of the people of Flagun had apparently climbed into the trees and were shooting at them from there.

He barked orders for his soldiers to back up and reassess, but more archers appeared behind them. It was a neat ambush, much too sophisticated for the likes of peasants like this.

Milo couldn't think. There was no time to think. He just did what years of experience told him to do — go the other way.

He led his men forward into the heart of Flagun, but when they got there, peasants began stepping out from random homes to knock his men from their horses with pickaxes or long, wooden staffs.

Suddenly desperate, he yelled a command to fire the homes, but of the four men who'd been bearing torches, three were already down. The fourth managed to set one of the huts on fire before he was pulled from his saddle by two peasants with swords, but the damage that fire wrought would be limited. The hut was isolated.

He didn't know what to do.

This kind of organized resistance was completely unexpected, especially from a village like this. They hadn't even taken these people by surprise. Already men were swarming the hut they'd set ablaze to throw buckets of water on it. He watched them in detached fascination.

In the very moment Milo realized they were going to be able to put it out, something heavy slammed into his back. His legs lost their grip on his mount.

He tilted, slid . . . and then tumbled to the ground.

The impact knocked the wind out of him, yet somehow he was able to roll over onto his back.

A face smeared with thick dirt hovered over him. The peasant bore an expression of intense determination that Milo had only seen before in the faces of professional soldiers during battle.

The strange man brought his sword down.

And that was the last thing Milo ever saw.

***

The day the siege began, since the church was outside the castle walls, Brother Geoffrey moved into one of the small outbuildings within the castle's courtyard. He led the people in daily masses, worked to comfort the sick and wounded, and generally encouraged everyone.

This evening, Aidan found him inside his tiny new abode studying by candlelight.

"Hello, brother," he said.

The monk's face lit. "Aidan! Come in, have a seat."

Aidan took the only other chair in the small space.

"You've been indispensable, Geoffrey. The people . . . without you, where would our spirits be?"

"In God's hands," Geoffrey replied, smiling. Then, he switched gears. "What troubles you, Aidan? Besides the siege, I mean. I can see it written across your face, clear as day."

Aidan started to answer but couldn't keep his jaw from quivering. A thick tear escaped onto his cheek, and then he lost it. He leaned forward and covered his face in his hands, sobbing.

Geoffrey leapt up and shut the door so an inadvertent wanderer wouldn't pass by and happen to see their lord so distraught.

"Aidan, you've got to pull yourself together," he said firmly, laying a hand on Aidan's back. "This won't do."

"I know, I know . . . I'm sorry." He sat up and wiped his eyes. The stress was overwhelming him. "It's just . . . there seems no hope. They've surely fired the whole manor by now. My people are suffering, and it's all my fault . . ."

"You cannot say such a thing. You've done your best to provide for them. It's the greed of those outside that drives this invasion."

"Priscilla is pregnant."

Geoffrey sat back stunned, then smiled. "Well . . . that's wonderful news! But . . ." his face sombered, "I begin to see why you are so distressed."

"*Geoffrey* . . . you *must* swear to me that if something happens to me . . . you will make sure Lady Priscilla and my child are protected. Get them to St. Alban's, do whatever you have to, just make sure they are safe."

Geoffrey nodded, rendered mute by emotion.

"Swear it!"

"I swear it, Aidan. I will."

Aidan nodded. They embraced, and then Aidan exited into the cool night.

Chapter 49

The next morning, Aidan went up on the wall to reassess Chester's positions since the previous day's battle. This time, in addition to his knights, he took Brother Geoffrey. Men he considered all to be his true friends.

He'd decided not to risk an assassination attempt the night before. It wasn't their last opportunity, but time was running out. The water bucket was hitting the bottom of the well.

Alan's objections had paused the plot for now. Aidan could have held a grudge against the man for his stance, but he didn't. He understood Alan's point of view. Chivalry demanded bravery under all circumstances and a dedication to honor at all costs. It did not matter that their opponents were unscrupulous men who cared not a fig for such a code.

Aidan and William, though, embraced a more practical philosophy of fighting: When your life was at risk, you did what you had to.

He could tell Thomas was torn. He was not the bold fighter Aidan was, but in the end, he would side with Aidan if pressed.

Alan took the idea of chivalry to heart though. A more ethical man Aidan had never known. It was what had made Aidan trust him from the start, so it would be foolish to blame Alan now for the very quality that had made him a top choice then.

Not that Aidan's idea for an assassination plot even had a solid chance of working. The plan had been hatched in desperation.

First, they would have to trust that the enemy wouldn't be watching the woods at night for people exiting the tunnel. Even if Chester's men hadn't located its entrance yet, they'd have patrols about. Especially after the skirmish in town.

Second, Aidan's men would have to tip toe through hundreds of sleeping soldiers and somehow get all the way to the earl's tent unmolested. Then, even assuming they managed to kill Ranulf and/or Richard, without any commotion, they'd still have to make their way back through the enemy camp and reach the safety of the tunnel undetected once more.

It was a brutally risky plan, with little chance for success, so, for that reason, Aidan wasn't overly dismayed by Alan's objections. Why argue over something that probably wouldn't work anyway?

Thomas had been right anyway. The Earl of Chester was one of King Stephen's strongest supporters. If Aidan killed him, it would propel Aidan from being a small, annoying gnat in the king's eye to his royal majesty's number one enemy.

One of the castle watchmen cried out. "Look!"

A new troop of men, at least five hundred strong, rode into Chester's camp from the east. All of them bore the well-known standard of William Peverel the Younger, Sheriff of Nottingham.

Aidan shook his head in resigned defeat. "Nottingham must have gotten word of Grunnald's death," he muttered under his breath.

Far from vacating the field, the Earl of Chester was doubling down and reinforcing.

It was hopeless.

Brother Geoffrey laid a hand upon the back of his friend's neck.

"Trust in God, Aidan," he said. "Trust in God."

Aidan wanted to. He tried.

But the evidence of his pending doom encircled him daily and was only growing.

***

The Sheriff of Nottingham strode into the tent with a poise born of overabundant self-assurance.

William Peverel was fully clad in emblazoned armor and bore a shield painted green and red in the pattern of his coat of arms. He dipped his head in greeting to his son-in-law, the Earl of Derby, then fixed his attention on Earl Ranulf.

"Sheriff! Welcome! We are blessed by your presence," Chester exclaimed, "Have you come to help rid us of the Falconer disease?"

Nottingham grimaced. "I wish I had . . . Grunnald was a good man."

Chester's brow wrinkled with confusion. He thought he might know what Nottingham was about to say, but, with a certain hesitant reluctance, he asked anyway.

"So, what brings you out in such force then?"

"The king requires our presence in the south. The empress Maud has finally arrived in England herself and is now in Arundel."

"How long do we have?" Ranulf asked. "The lad is almost mine."

"You have *no* time. The king requires our immediate response. Stephen will lay siege to her in Arundel and is concerned she may soon escape. He calls for both Derby and Chester to join his side, as well as my men."

The Earl of Derby nodded and ducked out of the tent to round up his knights. His support for the king was instant, not to mention his allegiance with Nottingham was much stronger than with Ranulf. Aidan Falconer was merely a nuisance to him. Stephen, on the other hand, was the one who had made him an earl. He would not disappoint his king.

Ranulf cursed. Richard protested vehemently. It seemed young Falconer might slip through his fingers once more. If Derby left, it would only encourage the upstart the moment he saw some of the soldiers packing up.

"Ranulf," Peverel added, "If you ever want to regain your northern lands, you *must* support the king. Now is not the time to go your own way. Not when Maud is finally making her move."

The earl cursed again. Richard kicked a table.

Ranulf stabbed a finger at him. "Calm yourself, man."

To Peverel, he said, "Then, of course Chester will ride out as well. Will you at least stay the night? Falconer may give himself up by morning. He's almost out of water."

"As you wish. A half day delay will not matter, and my men's horses need to rest anyway."

"Hugo!" Richard barked, "Run tell Derby that we're not breaking camp till morning!"

***

Aidan dreamed his enemies had all gone, but when dawn broke, they were still there. Just as many as the day before, if not more.

Yesterday afternoon, the well had gone dry. People were already complaining. Not everyone had gotten a share before it had. Children were beginning to cry from thirst.

He knew that before the end of this day, no matter how loyal, his people would be ready to throw the gate open from desperation. By then, the thirst would be maddening.

And Aidan wouldn't even try to stop them. It wouldn't be long before people started dying. Why force such a tragedy? It'd be better to give himself up.

This morning, Priscilla was the only one up on the wall with him.

He put his arm around her shoulder and squeezed. He glanced at her belly.

There was yet no sign of the child she bore within her girlish figure.

"What does your father say?" Aidan asked.

"He's worried. I think for me more than anything. He says we must trust in God."

"That's what Geoffrey told me last night."

"Then, that is what we must do."

Aidan squeezed her shoulder again and let go.

"It's *so* hard, my dear."

"I know."

"Trust is an easy word to roll off the lips, but when thousands of armed men are ringing your home, ready to slaughter you and the ones you love . . ." He paused.

"Wait . . . what is *that?*"

She squinted through the sunlight's glare to see what he was talking about. Then, she saw it too. Movement on the eastern side of the camp.

"Derby's men," Aidan said. "They're packing up."

Indeed, soldiers were rolling up sleeping mats and strapping them to their horses. Tents were coming down and standards were going up. In less than an hour, Derby's men had ridden out with Nottingham's not far behind.

News of the change spread like wildfire. A crowd gathered around Aidan and Priscilla on the ramparts.

Then, when Chester's men began to pack their things up as well, Aidan shouted with joy.

The siege was over.

Aidan noticed Geoffrey standing next to him.

"I told you so," was all the monk said.

Chapter 50

The sight of the burned-out town rent Aidan's heart.

It was all gone.

Becca's Well had been reduced to a jumble of blackened skeletal ruins scattered across splotches of muddy brown. The fields were just as destroyed, only distinguishable from the village by streaks of green that had survived among the black.

Just the stone church had escaped unscathed.

Reports coming in from the villages were mixed. Pilsley, Maneis, Conksbury, and Flagun had fended off the bands Ranulf had sent — an amazing feat that frankly surprised everyone.

The militias were what had made the difference. Aidan's decision to arm and train his people had allowed them to effectively defend themselves.

Nevertheless, Edensor, Taddington, and Brushfield had been wiped from the map. Crops ruined. Villages burnt. Eric took the worst of it, as both of his fiefs had been decimated.

Unfortunately, those that had lost crops wouldn't be able to replant. Namely because it was already too late in the year, and the people had to busy themselves with rebuilding their homes before winter set in.

The silver lining was the taking of Pilsbury Castle. Pilsbury oversaw its own small village as well as four others. Not as large a manor as Falconer, but it was a nice boon, and the crops would go a long way toward recouping what Becca's Well had lost.

Still, Aidan didn't want to steal those crops from its people, so he paid them from his treasury and issued everyone on Falconer Manor rations to take them through the winter.

The herds were the bigger loss. Chester's army had slaughtered most they could get their hands on, even what they couldn't eat, and the rest they'd driven in front of them as they departed.

Aidan couldn't replace those as easily, and he certainly didn't have the funds to try, even if he could find enough animals nearby somewhere. He had no choice but to trust the people would find creative ways to make do.

Their defenses had held up well. It looked like repairing the gate wouldn't be much trouble. Aidan was much more concerned about the water issue though.

Richard and Earl Ranulf would most definitely return and besiege them again someday. Aidan *must* be more prepared for that day when it came.

Eric pointed out that the exit from their secret tunnel was only fifty feet from the river and the underground passage ran slightly downhill most of the way from the river to the castle. He suggested they could extend the tunnel a little farther to get the entrance closer to the river and then hide a smaller channel in the riverbed itself.

The idea was that if ever needed, a sluice could be opened to allow part of the river to flow down the floor of the secret tunnel all the way to the castle through a small, sealed stone aqueduct. At the point where the tunnel met the castle wall, they would begin digging a new passage under the castle grounds that would allow the water to keep flowing all the way to the well.

If it worked, it meant they could control their access to water from a sheltered place without attackers being aware of their source. Needless to say, Aidan clapped Eric on the back for the idea. They'd begin on it as soon as he had enough available labor.

The city wall would have to wait until Spring. Most would be focused on building their homes and by the time they were done, it would be too cold for the mortar to set.

Though that didn't stop the people from filling in the gap in the wall with a wooden palisade in the meantime. They were skittish after the siege and wanted to protect for the future. Within a couple weeks, they'd complete the circuit, and it would effectively stop future invaders from getting into the town below the castle.

The problem was that wood could be set on fire during a long siege. Only a stone wall could save them in the long run. Aidan hoped the setbacks with their crops wouldn't hurt his treasury so much it would prevent him from funding more construction. They *needed* that wall.

John de Bayeux tried to raid some of his own, former villages that surrounded Pilsbury Castle, but Aidan had previously sent his militias from his burned-out towns to guard the new ones in Pilsbury, so they successfully fought the man's small forces off.

Ostensibly, Bayeux had done it to regain what he claimed was his, but to Aidan, hurting the people you hoped would welcome you back didn't make any sense.

Aidan asked William to oversee Pilsbury and all of its lands. William was very loyal, and Aidan knew he would manage it well. Pilsbury could support at least two more knights, so once they found a couple of good candidates, Aidan's total would be up to seven.

Tom returned to get his villages back in order and then went to help Eric rebuild Taddington and Brushfield. Alan would be busy rebuilding Edensor for a while. The destruction there had been enormous.

Adelard's wounds were healing, but slowly. Aidan estimated he'd probably recover fully in a month or so, provided he got enough rest.

For Aidan, this autumn would be a time of rebuilding while the rest of England was burning.

***

Priscilla peered into the church, squinting as her eyes adjusted to the dimmer light. She let out a small gasp at the transformation.

Geoffrey had pushed most of the rustic pews toward the altar and replaced them with crude tables and chairs clustered throughout the front of the church. At least twenty villagers sat around them, hunched over, studying tiny, delicate scrolls and papers.

Geoffrey was teaching them to read.

He raised his head, having heard the scuff of her feet as she entered. He flashed an immediate smile and rose to greet her.

"Welcome, milady," he dipped his head.

"Thank you, Geoffrey."

"I understand congratulations are in order."

"Yes, thank you again."

"When are you expecting?"

"Sometime in the Spring most likely. I see you are very busy," she changed the subject, looking around, "I did not expect so many students."

"Yes, I never had more than ten or so before the fire, but since then, I've run at least double that most days."

She strolled from desk to desk with him. Most were reading from scraps of letters or partial scrolls.

"Why the sudden jump?"

He shrugged. "Some want a more secure future than a field of crops which can be burned up at the drop of a torch can provide. Others are just bored without any fieldwork to do."

"I'm surprised the bishop hasn't tried to put a stop to you yet."

"He's in Rome. Regardless, I honestly can't keep up with this many people. A parish priest has other duties besides teaching, you know. I haven't even been able to finish my consolation rounds yet to families who lost loved ones during the siege. Not to mention my normal duties."

"I see."

"Which brings me to why I asked you here, milady. I'd hoped you might help me with the tutoring? Maybe your father as well? Otherwise, I'm overwhelmed."

She smiled. "I'd love to! But I think we should get them reading from the Gospels, or even some histories."

"Agreed!" Geoffrey smiled. "Prior Andrew has promised to send me more copies of Scripture in English. At the moment, though, I only have one set."

"My father on the other hand," Priscilla continued, "Is busy with students of his own . . ."

She trailed off as her eyes fell upon a voluptuous young woman on the left-hand side of the church. Her head was bowed forward, concentrated on a small book in front of her.

"You are teaching women?" Priscilla asked. "I am surprised."

Geoffrey cocked his head and looked at her quizzically. "Why should that surprise you? I'd think that *you,* more than any other, would approve."

"Well . . . I do. But *her?*"

"Ah, you mean Ysabella? She is one of our best students. Sharp mind, hard worker. She's had it rough, and now her fields are burnt, but she hasn't given up. She'll plant again in Spring — knowing her, probably double what she did before."

"I see." Priscilla frowned.

"Is something wrong, milady? She is one of the ones I'd hoped you could tutor."

She pursed her lips. "It's just . . . eh . . ."

There was a clever glint in his eyes, but she couldn't tell if he knew the reason for her hesitation or if he was just playing with her because she was resisting. He wasn't giving away anything with his expression.

"Of course," Priscilla said, "Tis the Christian thing to do. If she wants to learn, then I will tutor her."

Ysabella started when Lady Priscilla sat down in the chair next to her. For a moment, she felt uneasy, but then pushed the fear out of her heart.

Honestly, she admired Priscilla more than anything. For the woman who held Aidan's heart, how could Ysabella feel anything other than affection?

Regardless, she dropped her gaze to the table. Priscilla was nobility. She, only a peasant.

"Milady," she said.

"Hello, Ysabella. Geoffrey has asked me to tutor you in your reading."

Ysabella flicked her eyes up to meet the other woman's. In Priscilla's, she sensed a discomfort, an unwillingness she didn't understand . . .

. . . or perhaps she did.

Nevertheless, she needed the help.

"Thank you, milady."

"You don't have to be so cursed polite about it."

Chapter 51

"**A**idan!"

Martin the Red rose from the log where he'd been sitting and clapped his arms around his friend in a tight embrace.

"Come by the fire. Warm yourself. Would you like some gruel?"

The smell of it wafting from the blackened pot hanging over the embers brought back memories.

Aidan had arrived just as the outlaws were about to have breakfast. Several were perched on other logs, primed to leap into action to serve themselves as soon as the meal was pronounced ready.

"No, thanks. Already ate."

"Very well. How are you, my boy?"

"Fine, Red. You?"

"We're well. Just trying to keep warm in this cold," he said, stomping his feet on the ground to emphasize the point. White snow dust billowed up from the tops of his boots as he did.

Aidan laughed. "Well, you can always join my guard in the castle. They stay warm."

The others guffawed at the thought.

Red grinned, "No, that is not the life for me, my friend."

They bantered a bit, catching up on the latest news to pass through the forest.

"Red, I never got the chance to thank you for helping us during the siege. Without you, I don't know how we would have fared."

The mood turned serious.

"It *was* a close one, wasn't it?" Red said. "We weren't so sure you were going to make it out of that particular noose."

"Thanks to you we did."

"I'm not sure we did that much, but you sure put on a splendid battle, I'll tell you what."

"Everyone fought bravely."

Aidan drew near the fire and held out his palms to warm them. "Listen, you know that Chester raided all of our livestock."

"Yep." Red's mouth firmed into a thin line.

"I happen to have learned where he's keeping a large number of sheep that are poorly guarded . . ."

Red was already grinning again.

". . . and," Aidan continued, "I also happen to know the earl is down south helping the king assault those bishops who have defected to Maud.

Aidan seated himself on an upended log. "It occurred to me that if someone were to raid those sheep and bring them to Becca's Well, the local baron would probably be so happy he'd gratefully give the raiders a cut of the flock."

"That is a very interesting idea, Aidan. Let's have some mead and talk more about it. Now what *exactly* would a band of outlaws living in the forest do with sheep?"

"You could always sell them . . ."

***

Later that afternoon, Aidan rode home. He'd almost reached the castle and was glad for it.

The day's chilly air had started to set into his bones. Rubbing his arms didn't help because it just pressed the cold metal of his mail into his tunic, which in turn seemed to sap the warmth from his skin.

He should have accepted the overcoat Priscilla had offered him this morning, but he hadn't wanted to show up in Red's camp wearing luxurious furs. He was still one of them at heart.

He was close to the fields around Becca's Well now. His courser was struggling through the last snowbank before he broke out of the woodline. The winds had blown the thick snow into a heavy drift right at its edge.

All of a sudden, something heavy slammed into the side of his head.

Stunned . . .

Aidan watched with detachment as his hand slipped involuntarily from the pommel of his saddle. He couldn't understand why he couldn't control it.

Then, he felt himself sliding. He toppled from the saddle into the snow.

His world went black.

Chapter 52

With reluctance, Ysabella rose from her chair to get the door. This afternoon, the cold was terrible. She only had a small fire, and it seemed like every time she got warmed up under her wool blanket, the wood would run out and she'd have to get up to fetch a few more logs.

Now, someone was knocking on the door. It didn't sound like they were going to go away. It'd be hard for them to knock any louder, that was for sure.

She pushed the heavy door outward and saw John, the steward of Falconer Castle, standing there.

"Lady Priscilla requires your presence in the keep," he said.

Ysabella didn't have many options when it came to attire. She'd thrown on the best she had, as ragged as they were, hoping she'd look halfway suitable for the visit. She had no clue why the lady wanted to see her, but the urgency of the steward's summons had been clear.

It felt like there were a hundred butterflies fluttering in Ysabella's stomach.

Had she offended Priscilla in something?

The lady was waiting for her at the door of her bedchamber. Her rounded belly visibly shaped her beautifully embroidered tunic, promising that it was only a few months before Aidan's child was born.

A twinge of uncharacteristic jealousy raced through Ysabella at the thought. Sometimes, she couldn't help it. She often had dreams she were Aidan's wife instead, bearing his child, as impossible and immoral as that was.

Priscilla caught the slight, if ever quick, sign of envy and responded with an equal flash of her own.

"Come inside," she said.

Ysabella didn't understand what was happening. The tension in her gut tightened its grip.

Then, she saw *him* . . .

Aidan lay in a very large bed. The coverlets were stained with streaks of blood and mud, but they were nothing compared to the mess that was Aidan's face.

He was unconscious.

"Oh no . . ." a gasp escaped Ysabella's lips. She clutched her hands. "What happened to him?"

She turned and saw Priscilla's eyes welling with water, her worry freshened by Ysabella's reaction.

"Outlaws . . ." Priscilla choked. She sniffled and then worked to regain her composure.

"Outlaws? It can't be! Surely not Red . . ."

"No, Red's the one who found him. Aidan was lying in the snow. It must have been one of those bands of vagrant soldiers. They hit him in the head with a log and then beat him mercilessly. They stole his horse and left him for dead. Much longer in the cold and he would have frozen to death. It's a miracle they found him when they did."

Ysabella didn't know what to say. Her heart was in her throat. She couldn't control every tear that tried to escape, but she wiped them away as quickly as they came.

"Is he . . . going to live?"

"We don't know. He hasn't woken up yet. Geoffrey has sent for Brother Henri, but he says Aidan may be like this for a long time."

"What can I do?" Ysabella asked.

"This baby is starting to cause me a lot of pain. Geoffrey thinks I may have to take to the bed soon or risk losing it."

Priscilla winced and put a hand to her side as if to add visual emphasis. It took her a full minute to recover her breath.

"When Henri gets here, he'll give me a better prognosis. Regardless, my husband needs a lot of nursing, and I am unable to do it myself. The servants can help, but it needs to be directed by someone who . . . *cares* for him."

She winced again.

"Honestly, I don't like the idea very much, I tell you, but I can't help it. I need you to make sure he is cared for if I can't."

Ysabella nodded.

"I'm willing," she said.

"Very well," Priscilla said, "Get your things. You'll have to move into the castle."

Chapter 53

Weeks later, Aidan's eyes finally fluttered and cracked open. The sudden inflow of light felt like it was going to split his head apart. He clenched them shut them again, but the terrible pounding in his brain didn't go away.

He struggled to get fully awake.

"Ugh," he muttered, trying to raise his hands to clamp them over his temples and ease the pain, but his arms were stiff and encumbered by heavy blankets.

He wrestled to free his right arm, but a feminine hand clamped it in place gently.

He cracked his eyes again and turned to see Ysabella peering over him intently.

He was in a bed. She was seated in a chair next to him. She held a wooden bowl in her other hand that was filled with water and a wet towel.

It was all thoroughly confusing.

What was happening?

He recognized he was in his chambers, but why was Ysabella here? Clearly, something had happened to him, but had something happened to Priscilla too?

"Stay still, Aidan," she soothed.

She placed a cool hand on his brow to feel for a fever. "You've been unconscious for more than two Sabbaths. We were worried you wouldn't wake."

"What happened?" he croaked.

A severe thirst suddenly overcame him. He struggled to sit up. "Water . . ." he managed to get out.

She pressed him back down. "Stay there. I'll get it." She rose and fetched a cup. She placed a hand under the back of his head and helped him tilt forward so she could tip the wooden vessel to his lips.

The water was deliciously cool on his tongue. It trickled down his throat and soaked into his parched tissues, relieving what felt like dry fissures all the way down.

"We tried to give you water, but it was hard without choking you in your sleep," she said.

With each sip, the pounding in his head seemed to diminish just a bit. He shuffled himself in the bed so he could sit up all the way. Ysabella tried to stop him, but he waved her off.

"I'll be all right," he said. "I need to sit up."

"I'll get Priscilla," she said and left the room.

A few minutes later, Priscilla appeared in the doorframe, large with child. She held a hand to her lower back and was in obvious pain.

Still, she smiled through it.

"Aidan, my dear, you're awake!"

She slowly waddled to the bedside. She was in greater pain than he first realized. Ysabella hung back by the doorway.

Priscilla took the chair next to him and lowered herself into it with effort.

"You're in pain," he croaked.

"I'm fine," she said.

"You're not. You're in pain. What's wrong?"

"I'm fine," she repeated.

"The baby? Is the baby...?"

"The baby's fine as well."

"What happened to me?" he asked again.

"A band of rogue soldiers attacked you. Red found you in the snow just in time or you would have frozen to death."

"Soldiers?"

"Yes, but don't worry, Red and Ranulf tracked them down and they won't be bothering anyone again."

He closed his eyes momentarily. The headache was still there.

"And Richard? Chester? What do we hear of them?"

"Nothing, darling, you don't need to worry about them. They are occupied in the south helping the king. Though Red said to be sure and tell you about the sheep."

"The sheep?"

"After they found you, they set out after Chester's sheep as you'd asked. They captured over two thousand and drove them back here. They didn't even take a cut of the flocks. Just dropped them off at the castle and told John to distribute them to the people to compensate them for their fields."

Aidan nodded and a half-smile slipped onto his face.

"And you?" he asked. "Tell me the truth. What's the matter? You don't look well."

"Aidan! That is a terrible thing to say to a lady," she ribbed him. "I'm fine. Don't worry about me."

"And her?" he said under his breath, jerking his chin toward the door where Ysabella stood. "What is she doing here?"

Priscilla's smile faltered. "Yes, well . . . all right. I've had some pain and Brother Henri has ordered me to bed rest. I asked Ysabella to care for you in my stead."

The expression on Aidan's face could only be described as a strange mixture of shock and stunned confusion.

He shook his head. "I don't understand you sometimes."

She smiled.

"Ysabella has been very dedicated, Aidan. She's not left your side in all this time except to sleep."

Aidan shook his head again and tried to turn so he could get out of the bed. He was uncomfortable in a lot of different ways.

Priscilla leaned forward and gently pushed him back.

"No, Aidan. Take it easy."

"I've got to get out of this bed."

"No, you've got to make sure you're all right. You suffered a terrible blow to the head."

He tried to rise anyway, but dizziness overcame him. Finally, he relented and sat back.

"Perhaps you're right."

***

As soon as Aidan was strong enough to move about on his own again without pain, Ysabella silently packed her meager belongings and left the castle to return to her modest reconstructed hut in town. She left so suddenly Aidan didn't get a chance to thank her.

He thought about going in person once he was well enough to ride, but then remembered Priscilla's volcanic reaction the last time he'd visited the woman at her home and thought better of the idea. No, he'd have to send someone else with a gift and a message.

There wasn't much time to dwell on it though. The manor's business had limped along while he was unconscious, but much had been on hold. Appeals and requests from the peasants poured in. His knights had been waiting for him to deal with several issues. His head was still a little foggy, so it was almost too much to handle all at once, but he managed.

All that was overshadowed, though, by worry for Priscilla. She hadn't been able to leave her bed since the day he'd awoken. It was his turn to care for her.

His strength returned fast. He itched to resume his normal combat training regimen again. He poked his upper arm — a little too soft to suit him, for sure.

For every day that he gained strength though, it seemed Priscilla's waned. And he could see his anxiety mirrored in the faces of the servant women.

He crammed his fears into determined focus, exercising and sparring with the other knights as much as time allowed, even on the coldest days. In just a few weeks, his muscles had regained their tone.

Priscilla, though . . . her battle was one he could not resolve with his strength.

Chapter 54

March 1140 AD

It was the middle of the night when Priscilla woke him with a start. She was gripping his arm so hard, he thought it was a man at first.

Something was wrong.

Her breathing came shallow and fast.

He slipped from the bed even as she held onto his arm.

"Priscilla! What is it?"

"Aidan . . ."

It was too dark to see her clearly. There were still some hot coals in the hearth. He lifted her hand from his forearm, grabbed a rushlight from the side of the hearth and lit it with the coals.

He came back to her. She seemed to be regaining her breath. Her face gleamed pasty white and dripped with sweat.

"Don't worry," she whispered. "I think the baby is coming."

She tried to sit up and winced.

"Don't, dear. I'll get the midwife." He laid her back upon the pillows.

Aidan ran from the room and down the hall. He pounded his fist on John's door. The sleepy steward answered with wild tufts of hair pointing in all directions.

"It's time. The baby's coming!" Aidan yelled over his shoulder as he raced off to wake the servant girls.

Next, he went outside. The night was cold, and the air burned his lungs. He reached the side of the church and banged on Geoffrey's door. The monk finally answered after what seemed an eternity.

"Fetch Brother Henri! He should still be at St. Alban's. Baby's coming! Please pray!" Aidan exclaimed before running back to the castle.

When he got back, Priscilla was in the middle of another contraction, but the midwife and two servant girls were already in the room. The midwife had moved into the castle a number of days ago in anticipation of the coming birth.

A third girl entered with a bucket of warm water and some cloth. Aidan watched helplessly as his bride gripped fistfuls of her blanket in pain.

When the contraction finally faded, the midwife took him aside.

"How is she?" Aidan asked, unable to tear his eyes from Priscilla.

"She's fine. Everything's normal. The baby will be here very soon. Even though this is her first, I think it will come fast."

"But how is she? She doesn't seem fine."

"Well, she's not. She's in a lot of pain, but that's normal. Now, this is women's work, so you need to go outside and leave her to us."

He didn't want to go, but the midwife was used to dealing with stubborn husbands. She wrapped an arm around his shoulders and deftly turned him to the door. He was facing its closed surface from the other side before he knew what had happened.

He didn't go far though.

He laid his back against the wall and slid to the floor, listening to those excruciating cries the thick door did not muffle.

John came along and put a cloak over his shoulders.

"Why don't you come down to the hall," he said. "The servants have laid out some food and they've got the fire going. It's cold up here."

Aidan didn't want to go.

"Come on, Aidan. You're not doing any good here."

Reluctantly, Aidan relented and followed the steward down. William was there, as well as rest of the castle staff who weren't helping Priscilla directly.

The ambiance of the room was in stark contrast to his mood. Here, everyone was fully festive, celebrating the coming heir of Falconer Manor. Of course, he was also excited. He just couldn't shake his worry for Priscilla.

After a time, he went outside and walked over to the church. Geoffrey had left the door unlocked, so he went in. He knelt before the altar and supplicated God for help and protection.

Aidan's son came with the breaking of dawn. The servants couldn't find him until someone thought to look in the church.

He emerged into the bright morning light, hopeful and emotional.

They said Priscilla had made it through.

She would be all right.

Inside the castle, the mood had not dimmed in the least. Banter and well-wishes followed him all the way up the stairs.

Priscilla still lay in their bed, propped up on the pillows.

Someone had lit every candle and drawn the curtains to let in as much sun as possible. The room felt light and cheery, quite different from the night before.

In her arms, Priscilla held a small cloth bundle. She smiled as he approached and turned it to him. A tiny round, pink face peeked through the cloth up at him.

His eyes met Priscilla's.

"I've . . . I've given you a son," she breathed, her eyes lit with satisfaction.

Aidan moved to her side and laid a hand on the child's head.

"His name will be Andrew," he said.

He looked to Priscilla. Her face was puffy, still pale. Her eyes seemed sleepy like she was having trouble keeping them open. Of course, after childbirth, every woman is exhausted. Yet, she didn't look well to him.

"How are you feeling?" he asked.

"I'm tired," she said, "Would you like to hold your son?"

"Of course." He reached out and took the bundle from her.

His son.

The child felt light, yet solid in his arms.

***

Brother Henri met him a few hours later.

"I came as fast as I could," he said.

"I appreciate it, brother."

"I congratulate you on your son."

"Can't believe I'm a father now. It's hard to take in."

"Aidan . . . I've examined Priscilla, and we need to talk."

He could see the fear envelop Aidan's face. He'd obviously suspected something was wrong already but had been doing his best to hide it.

Aidan dropped his eyes to the ground.

"What is it?" he asked flatly.

"The afterbirth came out, but she still bleeds. The flow is dark and heavy. I've applied all the medicines I know, but nothing has worked."

Aidan said nothing.

"I fear she is likely to die," Henri said finally.

Aidan stared at Henri then with water-filled, trembling eyes.

"No . . . that's not true. *That cannot be true!*"

It broke Henri's heart to see Aidan so distraught, but there was no point in hiding the truth. If the bleeding didn't stop, Priscilla would die. There was no doubt.

Henri laid a hand on his shoulder. "I think you should go see her. You may still have a few hours."

Aidan broke into sobs and walked off toward the keep.

The baby lay in a wooden cradle in front of their small window. Priscilla was smiling, but her skin looked paler than ever.

Aidan had wiped his eyes before coming into the room, but she could tell they were red and swollen from crying.

Her smile was weak. "Aidan . . ."

He sat on the edge of the bed and leaned forward to hug her. Her skin was cool to the touch. Too cool. It wrenched his heart. He almost broke into sobs again. He sat up, took her hand and held it in both of his.

"Priscilla . . ."

"It's going to be all right, Aidan."

He shook his head. "I spoke with Henri."

The facade she'd put on for his benefit broke, and thick tears rolled down.

"I guess you're right . . . I can feel myself getting weaker." With effort, she lifted a hand to wipe her eyes. She smiled again through the tears. It sparkled like a jewel behind a stream of water.

Aidan kissed both her cheeks and pulled her into a long embrace.

"I feel sleepy," she said.

He sat up. "Don't try to talk."

"I must . . . we don't have much time."

"I cannot bear this."

"You've endured worse, my husband."

"No, I *haven't*."

"Aidan . . . I knew this was going to happen . . . you are not the only one to have dreams. It's God's will."

"What? When did you have a dream?"

"The night after they found you in the forest . . . You will be all right . . . I know you will . . . I've seen it."

She turned her head to see their baby. "I gave you a son," she breathed. "That . . . makes me happier . . . than anything."

She tried to sit up but couldn't. Her energy was draining fast. "Can you bring him to me? I want to feel him in my arms."

He choked.

He rose and picked up the baby, bracing its small head as he carried him to her. He laid the bundle in her arms and then wrapped his around them both in a giant hug.

He nestled his head in her shoulder and felt the baby stirring against his cheek. Her breathing was light but rhythmic under his chest. They stayed like that for a long time.

For those few hours, they were a family, united by their embrace. Dreams of future memories flitted through his mind, of their son growing up before them, of taking meals together in springtime pastures under a bright sun as the boy chased insects he'd spied. He could see her, in the tall grass, calling out to him, laughing.

She turned her head.

He broke his reverie and looked at her.

"He will be strong . . . like you." She smiled again, but this was the weakest of them all and would be her last.

"Aidan . . . remember me."

"I will," his throat caught, and he began to cry. He brushed the back of his hand against her cheek.

"I wrote you a letter," she said.

"A letter? Where is it?"

"It's . . . in my vielle case . . . don't open it yet . . . wait . . . until Andrew's first birthday."

He nodded.

"Promise me."

"I promise."

"I love you, Aidan."

"I love you too, Priscilla. I always have, and I always will."

"Don't bury my cross with me . . ."

She had worn the delicate, golden cross around her neck every day since Aiden had gifted her with it.

"What do you mean? I can't take your . . ."

"No," she was firm, "Don't . . . you must keep my cross . . .

"My love," he choked, unable to stop the tears from flowing.

She fought to stay awake, but eventually her eyes fluttered and then finally closed.

"Can you still hear me?" he asked.

"Mm-hmm."

"I love you."

"It's so *beautiful*," she said softly.

A few minutes later, a long sigh escaped her lips.

Chapter 55

The letter was right where she said it would be, tucked into a pocket in the leather case she used to house her vielle.

It suddenly occurred to him that he would never hear her play it again.

The letter was folded into three parts and sealed with red wax. She'd written *Aidan* across the front. He laid a finger against the scrawl, treasuring the flow of lines created by her hand.

He carefully laid the vielle back in its case and buttoned it up. He would keep it safe for the rest of his years.

The letter he took to the study and placed in the center drawer of his father's writing desk. He yearned to know what it said now, hoping its words might relieve him of some grief, but he couldn't. He'd promised to wait a year, and he would.

He shut the drawer and blew out the candle.

That night, the crystalline air did nothing to assuage his heart. It was torn in all the wrong places.

The stars above glittered like jewels. Like lost loved ones, he realized. Distant, cold, too far to reach, yet still shining a little light through the darkness of one's night.

Priscilla was like one of them. It would not be cold where she was now, but her warmth was gone from him. Yet, she still glittered for him and always would.

He paced the castle walk, unaware that his mother had done the same thing on so many evenings. Tears constantly threatened to break through again.

Tonight, though, a certain resolve had entered him — a determination to provide for and protect his new son.

Priscilla's son. Her last gift to him.

He stopped and surveyed the quiet countryside illuminated by the light of the moon. The town was almost back to normal as most of the houses and shops had been rebuilt thanks to Aidan's funds. Yet, the burned-out fields were still visible in many places — a constant reminder of the serious threat they'd faced just six months before.

Suddenly, a certainty gripped him.

He had to kill his uncle.

He gripped the stone parapet, ignoring the abrasions its rough surface dug into his palms. His determination to protect Andrew condensed into a steely resolve to be done with Richard once and for all.

Baby Andrew would never be safe until Richard was dead.

***

April 1140 AD

Richard strode into the earl's hall, ignoring the servants and other supplicants.

He bowed at the waist.

He and the Earl of Chester had spent the first months of the year helping the king tamp down rebellions across southern England. Several bishops had revolted after Stephen ordered their arrest, and they'd had to be dealt with.

Before that, King Stephen had besieged Empress Maud in Arundel. This was the event that had interrupted Richard's siege of Aidan as all forces sympathetic to the king had been summoned. To not go at that time would have been considered treason.

Richard cursed the empress more than ever. Her arrival had prevented him from recovering what was his.

Most frustrating of all, Stephen had foolishly negotiated a peace that included letting her walk away scot free. The king and many other nobles could not stomach harming a woman, and they believed their true enemy was her illegitimate brother, Robert of Gloucester. Of course, that was exactly where the empress had fled, to her brother's arms.

Richard knew that Ranulf was as bothered as he was by that development. Stephen had had Maud in his clutches and he'd let her go. The war would now escalate rather than fade away and many questioned why they should lend their support to a king who could not close the deal.

Richard cleared his throat to get the earl's attention.

"To what do I owe the pleasure, my dear Richard?"

Ranulf seemed sincere, but Richard could have sworn he detected a faint note of sarcasm in his tone.

"I came to inquire as to your plans? What will our next course of action be regarding Aidan Falconer now that the king has given us rest from our service?"

"Rest he has not given. Many lords have merely taken leave for the time being. Our manors require attention, and he has proven ineffective in many respects."

"I understand fully. Yet . . ."

"I am in no mood to waste men or resources on Falconer at the moment," the earl interrupted, "I give you he is a thorn in my side, but sieges cost money, *Richard*."

"Have you forgotten the insults he uttered to your very face?" Richard did not like the direction this conversation was taking. The earl had evidently mellowed toward the young lad.

Ranulf offered him a chair. "Patience, man. I've not forgotten. But you must remember that the interests of my earldom come first. The king has not supported my interests as well as I have his. My northern lands are still in the hands of Scotland. If Stephen cannot deliver them back to me, perhaps Maud can . . ."

"You cannot be serious!"

Ranulf's eyes narrowed. "You forget your place, Richard. I treat you as a friend, but we are not equals, you and I. Remember that."

Richard bowed his head and nodded.

"I assure you I am very serious. I also assure you that I've made no decision, but *my* interests will come before the king's. I must measure my path well. If I intend to seek Maud's help, it would not do me any good to have just assaulted one of her most ardent supporters, now would it?"

Richard clamped his mouth shut. He tried to dissimulate his clenched jaws.

"Relax," Ranulf half-heartedly tried to soothe him, "Even if I were to switch my support to Maud, it would only be temporary until I could recover my lands. Maud isn't fit to rule, of course, so after that, I could come back to the king."

The earl stood.

"As I said, I've made no decision, but for now, we do nothing."

Chapter 56

Six months later – October 1140 AD

Hugo threw out an arm to block Richard's forward movement.

The sudden effort of it evoked a sharp twinge of pain in his chest. During the fight with the boy, Aidan had slammed his feet into Hugo's chest. It had broken two ribs. The injury must not have healed right because the wrong motions still hurt him. He was starting to think the pain might not ever go away. So, whenever it reared its head, he used it to fan the flames of vengeance.

The *boy* (he knew he could not truly call Aidan a boy anymore — he had proven himself too well) had bested him twice now. Hugo didn't share Richard's virulent hatred for the young man, but he did share an equal determination to see him vanquished.

To Hugo, any man who could outfight him was a threat, plain and simple. More so if that man had reason to hate him — and if Hugo were in Aidan's shoes, he wouldn't rest until his enemies were dead. So, he expected no less from young Falconer than he would himself.

Which meant he must do away with Aidan before Aidan could do away with him.

And that was, theoretically, what Richard said they were currently trying to do here, crouched behind a line of shrubs along the king's highway, waiting to ambush the Prince of Scotland.

Yet, Hugo wasn't as sure as Richard of the connection between the two.

The distinctive sound of hooves clopping the road's hardened dirt had just reached their ears, but to Hugo it seemed like there were a lot more horses approaching than expected.

Richard had been edging forward to engage as planned, so Hugo had stayed him.

"Something's wrong," he muttered.

The men behind them had not stirred either, sensing the same indicators as Hugo, but Richard had been so overly eager to jump into combat he'd ignored the clear warnings.

Sure enough, whispered orders to "hold steady" soon filtered down the line.

The son of David of Scotland, a prince named Henry, had come to visit King Stephen for Michaelmas. Prince Henry was the man to whom Stephen had ceded Chester's northern lands.

Given the king's tepid support for Ranulf's interests, the Earl of Chester had made the executive decision to kidnap the Prince of Scotland on his way home from the English court.

Richard Falconer had long since tied his banner to Chester's because the earl had seemed the most willing to intervene on his behalf to recover the Falconer lands.

Hugo had no place in this fight today — he didn't give a lick whether the sun rose or fell on Ranulf de Gernon — but Richard was committed to the cause. He was convinced that once Ranulf recovered his own lands, he would be willing to take on Aidan again.

Still, Richard Falconer's star could be waning.

Without Falconer Manor in hand, or any real chance to get it back in the near future, Richard had no power.

Hugo was not ignorant that his current standard of living was financed by the Earl of Chester and continued only at the earl's continued good will. So, he knew it was a good idea to distinguish himself in the earl's service in case he needed to seek a new lord. Chester was much more powerful than Richard would ever be anyway.

Nevertheless, Aidan remained a real threat to Hugo personally and must be dealt with one way or the other — *and soon.*

From the noise alone, it seemed the Scottish prince's band must be much larger than Chester had anticipated, and the earl had only brought a hundred men to this foray in order to maintain secrecy.

As the first horsemen came into view, it quickly became obvious they were going to let the party pass unmolested, and not only because of numbers.

The knights leading Prince Henry's band bore the king's standard.

As the prince himself passed, they saw King Stephen riding right next to him. Stephen had apparently gotten word of Ranulf's plot and was escorting Henry back to Scotland himself.

After the last of the soldiers passed (all of them blissfully unaware of the unsprung ambush), Ranulf rode up on his destrier, more red-faced than Hugo had ever seen him.

"The king will regret this insult," he seethed. "He chooses Scotland over his own earls."

All present seemed to have the wisdom to know that now was not the best of times to speak — about *anything*.

Ranulf trotted his horse in circles, glaring at everyone, yet really at no one in particular.

"It's the last straw," he said. "We're going to take Lincoln."

***

Lincoln Castle was a formidable fortress.

It overlooked the city of Lincoln and was a major power hub in England. As the Earl of Chester, Ranulf had claimed rights to it for years, but his claims had fallen on deaf ears. Now, he'd decided to take what was his by force.

He'd considered a siege, but that had no hope. Such a tactic would take forever and provoke a direct confrontation with the king — which was not what Ranulf wanted.

He just wanted Lincoln.

So, he opted for subterfuge. His wife and his sister-in-law were already inside the castle paying a social visit. While they visited with the ladies of Lincoln, he, his half-brother, William, Richard, and two other knights arrived at the front gate, all dressed in the attire of humbler men. They were ostensibly servants there to fetch the women and escort them home.

The two guards in the gatehouse were unsuspecting, more concerned with what hour they would get off duty than in preventing an unexpected attack. It was an easy matter for their small band to subdue them.

After that, Ranulf threw the gates open and ushered the rest of his men inside. The royal garrison was ejected, and as simple as that, Lincoln Castle was his.

The break with Stephen was now complete.

Richard participated in the move, but without the fervor he'd once had. He saw the inevitable slide toward Maud that Ranulf was taking. He sensed the change in the political winds. It put him in a precarious position.

Maud would never turn on Aidan. His nephew had showed too much ardent support for her cause. If Ranulf switched sides, Richard would wind up in limbo, either destitute without Ranulf or impotent to recover the Falconer lands with him.

Chapter 57

King Stephen was an effective military commander, but many would argue that he had a fatal flaw – that he showed too much mercy to his enemies.

The Earl of Chester had confounded him from the beginning. As the son-in-law of Robert of Gloucester, he'd originally expected Ranulf to defect to the Empress Maud. So, early on, Stephen had sought to weaken his power and simultaneously pacify Scotland by ceding Ranulf's northern lands to the northern king.

Yet, the earl's antipathy to the idea of a woman ruling him had outweighed his loyalty to his wife's family in Gloucester. Surprisingly, Ranulf had not defected, even after losing his northern lands, but had shown loyalty to Stephen's cause.

Still, he'd known Ranulf was truly loyal only to his own cause. Chester supported Stephen because Ranulf thought it was his best shot to acquire more power.

Then, he'd received word the earl had taken Lincoln Castle and ejected the royal garrison.

Rather than fight, Stephen's immediate reaction had been to ride north and sue for peace.

If granting the self-serving earl that city for a time would pacify him, he'd do it. He was having enough trouble putting down the other rebellious fires that kept popping up all over England.

The last thing he needed was to face another powerful earl like Chester on the field of battle. Gloucester was enough. The two of them together . . . it could cripple his reign.

Equally surprising, Ranulf had accepted his peaceful overtures and they'd made a pact. Ranulf's half-brother, William, would be named Earl of Lincoln, and Ranulf would be given powers over the town of Derby, but not over Derbyshire. That would remain under Robert de Ferrers. (Now, Stephen would have to pacify Ferrers as well.)

He rubbed his temples, feeling the beginnings of a headache coming on. "Yes, what is it?" the king asked.

A messenger had arrived several minutes ago, but had stood patiently in the back, not wanting to disturb the king's court.

The servant bowed. "A message, sire."

"Very well, let's hear it."

The messenger unrolled a small scroll and began to read. It was a message from the citizens of Lincoln complaining about Ranulf's treatment of them. The earl and his half-brother were torturing merchants and commoners alike to force them to reveal their wealth.

The king grimaced.

Such stories caused him great distaste, and they were unfortunately becoming too commonplace throughout the land. Men, even women, strung up by their thumbs, hung from rafters with weights tied to their feet, thrown into dungeons with poisonous snakes, and even worse tortures, all simply to force them to turn over what little gold or silver they might have.

Everywhere, barons with even just a little power were throwing up castles against him and filling them with evil men, men without conscience or fear of God.

All of it was a result of this blasted war for succession of the throne.

Stephen shook his head.

Didn't Maud know what she was causing?

"Is that all?" he asked.

The messenger shook his head.

"They also say to inform you that the earl is resting unafraid in the castle with a very light garrison."

Stephen's face lightened. Here was a possible opportunity. Perhaps in one fell swoop he could put a stop to one of these merciless lords, recover Lincoln, appease the Earl of Derby, strike a powerful blow to Maud, and humble Ranulf once and for all.

If the earl had foolishly left himself unprotected, Stephen could advance, and the battle would be quick. He could kill five birds with one stone and not risk a long commitment of his forces.

He smiled for the first time that day.

***

"Aidan! Aidan!" Eric called as he ran breathless into the great hall. "Have you heard?"

Sir William entered right behind him.

Aidan stood to greet them.

"No, what is it?"

"It's Stephen! The king . . . he's been captured. Robert of Gloucester has him!"

"What?" Aidan sat back down heavily.

They'd heard about the battle forming up at Lincoln, how the Earl of Chester had switched alliances in favor of Maud. That alone had been such welcome news. It meant the earl would be forced to leave Aidan alone for a while . . . and without Chester's soldiers, Richard had no resources.

Now, to hear that Stephen had been taken prisoner . . . it was almost too good to be true.

"How did it happen?" Aidan asked.

William explained, "The king tried to take Ranulf by surprise inside Lincoln Castle, but the earl escaped and ran to Robert of Gloucester. Gloucester and Chester returned with a large force of men."

Aidan smiled. Gloucester was a friend. He was a distant, powerful lord, but he'd also been the man who'd knighted Aidan while he was still a nobody outlaw in the woods.

"The two armies engaged each other directly," William continued. "The fighting was fierce. Stephen's sword broke, but he picked up a battle-axe and destroyed many men with it. Then, Chester rallied his men and swarmed Stephen. The king's earls deserted him, and it was actually one of Ranulf's men who took him. The Sheriff of Nottingham was taken as well."

Aidan didn't know what to say. It seemed so unbelievable that he hesitated to even sigh his relief.

"Do you know what this means, Aidan?"

"Of course."

"It means the rightful heir will finally rule and Richard will be without hope."

Aidan studied little Andrew crawling by the hearth, playing with some wooden toys. Could it be that his son would grow up not having to worry about war and treachery?

"I know," Aidan said. "Clearly, this news is reason to celebrate . . . yet, let's not count our chickens before they're hatched."

Chapter 58

It had been a year since Priscilla died.

Andrew was already walking and generally causing trouble as the maid-servants struggled to keep up with him. The boy certainly didn't seem to understand the danger of staircases.

Every time Aidan picked him up and felt the solid thickness of his little body against his chest, he couldn't help but feel the weight of her still with him. Andrew's hair was the same chestnut color as hers, and he had her eyes. Sometimes, Aidan even caught a glimpse of her smile in his.

Nicholas Fontaigne had not been the same since Priscilla passed. Aidan had only seen him a couple of times since the funeral, and he'd looked pretty haggard. He'd feared losing her when she married Aidan, and now he literally had.

He would have thought Nicholas would want to spend time with his grandson, but it was almost as if the boy reminded him too much of Priscilla. The pain was too great to bear still.

Aidan had buried her right next to his own mother and father.

This morning, he stood alone in front of their graves.

The soil above his parents was flat. Their marker stones had weathered. Priscilla's grave, however, had maintained a rounded shape a year later, even though rains had flattened it a bit. Grass was finally growing over the hump, but there was still a lot of bare dirt.

Her stone looked as new and fresh as the wound in his heart.

"I suppose it's time, darling," he said.

With trembling fingers, he broke the red wax seal covering her last letter to him. The scroll crackled as he unrolled it. Its texture felt rough and stiff. The paper was already yellowing.

My Dear Aidan,

I write this knowing I shall soon pass from this world. This was revealed to me in a dream, long before you were hurt. God showed me that I would give birth to our son, but that He would take me home soon after that. These constant pains in my belly only confirm the truth of what I am convinced is coming.

I've also had glimpses of your future, but I shall not speak of those here.

Please do not grieve for me too long. I go to be with God. The reality is that we shall be together again someday, my husband.

I know you love me, more than most women can ever hope to be loved. You are a true and kind-hearted man. I only wish I could live long enough to see you be a father, though I have no doubt you'll be wonderful at that too.

My dear, I do not wish for you to remain alone. You need a woman to love, to live life with, and our son needs a mother. Please do not withhold from him the caring hand only a mother can give.

I wish for you to marry Ysabella.

I know what a shock that will be given the sharp words I've spoken regarding her in the past. Yet, you must know that I never did so out of dislike for her, but because of my own fears that I could lose you.

At Geoffrey's request, I tutored her in reading and other studies as long as I was able. She is a very intelligent and capable woman, as well as a hard worker, and I believe she has a good and honorable heart. She may be surprised to learn that I consider her a friend, but only because my insecurities never allowed me to be so familiar.

I watched her minister to you while you were hurt. She cared for you so tenderly, I know she loves you. Yet, she has never acted as a common woman would, throwing herself at her lord to provoke his desires, but instead has respected me. I can think of no better mother for our son, nor a better wife for you, assuming you will have her, and I believe you will.

Please give her my cross, the one you gave me. She is not replacing me but doing that which I cannot — loving you and raising our child. The cross is to remind her that she serves God in my stead.

Aidan, I will ask you to wait a year before reading this, and I've no doubt you'll keep your word. Therefore, I tell you that a year is enough time for a man to grieve his wife.

Tell my son how much I love him, that were it in my power, I would have never left him this way. Yet, God's ways are not our ways.

You will raise him well, of this I am sure. I have always admired your

strength, your whole-hearted dedication to the welfare of others.
You loved me so well, darling. We shall see each other again.

Her Heart Is Forever Yours,

Priscilla

So many emotions whirled within, he couldn't process any of them. Thick tears streamed down his cheeks and dripped to the paper. Hastily, he wiped them away and held the letter out from his body so others wouldn't make the ink run.

Ysabella?

She wanted him to marry *Ysabella?*

There was so much he'd wanted to say to her. So much time he didn't get. The idea that her last words to him focused on urging him to marry again was confounding. The fact that it was Ysabella she wanted him to marry was terrible.

There was no denying Ysabella had attracted him from the start in a powerful way, but he had not thought about her at all over the past year. Perhaps because of guilt — guilt because in his mind she'd once competed for his desire — something that could only seem like a betrayal to Priscilla's memory now.

Even now, thoughts of the girl from the forest, remembering her face leaning over him as she ministered to him after the attack, it provoked such conflicting sentiments he didn't know what to do with them. It was just easier to close them out of his heart.

Of all the women on the manor, why did Priscilla ask Ysabella to be the one who watched over him while bedridden? Perhaps it had been a test. Perhaps Priscilla had wanted to see for herself how Ysabella would care for him?

Aidan shook his head.

For the entire past year, he'd anticipated reading this letter. In all that time, he'd never once imagined that these would be the words it would contain.

He reread it several times, searching for something more, longing to hear more of her voice . . . *and hear it he could.* The faint echoes of her were clearly transcribed across every carefully-penned word.

Her purity, her passion, her beauty.

Why had God taken her?

He clenched the muscles in his forearms to prevent them from involuntary-ily crumpling the letter in frustration. It was the last. It was precious.

Ysabella or not, they were Priscilla's last words to him. Even if he wished her to have spoken more of her heart, or of other things, these were the ones he must treasure. They were what they were.

He would do his best to love them. And to decipher the meanings he did not yet understand.

***

Richmond Castle, Yorkshire, England

Water splashed onto Richard's leggings as his horse charged through the shallow River Swale. Above him, the imposing walls of Richmond Castle loomed atop the cliff.

Since the capture of the king and Lincoln, Ranulf had been on top of the world. He'd personally taken the king prisoner and turned him over to his father-in-law, Robert of Gloucester. It seemed Maud would have the whole country under her rule sooner rather than later, and Ranulf was set to be one of her most powerful earls.

The man was full of himself at this point, not that he hadn't been before, and not that Richard blamed him for it — he'd be full of himself too if he were in the earl's position — but Ranulf felt he was untouchable after the Battle of Lincoln. The master strategist.

Richard might have been elated as well except for the fact that Ranulf's latest strategies were eliminating Richard's best shot to recover the Falconer lands.

Now, Chester had decided to go after the Earl of Richmond's northern holdings to replace what Stephen had given to the prince of Scotland. Never mind that the capture of Lincoln had theoretically been to make the same reparations.

Nevertheless, Alan the Black, Earl of Richmond, was a strong ally of Stephen. In Ranulf's view, that not only made him fair game, but a vulnerable baron without support from a sovereign now that the king was a prisoner.

Alan the Black had heard Ranulf was marching upon his lands, so he'd attempted a pre-emptive ambush to capture him. Ranulf, however, had turned the tides on him and instead captured Alan.

Richard couldn't help but admire the Earl of Chester. He had a knack for coming out on top no matter who opposed him.

Alan the Black was now a prisoner in his own castle. Ranulf was torturing him and would continue to do so until Richmond submitted and paid him homage. The screams only bothered Richard because they kept him up at night.

He wondered if there would be an end to Chester's campaign for power. He was beginning to feel like he was nothing but the earl's puppy, following him everywhere.

The raids made up for it though. Every day was dedicated to decimating the Honour of Richmond. Chester surprised Richmond's lesser barons, one after the other, through clandestine assaults upon their castles in similar manner to the way he'd taken Lincoln.

Fields were burnt, silver was stolen wherever it could be found, and peasant women were ravaged. Richard engaged in the latter from time to time but accruing all that silver was nicer. Ranulf's men tended to get especially stupid when drunk, and he could usually take their pennies from them through some gambling game or other. He was building up a small fortune.

Hugo rode up on his destrier. He briefly shot Richard a sly glance that dissipated once their mounts drew even.

"What's on your mind, Hugo?"

"How long are we going to do the earl's bidding?" he asked, peering into the distance at a band of soldiers riding toward the castle from the west.

"Why? Aren't you enjoying these raids? I thought the chance to line your pockets with silver would please you."

Hugo lifted a small pouch tied at his waist and let it fall to accentuate the jingling of coins. "Of course," he replied, his mouth pulled into a tight smile, "But all the silver in the world won't do me any good if Aidan decides to have me assassinated."

"You don't know the boy the way I do. He's not that kind."

"It's what *I* would do," Hugo hissed, "And that's *all* I know."

Richard said nothing. They rode in silence.

"We must move on him now," Hugo insisted. "Chester has an insatiable thirst for more land and he's not going to stop any time soon. It's distracting us."

"For now," Richard replied, "I cannot leave Ranulf's side. If he wants to invade France, I'll have to follow him there. Unless you've got an idea for another patron . . ."

Hugo shook his head.

"Then just save your silver, man. Our time will come."

Richard spurred his horse and rode off.

Chapter 59

Almost two years after the siege, Falconer lands were once more overflowing with people and crops. Free tenants and serfs alike had flocked in from both Lincoln and Richmond, fleeing the Earl of Chester's oppressions.

Rumors flew across England about how Aidan had defied the powerful earl and won. People were beginning to view the Falconer lands as an island of safety in the sea of chaos flooding the English Isle.

Some refugees had even come in from Nottingham to escape William Peverel. Robin of Locksley was still harassing him, of course, but Locksley had not yet regained his lands, so people were looking for a place to farm in peace.

The administration of it all grew to be so much that John Steward had to hire an assistant. The number of castle servants had nearly doubled. Aidan now had a small retinue of household knights. Men of honor who had grown weary of the civil war and refused to fight for morally bankrupt lords like Chester, men who were content to serve Aidan for less pay as long as they could serve someone they believed in.

Recent harvests had been so abundant the treasury was also growing for the first time. Trees were felled right and left. It seemed like new fields popped up every day to satisfy the needs of the newcomers.

The town of Becca's Well was stuffed so tightly that some were building two story homes instead of one. They'd finished the city wall last year, but at the rate everything was growing, they might have to build a second one in a few years that extended further out.

He ran his fingers along the wall's stones as he walked, almost caressing its rough surface. The people had worked so hard to complete it. They'd finished in two years what normally would have taken five.

This wall was what stood between them and the anarchy outside. If Richard ever returned, the wall is what would save his people. Aidan could at last breathe a sigh of relief knowing that many would be saved from the ravishings occurring elsewhere.

They'd finished the channel that could siphon the river into the castle's well if needed. That little project would ensure that they would never run out of water again.

The sudden influx of people and prosperity made Becca's Well and its surrounding villages prime targets for raids and thieves, so Aidan was constantly having to issue arms to the people and make sure the militias were receiving proper training.

Outside of his barony, it looked as if Maud would take the throne any day, which should permanently ensure Aidan's claim to Falconer Manor. That event would eliminate the Earl of Chester as a threat, as well as anybody else except for Richard.

No matter what though, his uncle had to be dealt with, and sooner rather than later. Once he were out of the picture, Aidan could finally relax.

For this, and because he was tired of being patient, he'd put a four-pound bounty on his uncle's head and told Red to spread the word among the various outlaw bands in the forests.

For a commoner, four pounds of silver was a fortune. Enough that certain men would jump at the chance. The idea of participating in an assassination left a distaste in his mouth, but the alternative was unbearable. His son's life and the barony remained at risk as long Richard remained alive.

A peal of thunder suddenly rumbled through the heavens. Thick, grey clouds were drifting in from the west, turning the afternoon dark. He guessed a downpour would break out soon.

He studied the skies and then glanced back at the castle. He thought he probably had enough time to finish his circuit before it erupted. He often liked to walk the wall's perimeter to check for weak spots or cracks that might have appeared in the mortar. It was not a large risk, but he was becoming fanatical about security, especially now with little Andrew depending on him.

He wasn't anxious to get back anyway. Wasn't much to go back to. Without Priscilla, the halls were cold and dark and lonely. There was no one to celebrate his victories with. No one to help him think through problems. At times, it all seemed kind of pointless.

The rain opened up much sooner than he'd expected. Thick rivulets of it were soon drenching him, penetrating his hair like frigid fingers trailing across his scalp.

He broke pace and sloshed through the rapidly deepening mud toward the castle. The sky had suddenly darkened so fast it felt like the onset of night.

The cold that flooded in with the wind was drastic.

He shivered involuntarily.

A single, thatched-roof home caught his eye. He stopped in front of it.

He knew it would be warm inside.

The shutters had been closed against the storm, but light glowed out from between their cracks.

He swiveled his head and looked back to the keep.

It loomed coolly in the distance like a tall, grey sentinel rising to greet the lonely wind. Emptiness filled its rooms.

He turned back and knocked on the modest door, hopeful for warmth.

After a moment, the door swung open.

Ysabella stood in its frame, backlit by firelight.

"Aidan . . ." she stumbled for words, caught off guard, "...um...come in."

He didn't budge. He stood there, in the rain, staring at her silently.

She stepped back and beckoned him in. "You're soaked," she said.

The words broke his paralysis. He stepped across the threshold, rubbing his hands against each other.

Thunder echoed behind him and shook the fragile hut as the door swung shut.

Inside, it was as warm as he'd hoped. She had a healthy fire going. Her hearth was small but effective. She hurried to fetch him a cloth to wipe his face and hair dry.

"Aidan . . ." she repeated his name, "how . . . have you been?"

He studied the lines of her jaw, her cheeks, the swath of her brow, all glowing in the flickering light. It danced upon her skirts, revealing the familiar curve of her hips and her narrow waist. Her skin had a bronze tone in the dim room.

Her eyes sparkled with a mixture of sadness and hesitant expectation. Over the past several years, she'd grown to see him more as a lord to be respected and less as the young man she'd loved as an equal in the forest. She was just a peasant girl after all.

A trembling entered her limbs, almost like a fear.

The wetness of the rain still rolled down his arms. Drops of it trickled from his scalp to his neck. It was the only sensation he could feel, like an electric tingle standing his hairs on end.

His heart felt seized. Seized by memories of Priscilla. Of her beauty. Of her purity of heart. He'd never been unfaithful to her. Not once.

Within him, his vows clashed with her last words to him, her stated will. Rebelling, refusing, relenting, then rising up again.

Thunder exploded overhead once more, vibrating the home and even their very chests.

It broke his reverie.

He stepped forward and reached out for her. She didn't pull back but let him wrap her in an embrace. He gazed into her eyes, searching for answers, their faces just inches apart.

"Aidan . . ." she breathed, anticipation overwhelming her fear.

"I've been lonely," he rasped, finally answering the question she'd forgotten she'd asked.

Desire welled up and pressed his lips into hers. They felt warm and soft and giving. It was as if he'd been waiting his whole life for this kiss.

A thought that confused him all over again. She evoked physical desire in him in ways that were different from Priscilla, yet *how could that be?* He didn't understand.

He broke the kiss and stepped back, embarrassed. "I'm sorry," he said.

"Don't be," she answered.

This time, it was she who kissed him.

***

Two weeks later

Ysabella had never stopped loving Aidan. She *had* tried to forget him, especially after his marriage, but her heart had never truly let go. None of the young men in Becca's Well seemed to measure up.

It wasn't just that they were peasants, and it wasn't really about Aidan's position or title. If she were honest with herself, his prowess as a fighter did excite her. Of course, none of the other villagers had the time to practice the way he did, so they didn't have the chance to match his abilities. The same went for his education.

Secretly, this was one of the reasons she'd wanted to learn to read. Not to try and steal him away from Priscilla — she certainly hadn't thought to do such a thing. But, if on the off chance she ever had the opportunity to speak to him again, she'd wanted to have something intelligent to say.

Things like his strength, his education, and his position gave him his confidence, which was one of the most attractive things about him. But all of that paled in comparison with his heart.

Aidan had a good heart.

Early on, she'd watched him lead and care for their people in the forest. His sense of duty and compassion stood out like a shining beacon amidst the darkness enshrouding the country. She'd heard stories — they'd all heard stories — of barons and earls everywhere who were taking advantage of the lawlessness. The absence of authority seemed to reveal their true hearts.

Yet, while they bent to evil, Aidan had created an oasis of peace and prosperity. It was as if everything he touched were protected by a large bubble.

There were many reasons to love him.

Ysabella bent down and dipped her finger in the river, swirling it in circles and watching the ripples.

After their first stormy kiss, he'd looked into her eyes for a long while and then left, but not before promising to seek her out on the morrow. Since then, he'd come to visit her every day. They usually strolled the country lanes together, making no effort to hide their budding courtship.

The village women were chattering about it, of course, some jealous, some happy, but most just enjoying the gossip.

Today, they'd come down to the river for a picnic. Aidan said he liked the sound of its currents against the rocks.

These walks were teaching her that she didn't just love *him*, she loved *being* with him. He made her feel safe and secure, and she liked his humor. Being with him felt natural and easy. Relaxed. As if he weren't a lord and she weren't a peasant. They were just a boy and girl in love with no outside world pressuring them for answers.

They'd had a pleasant meal. Some songbirds in a nearby tree insisted on serenading them. She'd been feeling quite content.

Then . . .

. . . he'd shown her the letter.

Priscilla's letter.

At first, her words shocked her. She'd always suspected Lady Priscilla had detected her true feelings for Aidan in spite of her efforts to suppress them. But the idea that she'd *chosen* Ysabella . . . *named* her for her husband . . . it was all very strange.

She couldn't decide what to make of it. She supposed she should be flattered, or grateful, and in a way, she was, but she also didn't like it.

After Aidan had read the letter to her, she'd fallen mute. A cool hand had closed around her heart.

She wanted Aidan (she didn't doubt *that*) but she wanted to have him on *her* terms. Not Priscilla's.

After they'd married, she'd never let herself believe there could be a possibility for her, but now that the chance was here, she realized she would have preferred to never have it than for Aidan to marry her out of a sense of duty to his former wife.

She didn't want him like that. She wanted him to desire her because he did, not because he thought he should. Could she ever be sure his feelings were true now? Or had the blasted letter ruined it all?

"What are you thinking, Bella?" Aidan asked expectantly. He'd actually tolerated her silence for quite a while considering the weight of what he'd just shared.

She tilted her head and shot him a coy look from her crouched position.

He laughed. "You do have a spirit about you, don't you?"

Ysabella stood up. She liked that he'd started calling her Bella. She'd never had a nickname before. Geoffrey said it sounded like a Latin word for beautiful.

"Aidan," she began, "I was happy . . . but now I'm not so sure. I know what she wrote you . . . but I don't want to be with you because you think you have to."

He blushed and shook his head. "No . . . um . . . that's not it." The objection took him off guard.

He reached for her hand, but she pulled away.

He dropped his arm back to his side, stunned. He turned his gaze to the sky above the forest line.

"Bella . . . I think I understand . . . but that's honestly not the reason I'm here . . . well, I take that back. It is *a* reason . . ."

"See!"

"No, I mean . . . listen. Priscilla was a wonderful woman. She was the love of my life. I'll always hold her memory dear to my heart . . ."

"I'd have it no other way."

"In fact, she was so wonderful, she knew my needs before I did, and tried to provide for me the only way she could before she passed."

"But the letter forces you . . ." she objected.

"No, it releases me. I was so lost I might have gone years and years without opening my heart again. Somehow, she knew I would do that and perceived she needed to release me. So I could live my life and be happy."

"She was an amazing woman, Aidan. I'll never compare with her. And *that's* my fear. She didn't really free you but *chose for you*. I can't bear the thought that you might be with me only because of her."

Aidan moved toward her. This time, he succeeded in taking both her hands in his.

"No," he tried to assure her, "She didn't just perceive my needs, but also my wants. Ysabella . . . I've always desired you."

She didn't believe him.

"Don't you understand? I've been drawn to you since I first met you in the forest. When we danced, when you sang to me, when I saw you dancing in the glade . . ."

"Wait . . . *what?*"

He waved a hand to cut her off. "Yes, one day, I saw you dancing among the trees by the river . . . and singing. If I'm being honest, that wasn't the only time . . ."

Her eyes grew wide at the admission.

"But I thought . . . you never showed interest . . ."

"I couldn't! The pull . . . it was so strong. If my heart hadn't already belonged to Priscilla, I would have been lost to you. As it was, it was all I could do to resist."

"But . . ."

"I think Priscilla knew that. I think she knew what I wanted more than I did, and that's why she chose you. Believe me, she was very jealous of you. She was furious the day I went to see you about Mark and ended up saving your life. She wouldn't talk to me for days, so it shocked me as well when I read what she wrote."

"I . . . I just don't know what to say."

"Don't say anything. Just believe me. I'm with you here because I care about *you.*"

"You see? You say you care about me, but I *love* you! I love you with all my heart, Aidan! Yet, you only have care for me."

He looked away. She saw tears welling in his eyes. "Bella, love is a serious word. Priscilla is the one who taught me the meaning of it. I feel guilty even saying it . . ."

"I know. Again, I don't ask you to pretend . . ."

She tried to pull away, but he held her hands tight in his grip and looked in her eyes.

"I do, Bella. I do love you. That's what I'm trying to say."

A flood of emotions flowed through her. Elation, disbelief, joy, confusion.

"It's true."

"But when . . . how?"

"When? I don't know. Perhaps that night when we first danced, and I felt the curve of your hip under my fingers and the tickle of your hair against my cheek. Perhaps right now. I just know I do, and I wish to marry you, if you'll have me."

He dropped to one knee in front of her.

"Marriage? I don't know . . . how can you be sure?"

"I want no one else, Bella. I can't stop thinking about you."

She smiled and touched his cheek. "Um . . . *no* . . . wait, I mean, I'm not sure."

"*Why?*" he stood back up.

"Even if what you say is true, I'm just the daughter of a serf. I'm no lady. How could I run a castle?"

A look of confident determination entered Aidan's face, an expression she'd only seen when he was about to go into a fight.

"There's no doubt you're lady enough," he said, "So if it's my love you question, I'll just have to prove it to you."

Chapter 60

"Where are you going with that sprig of flowers?" Alan called with a teasing tone.

He was the fifth person to rib Aidan about it this morning.

"To find your mother," he called back without stopping. Best way to win a battle of insults was to get the last one in and be gone so quick you couldn't hear the reply.

He found Ysabella waiting for him in the great hall.

For the past month, Aidan had done literally everything in his power to court her and prove his love. He'd brought her flowers almost every day. He'd sung her songs and taken her on long rides through the forest on his courser. He'd even tried to write her a poem . . . though that hadn't come out very well.

Everyone in Becca's Well knew about the courtship now...and they knew she was still rebuffing him.

He was starting to think she was doing it now only because she was enjoying how much he was pursuing her. Her latest marriage rejections had been accompanied by a coquettish smile.

His knights were even making fun of him now, calling him a lost puppy, and that was one of the nicer jabs. Neither his servants nor soldiers dared joke with him openly, but he caught knowing smirks being exchanged every now and then.

He didn't care though. He loved Ysabella. If this is what he had to endure to prove it, so be it.

Short of some villain attacking her and him riding in to save the day, he didn't know what else he could do to prove himself though. Frankly, he *had* done that once, and if he did it again, she'd probably just say he was only being himself.

Courting her persistently was the only way to show his expressions of love were not just thin sentiments fabricated to please his deceased wife.

If she didn't give in soon, though, he thought they were going to have to have a serious talk.

When he reached the hall, she was standing by the long table in the center of the room they used for meals, holding Andrew on one hip and balancing him as she whispered to him playfully.

The scene shocked him to a halt. His eyes welled with tears. He could suddenly see her in the role of Andrew's mother like never before. How well she would fit into life in the castle.

She broke her game with Andrew and turned to him.

"Are those for me?" she asked in what was becoming her all-too-common, coy tone.

He crossed the room to her.

"You know they are," he said huskily.

"Well, thank you." She mimicked a mock curtsey as best she could while still holding the child.

"You look good with him," he said.

She blushed.

"How long will you refuse me, Ysabella? Why can't we be married?"

She set Andrew down, and the boy waddled over to a group of toy wooden horses scattered across the floor.

"That's actually what I came to speak to you about, Aidan."

His heart leapt into his throat. Suddenly, he was ready for the worst.

In his wildest dreams, he'd never imagined she might actually turn him down once and for all.

"I love you, Ysabella. I don't know how else to show it."

"I know, Aidan," she said. "I know you do. So, I came to tell you . . . *Yes*."

"Yes?"

"Yes!"

He grabbed her shoulders and pulled her into a tight hug.

"That's a relief," he breathed. "Frankly, you were wearing me out."

Aidan released her and withdrew a small leather pouch from a pocket in his tunic.

His fingers trembled as he undid the drawstring and pulled out Priscilla's cross.

He trembled because after winning Ysabella's belief in his love, he didn't want this to ruin it. He trembled as well because no one else had ever worn it but Priscilla. He'd given it to her, and in spite of her clear wishes, he couldn't help but feel this was a betrayal of sorts.

Ysabella had read the letter, so she instantly knew what it was — and what it meant.

Aidan didn't know what to expect. Would she be angry . . . hurt?

Instead, Ysabella smiled and pulled her hair back so her could set it over her head. The chain lay upon her neck like it was made for it. The cross pendant came to rest right above her heart.

It looked good.

Their wedding was a much smaller affair than his and Priscilla's had been. Ysabella didn't want to compete with the people's memory of their lady. She was shy of attention and preferred a humble ceremony inside the church.

The people defied her though and still turned out in droves in spite of her embarrassment.

Geoffrey administered the vows and the church erupted into enthusiastic cheering when Aidan bent to kiss his new bride.

Chapter 61

The woodsman knew how to blend in.

Until recently, he'd served as a king's forester. These days, however, neither the king nor the sheriffs had the time to deal with those who broke forest law. He hadn't been paid for months — nor had any other foresters he knew — so he'd been forced to make his own way.

He came from a family of foresters who knew the English woodlands better than anyone. They not only possessed the knowledge to reap its fruits, but also an innate sense of authority and willingness to prohibit anyone else from doing the same.

His brothers and he normally dominated the forest region north of Leicester. Since the king's pay had stopped, they'd been hunting deer and boar and selling the meat in local villages. They also felled trees and sold the wood to millers and builders. When others tried to do the same, they ran them off.

They'd been aware of the rumors of Aidan Falconer and his liberal policies in Derbyshire for several years. Any news from that part of the country always left them shaking their heads. If they'd been in Falconer's position, they knew they would have never done such things. The man was squandering his advantage.

Then, word of his offered reward reached their ears. Without missing a beat, they saddled their horses and rode north in search of their prey. A price on a man's head can have a way of crystalizing more solid support for the cause.

The woodsman and his six brothers now lay in wait inside the tree line along an unfamiliar road, each of them dressed from head to toe in forest green. They'd streaked their tunics with brown mud to break up the solid greens and camouflage themselves better amongst the bushes. From the previous night's fire, they'd mixed charcoal with animal fat and smeared the black grease under their eyes and across their faces to prevent a splotch of skin color from giving them away.

They'd abandoned their traveling boots for softer shoes that made no noise when they walked and positioned themselves downwind from their target so his horses wouldn't sense their presence ahead of time.

At last, the awaited party of soldiers came into view from around a bend in the road. Twelve men total, bunched in groups of two and three.

But only one of them was important.

They were seven woodsmen against twelve armed men. He and two of his brothers were the advance team. They would ambush the group and kill their primary target along with each of the men on either side of him. Then, they'd retreat back into the forest.

Two more brothers would cover their trail and surprise any pursuers, which they hoped would dampen the soldiers' desire to flush them out until they could gather reinforcements. Long before that could happen, the woodsmen would have melted off into the forest again.

While the soldiers were still scattered and distracted, the last two of his brothers would take advantage of the chaos and roll their target's body from the road to load it onto a waiting horse. They'd need it to collect their bounty.

The woodsman lifted his bow and pulled the string back until it was taut. He held it steady, feeling its power stored in the tension of its curved length. A simple release of his fingers and that power would flow into the arrow he'd already nocked.

He took aim and lined up Richard Falconer in his sights. He noticed the man didn't look like he was having a particularly good day as it was.

It was about to get worse.

"What would you have me do, Hugo?" Richard asked, grimacing as his horse stumbled in an unexpected pothole in the road.

"Seek a new sponsor. Why not go see Derby? He's not keen on Aidan either."

"I'm not a common knight to go around seeking a sponsor! Derby? . . . I don't know. He's with Stephen to be sure, but if I did that, I could never come back to Chester . . ."

"It's an opportunity to get back on the king's side. You've no hope as long as Chester fights for Maud . . ."

Hugo was interrupted by a sudden breath of air that passed in front of his face.

It had been more than a breath . . . there had been something solid in that wind.

Richard was startled as well, but before Hugo could say anything, some-thing slammed into his shoulder. The pain was piercing. Hugo looked down and saw the fletching of an arrow shaft protruding from his shoulder.

His hand moved to his sword. "To arms!" he cried.

In that instant, a third arrow sliced through the middle of the throat of the knight on Richard's other side.

The woodsman cursed angrily.
Right as he'd released his shot, a squirrel, a stupid *squirrel* of all things, had leapt onto his back and thrown off his aim. Never, in all of his years of forest life, had a squirrel jumped on him.

It had been *his* job to kill Richard himself, but because of that stupid rodent, he'd completely missed. His brothers' aim had been truer. At least one of them had killed his man, the other was only wounded.

He was shamed, but nothing could be done for it now except to retreat. He even wondered if they should consider abandoning the job. A squirrel? Who'd ever heard of such a thing. It felt like this Falconer man was protected by the very forest itself. How else could they have performed so badly when otherwise their bows knew not how to miss.

"They got away, sire," a soldier called, "They had bowmen waiting for us among the trees. We've got one more dead."
"Who was it?" one of Chester's knights demanded.
Richard glared at the trees but said nothing. It was clear to him he'd been the target.
"I know who it was!" Hugo spat. He snapped off the arrow shaft jutting from his shoulder without a blink. "Aidan Falconer! *I told you*, Richard. I told you it was just a matter of time."
Richard remained silent.
Hugo met his eyes and was certain he detected a twinge of cowardice there. Sure, Richard was brave enough when supported by others, like the day he'd evicted Aidan from Falconer castle. Back then, he'd had three knights to back his move against a boy.
Now that Richard was alone, though, he hesitated with every decision. He clearly feared stepping out on his own.
"That's it!" Hugo growled. "I'm done sitting here doing Chester's bidding! I'm going after Aidan. Are you coming?"
Richard stared at him blankly. After a moment, he slowly shook his head.
"Then, this is the last you'll see of me. Pray it's the last you hear from Aidan as well," Hugo hissed.
He reined his horse around and spurred it into a gallop, racing south at full speed.

Chapter 62

"Let's have another mead, Brewer!"

Grunting, the innkeeper poured a mugful and walked it over to his bleary-eyed customer, who was already sloshed and not letting up.

"Your woman said not to get you drunk anymore," the brewer said as he handed it to him.

"Aw, so what? Ya gonna listen to a woman? Just keep 'em coming."

Hugo watched the exchange silently. After the tavern keeper left, he picked himself up and slid over toward the man.

"Weren't you part of the castle guard?" He asked quietly.

The patron shot him an appraising eye.

"What's it to ya?"

"Just a man looking for a job. Someone said you'd been in the guard."

"Ya have the bearing of a man of means about ya. Why would you need a job?"

"Times have been better . . ." Hugo shrugged as if to admit a whole lot of nothing.

"Well . . . yeah, I was in the guard. Till last year, anyway. Bunch of hard cases over there, I tell you what."

"Why? What happened?"

"Borrowed a piece of equipment that didn't belong to me an' that steward kicked me out."

"Scummy thing to do."

"Here, here!" The man raised his mug to the sky as if toasting.

"So, what? You think I shouldn't go ask for a job?"

"More power to ya if they give one to ya. They pay well, I'll give 'em that." The former guard put his cup to his lips and drained it.

"I heard the baron had some kind of secret project going on here a few years ago?"

"Yeah, there were rumors an' such, but I wouldn't know much about that."

"Who would?"

The man set into deeper thought. "Probably Tim o' the Dale. Falconer chooses who he trusts, and he trusts Tim. Other than that, I don't know."

***

Timothy stopped to readjust the pack on his shoulder. It kept slipping. His wife would be pleased. He'd had enough pennies to bring a few good cuts of meat home from the butcher. They'd have a good meal tonight.

He was thinking about how they'd had more good times than bad of late, so he was smiling when he pushed open the front door with his foot.

Then, his smile fled like sand in a river current.

His wife was gagged and huddled in the corner with her arms around their children. The second thing he saw was a strange man seated in his chair by the fire. The man's sword lay loosely in his lap, and it didn't look like the kind of sword that never got used.

Tim started to yell, but the man cut him off.

"You scream, I'll slit their throats and leave."

His mouth shut like a trap.

The stranger's face revealed a certain viciousness that chilled the soul, and a sneer that conveyed contempt for all. His chain mail was worn and scarred in many places. He was familiar with war.

Belatedly, the beginning of recognition dawned. Tim realized he knew the man from several years ago. It was Sir Hugo, Richard Falconer's top knight. And he remembered Hugo's reputation. A reputation that matched the cold cruelty shining in his eyes.

He didn't doubt Hugo would kill them without the slightest remorse.

"What do you want?" he breathed.

"Come in and close the door," Hugo said.

Tim obeyed.

"For starters, why don't you tell me about Aidan's secret building project. I hear it was something to do with a tunnel?"

Chapter 63

"How long do you think you'll be, honey?" Ysabella wrapped her arms around Aidan. He could feel her warmth through his tunic. She began kneading the muscles in his shoulders.

He smiled. "Not long. I just want to read through these again."

He was seated at the desk in his father's study. He still had trouble thinking of this study as his own. Everything in it reminded him of his father. Its books, its smell . . .

"Are those the new steward's reports?"

"Yes."

"What do they say?"

"That everything looks great. The harvest this fall is predicted to be our best yet."

"That's good," she gave his shoulders a last squeeze. She moved to the door and smiled suggestively. "I'll be waiting up for you."

"Then, I'd better hurry," he agreed.

Through a peep hole in the backing of the bookcase that covered the entrance to the secret passage, Hugo watched Aidan and the woman. Out of fear for his family, Tim O' the Dale had quickly confessed the location of the tunnel's entrance. Hugo hadn't even had to ask twice.

He'd left the family tied up in their home. They only reason he hadn't slaughtered them outright was because he didn't want to risk the alarm their screams might raise. Once he was done here, he'd go back and finish them off. Had to eliminate the witnesses.

He'd located the tunnel entrance by the river easily enough, right where the Tim had said it would be.

An hour earlier, he'd popped the latch on the back of the shelving unit and snuck into the study. He'd figured Aidan would come here alone at some point and realized the study was the perfect place for an ambush. He'd removed one of the books from the bookcase and poked a tiny hole in the paneling behind it. The hole was so small, no one would notice it from the study side, but from the tunnel, he could put his eye to it and see everything.

He didn't know the woman. As far as he'd heard, Aidan had married Priscilla Fontaigne. *So, who was this one?* Surely, he wasn't brazen enough to court a mistress right under his lady's eye . . .

It didn't matter. Aidan would die either way.

The woman left, but not before sending her man some very seductive messages. Perhaps before the night was over, he'd go find her and have some extra fun.

Finally, Aidan was alone, his back to the bookcase.

Hugo brandished his long knife. He'd spent hours sharpening it, looking forward to the work it would do this night.

He inched the shelving unit open far enough he could slip out. He'd left the latch sprung and oiled the hinges before Aidan came in. So, the hidden door was perfectly silent now as it swung.

Hugo had also removed his boots to ensure his footfalls would be soft and undetected. Step by step, he creeped closer to Aidan's back. The boy was clueless, too engrossed in study.

Hugo loomed directly behind his prey. Still no awareness. Aidan was busy scribbling on the papers in front of him. The boy leaned forward slightly as if trying to see something more clearly in the candlelight.

Hugo raised the long knife high. The blade gleamed wickedly in the dim light. He paused for the tiniest of seconds to relish the deliciousness of the moment.

Suddenly, Aidan whirled around and plunged a dagger in Hugo's chest.

Stunned, he stared at Aidan as the long knife tumbled from his fingers, even as he willed it not to fall.

How had the boy known?

Too late, he realized Aidan had been writing with his left hand. The boy was right-handed. He should have remembered.

Hugo sank to his knees as Aidan stood from his chair and hovered over him.

The dagger had struck exactly where Aidan intended. The wound was mortal. Sharp agony gripped his chest. Hugo's vision began to fade.

"I guess . . . you're not a boy after all . . ." He tried to grin at Aidan.

Then, he toppled over.

The moment he'd entered the study, Aidan had seen that a book had been moved. A longer glance revealed the bookcase was just a fraction of an inch ajar. Without giving away his awareness, Aidan had simply seated himself at the desk with his back to the tunnel and waited.

That someone had used the secret tunnel was for sure. That they had left the panel ajar meant they were still there. Otherwise, they would have closed it fully and not risked detection.

Unfortunately, the only kind of person who could be lurking there must intend him harm. Most probably, an assassin sent by Richard.

He'd decided to wait them out, whoever they were.

The only point of anxiety had been when Ysabella came in. It had been emotional torture worrying the assassin might make his move while she was in the way. He'd forced himself not to breathe a sigh of relief when she exited unharmed.

His surprise was to see the assassin was none other than Hugo himself.

Hugo had helped poison his father. Now, he was agonizing like the dog he was on the floor of his father's study.

It fit.

Once he was sure Hugo was dead, Aidan called the guards to come and remove his body. There would be no ceremony celebrating the honor of a fallen knight. They would simply take it outside the grounds and burn it.

He didn't even want to strip his mail or weapons for the armory. After the burning, he'd send the metal to the blacksmith and have him melt it down for complete refabrication.

He felt lighter. Richard was weaker, and Aidan had one less enemy.

Ysabella would find out in the morning. He wouldn't tell her tonight. It might steal the peace of her sleep.

Chapter 64

September 1141 AD

S ince the day Becca's Well had been burned to the ground, it and the rest of Falconer Manor had boomed back like nothing Aidan had ever heard of. No one doubted Nicholas Fontaigne's freedom policies now. They'd proven themselves over and over.

Aidan eventually decided to lower his baron's share to a mere 12%. He found himself wincing as he gave the order, expecting to hear in the not-too-distant future that the treasury was emptying itself out again, but such news never came. At the first harvest, the results were clear. The more people were freed to work for their own benefit, the more they produced.

A small drop in taxes was a big deal to each peasant, so they worked harder. John estimated most Falconer families were earning around 60 pennies per month, *double* the average income of a peasant family elsewhere. Just because they worked harder and were free to try new things.

All of that meant more silver came into the treasury from every holding, in spite of the lower tax rate. And as more people were inspired to immigrate to the manor each month, they had to create new fields, which increased the *number* of holdings producing silver. Then, as the population increased and people had more money to spend, there was naturally more opportunity to be had. The town merchants were the most ecstatic of all.

Nicholas hadn't been himself since Priscilla passed. As much as Fontaigne had rubbed him wrong before they were wed, Aidan could not fault him as a father-in-law. He'd been instrumental in Aidan's success, and, of course, Priscilla had been who she was because of him.

Nicholas came around once in a while to see his grandson, but he was still clearly depressed. Even the sight of young Andrew caused him pain. Aidan lit candles in the church for him regularly.

John Steward had just informed him that Falconer Manor now had almost 1,700 families. That include the lands around Pilsbury Castle. As soon as Aidan had instituted his policies on Pilsbury, its villages had immediately launched into prosperity like his own. And more families seemed to arrive every week — every day even.

He'd hired more knights for a total of ten and had double that in men-at-arms. The castle servants numbered so many the keep felt like a tiny bustling city at times. The best part was that even after all their pay, he still had close to ten pounds of silver flowing into the treasury per month. A true fortune. Well, at least for him it was a true fortune.

He doubted it compared with what Chester took in, but it was a great start. It would allow him to continue to beef up the castle's defenses and even hire temporary soldiers if he needed to.

With the exception of Hugo's attempted assassination, he hadn't heard a peep from his uncle. He didn't doubt Richard still stewed in hatred, but without Hugo, and with Chester having abandoned the king, he was most likely stuck. For now, he didn't have a path forward.

Which meant, for the time being, Aidan could relax.

He looked up from the report. "Are we collecting all the revenue from the felled trees in Pilsbury?" he asked his steward.

Ysabella entered the hall in the middle of his question.

"Yes, sire. William is doing an excellent job at managing Pilsbury and implementing all of your policies. He's begun improving Pilsbury's defenses as well."

"Very good," Aidan replied. He turned to Ysabella. "Yes, dear?"

John bowed and excused himself from the room.

"Want some good news?"

"Sure," he smiled.

She rubbed her belly. "I'm with child!"

The blood drained from his face. Panic clutched him hard.

He couldn't help it. Sudden fear that Ysabella might share Priscilla's fate seized him. He loved Ysabella now as fiercely as he'd ever loved Priscilla.

He knew she wanted a joyous greeting for the news. *He* wanted a better reaction.

He struggled to shove the anxiety to the bottom of his heart and forced the biggest smile he could muster.

She'd seen the battling emotions and understood. She'd almost expected as much. She was actually impressed by how fast he'd been able to control them. She knew he loved her, and the fear was for her well-being, not disappointment that they would have a child.

He would share that joy as much as she.

"How long have you known?" he stammered.

"I've had the signs for a month or so?"

Just then, a clamor arose from the front of the keep. A messenger rushed into the hall flanked by Alan and Adelard. The messenger hurried to Aidan's chair and kneeled before him, dipping his head.

"I bear news, milord."

"What are they?"

"Robert of Gloucester has been captured at Winchester."

"What?"

Everyone knew Robert of Gloucester was *the* force behind Maud's attempt to claim her throne. With him captured, Maud's war effort would essentially collapse.

As Stephen's should have when he'd been captured by Gloucester. Yet, things had not turned out that simply. Stephen's queen, Matilda, had rallied his armies and carried on the war in his stead.

With the king imprisoned, Maud had entered London to be coronated, and the church had voiced its support for her reign, including Stephen's own brother, Bishop Henry.

Yet, within weeks, the people of London had risen up against Maud and she'd fled just in time to escape with her life and her forces intact.

Bishop Henry had then switched allegiances back to his brother Stephen, and so Maud and Robert of Gloucester began a siege of Henry in Winchester with the accusation that his behavior was much closer to that of a baron than a bishop.

Queen Matilda had come to his rescue though, and now Gloucester had been captured. A disaster for Empress Maud.

A disaster for Aidan.

"That's not all, sire," the messenger continued, "There is talk of exchanging Gloucester for Stephen."

"Stephen is to be released?" Aidan sunk his face into his hands. "This war is never going to end," he muttered.

All he could think of was Ysabella's beautiful belly that would soon begin to swell.

And the future he'd hoped to provide had just gotten a lot dimmer.

Eleven Years Later

Chapter 65

Richard's horse stumbled in the mud and almost threw him. It would have been a wet, unpleasant fall, given the cold temperature that was setting in.

The weather matched his mood.

After all these years, he still rode with the Earl of Chester. His life had devolved into that of a landless knight.

The earl had flipped sides so many times in the civil war, Richard had lost count. After they'd attacked the Earl of Richmond and taken his lands, Ranulf had begun a war against the Earl of Leicester.

In 1142, King Stephen had persuaded Ranulf to switch his allegiance back to him. Richard, of course, had encouraged this whole-heartedly with the hope it would allow them to attack Aidan again. They'd then fought alongside Stephen for several years against the castles held by Maud, but Falconer Manor always seemed to be perceived as too small to matter in Chester's eyes.

Richard often threatened to withdraw his support if Ranulf never chose to help him, but the earl was too obsessed with amassing entire earldoms for himself to be bothered with a small barony, and he knew Richard had nowhere else to go.

Two years later, Ranulf conspired with the king's brother, Bishop Henry, to rebel against the king and divide northwest England with the bishop. The king had come after them in Lincoln but abandoned the effort when a siege tower collapsed and killed eighty of his soldiers.

The following year, Ranulf switched back to Stephen for a third time. He'd felt his other holdings were secure and wanted to attack David, the King of Scotland, to recover the rest of his remaining northern lands. Since David was allied with Maud, he couldn't do that unless he allied himself with Stephen again. So, he did.

Sometimes, Richard just stood in awe of the man. No one played politics like him, and no one fought as fiercely as him. He seemed to have a knack for escaping sticky situations just in the nick of time. He was about no one's cause in any true sense but his own, and he knew just when to switch sides to advance that cause. Over the years, he'd amassed quite a bit of territory, but angered most of the nobles of England in the process, including both of the warring sovereigns.

Nobody trusted him, yet everybody needed him.

In 1146, rumors reached them that the Welsh were mobilizing to attack Chester. Richard had suspected the movement was instigated by many of the nobles that had lost land to Ranulf.

Chester had recently shown very real support to the king in battles like the one at Wallingford, so at the time, the earl had asked the king to help him put down the Welsh. But the same nobles stirring up the trouble with the Welsh whispered to the king that the earl's request was a trap to capture the king again.

Stephen had believed them and arrested Ranulf when he arrived at the king's court. When the news of the earl's capture reached Wales, the Welsh had immediately marched on Chester and laid waste to it.

The king had ordered Ranulf to forfeit all his lands or be executed. Ranulf pretended to agree, but as soon as the king released him, he'd immediately rebelled again and went back to Maud for the last time. He was furious at what had happened to Chester, at being arrested after arriving peacefully at the king's court, and at being forced to relinquish all the lands he'd worked so hard to acquire. He would evermore be a determined enemy of Stephen's.

That was the point when Richard had become most discouraged. First, when Ranulf was arrested and threatened with execution, but even more so once he was released and set upon such a vengeful path against the king. He knew there would never again be any hope to get Stephen's help in taking back Falconer Manor. Nor would Maud help since Aidan had shown her such support.

The Earl of Chester could have easily gifted Richard with one of the smaller holdings he'd taken from the other earls, but Ranulf only trusted family and rewarded family. Mere friends were out of luck. Richard had learned this unfortunate fact about the man too late.

Of course, he always promised the moon. Saying when he got this land under his belt or that land back, or when the king did this, or when Maud did that, *then* they would go after Aidan, but the only siege Richard cared about never materialized.

By 1149, things finally began to subside. Maud's supporters continued to launch sporadic attacks on the king, but her personal involvement in the conflict had waned. Robert of Gloucester had died in 1147, which had ended a lot of the fighting. After that, Chester had begun making peace with all the neighboring earls, perceiving the time for taking lands by force was coming to an end.

Then, news reached them that Maud's son, Prince Henry, now sixteen years old, was ready to command an army and return to England to reignite his mother's cause. Ranulf had the bright idea to form a coalition with him and David of Scotland to attack York in the north. King Stephen had come north to stop them, and they'd fled the field of battle. Yet, for the first time, young Prince Henry had been seen as a force to be reckoned with and a potential contender for the throne.

So, of course, the fighting soon began anew.

In the middle of that, Stephen's eldest son, Eustace, the sole viable heir to his throne, had died four months ago. Suddenly finding himself with no heir, and with Prince Henry growing in strength, the king had finally agreed to a peace treaty with Maud's son. That had been one month ago.

Prince Henry had agreed to pay homage to Stephen as king, but when Stephen died, the throne would pass to him instead of Stephen's younger son.

As news of the peace spread, all of England rejoiced.

Everyone was tired of war. No one was in the mood to begin a new siege or pick a fight where there had not been one before. The Earl of Chester had alienated just about everybody on the island, and Richard had no other resources to help his cause.

He'd once approached the Earl of Derby about the matter since Derby hated Aidan for taking Pilsbury Castle, but the loss of that manor was just an annoyance to him. He was too busy advancing Stephen's cause and had neither the time nor the resources to spend on it.

This evening, they would be attending a party hosted by William Peverel, Sheriff of Nottingham, to celebrate the end of hostilities and the coming Christmas. A significant marking moment for many. For Richard, though, it made him feel the pressing gloom of time running out like never before.

Then, it occurred to him on the way to Nottingham that the sheriff might be an option. He, more than anybody, had been harassed by Aidan and the outlaws of Newhaven Forest. Richard knew the man had experienced a lot more trouble from closer quarters like Sherwood, but still, perhaps Richard could get a word alone with the sheriff tonight and make him a proposal of sorts.

The wine flowed and the food was abundant.

Nottingham and Chester toasted each other with one flowery speech after another, with a good bit of raunchy humor thrown in as well, as if they'd never been on opposing sides of a war. There were moments when the other attendees literally roared with laughter at the exchanges.

Later in the evening, as things cooled down, Richard noticed one of Ranulf's knights looking especially green in the face. Honestly, the man looked like he was about to puke right there at the table.

Richard was wondering if he was actually going to do it, when he realized two more knights also seemed sick.

Then, Ranulf himself uttered something unintelligible and suddenly stood, gripping his stomach.

The other two knights fled the hall for the privy while the first one did exactly what Richard had expected – spew vomit all over the table.

Ranulf swayed on his feet, searching fruitlessly for something to grip for balance.

Richard rose and moved to him, but the sheriff was already at his side. With an arm around his shoulder, he neatly caught the earl as he collapsed and slowly laid him on the floor.

"You've poisoned me," he heard Ranulf say to him.

"Now, now, Ranulf," Peverel responded softly, "Did you think anybody believed we could hold the peace as long as you were alive? Why, your own wife has even had a hand in this."

A clear glint of malice shone in Peverel's face as he said it. Chester's eyes flicked opened wide.

The sheriff laid the earl's head down on the cold stones and exited the hall to make arrangements.

Richard moved to Ranulf.

"Get me out of here," the earl rasped.

Richard gathered Chester's remaining men, and they helped the earl to his horse.

Chapter 66

The pageantry was impressive, but Richard Falconer refused to let himself be intimidated by King Stephen's court. The king knew of him from the countless battles he'd fought alongside the Earl of Chester, and Richard was counting on that.

Stephen and Prince Henry had made their peace, and the two of them had toured southern England after the New Year so all the barons could do homage to both of them under the treaty. In February, Henry had returned to Normandy, presumably to wait until Stephen died, and this month, the king was holding court in York to reestablish his authority in the north.

Back in December, soon after the poisoning, Ranulf de Gernon, the Earl of Chester, had died. His three knights who also took sick that night had died right away, but Ranulf had held on for a while. It had begun to look like he might actually pull through, but then, the poison finally took him too.

No one doubted that the Sheriff of Nottingham was behind the poison, though everyone also knew the king would do nothing about it. At the very minimum, he was sympathetic with the killing of Chester. Some believed he might have even *ordered* it for the peace of the kingdom.

Whether or not Ranulf's wife had anything to do with it was a matter for gossipers. There were a number of reasons she could have wanted him gone, but there was no proof.

Richard had mixed feelings about the earl's murder. After all was said and done, he hadn't considered the man a friend, but his demise meant Richard's financial support was about to dry up.

On the other hand, it also freed him up to pursue the Falconer lands by other means.

Yet, the only means that seemed available at this juncture was a direct appeal to the king.

So, for good or for ill, that was his plan.

It had cost him a good bit of silver in the right hands to get an audience with Stephen. All of England wanted to see the king these days. Everyone and their brother sought restitution for losses or rectification of wrongs committed during the long war.

The herald announced his full name as instructed.

"Baron Richard of Falconer Manor to see the king!"

Stephen turned his attention Richard's way. The king had a sharp nose, a mild gaze, and a thick, fair-colored beard. He nodded for Richard to approach.

"Ah, yes. Richard Falconer, you were Ranulf's man, were you not?"

Richard bowed at the waist. "No, your majesty, he supported my cause, and so I, in turn, supported his, but that was all."

"It was quite shocking his sudden passing, was it not?"

"Yes, it was. Nevertheless, I imagine the minds of many in England are at peace now that he's gone."

The king laughed then grew serious.

"Yes," he said, "He certainly stirred up a hornet's nest wherever he went. If it hadn't been for his rapacious lust after lands that were not his, I wonder if I could not have ended this war much sooner, and much more to my favor."

Richard winced. "I wish to assure your majesty that I constantly pressed him to remain at your side. I never agreed with him going over to Maud, and much of the reason he came back to you several times was because of my counsel."

Stephen eyed him curiously, as if trying to determine just how much truth lay in his words.

For one of the few times in Richard's life, everything he'd just said had been the absolute truth. Except for how much weight Ranulf had given his counsel. Yet, in such an age of treacherous duplicity, the king would believe no one on simple faith.

"Very well," he said, "What is it I can do for you, Falconer?"

"Your majesty, I come to petition you for my lands. Years ago, my nephew, seeing that you were occupied in repelling Maud, violated the king's peace and through treachery took my castle and my lands from me.

"From his earliest days, my nephew has been an unwavering supporter of Maud's. As an outlaw, he stole countless sums of money from myself and the Sheriff of Nottingham that were intended to raise soldiers for your cause. It is also conceivable that you could have ended the conflict very early on had he not done so."

A shade of red entered the king's cheeks. It grew with each new piece of information.

"After he took control of Falconer Manor, his assaults upon the king only grew worse. He abolished serfdom on his lands. His people cut down the king's trees without limit, and he currently lets them take game from the forest with impunity.

"Not only that, milord, but he's also taken Pilsbury Castle through treachery, a fief under the protection of one of your most faithful supporters, Robert de Ferrers, and held it ever since in violation of the king's command, reaping its fruits for his own benefit."

Stephen's face burned crimson now.

"I understand your predicament, Falconer," the king said, "I have heard the occasional rumor about this Aidan. I will send him a letter immediately . . ."

"With all due respect your majesty, his impertinence deserves much more than a letter. After all the defiance he's shown, a communication will not make him vacate the castle. Only force."

"The land is weary of war . . ."

"My king, I know Falconer Manor seems small by itself, but with the taking of Pilsbury, he's already doubled his holdings. All of the nobles surrounding him are concerned. He offers higher wages than are custom, which has caused serfs and yeomen from surrounding shires to flock to the manor.

"All across Derby, Stafford, Nottingham, Leicester, and even York, lands have been abandoned as men have run away to serve him. This puts in jeopardy those shires' ability to serve the king.

"Your majesty, thousands of families work his lands now. It was just a few hundred when he began. In another few years, he could easily grow to be as powerful as Chester."

That got the king's attention.

"Surely not!"

"It's true."

The king looked away, contemplating what he'd just heard.

"For now, it is more pressing for me to reassert my royal authority in many parts . . ."

"You need not distract yourself, my king. Continue to do what you are doing. Just send a large army in your stead led by your best man and put down this insolence once and for all. I am confident Derby and Nottingham would also lend their full support to the effort."

Stephen fixed his eyes back on Richard.

"Very well," he said, "That is what shall be done."

Chapter 67

Aidan relished the sense of accomplishment and satisfaction his loved ones gathered around brought him.

Today, the hall's great table, which could easily seat forty people and ran most of the room's length, was full. Other, smaller tables on either side were also full. The hearth blazed and food bursting with flavor overflowed their plates.

Ysabella was to his right, as beautiful as ever. In her late thirties now, slight crow's feet had begun to show around her eyes. Her sensuous, yet sensitive face was still strong, and her figure was just as firm as the day he'd met her. Her dedication to Aidan had never wavered, and their love had grown with each passing year.

Ysabella had gifted him with four beautiful daughters, each of whom seemed like they would become as beautiful as their mother, if not more so. Needless to say, his girls had stolen his heart.

At the age of twelve, Aidan had begun training his son in the art of combat. Now fourteen, Andrew was already showing the beginnings of muscles that would eventually rival his father's, and a budding prowess with a blade that would one day be among the best in England.

When she saw them together, especially when they sparred, Ysabella often said, "the acorn doesn't fall far from the tree, does it?"

She'd proven to be a wonderful mother to Andrew in Priscilla's stead, loving him as much as she would have a son of her own.

In fact, Aidan knew she felt Andrew *was* her son. Early on, he'd noticed her clutching at Priscilla's cross on more than one occasion, especially when the challenges of being a lady or mothering Andrew had seemed too much. She'd eventually stopped though.

She still wore the cross every day, but now it remained out of sight under her tunic, and she no longer reached for it. It had become as much a part of her as her role as lady of the castle.

And she'd done an impressive job at that as well. She'd finished learning to read and continued to more advanced studies. Soon, she'd taken over where Priscilla had left off teaching others. Eventually, she and Geoffrey had established a full-fledged school.

Geoffrey continued to preach every Sunday, and he'd taken to visiting the neighboring villages during the week. Wherever he went, he drew large crowds as people were drawn to his practical teaching. Unlike most churches where the mass was held in Latin, Geoffrey would preach in English and quote the Scriptures in English.

The transformation among the villagers was astounding. Illegitimate births had become rare, and thievery was almost non-existent. The people seemed more content than ever, and donations to the church were up so much that there was even talk of building a cathedral. Now that England's political strife was coming to an end, and the bishops were free to refocus their minds on the daily business of the church, Aidan doubted their bishop would want to come down too hard on Geoffrey for preaching in English with that kind of track record.

After all, Geoffrey was accomplishing everything the church hoped to do in the world, and the only thing he'd rejected was the Latin language.

Aidan fully believed Geoffrey's efforts were an integral part of the freedoms Aidan had instituted. The chaos that reined in the rest of England for more than a decade had proven that prosperity goes hand in hand with strong morality.

For many years, freedom from royal interference had essentially been the norm across the entire nation. Elsewhere, the morality of the English people had completely degenerated into full-blown lawlessness, and poverty had followed everywhere that lawlessness went. On Falconer Manor, however, the clear difference that allowed their prosperity had been the law and order implemented by Aidan combined with the general morality of his people.

Law and order cannot exist by the will of a ruler alone. If the people themselves do not submit to that law, a lord cannot create prosperity or even restrain all the evil that would raise its head. Theft begets theft and prosperity is the universal victim. Children born out of wedlock force their mothers into poverty, which then often forces them into selling themselves, which brings about more illegitimate children.

Murder begets war and wounds so deeply that a society is generations in healing.

Without morality, there can is no prosperity. Of that, Aidan was convinced.

And without Geoffrey's heart-felt preaching and constant exhortation of the people to pursue the good, they probably would have forsaken their morality just as easily as the rest of England had.

Aidan reached over and rubbed Andrew's head affectionately.

The rest of the seats at the main table were filled by his daughters and his knights and their wives. Men-at-arms and merchants occupied the surrounding smaller tables.

Over 3,000 families lived on Falconer Manor now, and half of those resided in or around Becca's Well. He had 17 knights and close to 70 men-at-arms, and an equal number of castle servants.

The knights managed the affairs of the estates and trained the men-at-arms. The men-at-arms guarded the castle and trained the militias in the outlying villages. It was a good system.

If called upon, he could raise an army of at least 1,000 strong within a day, much larger than when Chester had besieged him years ago.

Ever fearful of the renewal of hostilities, they'd constantly strengthened the keep's fortifications and even enlarged it several times. They maintained well-stocked stores that could sustain them for months on end, and the water problem would not repeat. They'd also built a second city wall about a hundred feet farther out than the first one to accommodate all the new families and begun work on a moat that when finished would surround the castle's curtain wall.

Hugo had been the only one to ever figure out where the entrance to the secret tunnel was, and that secret had died with him.

Aidan breathed easier these days. Becca's Well and Falconer Keep had never been so secure. Ranulf de Gernon was dead, and Richard had no patron. The Earl of Derby seemed content to let sleeping dogs lie.

Between the manor and the lands around Pilsbury, Aidan's income was approaching *fifty* pounds per month. His treasury seemed near to overflowing at times. Honestly, he'd never imagined such wealth, though he knew it was still less than what some of the larger earldoms took in.

Regardless, for a barony the size of his, it was an inconceivable amount. He wondered if perhaps he should gift the king with a large sum in order to secure his confirmation of Aidan's title. Perhaps the king might even gift Aidan with more lands when he saw how well he was managing these.

A man-at-arms entered the hall from the front of the keep. He made his way over to Sir William and whispered in his ear.

The blood suddenly drained from William's face. Unconsciously, his fingers tightened their grip on the table.

Aidan was mildly alarmed but waited patiently as the messenger finished relaying whatever he had to say. As soon as he had, William got up and came over to Aidan.

A deep unsettling sunk into his stomach.

His enemies were gone or powerless. England was at peace. His loved ones were all here. It had been a long, hard struggle. Now, should be a time to enjoy life.

Yet, without a word even being said, the look on William's face told Aidan he wasn't going to be able to.

"What is it?" Aidan asked coolly, not lifting his eyes to meet his friend's.

"Pilsbury is under siege," William replied flatly.

It was Aidan's turn to go pale in the face, but he made an effort not to show it.

Ysabella had been laughing with one of the knight's wives, but she jerked her head around at the comment, instant fear etched into the lines of her mouth and brow.

"By whom?" Aidan asked as calmly as he could muster.

"By . . ." William's voice cracked, ". . . by *the king*. His banners are seen throughout their ranks. It appears Derby and Nottingham are with him as well."

He paused.

"Aidan . . ." he continued, "it's a *large* army."

Chapter 68

Aidan stood with Ysabella on the castle walk, watching soldiers swarm through the mist outside the city walls. His knights were arrayed in lines on either side of them. Andrew was also there, on Aidan's right, absorbing the scene with an obvious nervousness.

Bright banners and blazons swirled through the masses as troops circulated and began to make camp. They'd begun showing up about thirty minutes ago and already the fields were blanketed with them. Like a plague of colorful locusts.

It was a sight Aidan had hoped to never see again, but here it was. The only consolation was that this time, Ranulf of Chester did not lead them. Though, in many ways, that the king himself opposed Aidan now was worse.

His people were more secure now than during the siege fifteen years ago. They had much larger food stores, limitless water and several completed walls that would protect the town from burning.

Aidan prayed Stephen would be more merciful to his people than Ranulf had been and refrain from needlessly destroying crops and the outer villages. Of course, he knew the soldiers would take their sustenance from whomever they wanted though.

What his people needed most right now was courage. They were with Aidan to the man, but the knowledge that the king himself stood against them was enough to send tremors through the most solid of knees.

To oppose the king during the war had been one thing. Many a baron besieged by Stephen back then had been relieved by forces sympathetic to Maud. Now that the peace treaty was in effect, Aidan could not hope for any such relief.

"Bella, did I ever tell you the story of how Becca's Well got its name?" Aidan asked his wife. He said it loud enough for Andrew and the others to hear.

"No, my dear," she answered.

"Five hundred years ago, there was a great battle between the forces of Penda of Mercia and Oswald of Northumbria. Oswald, being a Christian king, was opposed by Penda, leader of the pagan forces who rallied his forces against the influence of Oswald and those sympathetic to Christianity. They did battle outside Oswestry in Masefield of Shropshire, and Oswald was killed.

"Penda's victory, however, was short-lived, as his own brothers were already Christians, and his descendants would all be as well.

"One of Penda's brothers was named Eowa. As Eowa was a Christian, he fought alongside Oswald instead of Penda. Eowa also fell during the fighting.

"Seeing that Penda had ordered Oswald's body to be dismembered and scattered, Eowa's men hastily loaded Eowa's body in a cart and fled for the hills of Derby, hoping to get him to the safety of Northumbria to be buried in peace."

Aidan glanced at Andrew and saw his son was hanging onto every word of the story.

"Well, those men and their cart passed right through this very village. In fact, they traveled right up that road there." He pointed at the village's main thoroughfare.

Andrew followed the movement of his hand.

"Yet, one of their horses went lame as they were passing the well in the center of town — which had a different name then, though I don't know it," Aidan continued.

"Now, a Christian princess by the name of Rebecca had been given as wife to the baron of the manor here. Seeing these soldiers were fresh from battle and exhausted from their haste, and that the townspeople were afraid to attend to them, she descended from the keep — which was just a small, wooden fortress back then — to fetch them water from the well.

"Just like the Rebekah of old, this Rebecca drew enough water for the men and their mounts. They were greatly refreshed by her hospitality and thanked her.

"Yet, when she poured the water over the dead Eowa's face to clean his wounds, the prince suddenly started sputtering and sat up, fully revived where just a moment before he'd been fully dead!"

Everyone was rapt with attention now.

"The water from the well, given in hospitality, had healed Eowa and even brought him back from the dead. Ever since, this place has been called Becca's Well in honor of that Rebecca and her story."

"What happened to the prince?" Andrew asked.

"He went to live with the Northumbrians and never returned to Mercia."

"That was a good story," Ysabella soothed, laying her hand on his back.

"Do you know what the moral of it is?" he asked Andrew.

"No."

"Where there seems no hope, there may actually be."

The enemy ranks were solidifying now. Tents were raised, camps were being staked, standards planted. The siege was serious.

Aidan had held out hope that the king's interest was merely to return Pilsbury Castle to the Earl of Derby, so upon hearing the news of that siege, he'd immediately ordered its garrison to surrender to the king.

Now, however, the king's intent was clear, and his uncle Richard's banner among the soldiers confirmed it.

Aidan turned to his knights.

"William, Alan, Eric, we ride out within the hour to parley."

***

The morning mist was just beginning to dissipate when Aidan and his men rode out through the front gate in full regalia, still thick enough it parted and swirled around them as they went.

Eric carried a pole bearing a white flag.

Several hundred feet of clear ground lay between the city wall and their enemy. The king's troops had camped outside the normal range of a bowman, as any wise army did. And in that same spirit, he would not ride all the way to them, but stop at a safe range and wait for the king's representatives to meet him.

Aidan's archers were up on the wall behind him to provide cover should anything go wrong, and a significant contingent of his men-at-arms waited just inside the gate, ready to rush out and escort him back.

They crossed the no man's land and stopped their mounts at the halfway point.

No one had anything to say. They waited in silence.

At last, a group of eight men, four of them bearing standards, broke from the enemy ranks and rode out to meet them.

As they neared, Aidan saw the king was not among them. Richard was, as well as the Earl of Derby, the Sheriff of Nottingham, and five others he didn't recognize who each bore the king's blazon on their chests.

The men formed a rough semi-circle around Aidan's group. One of the king's five was clearly their leader. Yet, it was the sheriff who spoke first.

He cried out as his mount paced restlessly behind the others.

"It's your day of reckoning, Aidan Falconer. We've come to exact justice!"

Aidan didn't budge. He noted a perverse smile peeking onto Richard's lips. He hadn't seen his uncle for more than a decade, but time had not been good to him. He seemed deflated by wrinkles and grey hair, not at all the towering threat Aidan remembered from his youth.

"That's rich talk, Peverel," Aidan called back, "especially from a cowardly murderer who uses poison like a woman."

Peverel sputtered, seeking words his fury momentarily blocked, glaring daggers. He dug his heels into his mount and whipped the reins as if he were going to charge, but the king's man held up an arm, ordering him to stand down without a word.

"We've just come for what's rightfully ours," the Earl of Derby said. "The king wants answers . . ."

"You've got Pilsbury back," Aidan replied.

"*I* will speak for the king," the king's man interrupted all of them.

He was tall and stocky, with the king's golden centaur painted on his shield among a field of red. A scar ran down the right side of his face, and his eyes told tales of many battles fought prior to this one.

Aidan immediately respected the man, recognizing a certain fairness in his spirit that was not present in any of the other nobles. Maybe it was a good thing the king's troops were here after all. Perhaps this would lead to an audience with the king that could resolve his dispute with Richard once and for all in Aidan's favor . . .

"My name is William de Falaise, commander of the king's forces. His majesty sends me to demand your appearance in his court for the purpose of answering the many accusations against yourself."

"It is well known that I was a supporter of Maud during the wars," Aidan said. "Are all of her supporters being treated this way? How can I be guaranteed my safety?"

"I will personally see to it that you are not molested," the commander replied.

"Then, why do you come with so many soldiers?"

Falaise cleared his throat. "It was assumed that you would not come peaceably."

"What are the accusations against me?" Aidan asked.

"First and foremost, will you swear fealty to Stephen de Blois, King of England?"

Aidan thought deeply about the question, though he knew the answer. All universally now acknowledged Stephen as king, including Henry, Maud's son. The question was settled.

"I will," he said.

Richard seemed surprised by that.

Falaise looked around at the other men to see if they were satisfied with the answer.

"It is rumored," he said, "That you have done away with serfdom and made all free tenants."

Aidan held his head high and met the man's gaze. "If I am able to provide the king with the knights and resources he requires, what does it matter how I accomplish it?"

"It's also said that you pay more than the customary wage."

"I do, and I repeat my previous answer."

"Your bishop says that you ejected his priest and allow the Scriptures to be read in English . . ."

"Isn't that a matter for the church to take up with me?" Aidan asked, cocking his head.

The king's man actually smiled at that answer. "You have allowed your people to pillage the king's forests," Falaise stated flatly.

"Ha! You cannot deny that one, Aidan!" Richard exclaimed gleefully. It was the most significant of the charges and carried the death penalty for a commoner. For a baron, the penalty should be less . . .

"I have retained every penny garnered from the sale of every tree for the purpose of handing the money over to the king's representative once his foresters returned. There have been many years of uncertainty, and the king was not available for petition. I have several hundred pounds that I can hand over right now."

The answer, and Aidan's ability to pay on the spot, shocked them. It visibly deflated Richard.

Falaise looked pleased by the idea that he might be able to return to Stephen with an oath of fealty and several hundred pounds to boot — and all without having to shed blood. There'd already been enough of that anyway.

He had one last item to bring up.

"Your uncle, Richard Falconer, claims that you took the barony from him through treachery and demands you turn it over. He says your father willed it to him . . ."

"I protest!" Richard cried, "Are we going to try the matter right here in this field or are we going to take him back to the king?"

Thwack!

Aidan had been looking at Richard because of his outburst, but the sound jerked his attention back to the commander.

An arrow shaft protruded from his chest rudely. The bottom dropped out of Aidan's stomach at the sight.

Who had shot it?

Weakly, Falaise reached up to grip it. The wound was mortal.

"Treachery!" Derby called.

Nottingham couldn't see what had happened from his position, but he'd heard the sound and echoed the cry without really knowing what was going on.

Richard's mouth fell open, completely taken off guard by the turn of events. The rest of the king's men were not so slow to react and were already pulling their swords.

Aidan pulled back hard on his reins and forced his courser into a rough turn.

"To the town!" he cried, digging his heels into the horses' side. He sensed his men were right behind him.

As the gates grew large before them, Aidan spied a lone archer on top of the wall with a face as pale as a ghost.

Chapter 69

Mark had watched intently as the group of nobles parlayed.

He'd been part of the castle guard ever since that day Aidan had caught him spying on the tunnel construction project. Before that night, he'd been a laborer for Ysabella, but he'd never gone back to working fields and was glad for it.

He'd hated Aidan at first for forcing him into a job and essentially holding him prisoner in the keep. Later, he'd realized he actually enjoyed being a guard. It was much better than plowing fields and pulling grass and weeds.

They'd trained him in sword combat, and Aidan himself had personally sparred with him a couple of times to show him some pointers.

He'd treasured those fights.

He loved his baron. Aidan Falconer was a man who'd never treated him with the contempt most had shown him since birth. He treated Mark with respect.

As he'd matured, Mark had grown to better appreciate the reasons for Aidan's tight security around the tunnel, and he'd never shared the secret with anyone since.

Due to the gusto with which Mark had embraced his new role, it wasn't long before he was allowed to leave the castle grounds and even entrusted with minor responsibilities.

He had a scrawny build, so his muscles never rippled in a way that matched his job description, not even as he approached the age of thirty. Yet, he did his best to make up for it with hard work.

He knew he would never be tapped for knighthood, but his fighting skills were good enough he hoped he might become a man-at-arms.

Mark had also taken up archery. The bow was a much easier weapon for him to manage than a sword, and curiously, it actually started making his arm muscles swell with new-found strength.

Enough so, that one of the kitchen girls was returning his smiles now. A very pretty lass of seventeen years. He thought he might even ask her to marry him. He was getting too old to be single.

Archery was making the difference in his build, so he practiced it with a fervor unlike anything else he'd ever undertaken. He'd initially used targets behind the keep, but when the inner yards didn't provide enough distance, he'd moved out to the fields.

These days, he could consistently hit a large target at two hundred yards. The captain of the archers had noticed his progress and invited Mark to join his bowmen just a few weeks prior. Thus, he was on the wall with them now, watching from a distance as Aidan and the other nobles met.

He could tell which one was Aidan even from this distance. There was no mistaking his confident frame. Only two of the king's men out there matched him in size.

On Aidan's left, one of the darker figures suddenly struck a chord of recognition. Over the years, he'd heard countless descriptions of Richard Falconer. Mark's vision was sharp, and he was sure that was him.

The realization seized him. He knew Aidan's history with his uncle. If Richard was with the king's men, this siege could be the beginning of something very bad. Not just for Aidan, but for himself too. A man like Richard would not let a man like him be part of his guard. He'd run Ysabella off her lands, and he'd let his guards abuse the servant girls just as he had before.

Mark was suddenly concerned about what treachery Richard might have in store. The whole parley could just be a ruse to get Aidan and his men out of the castle and vulnerable.

They should take precautions.

He lifted his bow and nocked an arrow.

The nobles were discussing something at length. One of them was pacing his horse back and forth behind the rest with a frantic energy. That kind of aggressive behavior only made Mark more nervous.

He glanced down the archer line. None of his fellow bowmen were at the ready. None seemed to sense the risk that he did. Though he was positioned at the far end of the line, he decided he could not remain passive.

He set his feet and laid his body into his bow, holding the string firm and pushing into the bow itself as if preparing to fire.

Slowly, he exhaled and sighted his weapon on the big man with the red blazon on his shield that was speaking with Aidan. He seemed to be their leader. If there was an ambush at foot, he would probably be the one to instigate it.

Mark would simply maintain the ready position, but he would not fire. At the slightest sign of treachery, he would release his fingers and save Aidan. They weren't that far away. Well within his practice range. He wouldn't miss.

He waited . . . and waited.

They were talking for a long time.

His arms were growing tired. Maybe he should share his suspicions with the other bowmen so they could take turns for as long as the parley took.

He was going to have to take a break. His left arm was starting to shake.

He relaxed his draw, took a few breaths, and inhaled.

He shook his hand out and wiped his sweaty fingers on his tunic to dry them. Next, he laid his body into his bow again, stretched it to its full length, and set his aim.

Then, his fingers slipped.

Mud spewed behind their horses as they passed through the gatehouse.

The moment the arrow struck Falaise, cries of shock and dismay rose up from the wall. The townspeople rushed forward to see what was going on.

As they entered Becca's Well, the streets were already filling up.

A group of guards escorted the lone archer Aidan had seen down from the wall. The man didn't offer any resistance. They descended the steps accessing the upper walk and reached the grass.

"Take him to the castle," Aidan called, pointing his sword first at them and then that way to emphasize.

He spurred his mount toward the keep, head down, focused. William, Alan, and Eric galloped right behind him. A mob of townspeople swirled around the guards and the archer as they walked through town following at a slower pace.

Inside the castle courtyard, Aidan dismounted and waited for the guards to arrive with their prisoner. Ysabella and his children, along with John Steward, were already there. She pulled their daughters closer to her side and shot him a very worried glance.

Word of the turn of events had already reached the castle, so its servants were spilling out the main door in alarm. The crowd milled about, buzzing with stress and anticipation.

When the guard contingent arrived, people parted naturally to allow it to pass through. The rest of his knights and many archers were with them. The group entered the hastily formed ring and threw the archer to the ground at Aidan's feet.

Ysabella gasped.

Aidan clenched his teeth. He flexed his jaw muscles in and out as he tried to maintain control over his boiling temper.

It was Mark, Ysabella's old field hand. *The ingrate.*

Mark kneeled before Aidan, head bowed, unable to face his baron.

"It was *you?*" Aidan growled.

Mark nodded weakly.

"Do you have any idea what you've done?" Aidan bellowed. "You've killed the king's commander!"

Cries and wails went up from the people.

"I'd almost convinced them to lift the siege and leave us alone!" Aidan said, "*Why? Why did you do it?* They'll slaughter us all now!"

Mark began to weep. He couldn't look Aidan in the face.

"I . . . I . . . it was an accident," he stammered then muttered something about trying to protect Aidan from an ambush.

Aidan stared at him. His mind didn't want to believe what he'd seen had actually occurred.

This man's guilt was inconsequential to the larger question of what the king's forces would do now. They wouldn't care about excuses or about it being an accident. The king's commander had been murdered under a banner of truce, and they would demand blood.

"Take him away and keep him under guard," Aidan commanded.

The guards that had brought Mark down from the wall dragged him away to the keep. They would chain him in the undercroft.

"John, William, a word please." Aidan glanced at Ysabella. She looked to him wide-eyed. He saw the tears welling there. She was in agony for all of them, not just the boy she'd once known.

John Steward and Sir William followed Aidan up to his study.

The three of them entered and closed the door. The faint smell of dust and book must hung in the air.

This room had to be his favorite in the whole castle.

Aidan moved to the small window and gazed out.

His fingers found a small mound of candle wax that had been pressed into a crack where its frame met the stone wall. He picked at it idly, thinking.

Finally, he turned back to them, but still said nothing. He just stared forward.

William cleared his throat.

"Are you sure he's dead?" he asked.

Aidan nodded. "If the arrow didn't hit his heart, it did a lung. Went right through his mail. It was mortal all right."

"Surely they will listen to reason?" John asked. "If we hand over the archer, perhaps that will satisfy them?"

Aidan turned back to the window. "So close," he whispered to himself, "so close . . .

"No," Aidan said more loudly to them, "Richard, Derby and Nottingham came for my blood and no one else's. They won't be satisfied by an archer. Falaise was the only fair-minded one in the bunch and now he's dead."

Silence reigned.

The faint bleating of sheep could be heard through the thin windowpane. The pasture behind the castle was filled with them. A testament to the prosperity Aidan had inspired.

"How do you think they'll do it?" he asked William.

"First, they'll fire the town and the fields. They may send troops to your outlying villages and raze them. They'll attack from the rear so they can get to the castle without having to breach the town walls. They may try to set fire to the keep with flaming arrows. They'll build siege towers, dig tunnels under the walls, a number of things. We can hold out for a while, but eventually they'll win."

Aidan took the news stoically.

"We've killed the king's commander under a white flag," William continued. "They won't go away. They may even build a counter castle."

"You've served in Stephen's army," Aidan asked. "What will they do once they're in? Will they show mercy?"

William clenched his teeth. "The king is not present, so if his men are bent on revenge, they can exact it while he pleads ignorance. In their eyes, we've violated honor itself."

"What do you think is *probable?*"

"They'll rape all the women and kill all the men," the knight stated flatly.

Aidan grimaced.

"That's what I was afraid of," he said softly.

He looked to his steward who had turned several shades paler.

"John, begin preparations to evacuate the people. We'll sit tight tonight. In the morning, I will go out by myself and try to reason with them. If that doesn't work, we'll start sending our people out through the tunnel at night and save as many as we can."

Chapter 70

"**P**lease don't go, Aidan!" Ysabella pled, eyes watering. She gripped his arm in both of her hands. He looked back at their children.

The sight of Andrew lifted his heart with fatherly pride. The boy was growing into a man and his body was starting to fill out. His daughters, each of them as beautiful as their mother, but each with a slightly different shade of hair, stood on either side of Andrew, their heights varying dramatically, from Rosa the youngest, to River the eldest.

"Andrew," he said, "If something happens to me, you will be the new baron. I am charging you with getting all the people to safety. Until you are an adult, listen to your mother and to your knights."

Andrew gulped and nodded. "Yes, sir," he croaked as strongly as he could muster.

"Aidan, please!" Ysabella cried.

He turned to his bride. How he loved this woman who had dedicated herself to him almost from the first day he'd met her in the forest. Now, her faced was stricken with panic.

He stared into her eyes and held her shoulders, willing her to understand his heart. "Bella, it's the only chance we have. If I don't go, they'll burn everything, and we'll all be killed."

"Surely, there's another way! Let's sneak everyone out as you've said. You and I will just go with them."

"Where would we go? Where in all of England could I hide if the king is after me?"

"We can be outlaws again. We can flee to France . . ."

Aidan shook his head. "Everything our people have built will be ruined, and there is no assurance we won't still be killed. This is my best chance to save everyone."

She stared back, alternating which of his eyes she pled with. "Aidan, *please . . .*" she whispered.

He pulled her to him and hugged her tight, taking energy from her. He kissed her on the lips and tasted the saltiness of her tears.

"It will be all right," he assured. He turned to his daughters and embraced each one of them in turn and then finally Andrew. His son was doing his best not to choke up.

"Hopefully, I'll be right back," he said with a smile. "The worst that can happen is they take me to see the king, and then I'll press my case with him."

Ysabella straightened and sniffed back her tears.

She'd tried with everything she had to get him to stay, but to no avail. He wouldn't change his mind. It was time to be strong.

Aidan swung up onto his horse, a smallish mare that could not be confused with a war horse. He was leaving his favorite courser behind.

The people who filled the courtyard parted to make way for him.

"Not even armor?" Ysabella called.

He shook his head again. "They must see that I am unarmed, or they'll kill me on sight."

He nodded to Brother Geoffrey, who was holding Aidan's sword for safekeeping. It was the same sword the prior of St. Alban's had given him so many years ago. The sword that had gotten him through so much.

He was leaving it in Geoffrey's charge. Should anything happen to Aidan, Geoffrey would give it to Andrew when he was old enough to handle its unusual length and weight.

He paused and turned to the corner of the courtyard where the archer Mark stood by himself, eyes to the ground, huddled with his arms wrapped around his chest as if shivering beneath a frigid afternoon wind.

Aidan had ordered the man released from his bonds this morning, but no one wanted anything to do with him.

Aidan raised his finger and pointed at Mark while casting his gaze around the crowd.

"No one is to lay a hand on him! No matter what!" he commanded loudly so all could hear. "He is to be left alone. Is that clear?" A few nods confirmed that his order had been received.

Aidan kicked his mount in its sides and spurred forward. He would not stop in the middle of no man's land this time but ride all the way to the besiegers' camp — and he would ride slow with his arms in the air. Meanwhile, his men would post white flags on the castle wall.

Aidan hoped that going alone and unarmed, and not asking the king's men to ride within range of his archers, would clearly communicate his desire for peace.

"It's time to *crush* him!" Richard stabbed his sword into the dirt to emphasize the point.

William of Ypres eyed him coolly. He was now the king's top commander in the field. He'd always been King Stephen's most trusted commander, but for Richard's excursion, he'd remained behind at York occupied with tasks there. Derby and Nottingham had sent for him as soon as Falaise had been killed. He'd just arrived this morning after riding all night.

The king had been infuriated by the news of the murder under a flag of peace and had communicated to him very clearly that justice was to be exacted. Still, the impertinence of this Richard Falconer was off-putting. Ypres would not allow the man to think he had any authority in the matter at all.

"I will decide when and where we act, and what we do," Ypres said firmly.

"But surely . . ."

"We will take action, I assure you, sir. Now, be quiet!"

One of Derby's men-at-arms ran up and whispered in the earl's ear. Derby turned and faced the castle in the distance.

"What is it?" The sheriff asked impatiently.

The earl pointed. "There's a rider."

William of Ypres stiffened and began barking orders. Soon, archers were forming lines behind knights and other soldiers who all began mounting their horses.

"He's alone," Peverel commented, "and they're waving white flags on the wall."

"Whoever it is, he's a fool if they think we're coming back out for another parley," Richard spat, "That arrow could have killed any one of us."

"He's not stopping," Derby said. "Maybe he's a defector. I think he's going to come all the way to us."

It was easy to read the shock written across all of the nobles' faces as he rode into their midst. Among them, Richard was the first to recover. His visage quickly twisted into a gleeful sneer.

He turned to the others. "Gentlemen, it's Aidan Falconer himself!" he cried, imitating a mock bow.

Aidan still had his hands in the air.

"I come unarmed!" he called to them. Then, he dismounted and began slowly walking toward the nobles, hands still held high. They relaxed when they saw he had neither sword nor armor.

The nobles formed a semi-circle around him. Each had drawn their blade.

Archers moved in on either side, bows ready.

"Mommy, is daddy going to be all right?"

Little Rosa peered up at her mother. She could barely see over the parapet, but she sensed her mother's stress.

Ysabella looked on from the city wall as Aidan dismounted in the distance and the men surrounded him. She could make out each one of the figures and could tell who was who.

Without taking her eyes from her husband, she reached down and caressed her daughter's head.

"I don't know, honey. I don't know."

"I am William Ypres, commander of the king's forces. You are Aidan Falconer?"

Aidan nodded. "I am. I come in peace to assure the king the tragedy that befell his man yesterday was the work of a lone archer who failed to follow orders, and was an accident at that."

Ypres glared.

"He killed an honorable man," he said.

"I have no doubt that is true. I saw it in his eyes. It is most unfortunate that we had almost reached terms of peace when it happened."

"Surely you do not think to argue peace after having violated it so recently!"

"I do not. I come to plead my case before the king and let him decide my fate. But I ask that you leave my family and my people alone. Take me and let them go."

"Where is this archer?" Ypres demanded. "Why have you not brought him so we can execute him?"

Aidan straightened and stood tall.

"I come in his place," Aidan said, "You may kill me now if you wish."

The commander shook his head.

"No, that will not be necessary . . ." Ypres said.

In a split second, Richard slung his ready blade up in a swift, wide arc and slashed Aidan across the throat. The cut passed halfway through his neck. Dark blood instantly gushed out.

Aidan felt the blade as it sliced through his throat. He'd seen it coming but had not moved nor defended himself. He'd come without weapons for a reason.

He'd come prepared to lose his life. It was truly the only hope he had to save his family and his people. That Richard had been so swift to accept his offer wasn't even a mild surprise.

Though he *had* expected more pain to accompany the wound. A strange humming filled his ears as thick, warm liquid ran down his chest.

He noticed the sun, bold and bright in the blue sky. Its glorious light felt so warm on his skin.

His vision swam and narrowed. The figures of the nobles and Ypres wavered before him.

Their expressions seemed stunned. He ignored Richard and the satisfied grin that engulfed his mouth.

He wanted to turn back toward the castle and see his family one last time, but his feet wouldn't obey. So, instead, he gazed into the forest.

The verdant trees were just as beautiful as they'd been so many years before when those woods had saved him from destitution. The same woods where he'd met Ysabella and learned to be a man.

His legs gave out, and he collapsed to his knees in the dust.

His vision blurred. Then came a bright, white light that overwhelmed the rest.

Familiar voices called his name, and a peace flooded his soul. A peace like no other he'd ever known. He strained to see into the light.

At last, he made out the form of Priscilla. She was beckoning him to come to her. His parents stood behind her. They looked so well. So happy.

Aidan reached out to her.

Then, he fell forward.

Chapter 71

Ysabella screamed when she saw Richard sling his blade up at Aidan. The cry was echoed by everyone else on the wall.

Aidan staggered and turned slightly. She watched in horror as redness grew large on her husband's chest. He didn't react for what seemed an eternity. She willed him to turn around to her, but he just stared forward at the woods.

Then, he collapsed to his knees. As he fell forward in the dirt, a low, wailing moan billowed up from the depths of her soul. She too staggered and almost went to her knees.

The only thing that stopped her were the expressions of abject terror on her children's faces. They couldn't see as well as she, but understood the tragedy told by everyone's cries. Her girls tugged on her dress desperately, peppering her with a thousand questions at once.

Andrew had seen his father die.

Pale-faced, he was struggling to assess, to believe that he'd really seen what he thought he'd seen.

She wrapped her arms around as many of them as she could manage and pulled them tight. Ysabella looked back to her husband and watched hopelessly through rivers of tears, not truly believing it herself.

"What have you done?" Ypres shouted.

"Only what he himself offered," Richard snapped, stabbing the bloody tip of his blade into the dirt to clean it.

His tone was firm. After all these years, his offensive nephew had neatly placed his neck on the chopping block, so he wasn't about to waste the opportunity.

He'd heard the beginnings of Ypres' prevarications. The man had been about to essentially forgive Aidan the transgression of killing Falaise, at least until they reached the king's court, and who knew what would happen there?

No, he wasn't about to let Aidan walk away. He'd offered his life, so Richard had taken it. No hesitation.

It had seemed like a dream the moment he felt his sword sink into Aidan's neck. A dream come true after so *many* years. A deep satisfaction had entered his heart, and he wasn't about to let Ypres steal it from him.

He was fascinated by the sight of his nephew bleeding out. Aidan had looked him right in the eyes as he'd swung. It had almost been like Aidan knew what was coming and had allowed it. He had to have. Aidan's battle reflexes were legendary among those that had seen him in action, and Richard was one of them.

He didn't care though. Whatever idiot thoughts had been running through Aidan's head to make him submit in such a way only proved him to ultimately be the fool Richard had maintained all these years he was.

And Richard was glad for it. Ultimately glad.

"You fool!" Ypres shouted. "He came in peace, and you've killed him!"

"He offered . . ."

"You *imbecile*! He was unarmed! Whatever offense you could have laid at his feet for killing Falaise under a banner of truce is now vacated, for *you've done the same thing!*"

A darkness began to settle in Richard's soul. A heavy sense that somehow Aidan was defeating him even in death.

The Earl of Derby silently mounted his steed, pulled on the reins and turned his horse back to the center of camp. A few of the others began trickling away, though most stayed to watch the spectacle.

Ypres dropped his tone to a harsh whisper. "Don't you understand that the king is a man of honor? He will never support your claim after he hears about this. You are a coward who cuts down unarmed men without a trial. Why don't you go ahead and kick his body too?"

Richard started to take a step forward, his instinctive hatred momentarily overcoming his good sense. Ypres whipped his sword up to Richard's throat.

"I cannot believe you! Furthermore, I cannot believe the king expended so much effort to support the cause of a worthless cur like yourself. I see why Ranulf never acted in your favor."

He pointed to Aidan's lifeless body. "You see that man? He was courageous like few I've ever known. And selfless. His remains shall not be disrespected, but we'll send them back to his people for a proper burial."

"As for this," Ypres continued, waving his arm over the camps behind them, "The king's forces will be retiring from this field, and I'll be reporting this matter directly to Stephen himself. Falconer Manor shall remain in the hands of Sir Aidan's offspring from here on out."

A flooding sense of doom overwhelmed Richard at the pronouncement. He was struggling to grasp the finality of it. Perhaps it could still be undone. Things changed in England from day to day. Surely, there was still hope.

"Very well," Richard mumbled, bowing his head. He sheathed his sword and began to walk toward the camp.

"Not so fast!" Ypres commanded. "Richard Falconer, you will remain right where you are! You are not to step foot back in that camp until every last one of us has departed. If I ever see you among the king's forces again, or in the king's court, I will have you run through on the spot."

"But . . ." Richard protested, glancing at the other men wildly, searching for an out.

"No buts." Ypres stepped forward and pressed the tip of his sword into the mail on Richard's chest. He gave a hard shove and pushed Richard backward onto his rear.

At that, the Sheriff of Nottingham also mounted his horse and turned away. William Ypres followed along with most of the soldiers. A small contingent stayed behind to guard Aidan's body and ensure Richard did not deface it further.

Richard sat in the dust, staring blankly, not understanding what had just happened to him.

Chapter 72

Ysabella ran down to Becca's Well when she heard Aidan's body was being returned. A small party of the king's soldiers were wheeling him on a cart up the main road. She ordered the city gates thrown open and met them at the well in the center of town.

She rushed to the wagon just as the soldiers were unloading him.

The sight broke her. There was so much blood.

Weeping, she knelt and hugged his head to her breast, not caring about the fresh blood coating her arms and tunic.

A man cleared his throat. "Madame . . ."

She lifted her gaze and saw a tall man in the king's colors before her. She stood to face him.

"My name is William of Ypres," he said, "I wish to offer my condolences for the loss of your husband. This was the work of one man, Richard Falconer, who acted contrary to my wishes. You husband was a bold and brave man. I had only intended to take him to the king. He should have been treated with honor . . ."

She nodded and started to say something in reply but was interrupted by the sound of frantic sobbing. They turned.

Andrew was kneeling beside his father's body splashing his throat over and over again with water from the well. Remembering Aidan's story of the miracle of the well water and the resurrected prince, in desperation, the boy was doing the only thing he could think of.

"Wake up, pa. Wake up, pa," he repeated over and over, tears streaming down. "Please wake up."

Grief ripped her heart as she watched him fetch another pail of water.

She moved to him and put an arm around his shoulder, but she couldn't get him to stop pouring the water on his father.

Hours later, the king's forces finished packing their gear and marched out of the cleared fields around Becca's Well. Slowly, they funneled into a long column and began disappearing down the road that led away to the north through the forest.

One lone figure, who she knew was Richard, sat in the dirt next to the bloody patch of ground where her husband had fallen. He hadn't moved from there since it happened. Nor, it appeared, did he intend to until the army was gone.

Ysabella reached up and fingered the cross she wore just inside the neckline of her tunic.

Priscilla's cross.

She pulled it out and laid it flat against the outside of her tunic, visible.

She called for Andrew to come to her side. The boy had somewhat recovered from the shock of his father's death, but his whole body was still tense with grief. His eyes were simply forlorn and distant.

Lost.

At fourteen, he was already as tall as Ysabella. She gripped his shoulders and looked him in the eye.

"Andrew . . . can you hear me?"

He nodded slowly.

"Yes, mother," he mumbled.

"I want you to get your father's sword from Geoffrey and your father's courser and take them to Red the Outlaw in the forest. Tell him what happened and give him the sword. Can you do that?"

Andrew nodded again, a new resolve lighting his eyes.

***

Richard stumbled along the primitive road, despising the very trees on either side. He hated this forest. Without it, Aidan never would have had a base of operations, and Richard would still be running the castle and manor. All the wealth Aidan had enjoyed over the years could have been his.

Again and again, he went over things in his head. How he might have done things differently. He realized now he never should have allowed Aidan to get a foothold with the outlaws. That had been his undoing. He should have pounced on the whelp the first time he'd ever caught wind of his activities.

Today, Richard had been impetuous, and it had cost him. He'd misread Ypres' willingness to be ruthless. He should have allowed them to take Aidan into custody and then murdered him in his sleep. Or poisoned him. Peverel could have helped him with that.

Still, a keen mind can always find a solution. He'd been far too patient and inactive while serving in the Chester court. He should have been planting seeds of mistrust between the king and Aidan from the beginning.

Which is what he would do now. Aidan's pup was far too young to run a barony efficiently, and his wife was a peasant woman. They'd run the manor into the ground in no time with Aidan gone. All Richard had to do was spread rumors that the woman and her child were conspiring with Prince Henry or David of Scotland to renew the efforts to oust Stephen.

Once the king heard that, he would take action. By that time, Richard's indiscretion today would be forgotten and there was only one man who could logically inherit Falconer Manor at this point . . .

Thunk.

It sounded like an arrow thudding into a tree, but a sharp, piercing pain told the truth. An arrow had shattered his kneecap and passed all the way through the back of his leg.

Richard screamed and fell to that knee, which sent new bolts of vivid agony throughout his body. He could do nothing but roll onto his side, desperate to alleviate the pain.

Thunk.

A second arrow shot through his other knee. He screamed again. He tried to reach for the arrow shaft, but the pain was too great. Panicked, he tried to use his arms to drag himself to cover in the woods.

Thunk. Thunk.

Two more arrows pierced each of his elbows. Now, the pain was beyond excruciating. Tears streamed down his face and wet the dirt below his cheek. He couldn't move. All he could do was suffer.

A group of fully armed outlaws emerged from the forest. The faces bore not the expressions of simple ruffians or robbers, but men full of stern wrath who held nothing for him but contempt.

Their leader was a man with flaming red hair. He bore a grim, determined air. He held an empty bow in one hand, as did three of the others. One of those archers was a huge bear of a man. The other two were unmistakably knights. Richard recognized one of them from the first parley with Aidan the day before, but he didn't know his name.

The red-headed leader threw down his bow and pulled a sword from its sheath on his back as he strode toward Richard.

"I'm Martin the Red," he said as he swung the blade down at Richard's neck, "And you killed my friend."

***

"What do you want us to do with him, milady?" The captain of the guard asked.

He held Mark down on his knees in front of her, waiting for her judgment. The courtyard was full, and the people's pain fresh. They all knew that while Richard had struck the life-ending blow, this scrawny man before them was the actual cause of Aidan's death.

A man that Aidan had essentially rescued from poverty and given every opportunity.

They wanted his head. They wanted her to demand it.

She could feel their anger sizzling in the air.

Ysabella cupped Mark's chin in her palm and forced him to look her in the eye.

"He did nothing but good to you," she said.

He could not answer, but only nod weakly as he burst into tears.

"Forgive me, milady," he croaked.

"It is not for me to forgive you, Mark, but my husband who forgave you before he died. You are free to go, but you have no future here. You must not return to Falconer Manor."

He blinked several times, unsure if he even wanted the reprieve.

"Set him free," she said.

Murmuring rolled through the crowd.

"Before he died," she called out, "Aidan made it clear he wanted nothing to happen to this man for what he did. No one, and I mean *no one*, is to lay a hand on him! Is that clear?"

Silence.

"*Is that clear?*"

Finally, several in the crowd began to nod.

To the guards, she ordered them to escort Mark safely to the west or the north but advised them to stay away from the outlaws to the east.

She watched as the guards took him away.

The crowd began to dissipate soon after.

Chapter 73

The funeral was the biggest Falconer manor had ever seen. The entire shire had wanted to attend. Even the Earl of Derby had sent some mourners as an act of contrition and solidarity.

It was all Ysabella could do to hold herself together, but she continually renewed her vows to do so. The future of their children, Aidan's legacy, it all depended on how she comported herself over the next days.

In private, she wept all night. In public, though, she must be strong. She had to build confidence of the people in herself and in Andrew, in their ability to run the manor.

She knew Aidan's closest knights would not abandon her in this time of need. Sir William, Sir Alan, Sir Eric, Sir Thomas, Sir Adelard, all of them to a man would offer their lives if need be to protect her and her children.

Still, confidence must be instilled. People would worry.

As they lowered Aidan's body down into the hole, a fresh lump caught in her throat.

She'd debated where to bury him. Next to Priscilla? Or somewhere else where *she* could join him when she passed?

In the end, she decided he belonged next to Priscilla, his first wife and the true mother of the new baron of Falconer Manor, though Ysabella's love for Andrew was just as strong as if he were her own. And as the men laid Aidan down next to his first love, he would also be next to his parents. He would have wanted that.

Perhaps when it was her time, she would ask to be laid on the other side of him. Or perhaps she would choose a place of her own, by herself. Perhaps it was her lot to be alone.

She laid her palm on the cross on her chest and looked at her children.

No, she was not alone. She had them. She had their legacy.

Ysabella stepped forward and tossed a bouquet of wood anemone flowers onto the casket. Their white blossoms spread across the wood as they landed.

Then, she burst into song, her voice vibrant and clear.

When the sun rose high
And our way seemed lost
Amongst the trees of Winster

With bare feet a'thorned
And in hunger shorn
In New'aven we did wander

One arose to us
Strong and tall in ways
Bereft of fief and manor

To allay our fear
And provide our bread
Aidan the Swift Hunter

As knights did plunder
And kings waged their war
Honor was his forever

Against traitors all
And corrupt king's men
Fought Aidan the Defender

Order to our lot
Shelter in the camp
Brought he our dear Leader
To support the queen
And promote her cause
Went Aidan the Defender
Went Aidan the Defender

Many blades slashed and flew swiftly
An' arrows pierced men through in number
Yet, there to stand against
Was Aidan the Deliverer
Aidan the Deliverer

He did save our camp
Brought us peace again
Aidan the Deliverer

Many maids looked on
An' to be chosen yearned
Yet, there was one who called
Yes, there's one who calls

I wish his days were long
I hope his nights were sweet
On the lands of Falconer Manor

May his children bloom
And his heart be e'er mine
Aidan the Deliverer
Aidan the Deliverer

My Dear, Aidan the Deliverer

With the last line, her voice lowered to a whisper, and then she fell quiet. Those gathered respected the sudden silence as if it were holy. Most cried openly. Especially those who had known him best.

Ysabella Falconer would make sure that Aidan's legacy never faded.

Until she could not breathe another breath.

Author's Note

Aidan Falconer died for his people so they might live.

It was painful to write that scene as I've grown to love Aidan, but the true mark of a good leader is a willingness to sacrifice him or herself for those in their care. To not have given Aidan the opportunity to do so would have been to deny him the chance to show true leadership — as a servant.

Of course, Aidan is a symbolic type that represents Jesus Christ, who also died for His people — you and me. Just as Aidan's policies resulted in freedom and prosperity for his people, so did Jesus come teaching in order to give us life abundantly (John 10:10)

Yet, this world is hostile to both truth and freedom. It actively fights to steal our joy, to keep us oppressed, whether it just be through happenstance or through the intentional, sinful acts of man. Just as Aidan's world constantly threatened to destroy the lives of the sheep in his care.

In the end, it was only through his death that his people could be ultimately protected.

It goes the same for us. We have no hope of being saved from the world's oppression . . . or even *ourselves* for that matter . . . without the death of Jesus Christ. Thankfully, our Father, in His great love for us, decided to provide Himself as the supreme sacrifice that would set us free.

All we have to do in response is to trust in Him as our Lord and Savior. To enter the Lord's protection, so to speak, and obey Him by staying within the city walls.

I truly enjoyed writing this book.

Every historical event described herein is accurately portrayed. A civil war did in fact ensue between Stephen and Maud for almost twenty years. The resulting chaos and terror that reigned over the land prompted one medieval monk to describe it as a time when "Christ and His saints slept." Modern historians simply refer to this period as *The Anarchy*.

Ranulf, Earl of Chester, was a true historical character and he really did switch allegiances between the sovereigns as many times as I've said, and in exactly the same ways. I've done my best to accurately portray his personality as well as those of Robert de Ferrers, Earl of Derby, and William Peverel,

Sheriff of Nottingham.

Yes, it is indeed possible that this William Peverel was the true historical Sheriff of Nottingham portrayed in the legends of Robin Hood. This time period and the events surrounding it much more match the lawlessness and opportunity for outlaw heroism as described in Robin Hood's tales than a century later during the reign of King John.

William Peverel was in fact a Sheriff of Nottingham who was not only very powerful, but truly did support a usurping king against the rightful sovereign, and it is a historical fact that he was involved in several schemes, including the murder of Ranulf of Chester.

Of course, everything involving Aidan, Falconer Manor, and the outlaws of Newhaven Forest is purely fictional.

Another major theme running through *Aidan Song* is the idea of a free-market economy existing in the middle of a world filled with socialism.

Make no mistake, socialism is not a new idea. In fact, feudalism is essentially socialism. In a fully socialist society, no one has rights to the land but the government (king). The government (barons, nobility) also dictates what people can produce (controlling which crops are planted), how much they can sell it for (price controls), as well as how much people can earn. In a socialist society, the markets are controlled by the unions (guilds) and the people can only live in collectives (feudalist estates), not in the King's forests.

In socialism, we are all serfs.

Except for those elites who run the government. They live above the rest, awarding each other with lands and titles and the spoils of war.

Unfortunately, socialism is the natural way of things and has been throughout history. Going back as far as the Roman Empire, 50% of the population were slaves. Yet, the Roman government gave free bread to the poor on a daily basis.

Falconer Manor serves as a simplified example of a free market sufficiently removed from modern political circumstances that we can hopefully shed the calcified scales from our eyes and see it with fresh ones.

When set in the context of Aidan Falconer battling against the designs of his Uncle Richard, the benefits of a free-market system become much easier to see. As well as the eventual and inevitable self-destruction of a controlling system such as Richard's.

Will not people be more productive when they know they're working to feed their own families rather than some distant, faceless bureaucrat? *Yes.*

Will not more people immigrate to a free nation? *Yes.* Will they not flee oppression? *Yes.*

If you combine more people with more productivity, won't the government necessarily receive more in taxes then, even if the actual tax rate is lower? Again, the answer is an obvious *yes.*

So, why do we make it so complicated?

I truly hope you enjoyed *Aidan Song*. Even if we respectfully agree to disagree with regards to my economic themes, I hope you were moved by the story of Aidan and those who loved him.

Who knows? Maybe we'll hear more from his son Andrew in the future.

~ Zack Mason

About the Author

Zack Mason loves the art of the word and the thrill of the story. He has wandered the countryside of Bangladesh, built churches in Costa Rica, roamed the desert in Arizona, hiked the Alps in France, and fought human trafficking in Atlanta. He has been a dishwasher, a house framer, a teacher, a waiter, a bookseller, and a businessman, just to name a few. He currently resides with his family outside Atlanta, GA and plans to continue writing for as long as he is allowed to do so.